The Veil

JUN 13

The Veil

K.T. Richey

www.urbanchristianonline.com

Urban Books, LLC
78 East Industry Court
Deer Park, NY 11729

The Veil Copyright © 2013 K.T. Richey

ISBN 13: 978-1-60162-759-9
ISBN 10: 1-60162-759-9

First Printing June 2013
Printed in the United States of America

10 9 8 7 6 5 4 3 2 1

Distributed by Kensington Corp.
Submit Wholesale Orders to:
Kensington Publishing Corp.
C/O Penguin Group (USA) Inc.
Attention: Order Processing
405 Murray Hill Parkway
East Rutherford, NJ 07073-2316
Phone: 1-800-526-0275
Fax: 1-800-227-9604

THE VEIL

a novel

by K.T. Richey

For JMADP

Now concerning spiritual gifts, brethren, I would not have you ignorant. Ye know that ye were Gentiles, carried away unto these dumb idols, even as ye were led. Wherefore I give you to understand, that no man speaking by the Spirit of God calleth Jesus accursed: and that no man can say that Jesus is the Lord, but by the Holy Ghost. Now there are diversities of gifts, but the same Spirit. And there are differences of administrations, but the same Lord. And there are diversities of operations, but it is the same God which worketh all in all. But the manifestation of the Spirit is given to every man to profit withal. For to one is given by the Spirit the word of wisdom; to another the word of knowledge by the same Spirit; To another faith by the same Spirit; to another the gifts of healing by the same Spirit; To another the working of miracles; to another prophecy; to another discerning of spirits; to another divers kinds of tongues; to another the interpretation of tongues: But all these worketh that one and the selfsame Spirit, dividing to every man severally as he will.

—1 Corinthians 12:1–11

Chapter 1

Misha could see. Not like the ordinary person. Yes, her vision was 20/20 but it went beyond that. Misha could see through the falsehood of everyday life displayed in the people she came into contact with. She could see through the lies people told. She could see the unspoken, the hurt and pain. She could see the secrets pushed back in time and memories. She could see the joy and tragedy of the future. She could see it all as she sat in her classroom, waiting for the bell to ring.

"Class, remember, there's a test next Friday on the Spanish-American War," Misha yelled, as her class of ninth graders ran to the door at the loud clang of the bell. It had been a long day. There was a fight between two girls in her second period class and Mr. Davis, the school principal, used her lunch break to discuss his upcoming vacation. She wished he would spend the time talking with the school superintendent or the school board about the outdated books she had to teach from, or the fact she only had twenty-six books for the thirty-two students in each one of her classes.

She had always wanted to be a teacher. When she was a child, she would play the teacher to all of her dolls and stuffed animals. History was her thing. She loved history. She loved the History and Biography channels and watched them religiously. The thrill of learning about ancient civilizations and people inspired her in many areas of her life. She felt it was important to learn from the successes and mistakes of other people. She engrossed herself in books dealing with history from all over the world. So it was no surprise she chose history with emphasis in education as her major in college.

Now, in her second year of the first teaching position she received out of college, she was beginning to doubt her career choice. Dreams of excited students and supportive coworkers were fading to the realities of uninterested students, mediocre test scores, demanding administrators, and gossiping coworkers. Her students did not see the excitement of history. The thrill of learning about the Spanish-American War, the Civil Rights movement, and other vital parts of American history were only backdrops to iPads, hormones, and whatever it took to be popular. No matter what she did to make history exciting for them, each class became more and more a torment for her.

She felt that possibly it could have been better if the other teachers did not keep her name as the topic of their conversations every day. As a fashionable twenty-three-year-old, she could not show up in colorful sweaters with characters on them like other teachers. Although her clothes were not expensive designer items, everyone thought they were. She was an excellent shopper and could smell a bargain before she entered a store. Fashion was more of a passion than history. Besides, she tried to look nice every day for herself and her man, Roger.

The thought of Roger put a smile on her face as she packed her cloth tote bag with the pop quizzes she had given her classes that day. They had been together since her junior year at Howard. They were inseparable and had so much in common. He was a Christian and he treated her with the utmost respect and honor. Her family loved him and kept hinting to them that they should get married. He was a minister in his church and busy social worker for a local nonprofit organization for low-income youth. He was passionate about his work but he always tried to find time for her. Tonight was one of those nights and Misha was looking forward to being with him. This was a big weekend for both of them, as Misha would step into the pulpit as a minister for the first time. She needed a distraction to keep the nervousness at bay.

She sat down in her classroom, waiting for the halls to clear and the buses to leave the parking lot, before she decided to leave. She did not like going to her car while the hallways were packed with kids. There was always some confusion going on and she did not like to discipline girls and boys who were much taller than her small five feet four inch frame. She felt threatened by them, although she did not want to show it. In the classroom she tried to act tough, as if nothing bothered her. But there were times when she was afraid she would get hurt, like today.

She sat at her desk, reviewing the lesson plan for the next day and listening to the sounds of all the people in the hallway, when she was interrupted by a knock on her door.

"Hey, Misha, you busy?" another teacher asked.

"No, I'm only glancing over some stuff. What's up?"

"Some of us are going to happy hour at the Curb sports bar. You wanna go?"

"I'm sorry. I thought you knew I was a Christian. I don't go to happy hour. But you guys have fun. Thanks for thinking about me."

"I'm a Christian too. But I need a break. You don't have to drink. That fight in your class today didn't stress you out?"

"I prayed during my break. It got better," Misha answered, knowing she was still stressed out about the fight. One of the girls threatened to hit her. Not wanting the girl to get kicked out of school, she left that bit of information out when she wrote their referral to the principal. Even though teaching was not what she thought it would be, she still cared about her students.

"Well, if you change your mind, we'll be there until about six."

"Okay. I'll keep that in mind."

The teacher left her sitting alone again in the classroom and Misha could hear the loud sounds quieting. She picked up her tote bag and sweater that lay on the back of her chair, walked down the partially empty hallway, dodging students idling around, and went toward the parking lot to her car.

"Misha, you're not going with us?" Judy, another teacher, asked, as she stopped her in the hallway.

"Thanks for the invitation. I have a date tonight and I have to grade some papers before he gets there."

"New love. Must be nice."

"What are you talking about? You should be happy. From what I hear you have a good husband and marriage."

"I can't complain. We've been married twelve years. He's good to me and the kids."

"Yeah, and it's going to get even better when he gets back and finds out he has that new promotion."

"What?" Judy stopped in the hallway and reached out for Misha's arm. "How did you know my husband was in France?"

"Your husband's in France? I didn't know that." Misha's eyes widened. She had no way of knowing Judy's husband was out of the country. Judy never mentioned it to her.

"But you just said 'when he gets back.' How did you know about the promotion?" Judy said, placing her hands on her hips.

"What promotion? What are you talking about?"

"Misha, my husband is in France working at the international headquarters of his company. He's in line for a promotion on his job. If he gets it, I may be able to quit teaching. How did you know about that?"

"I didn't until you told me. Are you sure that's what I said?"

"Well, I don't know how you knew, but I receive what you said. I want to quit this job. These kids and Mr. Davis are getting on my nerves. You spoke the word today and I receive it. Hey look, if you change your mind, call me on my cell," Judy said, dipping into her classroom.

Misha made her way to her gray Honda Civic and began her journey to her apartment on the other side of town. She was thankful that as a teacher she was able to get home before the evening rush hour. Traffic in Atlanta was horrendous during rush hour. With the Westdale High football team having an away game, she didn't have to collect tickets at the gate before tonight's game, one of the many other duties she had due to staff cuts. Not only was she ticket master, she had bus duty and was a hall monitor. But, tonight she belonged to Roger. He could massage away the stress she was feeling in her shoulders. Shrugging her shoulders, she wondered what food Roger was bringing to her apartment this evening. She did not want pizza. Chinese would be good.

As she stopped for a red traffic light, she quickly pressed the number one on her cell phone: the speed dial number for Roger.

"Hey, honey. Don't forget the food. Get Chinese," she said once Roger answered the phone. "You know what I like."

"Mimi, I forgot. Can you pick it up? We're having an emergency staff meeting for the community health fair we're having next month. Somebody messed up real bad and we have got to figure out how we're going to handle it. I'm going to be a little late. You can get you something and I can grab something on the way to your place. "

"How long do you think you're going to be?"

"I don't know. Look-a-here, I've got to go. I love you, baby. I'll see you later."

Misha sighed in disappointment. It looked like it was just going to be her and the exciting world of grading papers. She had so looked forward to snuggling with him while he watched the movie he picked out. She in turn would be dreaming about this or that and eventually fall asleep until he woke her when he was about to leave. It would take her mind off preaching her first sermon this weekend. But tonight, the plan had changed due to his work. Helping the community was a passion that he loved. His commitment to the community was one of the things she loved about him. He knew what he wanted out of life. His plan was to get in on the ground floor, then work his way up to executive director. He wanted to know everything about running an effective organization. His main goal was to start his own nonprofit focusing on helping children. Focused, goal oriented, and task driven—it was everything she envisioned would make him a good husband. But, why didn't it make her happy? She shook her head. She was only tired.

Hearing the blaring sounds of the car horns behind her, Misha breezed through the traffic light just as it was changing from green to yellow. Something inside her kept telling her Roger was not going to show up. As she continued the twists and turns to her home, her thoughts drifted to her conversation with Judy.

Judy's husband is in France? He's up for a promotion? How could she have known this? Outside of school, there was not much she knew about Judy and her family. To some it would have been strange for her to know this information, but not to Misha. All her life, she knew things she should not have known about people, events, and places. When people questioned her about it, she would try to deny she said anything. Never understanding how or why it happened, she just seemed to know things. There were times when she felt as if there were someone standing at her side, whispering in her ear about situations or important decisions she had to make. She could look at some people and know everything about their lives, even intimate details. Then there were times like today; she would say something in conversation and didn't realize what she was saying. Because of this, she didn't have many friends. People always thought she was spying on them. She wasn't. Somehow, she just knew.

"God, I pray if this is you, confirm it with Judy's husband getting the promotion," she prayed as she pulled into the parking space in front of her apartment.

Westdale was a small community near College Park, Georgia, in the suburbs of Atlanta. Although the area was filled with urban sprawl, it continued to have a country feel with farmland still embracing the community near her home. Sometimes, she would get up early in the morning to drive past the farms and look at the cattle and horses that dotted the two-lane road that led to her apartment. She knew it would only be a matter of time before the developers would convince the owners to sell the property. But, until then, she was going to enjoy everything it had to offer.

Roger is not going to make it tonight, she heard in her spirit. *But it will be okay. He will call.* She knew when she got that feeling, it was always right. So she settled into her routine, ordered Chinese for dinner, and began grading her papers for her class.

It was after eight when Roger called to say he had just gotten out of his meeting and was tired. Hearing his soft, faint voice she discouraged him from coming over. He did not put up a fight as he agreed to meet with her tomorrow.

"Honey, it happened again." She sank back into her sofa, leaning her head on the soft pillows and stretching her legs along the adjacent pillows. She placed the papers she had been grading on the floor and wiped her eyes as she listened to Roger.

"What happened?"

"You know. I knew something I shouldn't have."

"What was it?"

She told him about Judy's husband, and how relieved she was that Judy didn't get suspicious of her but accepted what she said as a sign her husband would be promoted.

"I don't know what's going on, but it seems like it's happening more and more now and I can't seem to make it stop. I don't know what to do."

"It's all right. It's a gift that's being manifested because you're about to go into the ministry. Have you talked to Bishop as I suggested?"

"Not yet. I might mention it to him after my initial sermon Sunday."

"Good, I know he can help you. I wished my meeting didn't last so long. I really wanted to see you tonight. I miss you."

"I miss you too."

They settled into a deep conversation about their love for each other. Misha could hear the sound of Roger closing the door in his apartment. Afterward he began to pray for her, asking God to give her direction with her gift and help her understand its purpose for her life and the Kingdom. Misha listened to his prayer, needing to feel the deep, wanting love she thought she ought to have, but something was missing.

"Baby, I'm wasted." Roger yawned. "I would like to get to bed early, but I have to finish this grant I'm writing by next Friday. So it looks like I'll be up until the late-night hours."

"Well, if you have to go."

"Mimi, I love you. One day I'm going to make you Mrs. Roger Dale Williams. I promise. I can't afford it now. My ministry is just beginning to get started and—"

"Don't think about all that. What's important is the two of us are together now. God has a set time for everything."

"I know, but there are days I really want to be with you. We've been together almost four years and I'm tired of coming home to an empty apartment."

"Then let's just do it. Let's get married. My income is decent." Misha sat up on the sofa. She was tired of coming home to an empty apartment too. With their combined salaries and the elimination of one apartment and its bills, they could make it just fine. She felt they had known each other long enough to get married, although she would get a nervous feeling every time she or he mentioned it. Even now her stomach trembled as she talked about it.

"Mimi, we have two car payments, two student loans, and don't forget my credit cards. We can't afford it right now. I promise you, soon. We're going to touch and agree our finances will get better and we'll be able to come together."

"Then pray, Roger."

Listening to Roger pray, Misha secretly prayed he would find another, better-paying job soon. Since he'd gotten this job, she was seeing less and less of him. It took so much of his time. She prayed it would be soon as she longed to be held and touched as a man would touch his wife on a daily basis.

It had been a long time since she had sex. But she wanted more than sex. She wanted to make love to Roger, as husband and wife. She wanted it to be special. Something that was fruitful in mind, body, and spirit—an act that would bear witness to their love and could be seen on their faces, spirit, and in their children. One day soon, she hoped.

Chapter 2

Sunday had finally arrived. Six months of counseling with Bishop along with six months of classes with Elder Pringle on the doctrine of the church, the day had finally arrived. Misha was nervous as she stepped into the pulpit to deliver her initial sermon. She sat down in the center chair, which gave her a clear view of the entire church. Familiar faces filled the pews, waiting patiently for her to speak. The children in her junior missionaries group were sitting together on one side of the church near the front. Her family was sitting in the center pews. The deacons, dressed in gray and black suits, were lined up across the front row of all three sections. The youth choir sat behind her in the pulpit. She could hear the children moving restlessly as they prepared to sing.

She finally stopped stressing about how she looked when Roger picked her up to take her to the church. He had always loved her natural hair. Today her kinky twists were pulled back in a conservative wrap. Her chocolate-brown suit made her feel as though she could be a preacher. It was uncomfortable and not what she was used to wearing. But Roger made her feel like she was the only woman alive who could rock the straight-laced suit.

Glancing to her left, she saw Roger smile as he stepped into the pulpit and sat in the chair next to her, his right eye giving her a quick wink. Watching the

other ministers file into the sanctuary and sit behind
the deacons in the second row of the center seats, her
legs shook nervously. Finally Bishop Moore walked
proudly into the sanctuary and everyone stood as he
entered. He stepped up to the podium and began ad-
dressing the congregation.

Everything looked different from Misha's view in the
pulpit. The church had three aisles of seats. Her family
was sitting in the center aisle. She leaned to the side to
get a better view of something other than Bishop's rear
end in front of her. Inhaling long, slow, deep breaths,
she hoped no one noticed her heart beating so fast
her chest moved up and down to the rhythm of the
beat. Leafing through the notes she held in her hand
in a poor attempt to keep her hands from shaking, she
briefly looked over them.

There was no reason for her to be nervous. She spoke
in front of people all the time as a teacher and at the
church. But this time was different. She could feel the
enormity of the occasion. It was a big step in her life.
God had placed her in a position to bring people into
His presence or drive them away by what she said. The
thought made her hands tremble even more.

Again, she tried to focus on the crowd. She could
see her family smiling. She looked at her mother: the
perfect missionary dressed in her royal blue suit and
large matching hat that only rivaled First Lady Moore's
large white hat with feathers. She couldn't believe this
was the same woman who whipped her with an exten-
sion cord many times for nothing, and locked her in
the closet to keep her from playing with the other kids.
Their relationship had been strained for many years.
Her mother didn't believe she would go to college or
make something of herself. College was her only escape
from the hell she called home. So she went to Howard

to get as far away from her as she could. However, she missed being with her father, brother, and grandmother.

Misha focused her attention on her grandmother's small body sitting between her mother and her brother on the pews. Their enormous size made her grandmother look frail and weak. Her stare caught Misha's attention and she waved at her. Misha smiled and slightly waved back. She was glad her grandmother was able to make it to the program. At eighty-two years old, she didn't get out much, especially at night. It was beginning to get dark outside and the darkness made her nervous. She liked to be at home when it got dark. But today, she made an exception.

Misha looked at her grandmother's face that had the perfect makeup on it. Always the elegant woman when she went out of the house. At home, she only wore housedresses, winter, spring, summer, and fall, without fail. Her hair was silver and rolled into tight curls that looked like she just took out the pink hair rollers Misha was so used to seeing her wear around the house.

Looking farther into the crowd she eyed the deacons sitting in the front row. She used to think they were nodding in agreement with Bishop. Now she could see some of them were only asleep. How could they be asleep at the beginning of the program? Other people in the crowd were already nodding off too. She shook her head as she began to focus on other people in the church. It was like she could see the joy, peace, hurt, and fear of the people who had gathered to hear her speak. She felt the weight of their pain in her heart. She placed her hand on her chest and continued to breathe deeply. Closing her eyes, she prayed silently to herself for strength to get through this day.

The lyrical voices of the choir singing brought Misha out of her prayer. Her hands were clammy, damp, as they connected with every clap to the music. Bishop stood again to introduce Roger. He seemed so formal to her. She knew this was serious, no time for joking.

"I don't know about y'all, but tonight, I'm nervous. This is one of my own. I'm not going to introduce her. Minister Williams knows her best. But I do want to say she is one of us. She got saved right here in this church and I have watched her grow as a person, a Christian. I love her like my own child. I love all my sons and daughters in the ministry," he said, turning to look at Misha. "Your family here?" he asked.

Misha stretched her finger toward her family. Bishop asked them to stand as the congregation applauded.

"I know y'all love her. We have adopted her here. We love the work she does here with the junior missionaries and the youth choir. I'm not going to get into all that. I'm sure Minister Williams will tell you all about it. I want y'all to know we love her and are looking forward to hearing her preach." He turned to look at Misha again. "Are you nervous?" he asked, smiling at her.

Trying not to look nervous, she lifted her hands and over-exaggerated them shaking; and the laughter that followed removed the tension in the pulpit.

"Minister Williams, come on up here." Bishop walked to Misha and embraced her. "You'll be all right. Take your time and let the Lord use you," he whispered in her ear. Misha nodded, hugging him tightly.

As Roger stood at the podium introducing her and telling the congregation how much he loved her, Misha sat back in disbelief of where her life had taken her. She was the same girl who used to come into this church with a hangover and only a couple of hours of sleep when Roger would come to pick her up and take her to church. She only came because of him. She did like the preaching, but she loved the party.

As Roger stood at the podium going through her list of accomplishments, including her nomination for rookie teacher of the year last year, flashbacks of how she met him quickly breezed through her mind. It was a cold October day and she was leaving a sorority rush meeting when she met him: standing outside, protesting fraternities and sororities. He walked up to her and called her a beautiful woman of God and began talking to her. She didn't care what he said. The smell of his Obsession cologne was taking her away deep into his beautiful gray eyes. She looked at his ebony skin and perfect smile and thought she would go anywhere with him. That night she had plans to go to the club, but she wanted to get to know him.

He walked her down Georgia Avenue to her dorm and prayed for her before he left. He later called her and invited her to church the following Sunday. When he arrived to pick her up, she didn't tell him she had just gotten in from the club. She had a little too much to drink and her head was pounding. The loud noise in the church was making her feel worse. She wanted to stay with him all day, but not with her hangover. After church, she made an excuse not to go to eat with him. Without complaint, he took her back to her dorm.

She was delighted when she found out he was from Atlanta too. He was so positive and involved with different organizations at the school, unlike some of the guys she grew up with. He was a volunteer at Loaves and Fishes, a local soup kitchen in Washington, and seemed to keep busy and stayed focused. She liked him so much she let him believe he convinced her she would go to hell if she pledged a sorority or a "secret society" as he called it. She never told him she didn't pledge because she didn't have the money.

Her lips curved slightly upward thinking about how they would go out and he always made it a point to get her back to the dorm by eleven. He didn't know that when he left, she would change her clothes and meet her friends to go to the club. She liked him but he was a square. He talked about God and his career all the time. She stayed with him because he was so fine and dependable.

He talked a lot, and although she found some of the things he was saying hard to believe, she stayed anyway. No one else was knocking on her door for a date. Besides, he was a free ride home to Atlanta. Somehow she became attached to him, although something inside of her was telling her to stay away from him. Against her better judgment, she stayed with him even when she began to realize they had little in common.

The day he took her to his home church in Atlanta was life changing. Bishop Moore stood to preach. She had never heard preaching like that before. It was so different from the preaching she heard in the church she grew up in. His message was more life application than repetitive statements. She held on to every word. There was something about him that drew her to the altar that day. Not only did she get saved, she joined the church. She was later baptized there and now she sat, waiting to preach her first sermon.

She heard the choir finishing their second song. She stood and walked to the podium. It was time.

"Daughter, where did you learn to preach like that?" Bishop yelled over the noise at the restaurant.

"I guess it was all those years of sitting in the Pentecostal church growing up, and your teaching of homiletics and hermeneutics."

The private room in the restaurant was filled with Kingdom Faith people. When they got together, they were loud. There was a feeling of family, with everyone happy and joking with each other. First Lady Moore complimented Misha's mother on her hat, and they were deep in discussion about shopping.

"Well now that you're a minister, we can really put you to work in the church. You ready?" Bishop asked Misha.

"Well, Bishop, I guess I'm as ready as I can be. I'll have to talk with Roger first."

"Anything we should know about? Should I get out my formal white robe? You know, the one I use for weddings?"

"Bishop, don't start. Let Mimi enjoy this day first," Roger quickly chimed in. Everybody at the table began laughing loudly as Roger wiped the imaginary sweat from his brow.

Misha looked over at her grandmother frowning at Roger. "Grandma, are you all right?"

"Chicken's kinda dry."

"Grandma, I'll go get you something else. What would you like?"

"No, baby. I'm fine. Ti'ed though."

"It's getting late. Mama, we better go. Y'all, I had a good time," Misha's mother said, getting up from the table and grasping her mother's arm and helping her up from the chair. She walked over and kissed Misha on the forehead and spoke to everyone as they left the restaurant.

The kiss felt cold and dry to Misha. She knew her mother only did it for show. She really didn't mean it like she loved her. They barely spoke to each other. She had forgiven her mother for the abuse, but it didn't change their relationship. Her mother was so bitter and negative that Misha didn't like being around her and only talked to her when she had to.

She watched as her mother left the restaurant and soon after, others followed. "It is getting late, Bishop. I have to get up early for school tomorrow because I have bus duty. Thank you for the gift. Thank you, everybody, for the gifts," Misha said.

"Is that all I get for the gift I brought you?" Roger asked.

"The robe is beautiful, Roger. I'll thank you later," she answered, flirting with him.

Part of their group in the restaurant said, "Oooooooo," and started laughing.

"Come on, y'all. It's not like that. Get your mind out the gutter. I'm a preacher now. The Bible says be holy."

"But you're not dead," someone said and everybody started laughing again.

Roger put Misha's gifts in the car while she hugged Bishop, First Lady, and all of the other people in their group leaving the restaurant. The day was over and she finally had some time alone with Roger. Getting into the car, he leaned over and kissed Misha softly on the lips. There was a knock at the window. "Be holy," the young lady outside the window said and started laughing. They laughed too as Roger started the car and drove to Misha's apartment.

Arriving at her apartment, Misha and Roger loaded the gifts in their arms and slowly climbed the flight of stairs leading to her apartment. Placing the gifts on her small dining table that divided the living room from the kitchen, Roger reached for Misha's waist, pulling her into him, allowing their bodies to rock from side to side. "Stay a few minutes," Misha requested.

"I thought you had to get up early."

"I do. This is the first time we've been alone all day. Stay with me. Just a few minutes."

Misha held his hand as she led him to the small brown sofa in the center of her living room and sat down. She kicked off her shoes, tossed a couple of pillows on the floor, and curled up on the sofa with her head leaning on his chest. He embraced her and they sat silently for a few minutes.

"Did you see my license?" Misha said, running to the table and picking up the framed certificate she was given at the end of the program. "Can you believe it? Misha Holloway, a preacher?"

"It is funny. All those days you thought you were fooling me, like I didn't know you were clubbing, I was praying for you. Praying you'd stopped drinking and going to clubs. The prayers of the righteous availeth much."

"You knew I was going to clubs?"

"Yeah, I knew. I liked you. So I started praying for God to pull you out of the world and into His kingdom. My prayers were answered more than I expected. I never thought you would go into the ministry. I thought you would make a good first lady."

"You're asking me to marry you?"

Roger sat up nervously on the edge of the sofa. "You know I would not propose to you like that. It's coming though."

"When?"

"It's coming. Good things come to those who wait."

"Sometimes if you wait too long, things can spoil."

"What does that mean?"

"Nothing. I'm just messing with you. I love you," Misha said, snuggling into Roger again and taking a deep breath.

"I love you. I promise you, it won't be long. You'll make a wonderful first lady if only I can find you a hat like your mother's."

Both of them laughed as they talked about the oversized hat that was folded on one side with a loop going over it and a peacock feather sticking out of it. They compared it to the fully feathered hat First Lady Moore was wearing.

"You won't catch me in a hat like those."

"Even if I wanted a private hat show?" Roger said, leaning over and lightly kissing her ear, his lips slowly moving down her neck.

"Roger, we agreed, no sex, and you know how hard that was for me," she said, sitting up on the sofa. She wondered if he knew about the other guys, since he knew about the clubs. When she met him, she wanted to have sex. He was adamant about his celibacy and this almost broke them up. She couldn't hold back. She had to get hers until about a year into their relationship; she began feeling guilty about cheating on him and decided to give up sex. She couldn't look Roger in the face. She confessed to her friend Sheryl, who convinced her she was in love with Roger and she should never tell him about the other guys. Since that day, she never cheated on him and committed herself solely to this Christian relationship.

"Roger, maybe you should go," she said, standing and walking toward to door.

"I thought you wanted me to stay."

"You're kissing my neck. You know what that does to me."

"I see we're going to have to get married soon. On a night like tonight, I really want to be with you. I'm so happy and proud of you," he said, pulling her body to his, their lips meeting, lingering for a more passionate kiss. "You're right. I better go. Minister Holloway, sweet dreams," he whispered as Misha wrapped her arms around his waist. "Aaaagh, do you think there's a flight leaving for Vegas tonight?" he said, leaning his head back.

"I'll go get my bag." Misha released him and started past him just as he reached out and took her hand.

"Hey, I was only joking."

"I know. Scared you, didn't I?" A smile spread across her face.

"Come here, girl. I promise you. Soon, we'll sit down and plan something, okay?" He pulled her into him again. Misha wondered if he was being honest with her. She had heard it all before. But she was willing to wait.

Chapter 3

Three weeks had passed and Misha was enjoying being called Minister Holloway, although sometimes she didn't answer when people called her Minister. It sounded strange to her. She was looking forward to Wednesday night Bible Study. Bishop Moore could teach unlike anyone she had ever heard before. He had a way of dissecting the Word in a way that made it so relevant to today's life. The first time Roger had taken her to his church, she was discouraged with all the things, scandalous things, that were going on in her home church. It seemed like family groups ruled the church and the older people made it hard for the younger people to take an active part in the worship service. In college, she attended chapel at Howard but with the multiple speakers she felt as if it was more political than spiritual. She visited multiple churches in the DC area but never felt comfortable in any of them. She saw too much.

So when Roger took her to Kingdom Faith Church, a midsize church of about 600 people located within the inner city of Atlanta, and she heard Bishop speak, it felt like that was where she belonged. It had been three years and she had become very active in the church, helping with the junior missionaries and the youth choir. She was also instrumental in developing the church's after school program. This project she was especially proud of since she and Roger worked on it together.

As she entered Bishop's office, she saw his many degrees, earned and honorary. There were multiple pictures on the wall, some of which looked very old and were in black and white. There was even one with Bishop and 1960s civil rights leaders. She smiled looking at the picture of Bishop in a dashiki and a very large Afro. There was a big maple wood desk and leather chairs scattered throughout the large office. She admired him because he was so wise and he helped her with a lot of the decisions she had to make after she graduated from college. He believed in establishing relationships with his members, like family.

He went to the hospital and visited her mother even though she was not a member of his church. He was so encouraging to everyone he met. He was well respected in the community and was a force to be reckoned with when it came to community revitalization and economic empowerment. He treated the ministers with utmost respect and just like they were his natural children. Roger would go on and on about the things he was being taught about church leadership and the ministry. Happy he was her pastor, she looked forward to finally discussing the gift with him.

Bishop Moore, a tall, stout, dark-skinned man in his late sixties, greeted her with a big hug and asked her to sit in one of the large brown leather chairs in front of his desk. He commended her for her work with the junior missionaries and advised her about their new project that would be starting at the beginning of the year. Finishing up the missionary work, Misha felt it was the proper time to talk to him about the gift.

"Bishop, I need to ask you something."

"Go ahead, daughter."

"Well this is kinda hard for me. I've only told one person before today and Roger said I should talk to you about it."

"Sounds important. Wait a minute. Let me close the door." Bishop managed to get his large body up from the well-worn chair behind his desk and went to the door and closed it. He returned to his seat and continued the conversation. "What is it, daughter?"

She took a deep breath and then started. "Bishop, all my life I have known things."

"Things? What type of things?" he said, sitting up in his chair and clasping his hands on the desk in front of him.

"I don't know how to explain it. But, I know things I shouldn't know, about people, places, things, and stuff like that. It's beginning to bother me. Like a few weeks ago, I knew the husband of one of my coworkers was out of town and he was getting a promotion. She told me today he got the promotion. I don't know how I knew. I just knew and I only met her husband once, briefly, last year."

"How long has this been going on?" Bishop asked, leaning on his desk.

Misha twirled her fingers nervously as she sat in the chair that sank in from wear. "All my life."

"I'm glad you came to me. What do you think it is?"

Misha searched for the words to describe exactly what was going on with her. How could she tell him her dreams were not ordinary dreams? They were insight into the future. She could not explain how she could look at a person and know their entire life story without them mentioning a word. Would he think she was crazy? Goodness, she was just ordained into the ministry. She did not want to appear weird.

"I don't know. It doesn't happen all the time. I've prayed about it. Roger seems to think it has something to do with me going into the ministry."

"What do you think?" he asked but Misha could not answer. She did not know.

Bishop began to minister to her about spiritual gifts and told her to study 1 Corinthians 12. He scheduled an appointment with her to give her a spiritual gifts questionnaire.

"Bishop, what do I do until then? This is becoming more irritating than anything. It seems like it's happening more and more. I can't make it stop. Like for instance, when I look at you, I see this dark-skinned woman with a short, natural hairstyle. She has two children, boys, standing beside her, and she is waving and smiling."

Bishop's eyes widened and he jumped to his feet, slamming his hands against the desk. His chair rolled back and hit the wall. Misha jumped, startled at his reaction. His smile was gone. She could see the veins beating through the skin of his forehead and neck. "What are you talking about? You don't know anything about me. How dare you walk into my office trying to trick me with gossip, pretending the Lord is showing you something. Do you think I'm some kinda fool?" he shouted.

"Bishop, I don't know what you're talking about. I need your help. I came for help. That's all."

"Do you think you're the first one to think they can pull something over my head? Who sent you here?" he said, walking around his desk and staring at her.

"Roger told me to talk with you. I didn't say anything to him about the woman."

"So you and Minister Williams think you can take over this ministry with your lies and gossip. You think you're sneaky. You need to try again. I built this ministry up to what it is today and I'm not about to let the two of you come in here and destroy it."

"Bishop, I don't know what you're talking about. I only came here for help. I need to understand what's going on with me." Misha could not believe his reaction.

"So you thought you could pretend you were a prophet and make me admit to something that's not true?"

"Bishop, I—"

"It's time for Bible Study. Please leave my office. I have to prepare for service. We'll continue this conversation later."

Misha left his office, bewildered at what had just happened. She didn't understand the reaction she got from him. Walking down the long hallway and down the short set of steps to the main sanctuary, she tried desperately to hold back the tears. She found a seat near the front of the church and silently prayed to herself about what happened and asked God for direction. Roger sat down beside her and kissed her lightly on the cheek, interrupting her thoughts.

"Mimi, what's wrong?" he asked, noticing her eyes on the threshold of tearing.

"We'll talk about it later," Misha whispered, holding her head down, trying to keep the tears from falling.

"Did you talk to Bishop?"

"I don't want to talk about it. I'll tell you after Bible Study."

The praise team got up and began service, and afterward the large group of people was divided into smaller classes with the largest, the adults, remaining in the sanctuary. Roger sat beside her with his arm around her shoulders. Bishop came out and began to address the congregation.

"There comes a time in everyone's ministry when we have to do things we don't want to. I've been praying in my office about this and I feel this is what God wants me to do." He stood at the podium, fumbling through the papers in front of him.

Something bad was about to happen. Misha could feel it. His every word was directed at her even though he did not look at her. He began to teach on witchcraft and the hold it could have on people. Misha fidgeted in her seat as she listened to him speak. Roger was engrossed with every word. At one point, he stood along with others, voicing his agreement to what Bishop was saying. He talked about the spirit of manipulation and how this was a primary instrument of the enemy. The congregation was taking it all in with such enthusiasm. Misha could not join in. That horrible sinking feeling in her gut wouldn't let go and kept getting worse. Fear ripped through her as she tried to prepare herself for the storm that was brewing. A cold chill swept through her the longer Bishop continued to speak.

"Today, a witch came into my office and tried to manipulate me. I will not tolerate a witch in this church. People who operate under a satanic anointing will tear a church up and I won't have it. Therefore, I want to say to that person she has to leave today."

Misha knew what was coming next. She could feel it in her spirit. She prayed he wasn't talking about her. But, she knew differently. He looked directly at her.

"Ms. Holloway, when you came to our church, we accepted you as family. But as with any devil, if you wait, the true fruit will appear. The Bible says you will know them by their fruit. Well, now I have seen your fruit. How dare you come in here and try to tell me something about myself? You don't know anything about me or what goes on in my house. You're a witch and have a spirit of divination. I will not let a witch come in here and destroy this church. Get out. Get out now and don't come back. Deacons, help her to the door," Bishop said, waving his arm in the direction of the door at the back of the church.

"Wait a minute. What's going on?" Roger's eyes were questioning as he looked at Bishop and then Misha.

"Minister Williams, if you don't like it, you can follow her."

Misha looked at Roger, his mouth open and eyes full of wonder. She waited for him to defend her. When he didn't say anything in her defense, she gathered her jacket and purse and was slowly escorted out the door by two deacons. She could hear the whispers in the crowd as she walked down the aisle to the door. Someone began clapping and there began a slow ascension of hands clapping from the congregation. They were agreeing with Bishop. Misha couldn't look at them. These were the same people who, only a few weeks ago, applauded her and celebrated her accomplishments. She couldn't believe they would turn on her so quickly.

She stopped at the door of the church, waiting to hear one voice stand and defend her. When no one did, she walked out the door. They were going along with Bishop even though they did not know the real story. They blindly followed him and put their trust in him. So whatever he said went. Today, the thing going was her. And where was Roger? Was he coming to her defense? She waited at her car for him to follow her out of the church, but he never showed. One deacon walked to her, apologizing for what happened, but asked that she leave the premises or he would have to call the police.

She began her journey home until her weeping became so bad she could not drive. She pulled her car into the parking lot of a grocery store and picked up the phone to call Roger, only to get his voicemail. What just happened to her? She didn't understand any of it. She only wanted answers to what was going on with her. This night she got none. If anything, she was more confused than ever.

"How could he treat me like that?" she wondered out loud. "He called me a witch. I'm not a witch!" She yelled alone in her car. "God, please help me!" She continued trying to get Roger on his cell until she arrived home. It was after ten when he finally called her back. She was in the bed but sleep eluded her. Tears fell freely onto her pillow. She leaped for the phone on her nightstand when it rang.

"Misha, what did you say to Bishop? He seems to think I had something to do with it. He wants to sit me down. What did you do?" Roger questioned her.

"I didn't do anything. I told him I know things and he got angry. That's all. He got so upset he asked me to leave his office."

"You know how hard I work in the ministry. How could you do something to destroy it? I thought you loved me."

"What are you talking about? I do love you. I didn't do anything. I only wanted help and he got angry. I don't know why. When I mentioned the woman and kids—"

"What woman? You told me you didn't say anything to him. What's the truth? What did you say about me?" Roger continued yelling in the phone.

"You told me to talk to him. I was only telling him what I saw. If he got so upset, then there must have been some truth to it. I thought of all the people, I would have your support."

"I thought I had yours. How could you do something to destroy my ministry? I thought I knew you. How could you do this to me, to us?" She heard the click of the phone as Roger hung up on her.

She was so overwhelmed with the situation she cried herself to sleep that night. She could not believe the man she loved was taking someone else's side in all this. He did not even listen to her. He didn't even ask her how she was feeling. He acted as if he didn't care about anyone but himself. This was a side of him she had not seen before.

The following morning she was beginning to question their relationship when he did not answer her phone calls to him. She went to school, pretending everything was fine, even though there were times when she felt like crying and had to leave her classroom to go into the hallway to get herself together.

At lunch, she stayed in her classroom with the door closed, trying to reach Roger on the phone. He still was not answering her phone calls. How could he treat her that way? He knew her better than anyone. She never would have thought he would do something like this to her.

Sitting in her car after school she again tried to call Roger on the phone. He still did not answer her. She called his job and was told he called in sick. He never called in sick. Upset, she left him an extensive voice message and asked him to call her back.

She started her car and tried to decide if she felt like eating. She didn't. She drove down the street, not really paying attention to where she was going, praying for God to reveal His will in her life. Her life was going well. She had a good job, so they said. At least, she had a stable job. She had a nice apartment, a saved boyfriend, and she thought she had found the perfect church. Now, with the snap of a finger, it had all changed. She was kicked out of the church and her boyfriend was not talking to her and she did not even know why. In addition to all of that, state testing was about to begin in the school and Mr. Davis was on everybody's case about test scores. This only added to all the stressors going on around her.

Suddenly, she could hear her grandmother's voice. She steered her car in the direction of her grandmother's house. She was the only one she could talk to about anything—if only she could get through the conversation without falling apart. Her grandmother would give her the answers she needed.

She pulled in front of the small white wood-frame mill house located near the center of the city. Her grandmother was sitting on the porch as usual, smiling, when she saw Misha's car slowly turn into the driveway. Before she could get out of her car, the tears were flowing down her cheeks. She ran to her grandmother's open arms.

"Baby, what's wrong?" There was concern in her grandmother's voice as she took her hand and led her into the small house. Misha looked around the room. She felt at home in the tiny room decorated with pictures of her family. The smell of fried chicken filled the air. Misha followed her to the breakfast nook and they sat at the small table.

"Everything. Everything." She wiped her eyes with the back of her hands.

"I just finished making some bread and peach preserves. Let me get you some. Have you had dinner? I think there is another piece of chicken in here. Let me see, where is it?" Her grandmother got up from the table and opened the cabinet and retrieved a large plate from the shelf.

"No, Grandma. I'm not hungry."

"Look at you. What you got yo'self all worked up 'bout?"

Misha told her grandmother everything that had happened. Her grandmother sat at the table listening attentively as Misha opened herself up to her. When she finished, her grandmother started a story of her own.

"You know you a special child." She picked up Misha's hand and patted it.

"Grandma, you say that about all of us."

"Listen to me. You a special child." She continued, "You the first born grandchild on both sides of yo' family. Everyone was so excited 'bout you coming to dis world. But the devil tried to take you outta here before you born."

"I know Mama had to be on bed rest before I was born so she wouldn't have a miscarriage."

"Yeah, that ol' devil tried to kill ya. But, God wasn't havin' no part of that. When yo' mama went into labor, your daddy was out of town driving that truck. He was trying to get back before you born. So, I had to go to the labor room wit' her. You came quick, unusual for a first pregnancy. But there you was, all seven pounds seven ounces of you, ready ta make your appearance in the world."

She got up and got Misha's baby picture from the mantel over the fireplace and gave it to her. "You was a beautiful baby. But, I knew that you'd be diff'rent. See when you was born, you had a veil."

"What's that? I never heard of anything like that. I don't understand."

"When you came out, yo' face was covered with a thin skin. This a sho sign that you have the gift to see thangs ordinary folk don't see."

"Like a prophet?" Misha was curious. This was the first time she had heard anything like that. No one ever mentioned it to her.

"Som'in like dat. Runs in our family. You the only child born this way. I know, 'cause I was at all y'all's birth. I wanted ta know."

She continued to explain to Misha, in her strong Southern-coastal Gullah accent, that when she was a child she had the ability to tell when something was going to happen. She even knew about things that happened in the family long before she was born. She had wisdom a child should not have and knew things she should not have known. Misha didn't remember any of the things she was hearing. She did admit she knew things like when people were going to die or private things about people.

"You have the gift. You have to be careful who you tell. When you went to the bishop, he upset 'cause you told him the truth. You can't lie 'bout things like that. The Holy Spirit using you to reveal truth and He reveal it to who He please. That was a warning to Bishop Mo'. I bet you not the first one God sent in there to warn him. You an easy target. He thinks 'cause he got rid of you, he got rid of the secret. I bet you anythang those chil'en you saw was his."

"Grandma, his children are grown and his grandchildren are teenagers."

"Don't know 'bout all that. But truth will be revealed. I know it hurt real bad for somebody to cuss you like that. But you gotta move on. God'll lead you. Pray. Pray hard. Now that you workin' for the Kingdom, devil don't like it. He be out to get you for sho. So you have to pray. Pray without ceasing. And do what the Lord tells ya. 'Til God sends you somewhere, you can come to my church. Pasta Smif won't kick you out. He'll be glad ta have a new memba."

"Grandma, Roger, he won't talk to me now. He's not answering my phone calls. They said he called in sick today at work. I don't know why he's mad at me. I didn't say anything about him."

"Roger yo' husband? You know who yo' husband is." She sat calmly at the table, looking at Misha as she began to cry again. She didn't try to comfort her. She stood and retrieved a glass from the cabinet. Opening the refrigerator, she poured a glass of water and gave it to Misha.

Misha took a small sip and set the glass on the table. "I love Roger. We talked about getting married but we can't afford it now."

"He yo' husband?" Her grandmother returned to her chair.

"I love him."

"You not answering me. You know who yo' husband is since you was a child. Now answer me, he yo' husband? I'll answer you. If he was, he be here supporting you 'stead of taking side of that man. He understand the gift and the purpose that God has for you. Now when you was a child, you had one name that you said was your husband, but when you found boys, you stopped talking 'bout him. You rememba?"

Misha did remember his name: Matthew. She remembered talking about marrying Matthew and having children and living in a big house with pretty flowers all around it. She said he was a preacher and she was the elegant first lady who wore big hats and had a successful business. That's all she talked about until she was about twelve. Dismissing him as a figment of a young girl's imagination, she found real boys to be more appealing.

"I know you remember. Now, I know it look hard now. What's important is you learn what you supposed to do with the gift. Rememba, you can't tell everybody about it. I may not understand everything you see and hear, but I do know that it comes from God and don't you let nobody tell you no different."

She went into one of the cabinets and returned with a bottle of olive oil that she had her pastor bless. Covering the open bottle with two fingers she slowly tilted the oil until it touched her fingers. Then she made a symbol of the cross on Misha's forehead and began to pray that God guide her through this process He was leading her into. Misha allowed herself to cry on her grandmother's shoulder. This was where she found the most comfort, the most peace.

Chapter 4

Misha looked around her classroom at the church. She missed the children in her class. She looked at every paper hanging on the wall with the names of her students on them. It had been two weeks since Bishop kicked her out of the church and she still did not understand why. Roger had not spoken to her and surprisingly she felt okay with that. She only cried a couple of nights but it was not a sad cry; it felt more of a cleansing. She learned a long time ago not to waste time on people who did not support her. But, she still had her moments when she wanted to pick up the phone and call him to see if he wanted to go out to eat or something. Old habits die hard. For some reason, she felt her load was lightened.

As she left the classroom, she noticed a hint of light peeking through the crack in the door of Bishop Moore's office. Since the church was almost empty, it would be a good time to talk with him. Slowly she walked toward the office and knocked on the door. Bishop was sitting at his desk, writing something in a spiral notebook. When he saw her, his eyes grew large and he leaned back in his chair. Misha tried to read the expression on his face. It seemed blank, without emotion.

"What are you doing here? I thought you understood you're not welcome in our church," Bishop Moore said to her.

"I had some things to get out of my classroom."

"So you're stealing from us?"

"No, I left my jacket and a couple of personal items in the classroom." She held out the jacket and small box filled with stencils she held in her hand so he could see what they were. "I saw your light on. Your secretary was not in. May I speak with you for a minute? I don't understand what happened the other night and I would like to talk with you for a minute."

Bishop looked as if he was ready for a fight—his lips poked out and his jaws locked in position. He did not invite her to sit down. "I have an appointment coming in."

"I won't be long," she said as she remained standing in the doorway.

"What do you want? Haven't you done enough damage?"

"That's just it. I don't know what happened. I came to you for help and you publicly embarrassed me by calling me out my name—accusing me of being a witch. How did you come to that conclusion? I have never practiced witchcraft. No one in my family who I know of practices witchcraft. I don't know where you got that from." She began to cry. "I gave my all to this church. When I wasn't at school, I was here or doing things for this church and yet it seemed like it didn't matter to you."

Bishop sat back in his chair and began swaying back and forth.

"Bishop, what did I do to you? Whatever it was, please forgive me. I didn't mean to say or do anything to hurt you or this church. I love this church. I don't want to leave. And Roger, he won't even speak to me. Was it about the woman and children?"

"There you go again." Bishop jumped up from his chair and walked to face her. "I don't know where you heard those rumors, but you can't fool me. I'm going to ask you nicely to leave this church, and if you come back again, I'm going to file a restraining order against you and have you arrested. Do you hear me?"

"Misha, what are you doing here?" She heard Roger's voice behind her. Her body stiffened as she turned to see him near her in the hallway. His eyes were puffy and his clothes were wrinkled. The smile he usually wore was absent. He slipped past her as if he was trying not to touch her as he walked into the office.

"Bishop, Misha, what's going on here? Misha, I didn't know you would be here. Bishop, I thought we were talking alone."

"Roger, I just came by to get my stuff out of the class-room, that's all. I've been trying to reach you. They said you have been calling in sick. Are you okay?"

"I got your messages. I didn't feel like talking. You hurt me."

"Hurt you? What did I do? You're the one who told me to talk to Bishop in the first place. How can you say I hurt you?"

"So, just like I suspected, you're in on this too, Minister Williams?" Bishop interrupted.

"No, Bishop. I didn't tell her anything. What she did, she did on her own."

"Roger, how can you lie like that?" Misha yelled. "You told me to come and talk to Bishop. I wouldn't have done it if you had not talked me into it."

Misha was stunned. This is not the Roger she knew. They had been together almost four years. He had been her rock. He was there to support her in all her efforts. She could count on him for anything—she thought. Of all people, he would never betray her. However, today, he was acting as if they never really knew each other. Her lips trembled as she tried to keep in the words she really wanted to say.

"Roger, why are you doing this? I love you and you said you love me. Don't do this to us. Don't, Roger, please don't."

Roger moved farther into the office and sat down in one of the big leather chairs, unable to look at Misha in the face. Misha watched as he sat in the chair, looking down at his hands clasped in his lap, and said nothing more.

"Ms. Holloway, I'm going to ask you again to please leave," Bishop said.

"Roger, you're going to sit there and not say anything? You're going to let them treat me like this when you know I haven't done anything wrong?"

He didn't answer her. He did not even look up. He acted as if he did not hear anything she said. She stared at him as if she stared long enough, he would turn around and talk to her.

"Ms. Holloway, I'm trying to be nice."

Bishop didn't need to tell her again. Misha ran from the office, her pulse racing as she picked up the pace to get to her car. The click of the door closing behind her only made her angrier. There was no telling what kind of lie Roger was there to tell. She gasped when she heard someone call her name before she reached the door. Turning, she saw a gray-haired lady come out the door of the main office.

"Come into my office quick," the lady said. It was Gertrude, Bishop's long-time secretary. They entered into the office and she offered Misha a seat and handed her a Kleenex. "I can't talk to you long. Pastor will fire me if he knew I spoke with you at all. I've been praying for you. It's about time you found out about Roger. His head is so far up Bishop's butt he could probably clean his intestines from the inside. He'll believe anything Bishop tells him."

"I don't want to talk about Roger."

"I understand. You're hurt and it'll take time to get over it. Count it all joy. It's best you learned this before the two of you got married. I want you to know I believe you. I overheard what you said. I didn't mean to pry, but the door was open and I sort of heard."

"You believe what?"

"Everything. I want you to know I'm behind you. I'm trying to find another job. I've had enough of this."

"I'm angry and upset. But, I'm not going to talk about Bishop, the church, or Roger." Misha wiped her eyes.

"That's because you have integrity. You're one of the few here who do."

"I'm going. Thank you for the tissue." Misha stood to leave the office. She knew better than to participate in church gossip. At this point, she didn't believe she could trust anyone in this church.

"Before you leave, let me encourage you. Everything covered will be uncovered. You just remember that. God will lead you where you need to go. Just continue to be obedient to what He tells you. You hear me?"

"Yes. Thank you. I better leave. Bishop said he was going to call the police."

"He won't do that. You take care of yourself. If you need anyone to talk to, give me a call. God bless you." She hugged Misha. Gertrude peeped out into the hallway to see if anyone was coming before Misha entered it, and hugged her again before watching her exit through the door into the parking lot.

Chapter 5

"Turn over your test and begin," Misha said to her class as they began taking the promised history test. She tried to get a jumpstart on grading the previous class's test while she carefully monitored the classroom for anyone trying to cheat. She heard an unusual ruffle and looked up in time to see a girl pass a piece of paper to another girl in the classroom.

"Bethany, can you bring me that piece of paper?" Misha requested.

"What paper are you talking about? I'm not finished with my test yet."

"If you don't bring me the paper that Amber just gave you, both of you will get an F on the test and a trip to the principal's office for cheating."

Both girls let out a long sigh as Bethany walked to the front of the classroom with the folded paper in her hand as the class watched to see what would happen next. Misha took the paper and opened it. She laughed at what she saw. The note said:

I really like Ms. Holloway's outfit today. I wonder where she got it.

Misha shook her head and thought that these two girls must have thought she was stupid. She had been warned while she was student teaching about this technique the students used if they ever got caught cheating. She knew there was another sheet of paper.

"Bethany, I asked you for the paper Amber gave you."

"This is what Amber gave me," she yelled. The other students stopped taking their test and looked at the two of them.

"Amber, come to my desk and bring me the paper or gather your things and prepare to go to the principal's office."

"I didn't cheat!" Amber yelled.

When she yelled, a cold chill went over Misha. What she heard was a call for help. She looked at Amber and saw a man, an older man, with his arms wrapped around her and Amber struggling to get free. She shook her head, trying to get the scene out of her mind.

"Amber, what did you say?" Misha asked, coming to her senses.

"I didn't cheat. It was a phone number for this guy I know. That's all. See? Here it is," she said, running to the desk, handing Misha the folded paper.

When she handed the paper to her, Misha saw the scene again. She sat at her desk with a blank stare on her face. She looked deeply into the brown eyes of Amber and she could see her life as clear as if it were a movie. What she saw frightened Misha.

"Ms. Holloway? Ms. Holloway? Are you okay?" Bethany tapped Misha on the shoulder to get her attention.

"What? I'm fine. You two go back and finish your test."

Both girls walked back to their desks and slightly laughed, thinking they got away with cheating. Misha knew they were cheating. But, there was something much larger going on with Amber and she knew it. She could feel it in her soul. She didn't know what to do about it. Amber was one of the most popular girls in the school. She was a cheerleader, a member of the student government, and in the honor society and numerous other organizations. She even managed to volunteer at the local hospital. She was from a wealthy family and she had received numerous awards and scholarships to go to college and she was only a junior. Misha continued to stare at Amber until the end of the class.

"Amber, can I see you?"

"I didn't cheat, Ms. Holloway," Amber said, placing her test on the desk.

Misha waited for the class to empty into the hallway and she closed and locked her door so the next class would not come in. There was a knock on the door and Misha told the students to wait outside.

"Are you okay?" Misha asked.

"I'm fine. I think I missed two on the test. I got a little confused about number six and fifteen. I think I did well though. I'm glad you put that extra credit question on the test. I really need it."

"How's everything at home?" Misha sat at her desk, looking at Amber—her hair long and blond, her skin tanned from the tanning bed she had bragged about having at home.

"At home? Everything's great. We're planning a trip to Aspen this Christmas. I can't wait. I love going there."

"No, really. How are you? Has anyone been . . . been . . ."

"Been what?"

"Has anyone hurt you?"

"Hurt me how?"

Misha saw the curious look on her face and realized the young girl had no idea what she was talking about. "I want you to know you can talk to me about anything, okay?"

"Sure, whatever. I'm going to be late for my next class. Can you give me a note?"

Misha wrote Amber a note and allowed her next class to come into the classroom. After handing out the test to the next class, she settled in to grade papers, but she could not shake the feeling she had about Amber. What she saw in Amber's eyes terrified her.

At the end of the day, Misha decided to stay longer at the school to grade her papers from the day's tests. She didn't want to go home anyway. All she would do at home was think about Roger. She was still upset about everything he had done, or not done, since she spoke with Bishop Moore. Just as she started to get upset, there was a knock at her door. It was Principal Davis.

"Ms. Holloway, is everything all right?" He noticed her wiping her eyes.

"No, my eyes are strained from grading all these tests. I'm getting ready to leave in a few minutes though. Can I help you with anything?"

"As a matter of fact you can. I'm still looking for people to help with the homecoming dance next week. Will you be able to do it? I could really use your help."

"I don't have any plans. I guess I can help."

"Good. I'll tell the homecoming committee you'll be there. Try not to stay here too long. It's the weekend and I'm sure you have plans with that boyfriend of yours; what's his name?"

"Roger."

"Yeah, Roger, that's it."

"No, we don't have any plans. Anyway, I'll be out of here in a few minutes. You have a good weekend, Mr. Davis."

She watched as the principal walked out of her classroom. She could hear him talking to the janitor who had started buffing the hallway. The sound of the buffer would not allow her to concentrate on her work. She wasn't looking forward to the weekend. She didn't have Roger to spend time with, nor did she have a church to go to or have all the activities being in an active church involved. She didn't know what she was going to do. At that point, she only wanted to go to the store, curl up with some ice cream, and allow the television to watch her.

"Misha, you still here?" Judy peeped into her room.

"I'm going now. I'm surprised you're still here."

"I didn't want to take any work home with me. My husband and I are going out of town to celebrate his promotion and leaving the kids with my mother. I stayed to grade some papers."

"Me too."

"Is anything wrong?"

"No, nothing's wrong."

"You sure? You don't look right. You haven't looked right in a while. You want to talk about it?"

"No, I'm fine."

"Okay. Well, if you need someone to talk to I'm just down the hallway. But, if I can't perk you up, maybe a look at that new soccer coach will do the trick. He's a cutie. Lord, have mercy. God allowed me to be married for such a time as this. That man is fine and if I weren't married . . ."

"Don't say it."

"You're right. We both are happy in our relationships and nothing or no one is going to tear them apart. Right?"

Misha didn't respond. She pretended to be focused on packing her bag to leave. Judy looked at her and could see the tears well in Misha's eyes. Then it came to her. "Oh, I'm sorry. Don't tell me you two broke up. I'm here running my big mouth. What happened? I thought the two of you were in love."

Misha could no longer hold back her tears. She hadn't talked to anyone about this except her grandmother. She thought Roger would be back by now. Her heart was now hurting so badly she couldn't breathe. She held her chest and sat down in the chair, trying desperately to catch her breath. She had tried to be strong. Suddenly she felt it all come down on her. Misha was crying so hard it felt like she was sipping air through a straw.

"Misha, are you okay?'

"I don't understand what happened. I can't talk about it." Misha gasped for air as the salty taste of her tears flowed into her mouth.

"Breathe slowly. Take your time. I'm sorry. I didn't know. Come on, breathe slowly." Misha couldn't control the tears that flowed down her face. Judy closed the door and walked to Misha and hugged her. "Do you want to talk about it?" Misha shook her head. "I understand. We won't talk here. Come on, get yourself together. We don't want these nosey people all up in your business. Here's a tissue. I don't want to be nosey but does this have anything to do with the gift?"

"What gift?"

"You know, your gift. I've been watching and listening to you since you got here. I know you have the gift. You knew about my husband's promotion among other things you shouldn't have known. Did God show you something about your boyfriend? You know not everyone can handle being around someone with the gift. They're afraid their secrets will be revealed."

"How did you know?" Misha looked at Judy.

"God told me. I know people think I'm a heathen. I believe in God and talk to Him every day. I'm a worshipper too. I don't go around talking like everyone else here trying to prove they're so holy. He reveals things to me too. I've been through what you're going through now."

Misha sat up in her chair. She wanted to talk to Judy more. She wanted to praise God for sending someone she could talk to. "I don't want to talk about it here."

"I understand. Here, get yourself together. Let's go to Roscoe's. We can talk there."

"I thought you and your husband have plans. I can't take you away from your family. I'll be all right."

"He'll be fine. We're not leaving until tomorrow anyway. I'll call him and let him know I'll be a little late coming home tonight. Right now you need me, and what kind of a friend would I be leaving you like this? Now get yourself together. Let's walk to my class so I can get my stuff and we'll walk to the parking lot together."

Misha reached into her purse to get out a wet wipe to wipe the now-dried white tearstain from her face, and walked down the quiet hallway with Judy. They quickly walked to the parking lot and on to Roscoe's. They sat at a table in the back of the restaurant. Misha looked around the almost-empty restaurant. She knew in a couple of hours there would be lines spilling outside the door and onto the sidewalk with people waiting to get in.

"Misha, what happened?"

Her tears started to flow again as she told Judy about the incident with the bishop and how Roger reacted. She even told her what her grandmother said about her being born with a veil over her face.

"You were born with a veil?" Judy's hands flew to her mouth.

"That's what Grandma said. I don't understand it. That's just what she said. I don't know if I believe that old wives' tale." Misha didn't fully believe the story her grandmother told her. She felt it might have been just a part of her grandmother's James Island background— just another Gullah tale.

"Well you better because it's true. If you were born with a veil, you're a prophet. There's nothing you can do about it."

"I'm not a prophet. Roger seemed to think the gift was manifested because of my trial sermon."

"Trial sermon? You're a minister?" Judy sat up with her hands fisted on her waist. "Why didn't you tell me? How long have you been in the ministry?"

"A few weeks."

"You just went in the ministry and you didn't say anything? I would have come to your trial sermon. I bet you did a good job. What did you preach?"

"I wouldn't call it preaching."

"Still, you should have told me. I would have liked to have been there. So how are you getting along? I know you still hurt."

"It's been hard. I don't know why Roger is treating me like this. We used to talk every day and . . ." Misha tried hard to hold back the tears but they seemed to escape no matter how hard she tried. She could no longer walk around as if she wasn't in pain and she didn't care. She had just given this man the last three years of her life.

Judy reached across the table to grip Misha's hand. "Hey, girl, it's going to be all right. Everything works for the good to them who love the Lord and are called for His purpose." She squeezed Misha's hand. "It will all work out."

Misha was hurting too much to let the words melt her pain. She didn't understand why she had to go through so much hurt in her life. First it was the abuse she received from her mother, now the church and

Roger. She wondered how long the pain was going to last. She only wanted it to stop.

"Misha, I don't know what's wrong with that bishop of yours. He'll probably never find another person to take your place in the church. From what you tell me, you did a lot in the church. A lot of people are not committed like that anymore. He may have to find several people to take your place." Judy tried to console her.

"I won't talk about Bishop. He did what he felt was necessary. I don't understand it. I did nothing wrong. What I really don't understand is the way Roger is acting. If it weren't for him, I wouldn't be a Christian. How could he just drop me after all we've been through?"

"It's his loss. You're a special person. Not everyone can handle the anointing on your life."

"I'm not that anointed. I don't even know what I'm doing. Maybe it wasn't meant for me to go in the ministry. I don't know."

"Don't give the enemy a foothold in your mind. He's messing with you right now. You need to find a good church that will allow you to operate under the anointing that's in you. Come to my church. You'll like it. Our pastor is kinda young, but he's a good minister. It's a new church and it hasn't been contaminated by the years of tradition a lot of other churches have. You don't even have to dress up. I would like for you to come with me."

"I thought you and your husband were going out of town this weekend."

"We are. You can come with us next week. I'm sure you'll like it."

"Well, I don't know. Seems like everybody has heard about what Bishop did to me. I don't know if I can—"

"Misha, don't let the enemy keep you at home. It'll do you good to be in a ministry where we believe in the operation of spiritual gifts. Try it, just once. You don't have to join."

"Thank you, I think I will go with you. I need to be somewhere other than my grandma's church. I don't understand a word her pastor is saying except 'ain't He all right?'" Misha chuckled at her own statement.

She loved her grandmother's pastor but he was old-fashioned and loved to eat the microphone. However, he and the church welcomed her in like they were family. Some of the members who had heard what happened to her called and tried to encourage her and support her.

Her grandmother was the church mother and sat in the amen corner every Sunday.

She enjoyed going to church with her grandmother. She was so wise. After church, they would go to a res-taurant and have dinner. Her grandmother would tell her stories about the old days and would minister to her in a way no one could. Misha took in every word her grandmother said. At this point in her life, she needed the support of her grandmother. She was the only one who made some sense out of everything that was going on in her life. Even if it was just Gullah tale, it was better than what anybody else was offering her.

Chapter 6

Seven months had passed and it was May, the end of the school year, and Misha was looking forward to taking the summer off. She was also glad she didn't have to worry about money, as she had taken the twelve-month pay option that divided her salary into twelve months of pay instead of nine. She didn't want to take another job during the summer. It had been a long winter.

Thoughts of Roger would sometimes enter her mind and she had to occupy herself with other tasks to keep from thinking about him and what could have happened. Her cousin told her he was dating a girl they knew at the church. She tried to act as if she didn't care, but she would cry all night and the pain would start all over again. With each report, the tears lessened until they were no more. That either meant she was closer to getting over Roger, or had just become numb to the fact that they may never get back together.

She was thankful that Judy had invited her to True Life Christian Fellowship. She enjoyed going there, although she had not joined. The pastor, Niles Simpson, welcomed her as a woman of God. He surprised Misha one Sunday by asking for a copy of her ministry license. When she gave it to him, he welcomed her into the pulpit and had allowed her to preach on several occasions. Because of this, people began asking her to preach on special days, like women's day and singles conferences at other churches in the Atlanta area. She was beginning to enjoy being a Christian and a worker in the Kingdom again.

Occasionally, the sting of Bishop Moore's words was still not far from her thoughts. When people asked her about it, she tried to change the subject or use it to minister to people about their own relationship with God. She had purposed in her heart she wasn't going to say anything bad about him or Roger.

It was the end of a busy week. She was preparing her students for the final exams the following week. She had given the graduating seniors their exam that day and graded them before the end of the day. She thought she would go see a movie. She was trying hard to do the singles thing they had taught her in singles ministry at the church. She was learning how to enjoy spending time alone.

"Hey, Misha, what are you doing tonight?" Judy walked into her room wearing a light blue pantsuit, looking so slim no one would ever imagine she had given birth to a bunch of kids. Her hair was cut short, cropped along the sides with tight curls on the back and a long bang that swooped across her forehead.

"Nothing really."

"Well I heard Pastor Shante Patrick is in town tonight at the Rock of Life church. You want to go with me? I know it's short notice. But I called the church. Service is starting at seven. How 'bout it?"

"Shante Patrick? Shoot yeah. How much is it?" Excitement filled her.

"You know she won't preach at a church that charges admission. It's free and you can wear what you got on. It'll be our girls' night out. Randy is watching the kids for me. You can leave your car at my house and we can go get something to eat. I don't live too far from here."

"Sounds great. But, I promised my mother I would pick up something from the store on my way home. Can I meet you at the church?"

"Okay. You better be there early. You know people at the Rock don't play. When they open the doors of the church, they're ready to go in. Try to get there about six so we can get a good seat."

Misha was excited to go to Rock of Life that evening. She had always wanted to go to that church. She had heard so many good things about it and their pastor. She was especially excited about hearing Shante Patrick live and in person. When she was going through her struggle with Roger and Bishop Moore, Judy had given her some CDs by Pastor Patrick. She listened to them over and over. She also went on her Web site and ordered more. She had never heard a lady preacher minister like Pastor Patrick could.

It was about six-thirty when Misha finally found a parking space near the church. She weaved in and out of the large crowd of people filing into the extremely large auditorium. Misha was taken aback by the mere size of the sanctuary. A man, who acted like he knew her and welcomed her to the church, greeted her at the door. She saw others doing the same. There was a spirit of anticipation in the air. She looked all over for Judy but could not find her. She decided to call her on her cell phone. She punched Judy's name on her cell phone and waited for her to answer.

"Where are you?"

"I'm in the bookstore, waiting in line. Go ahead and get us a seat. I want to get this book. I'm almost at the register."

Misha looked to her right and could see the crowd of people jammed into the bookstore. She walked through the doors that led to the sanctuary. At the door, a young lady greeted her the same way the man had and offered to help her find a seat.

They walked toward the front of the sanctuary. Misha could see that the floor of the sanctuary was almost filled, with the exception of a few seats in the first and second rows that had reserved signs in them. The usher took her to a section to the right of the pulpit and showed her a seat. When she sat down, she could barely see the pulpit. She stood up to see if there was a better seat available. She could not find two seats together on the floor. She wished she had arrived earlier.

Her cell rang. It was Judy trying to locate her. Misha stood until Judy spotted her in the crowd and joined her at their seats.

"You couldn't find better seats? I can't see anything. Well I guess we'll watch the screens tonight. It's just a blessing being in the atmosphere. Here, I got you something." She reached into her bag and pulled out a book and handed it to Misha.

Misha read the back cover and flipped through a couple of pages. "This looks good. Thank you. *Pure Satisfaction: Having an Intimate Relationship with God,* M. Bernard Taylor. I never heard of him," she said.

"Me either. The title sounded good, so I got it for you."

"How much do I owe you?"

"Nothing. It's a gift. How long before service starts?"

"About twenty minutes."

"Excuse me, ladies, are the two of you together?" An usher dressed in a blue suit with an ID badge on the jacket leaned down and whispered to them. They both said yes at the same time. "Come with me." They followed the usher to the center of the church, directly in front of the pulpit. Misha looked up into the balcony that was almost filled up with people. The usher walked to the second row and removed two reserved signs and told them to have a seat.

"Can you believe what just happened?" Misha was filled with excitement as she looked around the sanctuary at all the people there. She closely examined everyone sitting around them and wondered if they were VIPs of some sort. She wished she had changed her clothes before she drove to the church.

"Hey, that's the favor of God. These are great seats," Judy exclaimed just as a minister walked onto the pulpit and began prayer. The sound of people praying filled the auditorium. Some people walked to the altar and prayed. Misha clasped her hands in front of her, closed her eyes, and began praying. At seven on the dot, the prayer ended. Three women and a man walked onto the pulpit and began singing.

When Misha opened her eyes, she was surprised to see the first lady of the church sitting directly in front of her. Misha tried to hold her excitement—remembering she was there to worship. She made a mental note to get the video because no one would ever believe she was in the VIP seats. She nudged Judy and discreetly pointed forward. They both sat there feeling so special, and enjoyed the favor God had placed upon them.

The congregation gave Shante Patrick a standing ovation when she walked onto the pulpit. Misha scanned her from head to toe. She was dressed very classy, from her cropped hairstyle to her brown leather pumps. She was relieved to see a woman of God dressed in a way that did not make her look like the church lady on television comedy shows. After introducing her husband,

Max, and sons, who were sitting in the row in front of them, she began her sermon. Misha listened intently to every word that came from her mouth. She could feel the power of her words in her spirit.

"Y'all know I used to be allergic to bees." Pastor Patrick walked the stage as she preached. Misha was impressed she didn't have to use notes to preach. It was like she was talking naturally from her heart.

"Yes, I used to be allergic to bees. When one stung me, I would get upset, because it felt like I couldn't breathe. I would break out in hives and swell up. I had to be hospitalized for treatment. People who saw me would be alarmed at how I looked and it felt like I would die at any moment. I became fearful of bees and situations where I felt bees would be a threat. But one day, I went to an allergist. I was reluctant to be tested for bee sting allergy when the doctor explained how they would place bee venom right under my skin. First they would start in small amounts, and then increase the dosage to see how allergic I was and what type of bees I was allergic to. How many of you know that once you've had a bad experience, you just don't purposely jump into it again?"

Misha could relate to every word. "That's right," she heard Judy say. Others in the sanctuary were also agreeing with her.

"Well when they put the smallest amount into my skin, immediately I had a reaction. They gave me medication and watched me for about an hour to make sure I was okay. The doctor came to the conclusion I was indeed allergic to bee stings, from multiple types of bees. Duhhhhhh! I should have charged the doctor for that diagnosis."

The congregation was on their feet with laughter. Misha could see Reverend Patrick and their sons laughing hard in the front row. Just by the way he was so engaged in his wife's every word, Misha just somehow knew they had a happy marriage.

"Well anyway . . ." Pastor Patrick continued trying to hold back her laugh. "Y'all stop laughing. I need to hurry. Anyway, what the doctor did was have me come to his office each week and be injected with a mixture of venom from the bees I was allergic to. They gradually increased the dosage to build my immunity to the stings. This went on for about two years until my body had developed enough antibodies that a bee sting no longer bothered me."

Misha immediately caught on to what she was saying. She listened closely as Pastor Patrick left the pulpit and walked down the stairs of the altar and onto the sanctuary floor.

"See, some of y'all have been stung multiple times whether it was in the church, at home, at work, or in relationships. When you were first stung, you felt like your life was ending. You couldn't breathe. Your heart was racing. Everybody around you looked at you and wondered what was going on. Some people stayed away from you and others tried to help even though they didn't know how. When you look back, you'll see God put you in a place of safety so you could get over your hurt and pain. But each time you ventured out, you were fearful, afraid of being stung again, so you stayed in your own safety net. Each time you tried to venture out you were stung again. What you don't realize is God was trying to build your immunity.

"When your immunity is built up, little things don't upset you anymore. People can talk about you and call you out of your name all day and night and it won't have an effect on you. You can lose your job and it won't hurt you. Your spouse can leave you, but it won't hurt you.

Children acting crazy but it still won't hurt you. God is building you up so when you are attacked by killer bees they won't have an effect on you." The crowd was on their feet. "That's why you don't see old people getting upset about a lot of things. God has built up their immunity. God has to build your immunity. You can't be a leader crying all the time over little things. You can't be a leader scared of what people will say about you. You can't be a leader in hiding. You can't let fear confine you. You've got to move beyond your place of comfort and tell the devil that it's okay. I've been stung before. God is just building your immunity."

She looked directly at Misha. She was staring so hard at her that her husband turned around to see who she was looking at. Misha knew that word was directed straight to her. It felt like lightning had hit her body and she couldn't stand like the other people in the sanctuary who were already on their feet screaming. Being drawn back into her sermon Pastor Patrick continued, "You can't be a leader wanting to fight anyone who makes you mad. God has to build your immunity. Touch two or three people and tell them, God is building your immunity." People jumped to their feet and began touching people around them. Misha could not stand. This word was meant for her and its power held her to her seat.

After service, Misha and Judy waited in the long line at the bookstore to purchase the CD. Misha purchased the DVD and CD. Afterward, Judy drove Misha to her car that was parked in the shopping center across the street from the church. They met at the Waffle House to get something to eat.

"Pastor Patrick preached tonight. I'm so glad I came. Thanks for inviting me. I needed to hear that word," Misha said, lifting her menu from the table.

"You're not the only one. I needed it myself. When she talked about those bees . . . Lord have mercy."

"I know. She was preaching to me."

"I saw how she stared at you. I think she knew she was preaching to you, too. I thought she was going to call you out."

Misha looked up and saw Roger and a woman entering the restaurant. They were holding hands. Misha could feel her heart beginning to beat fast.

"Misha, you don't look so good. Is anything wrong?"

"Roger. He's here . . . with a woman."

Judy turned around to see Roger and the woman walking toward them. "We can leave if you want to."

"No, Judy. I've got to stay. I'm not running away from him." She set her menu down and flattened her blouse. She sat straight up and greeted Roger and the young lady, who she recognized from church. "Hey, Roger . . . Tracy." Misha waved to them to come over. Roger quickly let go of the woman's hand. She laughed to herself. But it still hurt to see him there with another woman.

"Mimi, I didn't expect to see you here."

"We're coming from the Rock. This is my friend, Judy." She turned her attention to the young lady. "Hi, Tracy."

"Hi, Misha. You guys were at the Rock? We were there in the balcony. Didn't Pastor Patrick preach? I got my praise on," she said, waving her hands in the air.

"We were sitting in the VIP seats behind the first lady." Judy invited herself into the conversation.

"Really? How did you get those seats?" Tracy continued her conversation with Judy. Roger was staring at Misha, but she'd had enough of the whole conversation and she picked up her menu just to have something other than Roger to look at.

"Tracy, there's a table opening up over there. We better hurry and get it," Roger said, pointing at a table on the other side of the restaurant where a man was tossing a dollar on the table.

"Okay. Well, it was good seeing you again, Misha, and nice meeting you, Judy," Tracy said as she quickly followed Roger toward the table.

He's using her for sex. It won't last long, Misha heard in her spirit. She thought it was jealousy and repented in her heart.

"Misha, you took that well. I don't think I could have done that."

"I'm building my immunity."

Driving home, Misha began to cry. She thought she could take seeing Roger with another woman but it still hurt. *Tracy Applewood, of all people.* She always thought something was going on between them. Tracy was always so touchy with him and constantly flirting. Roger denied he was involved with her. That night, she couldn't take seeing him with her and all the hurt began to pain her again. As the tears flowed, she noticed she was breaking out in hives and it felt like she couldn't breathe. She remembered what she heard that night. She began to pray. "God, it really hurts to be stung. I know you're building my immunity." She started to play the sermon CD and it gave her comfort as she took the freeway home.

Chapter 7

Misha could see Bishop Moore sitting at the head table in the large church gym waiting for the Urban Ministerial Society to begin their annual summer prayer breakfast, a kickoff of their revival. She could see the many people approaching him to shake his hands. As the presiding president of the group, she knew, he was in charge of making sure the annual prayer breakfast went smoothly, and preparing the member churches for the revival in the upcoming week.

As she entered the room, she could see people lined up at the buffet table loading food onto their plates. Others were seated at the round tables that dotted the church gym. Taking in the scene, she spotted Roger work the room, greeting people and laughing loudly as he spoke to them. She tried to keep her focus on her mission there. She wanted to hear Pastor Jarrod Fuller preach. Misha walked through the room, speaking to several people before finally taking a seat beside Gertrude, Bishop Moore's secretary. She could tell Roger had not noticed her in the room and if he had, he was playing it off really well.

She looked toward the head table and spotted Bishop Moore talking with Frank Wright, chief executive officer of the City Development League. She watched as he pointed toward Roger. Bishop placed a piece of paper in front of his face, hiding as if he did not want anyone to know what he was talking about. What was so secretive? Misha wondered. Bishop served on the board of the league and wondered what it had to do with Roger. She focused on Roger deeply engaged in conversation and watched as Bishop tried to get his attention. Spotting Bishop waving toward him, immediately Roger ended his conversation and practically ran to the head table. Bishop looked as if he was introducing Roger to Frank and they shook hands. Gertrude was watching the scene too.

"Something's not right with that," Gertrude leaned into Misha and whispered.

"What?" Misha still did not want to engage in gossip with Gertrude. She was sincere about not talking about Bishop or Roger. She had nothing to gain by doing so. She began to get an uneasy feeling. If she knew someone else, she would have sat with them. Instead, she was stuck sitting at the table with her.

"Roger, Bishop, and Frank Wright. He's up to something. I heard they got a big grant and they are going to hire about twenty new people. Roger's probably trying to get one of those positions."

Misha quickly changed the subject and began telling Gertrude about what had happened in her life since she left Kingdom Faith.

"Well you look good. You're doing something right," Gertrude said to Misha.

"I can't wait to hear Pastor Fuller preach. I remember when he did revival at the church last year. That man preached. I couldn't pass up the opportunity to hear him again, even if it meant running into Roger and Bishop. Besides, I saw Roger with Tracy Applewood last month. He's gone on with his life and so have I."

"That's old news. They broke up. She said she was tired of him acting like they weren't dating. She didn't want to be his secret girlfriend. She told a few people they were together and he said she was lying. She was so mad he was trying to make her look stupid, so she broke up with him."

"I see First Lady Moore; let me go speak to her." Misha got up from the table and walked over to the first lady and hugged her. Satisfaction filled her spirit with the news of the breakup. She had known it wouldn't last.

"Lady Moore, I want to be like you when I grow up. You're working that red suit and hat," she said, hugging First Lady Moore.

"Misha. Look at you. You look good. How have you been?"

"I've been blessed. I'm glad school is out. I'm finally taking a vacation. I wanted to thank you for the recommendation for that women's day program."

"Well, you're welcome. I happened to be at the church when St. Paul called to ask Bishop for a speaker. If Bishop knew I recommended you, he would go crazy. But you deserve it. Don't tell him. Sometimes I have to pray for my husband. I'm not saying what he did was wrong, I just didn't agree with how he did it. I don't want to know what happened between you two. I'm just praying. That's all I do is pray."

"That's all we need to do. Thank you. I'll never forget all the things you did and said to me. You are the first lady. If you ever need me, I'm a phone call away." She looked toward the stage. Bishop and Roger were talking to a group of men. "I see Bishop on the stage. I think I will go and say hello before service gets started." She hesitated, but she wanted Bishop to know there were no hard feelings between them. So she walked up the small stairs to the stage where the head table was located.

"Hello, Bishop."

Bishop Moore was deeply engaged in his conversation and had not noticed her walking onto the podium. He looked up and saw her standing beside him. "Daughter. Well, look at you. How have you been?" He stood and hugged her tightly.

Misha was shocked he greeted her with such affection. She expected him to be rude. Maybe he had gotten over what he had done and had a change of heart.

"I've been good, Bishop. You look good. I wanted to say hello before the service started."

"Well, I'm glad you did."

The man sitting beside Bishop cleared his throat as he stood to introduce himself to Misha. "Hello, I'm Pastor Willingham."

"Hello, Pastor. It's nice to meet you." She reached out her hand to shake his. He hugged her instead.

"You know the Bible said to greet the brethren with a holy kiss. You smell good. What's that perfume you're wearing, Essence?" Pastor Willingham said as his lips touched Misha's cheek.

"No, it's Coco by Chanel." Everybody turned to look at Roger. He said it before he realized it. "I mean, I know because someone I used to know wore it all the time." He immediately turned and walked away.

"Well, Bishop, I wanted to say hello. Take care." Misha walked off the stage as Pastor Fuller walked into the hall. Realizing she would not be able to greet him with the entourage surrounding him, she took a seat near the door.

When Pastor Fuller finished his sermon, she got up and slipped out the door. When she reached her car, her cell phone rang. She looked at the ID. It was her mother. She didn't feel like hearing the drama so she didn't answer the call. Driving to IHOP for a meal of pancakes and an omelet was far better than trying to eat the dried eggs or half-cooked bacon at the prayer breakfast.

She pulled into the parking lot of the IHOP and a flash went across her face. She sat in her car watching the fast-moving scene. She saw Amber and it looked like she was screaming. She was fighting the man. Her arms were flinging in the air, trying to break free from the man's grip. Immediately, Misha began to pray. She knew God was showing her something about Amber. School was out and she didn't know how to get in touch with her. She remembered Amber said her family was spending the summer at their lake house. She prayed God protect her wherever she was.

She shook off her vision and went into the IHOP and sat at a table near the window. After ordering, she reached into her purse and pulled out her itinerary for her trip to Daufuskie Island, off the coast of South Carolina. She was looking forward to vacationing alone. When she vacationed with Roger, they always went where he wanted to go. He never wanted to go more than two hours away from Atlanta. His idea of a romantic trip was going to Stone Mountain during the week when few tourists were there. She looked forward to relaxing on the island and enjoying the spa and beach there.

"Excuse me. Are you Reverend Holloway?"

"I'm Minister Holloway." Misha looked up and saw a young lady standing in front of her.

"You preached at Mount Moriah a couple of months ago, for singles day. I go to Mount Moriah."

"Hi. Are you with someone? Have a seat."

"I'm not going to take up your time. I wanted to tell you how you touched me that day. When you spoke, I was going through something and it was like you knew my situation. I wanted to thank you for being so honest with us. I'm doing better now. I listen to your CD over and over. It helps me out a lot."

"It wasn't me. It was God."

"Yeah, but God used you to minister to me. Thank you. Well I better go. Enjoy your breakfast."

Misha watched the young lady walk away. She thanked God for using her to touch others. She prayed silently for God to use her as an instrument of deliverance for other people.

After breakfast, Misha drove to the mall to do some shopping for her vacation. It seemed like every store she went in, she ran into Kingdom Faith people. Some of them acted like they didn't know her. Others were glad to see her and wanted to fill her in on all the gossip in the church, including gossip about Roger. She wasn't interested in hearing it and she tried to focus the conversation around her vacation.

As she walked the aisle of stores, she spotted a beautiful sundress in one of the windows. She quickly went in and tried it on. She stepped out of the dressing room to get a better look at herself in the full-length mirror outside the door. She looked at the price tag. She smiled as she thought about how cheap Roger was and how he would have never allowed her to buy a dress so expensive. But, she was no longer with Roger and she liked the dress.

"You look really cute in that dress," a woman said to her.

"Thank you." She turned around and saw Pastor Deandrea Fuller standing behind her. "Pastor Fuller?" Misha was surprised to see her there. She thought guest speakers and their wives hung out with the host pastor after service. "Thank you. I was thinking about purchasing it. But, it's a little too pricey for me. I enjoyed trying it on though."

"You know my name. So what's yours?" the tall, well-dressed woman said to her.

"Misha. Misha Holloway. Your husband preached this morning. I made a special trip to the prayer breakfast only to hear him preach. He's truly anointed."

"You were at the breakfast? I see I'm not the only one who couldn't wait to get to the mall. My husband knows I like to shop so he didn't say anything when I told him I wasn't going with him and the other ministers. So what are you shopping for?"

"My vacation. I'm going to Daufuskie Island."

"In South Carolina? That's where we got . . . Well I've been there and it's nice. You're going to enjoy it. That dress would be perfect for your trip. Why don't you let me get it for you?"

"You, buy this dress for me? Oh, I can't let you do that." Misha shook her head. "It costs too much."

"God blessed me to be a blessing to others. Besides, I want to bless you."

"Really, I can't let you."

"Tell you what. You can work it off. Why don't you take me to all the shopping places in the city and we can call it even."

"Go shopping . . . with you?"

Pastor Fuller stood smiling at Misha. She couldn't turn down the invitation. What an opportunity to go shopping with someone like her. She began to thank God for showing her favor again and allowing her to be in the presence of a woman like Deandrea Fuller.

They spent the day shopping at the various malls and boutiques around Atlanta. Misha had never seen anyone who could shop like Pastor Fuller. While they were shopping, Pastor Fuller advised her about financial matters and shared her testimony about overworking. She challenged Misha to always find the time to take care of herself.

At the end of the day Misha drove her to the Four Seasons Hotel. Having been alerted of their arrival, her husband met them to help with their purchases. Pastor Jarrod walked out of the door wearing a gray jogging suit. Misha barely recognized him without his suit on.

"Hey, honey. Did you leave anything for the other people in Atlanta to buy?" Pastor Jarrod said to his wife.

"You're real funny." She embraced him and kissed him like they were the only two standing in front of the hotel.

Misha thought about how she used to kiss Roger like that. She shook her head. She wanted to get that thought out of her mind. She saw him and allowed him to get in her head again and she did not want that. She tried not to look at the two of them until they finished. They walked over to her.

"Misha, this is my husband, Jarrod. Honey, Misha was at the prayer breakfast this morning," Deandrea said as she caressed her husband's back.

"Misha, nice to meet you. I hope my wife didn't wear you out. When she goes shopping she can do some damage." He shook her hand as they talked. Misha noticed his wide smile and how informal they both acted. She wasn't used to preachers acting like that. Most of them were so formal.

"No. I had fun. I enjoyed the sermon this morning. It was a blessing."

"I'm glad I had the opportunity to preach." He looked at his wife. "So, honey, where are your bags?"

Misha popped the trunk of the car and reached in and handed him several shopping bags. They stood outside the hotel chatting about her upcoming trip to South Carolina until the doorman walked over and asked her to move her car.

"Well it looks like I have to go. It was a pleasure meeting both of you. Thank you, Pastor Dee, for everything."

"Oh, Misha." Pastor Jarrod looked directly at her. "The gift is special." Misha could feel the power of his statement. "In the ministry you'll be persecuted for preaching the Word. But you preach it anyhow. Don't worry about what anybody may say or do to you. Make sure you walk with the utmost integrity and believe God even when you're the only one who believes. You'll see. God will bring you out on top. Trust God. Always trust God." He paused and looked at his wife. "Thank you for taking my wife shopping. Do we owe you anything?"

"You've given me more than enough. How did you know I was a minister?"

He smiled, reached into his wallet, and pulled out a card. "Here's our card. Stop by and see us at the church while you're in South Carolina."

Misha watched as they walked arm in arm into the hotel, each one holding several bags in their free hand. How in the world did he know she was a minister? Was it the way she carried herself? She didn't remember telling Pastor Dee. *Maybe he has the gift too.* She felt like running after him. She needed someone to explain what was going on with her now. Would he respond to a letter? Would he take her phone call? She shook her head. For goodness' sake, he was a nationally known preacher. He preached big conferences and filled the sanctuaries of some of the biggest churches in the world. He didn't have time for her and her problems. Her only option was to trust God. He would show her the way.

Chapter 8

Misha arrived home after spending a week on Daufuskie Island. She finally had time to relax and read the book Judy had given her. Although it was interesting, it was tough reading while she relaxed on the secluded beach. It was peaceful and she didn't have to worry about Roger watching everything that went into her mouth and warning her about diabetes, heart trouble, and getting fat. Just being alone with no problems or work was refreshing.

She looked at her answering machine and noticed she had a number of phone messages. There was a reminder from someone at St. Paul about her speaking on their women's day program next Sunday. "Yes!" she said as she listened to the message. They still believed in her, even with all the rumors being spread about her around town. Someone told her Bishop Moore told the member churches of the Urban Ministerial Society not to let her preach because she was trouble. However, when he did that, God opened up the doors of other churches and allowed her to deliver the Word. She was winning without trying. She had a week to get ready for her sermon. She wanted to make a good impression. She wanted a return invitation.

During the week, she prepared for her sermon, studying for hours. The following Sunday, Judy and her children went with her to St. Paul. Her mother and grandmother met them at the church. Her mother was wearing a white suit to go along with the theme of the day: one hundred women in white marching for Christ.

Misha wore the white suit she purchased at the mall during her shopping trip with Pastor Fuller. She felt confident and positive as she walked into the church.

As the service progressed, Misha became increasingly nervous. Her legs were shaking, her palms were sweaty and the urge to run filled her. All week she had practiced her sermon. She had anticipated where the congregation would clap, say amen, and stand. She wanted to move the worshippers like Shante Patrick.

The women in the church created a sea of white throughout the sanctuary. Misha glanced to her left and could not help but notice a young lady sitting quietly at the end of a pew near the center of the church. *Tell her it's not so,* Misha could hear in her spirit as she looked deeply into the eyes of the young lady. She could feel the young lady's pain. She began to have a severe pain in her stomach. She took her hand and placed it on her stomach. It was probably nerves, but the pain would not go away. She continued to hold her stomach as she stood to the pulpit to preach.

Misha's sermon was not turning out like she anticipated. Where she thought people should have been standing, no one stood. When she anticipated people would say amen, no one said a word. As she continued to preach, her anxiety increased. So she decided to walk the aisle of the church like she saw Shante Patrick do. She was nearing the end of her sermon when she walked near the young lady. Their eyes met. She remembered what she had heard earlier in her spirit.

Ask the pastor if you can pray.

Misha ignored the voice in her spirit. She wanted to do something to move the congregation and she knew she heard the voice of God say to tell the young lady it wasn't so.

She began the close of her sermon as she walked back toward the pulpit. *Ask the pastor if you can pray.* Once again she ignored the voice in her spirit as she asked the congregation to stand. She stood on the floor in front of the communion table and spoke about healing and deliverance. She noticed the young lady crying. She asked her to come to the front.

"God said it's not so." She addressed the young lady as she placed her hand on the woman's stomach. The woman became limp and began to cry loudly. "God said it's not so." Two ushers ran to hold the young lady up. "Be healed in the name of Jesus." The young lady's limp body fell into the arms of the waiting usher. Misha felt such a sense of accomplishment as she walked the floor continuing her altar call.

People began to run to the altar. Misha helped herself to pray for a few more people and was thrilled when they passed out. Without doing a corporate prayer, she ended her sermon and altar call by handing the microphone to the pastor, who was standing at the edge of the pulpit watching her. She sat down and thanked God for using her that day to bring deliverance to so many people.

After service, the pastor asked her to meet with him in his office. As she tried to make her way to the pastor's office, a woman stopped her and told her they didn't believe in that kind of stuff at their church and she would make sure she didn't preach there again. Offended, Misha walked into the pastor's office.

"Minister Holloway, close the door. Here's your money," he said, throwing the envelope at her. Her arms flew out, catching it midair. Now she knew why his members were so rude. *The oil flows from the head.* "When I talked with Bishop Moore about you, he didn't have anything good to say. But I thought I would give you the benefit of the doubt and let you preach here anyway. But, what I saw here today, I see he was right. He told me you were trouble. I should have listened to him. Now I've got to undo what you did here today."

"What did I do? I preached what God told me," Misha said, placing her hand over her heart.

"I didn't have a problem with your sermon. It was what you did after your sermon. You know that girl you called out. She just found out she has stomach cancer."

"Stomach cancer? I didn't know."

"I'm sure you didn't. Now I've got to figure out how to handle this mess. You can't preach here anymore and if you come back here, I will personally remove you myself."

Misha got up and walked out of the office in tears. She thought she had done the right thing. She knew she heard God tell her to tell the young lady it wasn't so. As she walked to the parking lot, the young lady came up to her and thanked her for the encouragement. She had been praying all night for a word about her cancer and she believed God sent her there to give her hope.

As the young lady walked away, Judy walked up to her. "Misha, you did a good job. I've got to go. My husband's flight lands in thirty minutes. I'll call you later."

She watched as Judy and her children drove off in their SUV. Disappointed and trying to hold back tears, she continued walking in and out of the passing cars clearing the parking lot. She didn't want anyone to see her crying. Before this day, she'd only heard rumors that Bishop Moore was talking about her. Now she had proof. He was saying negative things about her to other pastors and trying to get them to not allow her to preach. Now with what happened at the altar call, she knew it was going to become more difficult for her to find places to preach. Yet, she was confused. She did what the Lord told her and the young lady and the pastor confirmed it. Was that the reason her stomach was hurting before she preached?

She placed her hand on her stomach. It was no longer hurting. Was that the reason she had to lay hands on the young lady's stomach? She didn't know what to think. What did she do that the pastor felt he was going to have to undo?

When she reached her car, her mother informed her she would have to take her grandmother home, and asked her for money. Misha handed her the envelope the pastor gave her. Her mother opened it up, peeped inside, and asked for more.

"More? How much was in there?" Misha took the envelope from her mother and pulled out the money. She counted it. "Twenty dollars?" There in her hand was twenty dollars in one-dollar bills. "There should have been more. Did you see how many people were in there? There were more than twenty people who came to the front to give in the special offering for me. I expected a few hundred dollars." She had anticipated at least $500. She needed the money to cover some of the items she charged on her credit card during her vacation.

"Well you didn't preach that good. That's why they didn't give you anything." Her mother walked away and got into her car and drove off.

Disappointed, Misha looked at her grandmother, who was waiting patiently at her car. She unlocked the door and helped her into the car. It was silent in the car as they drove down the busy highway home.

"You was out of order."

"Grandma, not you too," Misha said as she continued to drive in the heavy Sunday afternoon traffic.

"You was out of order. Did God tell you to do that?"

"Do what?" Misha tried to look at her grandmother while trying to keep an eye on the rapidly moving traffic.

"Pray for all dem people?"

"God told me to tell that girl 'it's not so.' I heard Him so clear. I know it was God. I was right. She and the pastor told me she has stomach cancer. I didn't know that when I put my hand on her stomach and prayed for her. I never met the girl before in my life."

"Did God tell you to do that?"

Misha didn't want to answer her grandmother. She knew God did not tell her to pray for the young lady. He only told her to say "it is not so."

"Did God tell you?" Her grandmother's voice grew louder and stronger.

"No. I thought . . . well, I thought."

"Only do what God tells you. It's important that you do exactly what God tells you. Nothing more."

"But, Grandma, I was right."

"Was you? What 'bout all those other peoples?" Misha couldn't answer. "You shoulda asked the pastor before you prayed."

Misha looked over at her. A sinking feeling came into her body. It was the exact same thing she heard. Too embarrassed to admit it to her grandmother, she felt so guilty. She was out of order. She should have listened to the Spirit. Instead, she went for the theatrics in ministry, like she had seen so many other people do. Maybe that was what God was telling them to do, not her. For her, it was pure selfishness. She was learning to follow God's direction to a tee. She prayed for God to forgive her for her disobedience.

"Always remember. Do only what God tells ya. You ain't no Tay Patrick. You Misha Holloway and you have to do it the way God tells you not like anyone else. They have to do it the way God tells them."

As they continued their journey, Misha's grandmother continued to minister to her about obedience to the voice of the Lord. Although Misha cried, her tears did not have an effect on her grandmother. She continued correcting and teaching her about the gift until they reached her home.

Misha helped her grandmother into the house and watched as she walked to the refrigerator and pulled out the big pitcher of tea she always had and poured two glasses full for them.

"Grandma, I studied and prayed all week for that sermon. Seems like they would've appreciated the sermon, even if I messed up at the end. I felt like a waitress who only received a penny tip after she went above and beyond the call of duty to serve."

"Don't worry yourself about money. Bible say, 'Bless the prophet, receive prophet reward.' Dem siddity peoples should have blessed you anyhow. They's pay, sholl will. They's should have blessed the prophet."

"Grandma, I don't wish bad on anybody." Misha sipped her tea.

"Me neither. But, that's the Word. Ask God to teach you how to use the gift. He'll show you. Yes, He will. You make mistakes. God know you learning. He forgive your mistake."

"Grandma, thank you for all you're teaching me. I don't have a pastor to teach me. Reverend Simpson doesn't teach us anything at the church. When I try to talk to him, he acts like he's scared or something. I found out today from the pastor that Bishop Moore is talking about me all over town. I think they're trying to blackball me."

"Why you worry yourself? Bible say, 'Touch not my anointed.' Let God handle it. You just do what God tells you and go where He sends you."

"But, I didn't do anything to Bishop Moore. I don't understand why he's doing this to me. I treat him with respect and I don't talk about him to anyone, especially people who come to me with mess."

"Lord, child, when you gon' learn? Peoples gon' be peoples. They's say all sorts of things. You just make sure your hands clean."

"Grandma, what would I do without you? You've taught me more in these past few minutes than any preacher has."

"Well, my time ain't long. My bones weak. I'm slow now. Not much left of me."

"Stop talking like that. You've got a few more years on you."

"Not sure about that. My time ain't long. Done got old. You know that. But I'll help you whiles I here."

Misha stood up and hugged her grandmother. "I don't know what I would do without you. You're the only one I can talk to."

"Child, you got the Lord and He hear a whole lot better than me."

Misha stayed with her grandmother until darkness slipped over the sky. She helped her grandmother get ready for bed, and began her journey home. As she drove through the quiet city streets, she thought about what she learned that day and repented again for her disobedience. She felt so bad. She kept saying to herself that she should have asked the pastor to pray. She repeated this even as she climbed the stairs and entered her apartment. Guilt flowed over her body as she closed the door. She fell on her knees and begged God for forgiveness. Even when she heard *I will honor your prayer* in her spirit, it did not give her comfort.

She thought she must have looked like a fool, trying to be like other female preachers. She vowed not to ever try to preach like other people and only do what God tells her. As she lay on the floor praying, she asked God to forgive her and to remove the spirit of offense she felt that day. She asked God to help her love Bishop Moore unconditionally and vowed never to speak evil about him even though he said negative things about her. She asked God to help her forgive him and when she saw him, help her to treat him like her father in the ministry with respect and honor.

Chapter 9

The summer went by quickly as Misha filled her time with work at the church, reading, and going to various places to preach. Fortunately, the incident at St. Paul's did not stop people from asking her to preach. Suddenly, she had become the star. The newspapers were calling her for interviews about being single and saved. She started to have her own little following of supporters, including her grandmother.

She made sure she took her grandmother with her everywhere she preached. She wanted to be sure she was walking in the will of God when she stood before the saints to share the Word. Afterward, she would spend hours talking with her grandmother not only about the sermon, but also about life in general. She enjoyed these moments and savored every minute.

School was scheduled to start in about a week for the teachers and the following week for the students. This meant one thing: time for her annual checkup. She wanted to make sure she was healthy before school started and she became exposed to the germs students always managed to bring to school with them. Although she knew she should have the exam done, she didn't like going through the process. It was a necessary evil.

It was the result of her HIV test that was most important to Misha. She started getting one every year before she met Roger. She wasn't exactly a saint then and she wanted to be sure she did not have the disease.

So far, her results were always negative. As a matter of fact, she'd always managed to walk away with a clean bill of health. She only prayed this year would be the same.

Misha's doctor called her back into the office to tell her the results of her testing. She sat in a cold exam room, playing games on her smartphone while waiting for the doctor to come in. After a few minutes of waiting Dr. Wilson came into the room.

"Ms. Holloway, I'm glad you could come back to the office today."

"I'm not so sure I want to be here. You've never called me back before." She placed her phone in her purse.

"Well, I see you are anxious. I'll just get right down to it."

Misha's leg shook in the chair as she watched the doctor move to the small sink and place her chart on the counter.

He lifted one page, then two. "Well, looks like your blood work is normal. The HIV test was negative. Blood pressure's okay."

"Then what's the problem?"

"Your Pap smear shows some precancerous cells. It could be nothing. However, I want to investigate it more."

"Cancer?" Misha slid to the edge of her chair.

"I'm not saying you have cancer, it could be nothing. But I would like you to see a specialist."

"A specialist? Is it that serious?" The words felt stuck in her throat.

"Like I said, it could be nothing. Sometimes, it may be the test or the time we did the exam during your cycle, or you could only have a very serious infection that can be treated with antibiotics. The specialist will repeat your Pap test. She'll probably want to do a biopsy."

"Biopsy? I'm going to need surgery?"

"The doctor we're sending you to can do the biopsy in her office. It won't take long. You won't need anesthesia. You'll be able to drive yourself home. But, I think this is something we need to look into further."

"What if the biopsy comes back positive? What then?"

"Well, we'll wait until we get the results of the tests before we start speculating. Right now, we need to get you over to Dr. Trinidad's office. Janie is scheduling an appointment for you. She'll be in shortly to give you that information. Do you have any more questions?"

Misha shook her head no. But she had questions, a lot of questions.

"Are you sure? I want to be sure you understand what's going on."

"No questions right now. I'll wait until I see Dr. Trinidad."

"Very well. Janie will be right in." He shook her hand as he walked toward the door. "Don't worry. I'm sure it's nothing."

Nothing? Why did he call me in here for nothing? Misha sat in the chair, trying to be strong but scared out of her mind. She began to talk to herself. "Cancer? I'm too young for cancer. I haven't even had children yet. Cancer? Not me. No, not me."

The door opened and Janie, Dr. Wilson's nurse, walked in. She gave instructions to Misha and handed her all the referral paperwork. She was to see Dr. Trinidad later that afternoon. She patted Misha on the shoulder as they walked to the front desk for discharge, trying to assure her everything would be okay.

All the way home, Misha prayed. "I believe. I receive my healing. God, you are the healer. By His stripes I am healed."

Whose report do you believe? There was that voice again. *Whose report do you believe?*

"God, I believe your Word. I believe I'm healed. Cancer cannot live in this body. My body belongs to you."

Later that afternoon Misha sat patiently in Dr. Trinidad's office, waiting for the doctor to return. The biopsy was the most uncomfortable thing she had experienced. There was no anesthesia or pain medication. She could feel every cut and pull the doctor made. Now, as she sat in the chair, the cramps the doctor warned her about were hitting her hard. She searched her purse for some Tylenol to take but couldn't find any before the doctor walked back in.

"Here's some Tylenol. It'll help you with your cramps." She handed her the pills and a small cup of water. "The cramping may last a day or two. We should get the results of your biopsy in about a week. I want you to come back in next week. I know you're anxious for the results. How are you feeling?"

"I'm cramping a little. Thanks for the Tylenol. Could you tell if anything was wrong? I mean, did you see anything out of the ordinary?"

"Well, I did see a couple of spots. I biopsied them. We should get the results before you come back in. Right now, don't worry. If it's anything serious, we'll call you back in before next week."

"School starts for teachers next week. Should I do any heavy lifting? I've got to get my classroom together before the students return."

"You should continue like normal. I'm sure it will be okay. I'll see you back next week." Dr. Trinidad walked toward the door.

Misha stood up but quickly sat back down as the pain of cramps filled her abdomen. She waited until it released its grip on her to stand and walk to her car.

"God, I believe you. I'm healed," she repeated to herself. She turned the radio up louder as the sound of Marvin Sapp's worship melody filled her car. This time it didn't comfort her. This time it depressed her. Then, the voice, another voice, began to trouble her mind:

You've got cancer and you're going to die without even having children. The results will come back showing cancer. You've never been married. You will never know the joy of seeing your own children grow up. You shouldn't have put your hands on that woman with cancer. That's what you get for being disobedient.

Tears ran down her cheek. "God, I believe, I receive my healing," she repeated but the other voice was tormenting her. She made a decision not to tell anyone and believe God for her healing. She assured herself loudly in her car everything was going to work out all right.

The rest of the week Misha fought the negative voices in her head. At night, when she couldn't fall asleep, she played a CD she made with scriptures on healing. She decided to fast and pray for a good report. She continued with her daily routine, acting as if nothing was wrong. She avoided her grandmother because she couldn't hide anything from her. She went to school and attended all the teachers' meetings, district meetings, and the statewide meeting. She busied herself with decorating her classroom and didn't mention anything about the biopsy to anyone.

Finally, the day arrived for her to get the results of her testing. Trying to be positive, she kept telling herself everything was fine, especially since they did not call her back. She knew if anything was seriously wrong, they would have called her. She praised God for her healing. Sitting in her doctor's office she continually assured herself everything was fine. She repeated her healing scriptures in her head, assuring her everything was okay.

"Miss Holloway, how are you doing today?" Dr. Trinidad walked into the room and sat down behind her desk.

"A little anxious."

"I understand. Well, we got your results. I'm afraid the news is not good. The pathology report shows the specimens we took last week were cancerous."

"Oh." Misha tried to look strong.

Whose report will you believe? she heard in her spirit.

"Are you okay, Miss Holloway? Is there someone here with you? Miss Holloway." Dr. Trinidad got up from her seat and shook Misha's shoulder. "Miss Holloway, can I get you some water?"

Misha came out of her intense stare and looked directly at the doctor. "What now?"

"Well, we have scheduled you for outpatient surgery. What I would like to do is go in and do a more thorough examination. It's possible, if the cancer has spread, we may have to do a complete hysterectomy."

"Hysterectomy? You mean I won't be able to have children?" She placed her hand on her lower abdomen. "I'm only twenty-four years old. I've never been married. How can I need a hysterectomy?"

"Well, we don't know for sure. What we'll do is go in your naval and use a scope to examine your entire reproductive system, looking for cysts, lesions, or anything that looks unusual. Then, I'll go in vaginally and look for the same thing. I'll remove any lesions I see and we will biopsy them to see if they are cancerous and it will tell us if it has spread. If we have to do a hysterectomy, you'll be hospitalized for a few days."

"Will I need chemotherapy or radiation treatment? Will I lose my hair?"

"We haven't gotten that far yet. Hopefully, since you have regular checkups, we only have a small spot to deal with and none of that will be necessary. Are you sure I can't get you anything to drink?"

"No, I'm fine. So when are you going to do the surgery? I'll have to notify the school. How long will I be out of work?"

"That depends on if you need a hysterectomy. If we have to do it, you'll be out about six weeks. If not, maybe a week. We have your surgery scheduled for Monday. You'll have to be at the hospital at six in the morning. You can't eat anything after ten Sunday night. The nurse will give you more instructions. You'll have time to talk with your family. If you want, I can talk to them with you."

"No. I can handle it." She took in a deep breath and wiped the tears from her eyes. "Surgery is Monday? I'll tell my principal tomorrow after the meeting in the morning. He'll need a note from you."

"I will make sure you get what you need. Anything else?"

Misha shook her head no. She had enough that day. She couldn't take in anymore. She never would have thought she would be diagnosed with cancer at twenty-four.

Misha walked out to her car and began to drive around the city. It felt as if her life continued to fall apart. Just as she was getting over Roger and Bishop Moore, then her health got bad. She drove to her grandmother's house and slowly walked into the house. Tears ran down her cheeks at the first sight of her grandmother.

"Misha, what's wrong?"

"I got cancer."

Her grandmother wrapped her arms around her. "Sit down. Calm down. Tell me 'bout it."

Misha told her about the two biopsies and how she was going to have surgery on Monday. Misha cried harder when she told her grandmother she would not be able to have children.

"You tell your mama?"

"No, not yet. You know how she is. I need someone positive around me now. I need some intercessors to pray." She leaned on her grandmother's shoulder.

"Child, not every sickness leads to death. That's what the Word say."

"I know. What if—"

"Don't say it. You got the power to speak life. Watch what you say. What the Lord tell ya?"

"I'm healed."

"Then whose report you believe, that doctor or God's?"

"I believe God."

Her grandmother got up and went into the kitchen and returned with her slim bottle of anointing oil. She tipped the bottle, placing a small amount of the oil on Misha's forehead, and began to pray for healing. After her prayer, she sat beside Misha and wrapped her arms around her. "Lord, child, the enemy wants to destroy you to keep you from preaching the gospel. But, his plan is not gon' succeed," she said as she turned Misha toward her. "You have a gift, a true gift from the Lawd.

Peoples wit' yo' gift experience a lot of heartache. But God will see you through it all."

She opened her Bible and showed her examples of prophets in the Bible and told her all they had to endure to deliver the Word. "This cancer is not gon' take yo' life. You have a lot to do. You got to pray hard. Pray for yo' life and pray fo' you child, one from yo' own body. You pray and I'll pray wit'cha."

Misha left her grandmother's house feeling better but still filled with anxiety as she fought the negative voices in her head telling her she was going to die. She paced the floor and recited scriptures loudly in her apartment. "God, I believe you." Just as she gained the strength to eat something, her phone rang. She eyed the caller ID. It was her mother. She didn't want to talk to her, but this time, she had to.

"Hey, Mom."

"Well, you could sound happier to hear from me. Where have you been? I've been trying to call you all week."

"Mom . . . Mom . . ." Misha hesitated. She couldn't bring herself to tell another person.

"What's wrong with you? You need to do something about your attitude."

"Mom, look, I got cancer. Now leave me alone." Misha pressed the end button on her phone. There was something about her mother that always made her angry. The phone rang again. It was her mother. She debated picking up the call. After about eight rings she pressed the green answer button.

"So what you trying to do, scare me or something? You know I don't believe that lie."

"Mom, it's true. Dr. Trinidad told me today. I have cancer. I'm having surgery at Emory on Monday."

"Ooooooooooh, Lord. My baby gon' die. I knew it. I knew it. That day you laid hands on that lady in the church that cancer got on you. I knew it. Something told me you was dying."

"I hate to burst your bubble. I'm not dying. It's outpatient surgery. I'm going home the same day of the surgery." Misha sighed and rolled her eyes, offering up a silent prayer.

"Don't matter. When you let them start cutting on you, that's it."

"Thank you, Mother, for all your encouragement and support. I've got to call my pastor now. I'll talk to you later." She hung up the phone again. She called her pastor and asked for prayer and told him about the surgery. By the time she hung up the phone, she had lost her appetite. She went to her bedroom and fell on her knees and began to pray.

The next morning, she got dressed for work as if nothing were going on. She joined the other teachers in the auditorium to await the start of the meeting.

Principal Davis got up and began his same old boring "welcome to the new school year" speech. "I know we are going to have a successful school year. We have a good team and I want you to keep up the good work."

He finally reached the end of his speech and Misha looked into her folder and spotted the work excuse she got from the doctor. Reading the note, she wasn't really paying attention to what Mr. Davis was saying until she heard Roger's name. She looked up to see Roger standing in the front of the auditorium.

"Mr. Williams is the counselor from the City Development League. His main focus will be to work with troubled kids and students from low-income families to prepare them for college. Y'all welcome Mr. Williams to our school."

Misha gasped. She couldn't believe it. Roger was working at her school. *Is there something wrong with the universe?* How could God let this happen to her? How could she deal with cancer and Roger at the same time? Uncertainty gripped her. How could she handle all that was being placed on her? Misha continued to stare at Roger until their eyes met. She turned away. If anyone could see there was something wrong with her, it would be Roger. He did not need to know anything about her.

After the meeting, the teachers were indifferent to Roger being there. They had seen so many agencies send people into the schools and they didn't like it because it only brought more work for them to do. So only a couple of people walked to the front to meet him. Misha walked to the front to try to catch Mr. Davis before he left.

"Mr. Davis, I need to talk with you."

"Sure, Misha. What can I do you for?"

"I need to speak to you privately," she said as she eyed Roger approaching them.

"Hello, Minister Holloway," Roger said when he reached them.

"You don't have to be so formal, Roger. You can call me Ms. Holloway, or Misha will be fine," she said as she turned to him, trying to act as if nothing were wrong.

"You two know each other?" Mr. Davis asked.

"Misha and I went to the same church. How are you? You look good."

"Mr. Davis, I really need to talk with you. It's important." Misha ignored Roger. There were more important things on her mind. Besides, she could not take his false friendliness after all he had done to her.

"Well, okay. Let's go to my office."

***

The surgery waiting room was filled with people waiting to be called back for surgery and their families. Misha sat alone in the big room. No one went with her to the hospital that morning. She drove herself to the hospital. Judy was going to meet her. Her pastor told her one of the deacons and a missionary would probably meet her there to pray with her before surgery. But there she sat, all alone.

When she looked over at a few groups of people, she could see people gathered in prayer. Some had their priest with them. A rabbi sat with one family. There was also someone there who looked like he was Greek Orthodox or a monk or something; she didn't know. All she knew was he was praying for someone.

She tried to hold back the tears as she thought about all the work she did at the church, and no one showed up at the hospital to pray for her during the toughest part of her life. She tried not to look around the room. Each time she did, she wanted to cry. Her family was not even there to support her. Even though she didn't want her mother to be there, it would have helped to have someone there, anybody. She heard her name called. She stood and walked toward the waiting nurse.

"Your family can come back with you," the nurse said.

"I'm here alone."

"Oh. Well, I'll take you back to a room. Come with me." Misha followed the nurse into a small exam room. The nurse handed her a hospital gown and blanket. "You need to completely undress and place your clothing in the bag on the bed." She pointed to the large plastic bag lying on the hospital bed. "I will be back in a couple of minutes to give you a shot to help you relax." She walked toward the door and stopped. "Is there anyone you would like to call before we get started?"

"No."

"Well, okay. I will be right back."

Before the nurse could return, the anesthesiologist came in and asked her a few questions and left. Then Dr. Trinidad came in and explained the procedure to her again and asked her to sign a surgery consent form for the hysterectomy if needed. She reluctantly signed the form and gave it back to the doctor.

"Your family can come in and wait with you until we're ready for the surgery."

"I'm here by myself."

Dr. Trinidad placed her chart on the metal table next to the bed. "Have you made arrangements to get home if we discharge you today?"

"I'll drive myself."

"You can't do that. Does your family know you're here?"

"My family, my church, my friends, they all know about the surgery. I'm here alone." Misha's eyes shifted downward; she was embarrassed that she had no support during this tough time in her life.

Dr. Trinidad patted Misha's hand. "Well, we'll have to make arrangements to get you home. You won't be able to drive with the anesthesia. We'll work something out."

Dr. Trinidad left her in the extremely cold room. She didn't know if she was shaking because of the surgery or the fact that it was so cold in the room. She prayed quietly to herself until a nurse came in and covered her with a warm blanket. She took a long needle and gave Misha the medication to help her relax. Another nurse entered the room just as the medication began to kick in. Misha was feeling groggy but could feel the bed slowly moving toward the operating room.

Chapter 10

Misha listened as the last bell of the school day rang. Today, she couldn't wait for the students to clear the hall. She had to get to the doctor's office to get the results of her surgery. As she picked up her bags and headed for the door, Judy walked into the classroom.

"Hey, Misha. You look like you're in a hurry."

"I've got a follow-up appointment with the doctor today."

"I know you've got to go. I just came in here to see how you were doing. Look, I'm really sorry I didn't go to the hospital with you. I feel so bad. I thought your family would be there and I didn't want to interfere."

"Judy, you don't have to apologize to me again. I appreciate you and your husband going to the hospital to get my car out of the parking lot and the food you brought me. That really helped me out a lot." Misha slung the shoulder strap of her purse over her shoulder.

"Are you going to the doctor alone? Would you like me to go with you? I can have someone pick up the kids."

"No, I'm fine. If anything were wrong, I would just be getting out of the hospital today. They sent me home. That lets me know everything's fine. Thanks for offering though. I've got to get out of here. I don't want to be late."

"Mimi, hi. I'm sorry. Did I interrupt something?" Roger walked into the classroom, interrupting the conversation they were having. Misha looked at him wearing the shirt and tie she gave him when he got the job at the community center.

"Do you want me to stay?" Judy whispered to Misha.

"No. I'll be fine. I'll call you later."

Judy walked past Roger and out the door without speaking to him. He stood in the doorway with his hands perched on his hips. He slid to the side, allowing Judy to get past him.

"Roger, what do you want? I've got somewhere to go."

"I heard you were sick. I wanted to see how you were doing."

"I'm fine. You could have called me at home. I was out a week."

"I started to but I didn't know how you would feel if I called your house."

"I didn't cut you off. You cut me off. I don't have time for this. I have somewhere to go," she said, walking toward the door.

"Do you mind if I walk you to your car?"

Misha stopped and stared him in the face. "What do you want, Roger? You haven't spoken to me in months. Now, you show up at my job and want to walk me to my car? What's up?"

"Bishop recommended me to be the pastor of New Horizon Worship Center. I preach there every week now. If you want, you can come sometime."

Misha couldn't pretend to be happy for him. She wasn't sure if he was ready to be a pastor. If he treated people like he treated her, he would make a lousy pastor. All the kissing up to Bishop was finally paying off. "Look, I'm happy for you. Thanks for the invitation. I'll think about it. Anything else? I've really got to go."

"No. That's all." Misha quickly headed for the door. "Mimi." She turned around. "You look good."

"I'll see you around." She walked through the crowded hallway as quickly as she could and ran to her car. She had arrived late that morning and had to park in the dungeon, as they called it. It was the area between the football field house and the baseball practice field. There were a lot of tall trees and shrubbery that shaded the parking area to look like a cave. Misha hated parking there because it was a long walk from the main buildings of the school. So today, she ran to her car.

She threw her bags into the car and turned to get in when she looked up and saw the field house. She saw the vision again. The man was attacking Amber again. This time, she heard Amber scream her name. She stood with one foot in her car, staring at the field house, listening to Amber scream her name, unaware of Coach Wells approaching her.

"Ms. Holloway, is there anything wrong?" he said, tapping her lightly on the shoulder.

"What?" She broke her stare to see Coach Wells standing in front of her.

"Are you okay? You haven't moved in a few minutes. I knew you were sick. Somebody said you had surgery. Are you okay?"

"Uh, yeah. I just remembered one of my students said he left his book in the field house after gym today. Do you mind if I go in and check to see if it's there?" Not that she lied. A student did tell her he left his book there. It was no big deal. However, it was a great excuse to go in there.

"No, I'll walk with you. Kids are always leaving things in the field house. If I had a dollar for everything they left in there, I could retire."

Misha walked quickly to the field house. She had never been in the field house and she was taken aback by the musty smell in there. She braced herself against the wall to try to get her breath.

"Are you sure you're okay? You don't look so good."

"I'm fine. It's the smell."

"I guess I'm used to it. Come on. I'll help you look for the book." He waved her to follow him.

Misha walked around the field house, not really knowing what she was looking for. Coach Wells talked the entire time as they looked through open lockers, under benches, and in the office. Misha looked for something familiar from the vision. She wanted to hear the sound again. She wanted answers. Admitting defeat, Coach walked Misha to her car and walked away. The parking lot had completely emptied and her car was the lone one remaining. She looked back at the field house, sighed, and hopped into her car for her drive to the doctor's office.

Misha arrived at exactly her appointment time. Since she was the last appointment for the day, she was taken right back to Dr. Trinidad's office. After waiting half an hour, Dr. Trinidad walked in, apologizing for the wait.

"Well, Ms. Holloway, the surgery went well. We scoped your uterus, ovaries, and fallopian tubes and didn't see any signs of cancer, cysts, endometriosis, or anything that look abnormal," she said as she flipped through the papers she held in her hand.

Misha wanted to jump from the chair and yell, "Praise God." However, she sat quietly, listening to the doctor, not wanting to miss anything the doctor said.

"There were some areas in your cervix that we removed. The biopsy showed they were cancerous. They were really small areas but we had to cut a large area around each spot to prevent any possible spread."

"What does that mean? I don't understand."

Dr. Trinidad leaned against the sink and folded her arms. "The good news is we got all of it. None of the specimens showed any spread of the disease through the walls of your cervix."

"And the bad news?" Misha rubbed her hands together.

"Well, we had to cut extensive areas of your cervix. These areas held the mucus membranes that allow sperm to travel to fertilize the egg. These membranes are also needed to lubricate the vaginal area during sex. With this area removed, it will be quite difficult for you to conceive naturally."

"You mean I still can't have children?"

"I'm not saying that you can't have children. I'm just saying having children naturally will be extremely difficult. When you're ready, I can refer you to a fertility specialist to help you conceive."

"Let me get this straight. You're saying it's impossible for me to get pregnant naturally?"

"I'm not saying it's impossible. It would take a miracle for you to get pregnant naturally. We're going to follow you closely for about a year to be sure everything's fine and monitor you on a regular basis after that to be sure the cancer doesn't return. But I want to see you back next week. I'm going to check to see how you're healing."

"Will I need chemo or any other treatment?"

"Since the areas were so small, we'll only monitor you right now. I want you to come in every other week for about three months and monthly for a few months after that. It's good you have regular checkups. We were able to catch it in its early stages."

Misha left the doctor's office emotionally drained. Dr. Trinidad's words rang in her ear: *It would take a miracle for you to get pregnant.* Driving down the road she began to pray for God to bless her with a child. She prayed God heal her body and allow her to conceive naturally. She pledged to herself she would continue to listen to her healing tapes and declare God's Word over her situation. She loved the Lord and she had faith to believe He would not let her down.

As the rush hour traffic slowed on Interstate 85, she became extremely hungry. She looked around to see where she was. She took the nearest exit to look for a restaurant that would satisfy her hunger. Instead, she pulled into the nearest parking lot. She reached for her phone and punched in her grandmother's number.

"I cooked. Figured you come by after the doctor. I'll be waiting on you." Her grandmother's voice rang over the phone.

Misha took the next exit and made her way through the bumper-to-bumper traffic to get to her grandmother's house. When she pulled up, her grandmother was sitting on the porch, waiting for her. They greeted each other with a hug.

"Well you ain't all to pieces. Must be good news."

They walked into the house and Misha could smell the fried chicken. Misha smiled when she saw the perfectly cooked chicken sitting on the stove. She knew her grandmother only cooked chicken two ways, fried and baked, with only salt and pepper as seasoning, but it was the best in Atlanta. She spotted a fresh pie in the oven. "Grandma, is that a blackberry cobbler?"

"Your brother brought them berries to me. I figured I'd make something with them."

As they sat at the table eating, Misha shared all the doctor had told her that day. Her grandmother encouraged her as Misha gobbled down the blackberry cobbler.

"You talk to yo' mama?"

"Not yet. I'll tell her later." Misha forked a piece of pie into her mouth.

"I don't know wha' it is 'tween you and yo' mama. She been upset. Scared you 'bout to die."

"Mama is so negative. That's why I don't talk to her. When I told her about the cancer, she started putting me in the ground. She kept calling me and crying. She didn't even bother to go to the hospital with me. Justin told me she got up in church and told everybody I had cancer and acted like she so upset she passed out. She is such a drama queen, always wanting attention."

"Don't talk about yo' mama. I know she spoil. We spoil her. I don't know how your daddy puts up with her sometimes."

"Now who's talking about her?" Misha pulled the foil from the cabinet to wrap a plate of food to take home. "I'm going to have to get you some of those cheap plastic containers so I won't have to take your plates to my apartment."

Her grandmother got up and went to the other room and came back with a shoebox. She sat down at the table again while Misha stood at the sink washing dishes. "Go in my room. Look in my closet. On the top shelf you see a quilt. Bring it to me."

Misha wiped the suds off her hands and did what her grandmother asked. She looked at the quilt as she walked back to the table and handed it to her grandmother.

"What's this?" Misha looked into the shoebox.

"This is the family heirloom. Nothing worth selling. Means a whole lot to the family. Look here." She pulled a small ring from the box. It looked as if someone had twisted two small wires together and joined it at the ends. The metal had darkened with time. "This here's my mama wedding ring. They's po' back then. Daddy made this hisself. Mama wore it 'til day she die." She picked up the quilt and opened it up.

Misha looked at the unusual pattern on the quilt. Her fingers traced the stitching in the cloth.

"When your mama got married I gave her a quilt. Gave yo' brother and yo' Uncle Paul and his children one too. You know men. Mean nothing to them. This here's yours."

"You made me a quilt? Why?" Misha sat down across the table from her grandmother and began to look at the different pieces of the quilt.

"This yo' wedding gift. This quilt special. It's a family quilt."

"You thought Roger and I were getting married?"

"Lord no, child!" She held her head back and laughed so loud it made Misha laugh too. "Child, you and I know Roger ain't your husband. This is for you and your real husband. What's his name?"

"Grandma, I'm not six years old. That was just a little girl's fantasy."

"What's his name?"

"It was Matthew. Matthew, okay?"

"Well I was planning to give this to you and Matthew. But the Lord tells me to give it to you today." She pulled the quilt closer to her and began to explain each block on the quilt. "This here is a piece of your granddaddy best Sunday suit. This one he wore on communion Sunday." She went to another square on the quilt. "This one is piece of your mama dress she wore to school. This is part of Paul Easter suit when he was a little boy. This is you and Justin's baby clothes. This a part of an old house coat I had."

"Grandma, you got something of everybody on this quilt?"

"Yeah. These two pieces belong to my mama and daddy. Daddy loved them coveralls. Wore them everywhere, even to church." She reached into the box and pulled out pieces of scrap cloth. "Now this is leftover for you and your children." She handed the scraps to Misha. She turned them over and each one had a small piece of paper pinned to it with the name of the person it came from on it. Misha looked over each piece. "Go in the living room and fetch me that old Bible on the fireplace."

Misha went and got the Bible and then handed it to her grandmother and sat down. Her grandmother pushed the shoebox to the side and opened the Bible. "This here is our family. See, this yo' mama and me and George and Paul and Mattie. This is my mama and daddy and your granddaddy's mama and daddy." She turned the page and pointed to the inscription. "Here is you and Justin and his wife and children. When you get married, you put Matthew name here and your children." She closed the Bible and handed it to Misha. "Take this. Take all this home with you. Don't tell your mama I give you that Bible. Let me tell her."

"Grandma, I can't take your stuff," Misha said, pushing the Bible away from her.

"I want you to have it. Not mine no mo'. It's yours, for you and yo' family. Don't you worry your head about what some docta said. Put yo' children's names in that Bible. Keep the family line going." Misha reached over and hugged her grandmother. "Now, child, go over yonder and get that phone and call yo' mama."

Misha picked up the phone and called her mother and told her what the doctor said. She left off the part about not being able to have children. She wanted only people of great faith to know her situation so they could touch and agree with her. As she spoke with her mother, she was looking at her grandmother and started to make faces.

"Child, bring me that phone." She reached for the phone.

"Mama, Grandma wants to speak to you."

"Ruth Ann, I gives Missy that Bible on the fireplace. It's hers now." Misha could hear her mother's voice screaming. Her grandmother held the phone away from her ear as she watched Misha cover her mouth, trying not to laugh out loud. "The Lord done blessed her with healing. Ought to be happy. I's ti'ed. Here Missy." She handed the phone back to Misha.

"Mama, I've got to go. I'll talk to you later." She hung up the phone and laughed so hard her side hurt. "Ooooooo, Grandma, you're soooo bad."

"I's know how to handle your mama. She be mad a few days. She get over it."

Misha continued laughing as she helped her grandmother finish cleaning the kitchen and enjoyed the evening with her grandmother, who had a way of helping her forget about her troubles. She always had a way of letting her know everything would be all right.

Chapter 11

Misha woke up suddenly from her deep sleep. *It's time to leave that church,* she heard in her spirit. She got up and turned on the light. She looked at the clock: 2:17. She groaned and turned on the television. It was just a dream. However, it was good she was awake because she could feel the start of her monthly visitor. It was late, she assumed, because of the surgery. She got up and went into the bathroom and did what she had to do and climbed back into the bed. She set the sleep timer on her television and curled up and went back to sleep.

She was awakened by strong cramps. Finding she was bleeding heavily, she was not alarmed because her doctor had warned her that this may happen the first month after the surgery. But she didn't expect it to be this bad. Rushing to the bathroom to take a quick shower and to take a Tylenol she prayed, "Lord, I don't want to go to church this morning. I'm supposed to help in children's church. Since I gave my word, strengthen me to do this today." The pain in her abdomen was severe. She walked slowly bent over as she dressed for church. The room began to spin and she braced herself against the table until the feeling went away. She had to go to church—she gave her word. After much debate she left for church.

Arriving in the pastor's study where the other ministers were gathered she was greeted by her pastor with a hug. "Hey, girl. You still going with us today?" Pastor Simpson asked her. She had forgotten about traveling with Pastor Simpson to a church where he was scheduled to preach. She looked at him, trying to decide what to tell him. She did tell him she was going. The associate ministers always traveled with him when he preached. She didn't feel like it today. But, she gave her word.

"Sure, Pastor." *I'm so sick, I can hardly stand. I want to go home and spend the rest of my day fighting these horrible cramps.* The thought was on the tip of her tongue. She kept it to herself. It would have been an inappropriate thing to say.

"We're going to eat after morning service and then we're going to the church."

"I have something to do after morning service. I'll meet you at the church."

After morning service, Misha drove as quickly as she could to get to her apartment. She hadn't spoken to anyone on her way out of the church. She had just been glad church was over and couldn't wait to leave. The Tylenol, which barely helped the pain, was wearing off. She could feel intense cramping and the heavy flow of blood. It seemed as if it was getting worse with each passing hour. She had never experienced anything like this before. She debated whether to call her doctor or stay at home and nurse her raging body. Since she gave her word, she would go to the service and support her pastor. She changed her clothes and put on a pair of black pants with a camisole and a long, flowing blouse that went to her knees. She changed her purse to a larger purse and filled it with sanitary napkins and tampons and headed to the church.

When she arrived at the church, she squeezed into the corner of the last pew in the back of the church.

Sitting there she wouldn't disturb the service when she had to go to the bathroom. Before she left the house she had taken one of the pain pills the doctor had given her after her surgery, and her eyes felt heavy. She prayed the service would be upbeat so she could move around and stay alert. The good in it all was the pill eased her pain.

The service started and, to her delight, it was an upbeat praise and worship service. The people praised like Kingdom Faith. They sang all the old devotion songs and rocked the house with them. Pastor Simpson and the other ministers entered the sanctuary and walked onto the pulpit. Pastor Simpson knelt down to pray and then sat down in one of the upholstered chairs. He leaned over and began talking with the other pastor. After praise and worship, the pastor stepped to the podium and kept the crowd hyped up with his words of exhortation.

"We'd like to thank all of our visitors for being with us to celebrate our ushers' anniversary. If you are visiting with us for the first time, stand up and let us welcome you."

Misha and a few others from True Life stood. Pastor Simpson stood and whispered into the pastor's ear.

"We have another minister from True Life with us today. Minister Holloway, it's good to have you visiting with us today. Come and join us in the pulpit."

Misha knew this was the wrong day to sit in the pulpit. She had to be close to the bathroom without creating a distraction. She stood. "Thank you, Pastor. I may have to sneak out early. I don't want to disturb the service. So, I think I will sit here," she said politely.

The pastor continued to recognize other visiting ministers and invited them to the pulpit. She was the only minister who did not go to the pulpit when invited.

She could feel the tightness that moved from her lower back to her front. She got up and went to the bathroom. *Made it just in time.* As she sat on the toilet, she could feel the flow like water streaming out of her body. She had no idea it would be this bad. She had never experienced anything like this before. What was wrong with her? Was she being punished for something? Did the doctor miss something during the surgery? Should she call her doctor? No, she would look like an idiot. She was told this would happen. Deciding it was best for her to go home, she walked out of the church and got into her car. She was no help to anyone and a danger on the road after taking the pill. Luckily she was not far from home. She could make it fine. Pastor Simpson would understand why she left.

Misha took Monday off and nursed her cramps and heavy flow. After calling Dr. Trinidad, she was assured it was normal bleeding after surgery. It didn't feel normal. She was told if it did not let up in a couple of days or she felt sick, to come into the office. This satisfied her and she spent the day curled up on her sofa watching television in between trips to the bathroom. She prayed for her healing and that this passed quickly.

By Wednesday, she was back to normal. Her flow was light and she felt comfortable enough to go to Bible Study. When she arrived at the church a young man told her Pastor Simpson was looking for her. She walked to his office and peeped in the already open door. "Pastor, you wanted to see me?"

"Yeah, close the door."

"What's up?"

"What happened to you Sunday?" he said, rocking back and forth in his chair.

"What do you mean?" She didn't want to tell him what was happening to her.

"You didn't sit in the pulpit and you left early. What's up with that?"

"I had an emergency and did not want to disrupt the service."

"You embarrassed me when you did that. I told him to invite you up and you didn't even bother to come." He leaned back in his chair and sat right back up again. "You know it's an insult not to go into the pulpit when you are invited. You insulted the pastor and embarrassed me. Bishop Moore told me, when I called him about your license, you would be an embarrassment to me."

"You've been talking to Bishop about me?"

"Yeah, on more than one occasion. He calls here to check up on you. Now I have to tell him he was right. I should have listened to him. You've been here almost a year and still haven't joined the church. I treated you like one of our own, like a member. If you're going to stay here, you need to be taught how to act."

"Pastor, I apologize. I didn't mean to embarrass you." She could not believe what she was hearing. Apparently Bishop did not know how to let things go. He was checking up on her and continuing to talk about her. Why? Why was he trying to tarnish her reputation? One minute she was his daughter, the next she was the enemy. What was he trying to prove? She did not do anything to him. She certainly was not trying to destroy his ministry. He was trying to destroy hers.

"You did. Try not to do it again. If you don't want to sit in the pulpit, don't go anywhere with me. All my ministers sit in the pulpit to support me. I need to know you have my back. It's all kinds of demons out there and I need someone praying for me when I preach."

"I'll remember that. Anything else?"

Pastor Simpson shook his head no. She exited the office. Another minister followed her into the ladies' room down the hall. As she hugged Misha she began to pray loud, drawing the attention of others. Now, Misha was embarrassed. None of these people had her best interest at heart.

Leave.

She wanted so much to go. However, they were having a prayer meeting in the bathroom. People were screaming, crying, and falling out. Misha sat on the sofa in the powder room looking at people laying hands on each other, prophesying and crying.

Leave.

This time when she heard it, she picked up her purse and eased out the door and to her car.

When she arrived home, she began to talk to herself. "I was an embarrassment to him? He has been talking to Bishop Moore about me? Neither one of them taught me anything about the ministry. Bishop Moore only taught me how to put a sermon together and that was with some books I read. He really hasn't taught me a thing. I didn't know it was an insult to not go to the pulpit when invited. I didn't know. And Pastor Simpson, he hasn't taught me a thing. Nothing. The cool pastor, the hip pastor, all of this was a disguise for the same old thing—same thing, new people. Well, if he thinks he has gotten rid of me, he has another think coming."

That night, as Misha slept, she heard the voice again. *It's time to leave that church.* She woke up and sat up on her bed. She shook her head. *Is this really the Lord or my fight or flight coming into play?* She prayed, "God give me the strength to stay at True Life. I'm not going to let those Negroes run me out of that church. I'm a strong black woman. I'm a strong Christian woman."

She lowered her body underneath her covers and quickly fell asleep. Her body rolled over the edge of the bed. It felt as if something pushed her out of the bed. She felt herself falling but couldn't stop it.

I told you to leave that church and you will not sleep until you leave.

"God, I'm tired. I've got bus duty in the morning. I have to get some sleep." She got up off the floor and crawled back into her bed. She was wide-awake. Nothing she did helped her get back to sleep. She got up and took one of the pain pills because she knew it would make her sleepy. She sat up and watched the clock until she could no longer see the numbers.

Her sleep was not a peaceful one. She was tormented by her vivid dreams.

I told you to leave that church.

Feeling the lightheaded effect of the medication, she sat on the edge of the bed. She looked at the clock. She had only been asleep for thirty minutes. She curled up on her pillow and dozed back off to sleep when she thought she felt the bed shake. She sat up again and turned on the light. The pill was beginning to make her body shake. Why was her body fighting sleep?

She walked around and watched a little television. She pressed the button on the remote until she stopped on Christian television. Shante Patrick was talking about how difficult it was for her to leave her church and start a new ministry with her husband. She testified about her walking in disobedience because she didn't want the people to feel they ran her out of the church. Then she realized she was out of order. Misha somehow knew this message was for her. She eased down the side of her bed and fell on her knees and began to repent. "God, tell me, what you want me to do?" She continued to pray until she fell asleep.

The next morning Misha woke up on the floor beside her bed. She felt extremely tired and nervous. She looked at the clock. It was 7:32. "Oh no, I'm late." Adrenaline flowed as she hurriedly got dressed and ran for the door to go to work. She called the school to tell them she was running late and finally made it before first period was over.

When she arrived in her class, Roger was sitting at her desk, looking at some papers. "Mr. Williams, what are you doing here?" She stopped in her tracks.

"The principal asked me if I could sit in with your class until you arrived." He set the stack of papers in his hand on her desk.

"Thank you for your help. I'm just running late this morning. Any problems?" She casually walked into the room.

"No. They're a great group of kids." Some of the students laughed. "I've been keeping them entertained. I didn't see a lesson plan for today on your desk. I would have started their work for you."

"I have it with me. Thanks. I can handle it now." She stared at Roger, waiting for him to move from her desk.

"I'm sorry. I guess you need your desk." Roger stood and walked to the door. "Bye, guys," he said, waving to the class.

"Bye, Mr. Williams," they all sang at once, sounding like an elementary school class.

She began to teach her class when one of the students raised his hand. "Yes, Daniel."

"Mimi, can I go to the bathroom?" The other students in the class laughed.

Misha was shocked to hear him call her Mimi. Only one person called her Mimi—Roger. What did he say to her students? She stood stoic, trying not to show her anger. She placed her hand on her hip and asked, "Daniel, who told you to call me that?"

"Mr. Williams, he said you would understand the joke." The other students continued laughing.

"What else did Mr. Williams tell you?"

"He said y'all went to college together and you used to party a lot."

"What was it like going to clubs every night?" another student asked. The class seemed to think it was even funnier. Misha could feel there was something more. He was only in her class about thirty minutes. What else could he have said about her?

"Class, that was a long time ago. We all make mistakes. Besides, I didn't go to clubs every night. If I did, I wouldn't have graduated and become your teacher and be able to give you a test tomorrow."

"Aw, Ms. Holloway," the class chimed.

"Just kidding." Misha laughed. "You guys do have a test next week. So I want you to study hard. The Mimi joke you don't understand. So don't call me that again. You can call me Ms. Holloway. That will be enough."

As the class was ending and the students were changing classes, one of the young ladies walked up to her and told her Roger told them she used to like him and stalked him when they were in college. He said they called her Mimi the Stalker in college. Misha tried to hold back her fury. Her body tensed listening to the student's explanation of their behavior. During her planning period she was going to pay Roger a visit. She wanted to do it then but her other class was about to start. Taking a deep breath and slowly letting it out, she began her class.

***

"Mimi the Stalker, Roger?" Misha said as she slammed the door to Roger's office. "How could you say that to my students about me? You told them I went to clubs every night."

"Mimi, it was a joke. They took it out of context." Roger leaned back in his chair, smiling the entire time.

"You got my students calling me Mimi the Stalker. What does that say to you, if you heard it about someone else?"

"I'll straighten it out. It was only a joke." There was a knock at the door. It was Mr. Davis. He walked into the office.

"Is everything all right here?" he said, looking at both of them.

"Sure, Mr. Davis. Everything's copasetic." Roger smiled. Misha turned her back on Mr. Davis—her arms folded around her body. She did not want him to see the rage in her eyes.

"I was told there was yelling coming out of this office. Is everything fine, Ms. Holloway?"

Misha took a deep breath and slowly turned around to face him, forcing a smile on her face. "Sure, Mr. Davis. We were only talking loud about a joke." She glanced at Roger, who was still smiling as if nothing was out of the ordinary.

"Well, keep it down. You know how everybody's all jittery about little things since the Columbine shooting. I'll see you two later." He walked out of the office and Misha closed the door again.

"Roger, I would appreciate it if you keep our—no, my—private life out of the school," she said, lowering her voice.

"It was a joke. Okay, okay. I won't say anything else," he said, waving his arms in the air.

Misha walked out of the office and started down the hallway when Mr. Davis stopped her. "What was that all about?"

"It was nothing. He played a joke on me. That's all. It's all good."

"Okay. But if you have any problems, let me know."

"I will. I better eat lunch before my next class starts." Misha watched as Mr. Davis walked away and into the counselors' office. She hoped he wasn't going to talk with Roger. Somehow she knew he was. She asked God to get Roger out of her school. He was nothing but trouble. She could finally see the real Roger and wondered how she could have gotten mixed up with him in the first place.

At the end of the day, Judy walked up to her as she was getting into her car. "Hey, Misha. What is this Mimi the Stalker thing I've been hearing about you all day?"

"Boy, news travels fast. Roger sat in my class until I got here this morning and told my students I used to stalk him when we were at Howard. He told my students to call me Mimi the Stalker."

"That . . ." She stopped herself before saying how she really felt. She had not liked Roger since he came to the school. "Did you tell Mr. Davis?" Her mouth twisted into a frown.

"Our wonderful principal walked in on us when I went to Roger's office to confront him. Roger played it off like he was so innocent. He made me look like a fool today. I'm going to have to pray him out of here."

"I'll be praying with you. He's got some nerve. Does he know how hard it is to win the students' respect? I don't know what you saw in him. He tells some of the wildest stories. It's hard to believe somebody let him pastor their church."

"Hey, Mimi," another teacher called to Misha as she walked past her car.

"Hey, girl, that's an old joke. You can call me Misha." Misha laughed it off and continued her conversation with Judy. "See what I mean? Why did I ever fool with that man?"

"The sex was probably good."

"I never had sex with Roger."

"You two never did it? Never?" Judy's eyes stretched, surprised to hear her say that.

"I'm not saying I haven't but not with Roger. He was a Christian when we met and he said he was celibate."

"Never?"

"Get over it, Judy. We never did and I'm glad. Just think what would have happened if I got pregnant by somebody like him. Look, I would love to stand around and bash Roger all day. But I have to go."

"Not one time in all those years?"

"Love you but I really have to go." She hugged Judy and slipped into her car. Her cell phone chimed. She looked at the caller ID. It was Roger. She hesitated, then answered it so she could really tell him off as she left school property.

"What do you want now, Roger?"

"Mimi, I'm really sorry. It was bad judgment. I shouldn't have told your students anything about you."

"You're right. You shouldn't have. Now everybody, including teachers, is calling me Mimi the Stalker. It wasn't funny."

"It'll die down in a few days. You have any plans for dinner?"

He had some nerve asking her out to dinner. She would not be seen anywhere with him. "Yeah, I have plans."

"Oh. Maybe another time."

"Maybe."

Why would he think she could just forget what just happened and go out to eat with him? She wished she still used profanity. It was moments like this that cussing him out the old-fashioned way would have made her feel a lot better. But she couldn't do that. She wasn't going to allow him to bring out the worst in her.

She ruminated over it so much it became funny to her. She laughed until she got home. He could not have possibly believed she would even have a desire to be with him. She tried hard to think what she saw in him but could not think of a thing now. Everything she believed him to be, he wasn't. She never really knew him. Now, she did not want to know him. She did not want to be near him. She had to pray him away from her. She needed to be completely free from him.

Chapter 12

Misha sat on the edge of her bed, contemplating what she was going to do. It was Sunday. She knew God wanted her to leave True Life but she didn't have anywhere else to go. She prayed for God to guide her footsteps. She didn't want to go to her grandmother's church. It was beginning to look like it was the place she ran to every time she left or got put out of a church. She got dressed and asked the Lord for direction. She got into her car, not really knowing where she was going. She figured she could drive through the city until God directed her to a church, finally ending at the Rock of Life.

This time a different person greeted her so friendly, like she knew her. She walked over to the information desk and noticed a Clark Atlanta brochure sitting on the counter. After getting information about the church and picking up a brochure, she found herself a seat as prayer was beginning.

She enjoyed service as much as she did when Shante Patrick preached. The Word that came forth was in agreement to everything God was telling her in her spirit. She felt the connection to the entire service. She left the church feeling so refreshed she decided she would attend that church until God led her somewhere else.

She stopped at a local restaurant and ordered some food. As she waited for her food, she began to look at the

Clark Atlanta brochure. It was more than a brochure. It was a folder with a lot of information, including an application. She hoped it didn't belong to someone and she picked it up without asking first. It was the only one sitting on the counter. She leafed through the information in the folder. They had a master of education program. She needed something to occupy her time, and returning to college was a good way to do it. The pay increase after she got her master's degree would help. She smiled. *God does have a plan.* She continued looking at the information until she finished her food. Folding it, she decided applying for grad school was the right thing to do.

Later that evening, she called Pastor Simpson and told him she felt the Lord moving her to another church. He apologized for what he said, stating he didn't know she was never told about the insult. He asked her not to leave. The longer she talked with him, the more she realized he didn't understand her leaving had nothing to do with him or the church. But it had everything to do with God and what He wanted to do in her life.

The next day, as Misha walked toward the library for the staff meeting, she was confronted by another teacher, Gloria.

"Mimi, I didn't know you liked Roger."

"That joke's old. Please don't call me that." Misha turned away toward the library. She wanted to get a good seat in the back before the other teachers got there.

"Well, I wanted you to know Roger and I are together now. He's not interested in you," Gloria said to Misha.

"Gloria, where did you get the idea I was interested in Roger?" Misha turned to look at her.

"He told me you used to chase him around. He said he had a restraining order against you. I want to warn you to back away from him or I'm going to Mr. Davis."

Misha nearly fell over laughing. That was the funniest thing she had heard in a while. Shaking her head, she responded, "He does not have a restraining order against me. You need to wake up. No, I'm not going to entertain this. I'm going to the meeting." Misha left her standing in the hallway and walked to the library, where she sat with Judy at one of the round tables.

Gloria and Roger walked into the room. Gloria reached for Roger's arm and directed him to a table near Misha. This time when she saw Roger with another woman, it did not bother her. She felt sorry for Gloria. She knew exactly what it was going to be like dating him. *Good riddance.* At least she did not have to listen to his negative comments or lies anymore. *Let someone else do it. If Gloria wants to be that one, more power to her.* Hopefully, she would not have to put up with this childish behavior every day.

"That woman's desperate," Judy said to Misha. "Does she think she has a catch?"

Misha tried hard not to look their way as the meeting progressed. It seemed as if Gloria was trying everything to get her attention. She laughed louder at Mr. Davis's jokes than anybody and then glanced at Misha to see if she was looking. She moved her chair so close to Roger they almost touched. Roger sat back, acting as if he was the life of the party. They both had the stares of the other staff members. Misha was glad when the meeting ended so she would not have to endure the spectacle that was distracting her from the meeting.

"Hey, Misha. Wait up." Misha heard Roger calling her as she walked down the hallway. She tried to speed up her steps and acted as if she didn't hear him calling her.

"Misha. Mimi, come on. Don't act like that." She had no choice but to stop. There was already a lot of talk going on about them around the school and she didn't want to give anyone else any more ammunition.

"Mr. Williams, what can I do for you?"

"I need your help."

"You mean Gloria can't help you."

"Gloria?" Roger smiled, then twisted his lip like he was disgusted. "Come on, girl. You know ain't nothing going on between me and Gloria."

"That's not what she said. What do you want? The first bell is about to ring." They stood in the hallway as teachers and students passed them by.

"We are having women's day at my church. The speaker canceled last night. I really need your help. Do you think you can speak Sunday? I know it's short notice but I couldn't find anybody else."

"So I'm your last choice?"

"You were my first. I was afraid to ask you. I'm desperate. Can you help me out?"

"Roger, I don't know."

"Please, pretty please," he said in a baby-like voice. "Do me this one favor and I'll forever be grateful to you."

"I'll tell you what. If you don't find anybody by the end of the week, I'll do it. Only if you don't find anyone."

"Thank you, Mimi. I owe you one," he whispered in her ear before he turned and walked down the hallway toward his office.

Don't go.

Misha's spirit was troubled as she walked to her classroom. Her body trembled as she heard that voice again.

Don't go. He can't be trusted.

She shook off the feeling as the bell rang and students began to file into her class.

That night Misha sat at her table, completing the application for admission to Clark Atlanta. She wanted to be admitted in January, but the deadline had already passed. She checked the proposed admission date as January anyway, just in case someone dropped out or failed to enroll and she could take their place. She completed the application, financial aid info, and the request for her transcript. Deciding to mail the information that night, she headed for the post office.

She hopped in the car wearing jeans and a Westdale Eagles sweatshirt. It was October and the air was beginning to chill in the evening. She rolled down the window so she could feel the cool breeze throughout her car. On her drive back home, the smell of barbecue filled her car. She looked up and saw the big red neon sign: SMOKIN' JOE'S RIB HOUSE. She could really use some ribs. She pulled into the parking lot. Before getting out of the car she reached into the back seat and picked up the Victoria Christopher Murray novel she had been trying to get to for weeks. She got out of the car with book in hand and walked into the restaurant.

The restaurant was filled with people laughing and enjoying the casual atmosphere. The rustic look of the restaurant gave it an earthy feel. She gave the waitress her order and opened her book and began reading. Her focus waned as the noise from a large group of people sitting together in the restaurant distracted her. Her eyes met the eyes of one of the men in the group. He was laughing with his mouth wide open. He saw her looking at him and he stopped laughing. She quickly reverted to reading her book. She could feel him staring at her as she tried to concentrate on her book. Each time she looked up, she could see him peering at her. She squirmed in her seat, uncomfortable at the man's attention. Looking at her watch she became impatient, wondering how long it would be before her food arrived.

"Excuse me." She looked up at the tall caramel-skinned man who stood before her. It was the man from the table. "Do you have the time?"

She saw the large watch on his wrist. *Time for you to get away from my table.* No one in the group had a watch that was working? Or could it be the bootleg Rolex he was wearing was not working?

"I apologize for interrupting you. Looks like a good book."

"It is. Your watch broken?"

He looked at his wrist as if it was the first time he noticed the watch on his arm. His lips curved in a crooked smile. "I just got in from Singapore. My watch is set for that time."

He was trying too hard. She gave him the time to get him away from her table. "It's eight-twelve."

"Thank you. You alone?" he said, standing with his hands slightly pushed into the front pockets of his jeans.

"No, I'm waiting for my husband." Misha slipped her left hand under the table, hoping he did not notice she was not wearing a ring.

"Oh. Well, thank you for the time."

"No problem."

It wasn't exactly a lie. She was waiting for her husband. She would have to use that line again. It could get rid of a man fast. She went back to reading her book in peace until the waitress arrived.

The waitress placed the plate piled high with ribs, potato salad, and baked beans on the table in front of Misha. "He looks better in person," she said.

"He? Who?" Misha asked curiously.

"That guy you were talking to. You don't know who that is?" The waitress poured water into the glass on the table.

"No. He was trying to pick me up. I told him I was married."

"I wish he would try to pick me up. I would go anywhere with him. That man is fine."

Misha looked over at the table. He was still looking at her. "Are we talking about the same person? You mean that light-skinned guy sitting at the table with all those people?"

"Yeah. You don't know who that is? Girl, that's Bernard Taylor, the gospel singer."

"Who is that? I never heard of him."

"You're kidding right? Bernard Taylor?" She began softly singing a song. Misha shook her head no. She didn't recognize the song. "You never heard of that? He's won Grammys. Didn't you see him on the Stellar Awards?"

"I don't like awards shows. Besides, I don't have time to listen to a lot of gospel music. He couldn't be all that famous. I never heard of him."

"If I were you, I would let him take me wherever he wanted to go. I better get back to work. You need anything else?"

"No. I'm fine." Misha looked over at the table just as two of the guys sitting with him turned to look at her.

She felt more uncomfortable. She decided to ask the waitress for a carry-out box. She couldn't enjoy her ribs with all those people staring at her. Besides, the unwanted attention made her nervous. She hoped she could make it to her car without incident. Should she ask the restaurant manager to walk her to her car? She shook her head at the thought. She would be fine. She was parked just outside the restaurant on the curb. She asked the waitress for a box, pushed her food into it. She paid for her meal and left the restaurant.

When she reached her car, she heard someone trying to get her attention. She turned around, prepared to kick and run, when she saw it was Bernard Taylor with two guys following him. Misha's heart raced. She pressed the unlock button on her car and picked up her step to get to it.

She had pulled the car door open when he reached her. The two guys waited on the sidewalk. All her defenses were up and she was about to press the alarm on her car keys when he started talking to her, apologizing for startling her and promising to do her no harm. Misha cautiously listened to him, standing with one foot in her car. Just because he was famous did not mean he wasn't crazy. Besides he had two other guys with him and they were big and looked mean.

"Miss, I'm sorry to bother you again. We're new in town and we need directions to the High Museum."

"It's closed now. What is it you really want?" This guy did not know how to approach anyone. Why was he bothering her? She looked at him. *A famous gospel singer?* He did not look like one. His skin was so light one would think he was white, which is unusual for a gospel artist. His striped shirt was not tucked in his jeans and he was wearing a pair of bobos. His clothing looked so cheap he almost looked like a bum.

"I guess I look stupid. What's your name?" He smiled. His white teeth with a slight overbite glistened in the lights from the restaurant.

"Look, mister. I'm very uncomfortable right now. Who are those guys?" She nodded in the direction of the men standing idly on the sidewalk.

He looked back at the two men pretending not to watch them. "Those guys? They're harmless unless something funny's going on."

"Funny? I've got to go." Misha dipped into the driver's seat of her car and locked her door. Bernard tapped on the window. She slightly rolled down the window.

"No, wait. What's your name?"

Misha placed her food and purse on the front passenger seat. "The waitress told me you were famous or something. I'm sorry but I've never heard of you. But I'm going to let you in on a life-changing secret. Once you hear this, you will never be the same. It will make you look at the world in a different light. What I'm about to tell you will revolutionize your life."

"Oh yeah. What is it?" He stood looking at her with a big, wide smile.

"Not every woman who sees you wants you. Not every woman who hears you sing wants you. Once you get that in your head, your life will be a whole lot better. Now if you'll excuse me, I have to go."

Misha started her car and pulled out of the space, leaving him standing in the road where her car had been parked. She looked in her rearview mirror and could see the two men on the sidewalk laughing as Bernard slowly walked toward them. She took a deep breath, letting out all the tension she felt. She handled that situation pretty good. She felt empowered. *A famous gospel artist. Be for real.* Her lips curved, smiling. She pressed the gas, trying to get home to eat her food before her ribs got cold.

***

Bernard Taylor stood alone on the sidewalk, staring in the direction Misha sped away from him. There was something special about that girl. He wished he had approached her differently. She was beautiful. He could still see her big, deep brown, doe eyes that smiled even when she wasn't smiling. Her voice was filled with sassafras and sweet tea, challenging him. No one outside his family had ever dared to do that before.

She never heard of me? He liked it. His lips curved upward, forming deep dimples along the sides of his mouth. He wished he'd had one of his guys get her tag number. He would really like to know who she was. Maybe they would run into each other the next time he was in Atlanta. He would send up a special prayer just for that. Shaking his head, he walked back into the restaurant.

Chapter 13

Friday evening Misha was surprised to get a phone call from Roger, saying he couldn't find anyone to preach and asking her to do it. She reluctantly agreed although everything in her spirit was telling her not to do it. She was already tired from taking up tickets at the football game and watching another brutal defeat of the West-dale Eagles, so she decided to wait until Saturday to begin studying for her sermon.

After all, it was just Roger. She did not have to impress him with her preaching style to get a return invitation. Besides, she needed the money. If she only got a couple hundred dollars, it would help. Her sermon would not be long. She could get in and get out without having to deal with Roger too much. She could show up right after service began, but in time to walk into the pulpit with the other guests. Hopefully, they would give her a check during a special presentation during the service. Then, she could leave immediately after benediction. Sounded like a plan to her.

Saturday went by and she did not have a sermon. No scripture popped out at her as she studied. She decided to preach one she already had. She had nervous tension as she drove to Roger's church wearing her white suit. She prayed along the way that God gave her strength to preach. She needed God's help to strengthen her since she was traveling alone. She did not dare tell her grandmother she was preaching at Roger's church, knowing how she felt about him.

She pulled into a space on the side of the church and watched the people going into the church. After praying quietly in her car, she walked into the church and asked an usher for the pastor's office. The usher escorted her to Roger's office. When she walked in, she noticed she was the only woman there. Roger was sitting in a large chair behind a desk and he jumped up as if he was surprised to see her there. She walked around the room, introducing herself to the men in the room. Roger asked her to have a seat and one of the men stood up to give her a seat.

There was another knock on the door. As the door opened, Bishop Moore entered the room. Roger jumped up and hugged him. The other men stood and Bishop greeted each one of them. When he got to Misha, he hugged her and asked her why she was there.

"Roger invited me to preach."

Bishop looked at Roger. Roger sat back in his chair without saying a word.

"When? It's men's day. I have on my schedule I'm supposed to preach this morning," Bishop explained.

Misha knew Roger had set her up. She knew he was a little too anxious to get her to come. He even called her Saturday night to be sure she was coming. Now, she was looking like an idiot in front of all those men. She knew why God did not give her a sermon. How could she have been so gullible? She wanted to believe he was sincere. He knew she would help him with his ministry. This was the final straw. She had enough of him. However, she had to get out of that office—that church.

Misha opened her purse and pretended she was looking for her calendar. "Bishop, I probably got my days mixed up. I was pretty sure it was today. I can't find my calendar. Well this is awkward. I guess I'll go out in the sanctuary and enjoy the service."

"No, you don't have to go. Sit here with us, daughter. I haven't seen you in a while. How are you doing? Roger said you were sick."

"It wasn't anything serious. I think I'll go out and sit in the sanctuary. It was good seeing you again, Bishop." Misha walked out into the hallway. She could hear the men in the office laughing loudly. She headed straight for the exit door. *How could I have been so stupid?* Roger was not going to ruin her day or any days to come. Something welled up in her stomach—a silent strength. She knew she had to experience this to see how far Roger was willing to go to make her look stupid. He was an idiot she did not have time for. The decision was made not to speak to him again and maybe, just maybe, he would leave her alone.

The next day, during her planning period, she was called to Mr. Davis's office. When she entered the room, she saw Roger sitting in a chair, crying. "I'm sorry. I'll come back." She turned to leave the room.

"No, Ms. Holloway. This concerns you. Come in and have a seat," he said stoically.

Misha walked into the office. Mr. Davis closed the door and returned to the chair behind his desk. Roger was looking out the window, sniffing. Now there was anger welling in her belly. She knew he was up to something dirty. How dirty was yet to be seen.

"Ms. Holloway, Roger tells me the two of you have a history. He's still pretty shaken up about yesterday."

"Yesterday? What do you mean yesterday?" She looked over at Roger, who was still looking out the window.

"He said you showed up at his church uninvited and tried to force him to let you preach. He said there are a number of witnesses who will testify to this."

"Testify? Roger?" She looked over at Roger again. He was sitting in his chair with his head lowered. Misha knew he was only pretending he was upset. Her heart began to beat fast. Sweat beaded on the palms of her hands. She wanted to go off on him but she could tell by the look on Mr. Davis's face it wasn't the time.

"Mr. Davis, Roger invited me to his church to preach. He even called me Saturday night to see if I was coming. When I got there, I found out it was men's day and our father in the ministry was preaching. If he said I showed up uninvited, it's not true. Is it, Roger?" she asked sternly.

Roger still did not look up. Misha shook her head in disgust, a frown forming on her face. Now Roger was trying to get her fired. "Roger, tell him the truth. You invited me. Tell him." Misha pleaded for Roger to tell the truth.

"Ms. Holloway," Mr. Davis said. "I'm trying to keep this between us. However, I cannot accept this type of behavior in my school. Because the incident did not happen on school property, there is really nothing I can do about it. But, if you bring it to my school, or me, then it will become a problem. You have been a good teacher. I nominated you myself for rookie teacher of the year. In all my years of working with the school, I have never had a problem like this before."

"He's lying. He invited me. Roger, how could you do this to me? We dated for almost four years and now you are treating me like this?" Misha exclaimed, not hiding her disbelief. "I haven't done anything to you. I've even tried to help you by referring students to your program. I know you are a good worker. I don't understand why you're treating me like this. I thought you were bad when you had Gloria come up to me and threaten me, but this is stooping too low."

"Gloria? What does she have to do with this?"

"Apparently, she and Roger have something going on."

"Is this true, Roger?"

He shook his head no.

"Ms. Holloway, I have to warn you I cannot allow this behavior in my school. I won't put this in your personnel records. But if something like this comes up again, I'm going to have to notify the district."

Misha was so upset she trembled. Her SWATs roots were deep in her soul and were about to show up. Girls from southwest Atlanta are too strong and don't take a whole lot of crap from people. Roger was about to push her back over the edge. Her hands gripped the armrest, preventing her from reaching over and choking him. Mr. Davis asked Roger to leave them alone. Roger exited the room without saying a word.

"Look, I know how hard it is to end a friendship. Roger said you were only friends. Just stay away from him. Don't have anything to do with him. I would hate to lose you as a teacher. You're a good educator and that's hard to find these days. Now, pull yourself together. Would you like some water?"

She shook her head no. "Mr. Davis, you have to believe me. He invited me. He said his speaker cancelled and he needed someone on short notice. I wouldn't have gone if he didn't say he was in a tight fix."

Mr. Davis wiped his face with his hand. "Just try to stay away from him. Please, I beg you. Leave him alone."

"You don't have anything to worry about. I didn't fool with him after we broke up over a year ago, and now with all of this, I definitely won't have anything else to do with him again."

Misha walked out of the office feeling emotionally drained. She walked into the teacher's lounge to try to get herself together, until she saw Roger and Gloria sitting closely at a table, laughing and talking. He looked as though he got over his emotional breakdown quickly. They stopped talking when she walked through the door and stared at her. She turned around and walked to her classroom. Why would he do something so childish to her? It was as if they never meant anything to each other. Her grandmother saw it from the beginning. She should have listened to her.

His antics did teach her one thing—to no longer accept any invitations to speak that were not in writing. She had nothing to prove he had, in fact, actually invited her to preach. She had no defense. It was his word against hers. She vowed never to be in that situation again, not only with Roger, but also with anyone who asked her to preach.

Misha walked down the hallways that were decorated for Spirit Week, trying to hold back her anger. Revenge would be so sweet—cut his tires, sugar in the gas tank, set up a "watch out for rats" Web site with his picture. So many crazy thoughts ran through her head she had to laugh at them. Amber came out of a classroom, interrupting her thoughts.

"Ms. Holloway, you're coming to the game Friday, right? Remember, you promised to help the homecoming committee with the parade."

"Sure, Amber. I'll be there. You better get to class before the bell."

"It's my lunch break. So, I'm cool. Besides, we still have work to do on the float. I've got to look good after they crown me homecoming queen."

"You're so sure of that. The students don't vote until lunch Thursday."

"Oh, I'm going to be homecoming queen, then Miss Westdale High. I rule." Amber began doing one of her cheerleader kicks, waving her arms in the air—her blond hair waving with her movements.

"That's enough of that. Now get to the cafeteria." Misha was glad she ran into Amber in the hallway. Her upbeat attitude and cheerful, positive outlook and silliness made her smile and for a brief moment made her forget about Roger.

The rest of the day passed by slowly as Misha continued to keep her mind on her work. She debated to herself if she should talk to somebody about the incident. She knew the only one she could trust was her grandmother. She did not want to tell her because of the way she felt about Roger. But she needed to talk with someone. She did not want to talk to Judy. For some reason, she felt Judy had some drama of her own. She didn't have a pastor she could talk to. She had to talk to someone. At the end of the school day, she took a deep breath and headed to her grandmother's home, deciding that was her only option.

Misha could see her grandmother in the front yard, raking leaves. She pulled into the driveway and got out of the car.

"Hey, Grandma. What'cha cook?" She tried to sound cheerful.

"Got some turkey neck bones and rice."

"You're the only one I know who cooks that kind of stuff. Do you have any left?"

"It's on the stove. Come on. I fix ya a plate." The two of them walked into the house and Misha quietly fixed herself a plate. "You're quiet today."

"I got things on my mind."

"Well, child, nothing a good meal won't fix."

"I wish it was that easy, Grandma. I think Roger is trying to get me fired." Misha began telling her grandmother about the invitation and the men's day program. She told her how embarrassed she was to be called to the principal's office and how she felt seeing Roger there crying like a little girl. "He was trying to make me look crazy. Like some lunatic stalking him. I hadn't talked to him or seen him in months until he came to my school to work. He's even got one of the teachers threatening me."

"I don't see why you fool with him anyhows. Tell he ain't no count."

"He was good to me."

"If he was, I ain't seen it. He talks to you so bad, almost made me cuss."

"I didn't realize it then. Looking back, now I do. He was real critical of me. How could I have gotten mixed up with him? I feel so stupid."

"Don't beat yo'self up. We all make mistakes. It's going to be all right. We'll pray him outta there. That's what we're gonna do. You needs your job. That's a good job."

This made Misha happy. If anyone could get a prayer through, it was her grandmother. She knew it wouldn't be long before Roger was completely out of her life. She began to attack her food like she did when she was a little kid. She loved her grandmother's food, even though she would never admit to anyone she ate neck bones. She licked her fingers and talked at the same time. "Grandma, I'm going to the Remnant Church Sunday. You wanna go?"

"Remnant? That one of those churches . . . What y'all call them?"

"Mega church."

"Whateva. Too big for me. What you going there for?"

"I don't know. It's been in my spirit to go. Maybe it's where the Lord is leading me."

"Well you just do what God tells you. I'm fine. The bus pick me up Sunday."

"Okay. Well, if you change your mind, give me a call."

"I sho' will. You tell yo' mama?"

"Now, Grandma, you know I don't tell her anything."

"You gon' hafta learn how to get along wit' yo' mama. She spoil but you spoil, too. I spoil both ya. I'm not gon' be 'round fo'eva."

"Stop talking like that. You ain't going nowhere."

"Chile, we all got to die. I feel a whole lot betta if you and yo' mama got along."

Misha scraped the last bite of food off her plate and forked it into her mouth. Her grandmother was right. It was time to call a truce with her mother. She had to forget all the things that was done and said in the past. Life was fragile and too short to hold a grudge.

Chapter 14

Sunday arrived and Misha woke up early to pray. She had never been to the Remnant Church before and she was looking forward to going. Although she had never attended the church, she felt an urgent need to go after seeing the pastor on television.

She wanted to make sure her hair and clothes were well presentable. The Remnant Church was known for its classic style. She unwrapped her hair and tried on several outfits before deciding on a navy blue pants suit. She wanted some bacon and eggs, but she ate cereal. She didn't want to go to a new church smelling like bacon.

She got into her car, reviewed her directions again, and started her journey to the church. When she got there, she could see people dressed in bright orange vests standing in the road, directing traffic. She followed their directions and pulled into a parking space. As she got out of her car, she could see people of many different races going into the large auditorium-styled church. Several people rushed past her without speaking. One lady almost knocked her over and did not apologize. However, Misha did not think much of it. She wanted to believe the lady was anxious to get into the presence of God.

Misha walked into the sanctuary and noticed how chaotic the atmosphere was. Some people were laughing and talking loudly to other people. Some people were crying and praying. There were some people in bright pink leotards and net skirts, running around, waving flags. There were others dressed in black, running around with electrical cords trailing behind them and carrying large video cameras. There was even a guy running around with a Jewish prayer cloth wrapped around his head. The music was so loud Misha could hardly hear herself think and service had not even started.

She searched for a seat. When she sat down, an usher rudely asked her to move. She moved to another seat and a woman sat down beside her. The lady set her large bag and purse down in the seat between them. She began to yell at someone on another aisle. Then she began searching wildly through her bag. Misha wanted to move again, but service was beginning. The woman was too weird with her bright red hair that was as chaotic as the church and the constant mumbling she was doing.

A slim white man with spiked, bleached hair walked onto the podium and began screaming in the microphone. "Praise God. This is a church on fiyah this morning. Praise Him. Praise Him. Praise Him." He began waving his arms in the air as people ran to their seats.

A group of singers walked onto the stage, holding microphones in their hands. Another man stepped out onto the podium with a large shofar and began blowing into the ram's horn. Misha placed her fingers in her ears because it sounded like large explosions. Three large screens, positioned at the front of the church, showed pictures of fireworks displays. Then the music started. It was louder than the music when she came in. The lights were dimmed and the people in the sanctuary began jumping up and down, screaming and clapping their hands.

The loud music was beginning to give Misha a headache. She picked up her Bible and purse and move toward the back of the church. She found a spot in the back of the first level that seemed much calmer. There were not many people there. From this viewpoint she could see people dancing in the aisle, both white and black. But, this was not a dance she was used to seeing. There was an influx of dancers with flags running up and down the aisle. The voices of the singers sounded like birds fighting. She prayed to herself that she receive what God had sent her there for and that she's wasn't self-righteous or judgmental as she watched the whole scene.

The pastor of the church stood to give his remarks and it seemed as if the people were over-exaggerating their laughter. The whole scene looked so choreographed to Misha. She felt very uncomfortable as she listened to the pastor. She had heard that same sermon somewhere. As she continued to listen to him, she realized it was Shante Patrick's sermon. She listened as this white man stood on the stage, talking about growing up in a church that sounded like a black church. He was even trying to imitate black deacons and black preachers.

Misha looked around the sanctuary at the people of different races standing up, laughing at what the preacher was saying. How in the world could these black people listen to this message? It seemed so racist to her. Then when the preacher told a joke about a girl name Shequana winning a "frigerator" on *The Price Is Right* and pretended to act like her, Misha was fed up. She stood to leave but she heard, *stay,* in her spirit. She sat back down and anxiously waited for the service to end.

Misha continued watching the service as people began walking, some running, toward the altar and throwing money at the altar.

This is not me.

The people running and throwing money on the altar were distractions to Misha. She was puzzled. Why were they doing this? Didn't they put their offering in the baskets when the ushers passed them down the aisle? She was no longer able to focus on the message the pastor was preaching.

The pastor gestured to the musicians. They began playing a fast, upbeat praise song. The congregation began their frenzy all over. The pastor then said something that didn't sit right in her spirit.

"Look over at your neighbor and do a hallelujah check. If they don't say hallelujah and not up praising God, then you need to get up and move. Tell them, 'I don't want to sit beside you. I want to be by people who are on fire for God.'"

A woman grabbed Misha's arms and tried to pull them in the air. Misha shook her arms away from the lady. She tried to get them again. "Don't put your hands on me," Misha said. She looked intently at the woman.

The lady began mumbling or speaking in tongues, Misha did not know which. The lady tried to rebuke Misha.

This is not me.

Misha picked up her purse to leave. Before she could step out into the aisle she heard it again.

Stay.

She sat down and continued watching the service. "God, why am I here?" Her head was still pounding from the loud music.

Once again the pastor gestured to the musicians and the music slowed. Large groups of people stood and ran to the altar. Several very large men with earpieces in their ears jumped up and surrounded the pastor. They looked like bodyguards. They blocked people from reaching the pastor as he continued speaking. A group of people fell to the floor and began rolling around. Others fell on their knees and cried loudly. Some just stood in front of the men with their hands outstretched.

The pastor walked up to a man and laid his hands on his head and immediately the man fell backward. He was caught by a collection of the ear-plugged men and gently laid on the floor. This continued one by one until several people were lying motionless on the floor.

Misha stood when the people on the floor began convulsing as if they were having seizures. What in the world was going on?

This is not me.

Finally, the service ended and Misha rushed to her car. Something about that place was making her sick. It did not feel right in her spirit. There was a strange smell in the air, almost like the pungent smell of sulfur. Delighted when she reached the door, Misha kicked up her pace to her car.

She reached her car, got in, and closed the door. She took deep breaths as if it were the first burst of fresh air she had all day. Her ears were ringing from the extra loud speakers in the church. Her head felt like someone had a hammer banging on it from the inside out. She got into the long line of cars exiting the parking lot.

"God, why did you want me to come here?" Misha prayed out loud in her car as she waited her turn to exit the parking lot.

Loud doesn't mean anointed.

"What?" Misha responded to the voice in her spirit.

Loud doesn't mean anointed. If you can hear me when I whisper to you, don't you think I can hear your whisper too?

Misha felt like a freed slave when her car exited the parking lot of the church. She didn't want to ever go back to that church again.

That night, alone in her apartment, as she began to pray, Misha felt a coolness come over her. She began to worship. She lay stretched out on her floor as she felt the calmness engulf her body. Then, suddenly, a scripture came into her spirit: Revelation 3:1–3. She stood up and opened her Bible to the scripture and began to read.

To the angel of the church in Sardis write: These are the words of him who holds the seven spirits of God and the seven stars. I know your deed; you have a reputation of being alive, but you are dead. Wake up! Strengthen what remains and is about to die, for I have not found your deeds complete in the sight of my God. Remember therefore, what you have received and heard; obey it and repent. But if you do not wake up, I will come like a thief and you will not know at what time I will come to you.

Misha read the scripture again. "God give me understanding," she prayed.

I sent you to that church so you can see a church that has the reputation of being alive but is really dead. Go back to the Remnant Church. Tell the pastor to repent. Tell the people to repent for I will surely come to them if they fail to obey my commands.

She began to talk to the Lord as if He were there in person in her apartment. "God, is this you? How can I go to that pastor? I saw how many bodyguards they had around him today. Even the people in the church could not get to him. How can I and he doesn't even know me?"

Go to the Remnant Church and tell them thus saith the Lord.

Misha was nervous. How was she going to get those people to listen to her? In a church like that, how was she going to be able to talk with the pastor?

The next day, she attempted to call the Remnant church to schedule an appointment with the pastor but was told he did not counsel congregants or set appointments with people he did not know. Yet, she was still being tormented by the voice in her spirit telling her to return to the church.

She tried to continue her week as normal. When she accidentally ran into Roger, she acted as if she didn't see him, and looked for the nearest escape. She was glad for the weekend. She tried to relax. But she felt more pressure on her to go to the Remnant Church. On Saturday night, she could not sleep. She awakened suddenly from her sleep.

You are walking in disobedience. Do as I have appointed you.

She tried to get back to sleep. However, fear raced into her room and into her body. She began to tremble. "God, they don't know me."

I have made a way.

Misha didn't sleep anymore that night. Sunday morning she got dressed and drove to the Remnant Church. She sat in her car, watching people walk into the church. She prayed to herself and slowly walked into the church. The same thing was going on as last Sunday. She sat down in a seat near the front as she felt led by the Holy Spirit.

The service continued as usual. However, this time, the pastor said he felt like someone had a testimony.

Raise your hand.

Misha hesitated but raised her hand. People started clapping and jumping up and down as the pastor walked up to her. She nervously took the microphone. She began to speak.

"I attended your service last week." Her voice trembled. "That night as I began to pray, the Spirit of the Lord came upon me and this is what He said." She began to tell them everything the Lord had said.

When she finished, the sanctuary was quiet. She looked at the pastor, who looked like he was totally disgusted with her. His face was blanketed in white as if all the blood had rushed from his body.

"I rebuke you, you ungodly witch," he said to her.

The congregation followed his lead. At the pastor's urging, they began speaking in tongues and trying to cast out the devil in her. He asked the bodyguards to escort her out of the church. Two large men took her by her arms and walked her to a room at the side of the sanctuary. They shoved her onto a small chair and began yelling at her as if she were a criminal. Then, they snatched her purse from her. Misha jumped out of the chair with her arms stretched, trying to get her purse back. Another guy grabbed her around the waist and pushed her back into the chair.

"We've seen psychos like you here before. You can't curse us. We have divine order. Our pastor is a saint and chosen by God."

Misha could only watch as a man rummaged through her purse, pulling out her wallet. He took out her driver's license and placed it on a copier. He wrote something on the copy of her license. Then, he tossed it back into her purse and gave it back to her.

The man tapped the earpiece in his ear. He turned. Misha could hear him talking but could not understand what he was saying. The man grabbed her under her arm and pulled her up. Three other men surrounded her. They quickly began walking her toward the vestibule of the church. Misha could hear the chaotic sounds coming from the sanctuary: service as usual. The men escorted her to the front door.

"Where is your car?" the front man asked.

Misha pointed to the right and the five of them began walking until Misha spotted her car. Before the man released his grip, another man took out a pen and wrote her tag number on a pad he held in his hands.

Misha felt totally humiliated and violated as she left the parking lot.

I will bless you for your obedience.

This didn't comfort her. She wanted to get home and take a shower. She had to get the residue of the Remnant Church off her body. She felt so dirty, as if she had been raped. She did not understand what happened that day. She knew she heard the voice of the Lord speaking to her. Doubt welled in her. Did she do the right thing by speaking up during service? Should she have waited until after service to try to speak with the pastor? She was embarrassed. Was there anyone she knew there to witness her being thrown out of the church? What would people say? All kinds of doubt ran through her mind.

That night, as she worshipped, the Holy Spirit began to minister to her and she finally had some peace with what had happened that day. She tried to focus on a television show when she heard, *I am sending you back to Washington and you're going to be there awhile.*

"Washington? Why do I need to go back to Washington?" Misha was curious of the thought. After graduating from Howard, she never expected to return except for reunions. Why would God send her back to Washington? She had no desire to live there. But, if that's what God wanted she knew He probably had a plan.

"God give me peace with moving back to DC," she prayed. The self-doubt began to walk through her mind again. She struggled all night to get rid of the negative thoughts. She prayed to God for strength, which was something she found herself doing quite a bit lately.

Chapter 15

Misha was looking forward to spending Thanksgiving with her grandmother. Her family always gathered together this time of the year. She looked forward to playing with India and Asa, her brother Justin's children. More than anything, she looked forward to the time off she had during the holidays. She couldn't wait. She already had it planned out. She was going to spend Thanksgiving Day at her grandmother's and try not to get into an argument with her mother. On Saturday, she was going shopping with Judy and her kids. Then on Sunday, she was going to church. She didn't know where. All she knew was she was going to church Sunday and nothing was stopping her.

Misha sighed, listening to yet another class complain about the football team's losing season. She wished Mr. Davis had not announced the Eagles lost their last game by a whopping thirty-six points. This was their seventh losing season and they had the reputation around town of being losers. The lower classmen on the team were vowing next year would be different. One of her students told her his father was hiring a pro football player to train them in the spring. He wanted to graduate with a winning team. With all the talk about the football season and the upcoming holidays, it was hard for her to get her students focused.

After school, Misha walked into her apartment with her arms filled with groceries and her mail. She placed the bags down on the kitchen countertop and began to sort through her mail. She saw an envelope from Clark Atlanta. She threw the other envelopes on the table and tore open the letter. She screamed when she read the first line.

Congratulations, it is our honor to welcome you to our School of Education, Master of Education program.

Misha jumped around the room. She didn't expect to get accepted so quickly. She read the letter over and over. She screamed when she realized she was able to start school in January. She picked up her phone and called Judy to give her the good news. Then she called her grandmother with the news. She wanted to celebrate and she knew exactly how.

Misha jumped in her car and began to drive to Whole Foods. She wanted chocolate cake and ice cream. She was really a party animal now. Misha laughed. It was not too long ago she would have celebrated at a club. Instead she was celebrating alone with a rare treat. Besides, to her it was a holiday week, a major pig-out holiday, so it didn't matter if she started on Monday or Thursday. She would think about her weight after the holidays.

Misha stood at the bakery counter waiting for the clerk to finish packaging her cake when she saw a man she knew approach her.

"Hey, Misha. How you doing?" It was Carlos Witherspoon, someone she knew from Kingdom Faith.

"Hey, Carlos. How are you? Look at you. You lost weight." They embraced each other. Misha was happy to see him. He was one of the few people she trusted at Kingdom Faith. "How's Bishop?"

"I don't know. You know, Nicole and I decided to leave Kingdom Faith a couple of months after you did. We couldn't understand what Bishop did to you. After he did that, rumors started all over the church. A number of people left. With all the confusion, we decided we wanted to go somewhere where we could hear the Word of God. Hey, Nicole's pregnant," Carlos said with a smile.

"You're kidding. You guys are going to have a baby? That's terrific. Congratulations. When is she due?"

"In about three months. We're happy and nervous at the same time." Carlos stood with his hands on his hips.

"I'm sure you are. I know it can be exciting."

"You'll find out one day."

"If the Lord's willing."

"Well, Misha, where do you go to church now?"

"Nowhere really. I'm still looking."

"Why don't you come to our church? You'll love our pastor. You'll love the church. It's in the country, but it doesn't have all the drama."

"Are you the minister of music?"

"No, but I do play keyboard for one of the choirs. Why don't you come? I'm sure you'll enjoy it."

"I think I will. You'll have to give me directions."

Carlos reached on the counter and picked up a napkin. Misha handed him a pen. He began writing directions to his church on the napkin when Misha spotted Roger walking toward the deli counter. Carlos turned to see who she was looking at.

"You two still seeing each other?" he asked her.

"Goodness no. I don't even know what I saw in him in the first place."

He handed the pen back to Misha. "You know, we were all wondering the same thing. We were praying you find him out before you got hurt. Nicole grew up in that church. She has known him for years. She said he was a user and loser. I stopped fooling with him. He lied too much for me."

"Well, it's too late for that. I don't want to talk about him. Let's talk about your new baby. Is it a boy or girl?" Misha took her cake from the counter and continued her conversation with Carlos.

Carlos received a call from his wife and he left to get her the Italian food she was craving. Misha walked to the freezer aisle to get her ice cream.

"Hey, Mimi." She heard Roger's voice behind her.

"Don't talk to me. I don't know you." Misha walked away from him.

"Come on. Don't act like that. We're not at school."

Misha continued walking as if she didn't hear him talking. She paid for her food and drove home. She prayed she would not have any drama at work the next day. She prayed for peace on her job.

By the time she arrived home, she had lost her appetite for ice cream and cake. As she placed her items in the refrigerator and freezer, she asked herself why Roger still had control over her. It had been over a year since they broke up and it shouldn't have bothered her anymore. But it did. He had a way of turning a good day into a bad one and she was sick of it.

That night she began to pray that God release her from every man she ever connected with who was not her husband. She asked God to release every physical, emotional, sexual, and spiritual connection she had with any man outside her husband. She asked God to cleanse her from the sins of her past.

The next day she dreaded going to work. She fully expected Roger to say something about her. If she could get through the day, she would only have Wednesday to deal with him and then time off for the Thanksgiving holiday. She avoided Roger all day by staying in her classroom. Thrilled that the day went by uneventful, she took a long sigh of relief.

That night she read her letter from Clark Atlanta again. She was at peace as she ate her ice cream and cake from the night before for dinner. Sorting through the mail from the previous day, she noticed another letter from Clark Atlanta. Opening the letter, she screamed when she saw it was a scholarship offer.

She leaped as she praised God for blessing her. This time she would not have to take out another student loan. Her phone rang. She looked at the caller ID. She did not recognize the number. Her hand reached out to pick up the receiver.

No. Don't answer it.

She drew her hand back and waited for the machine to get it. Her hands flew to her mouth when she heard Gloria's voice.

"I want to let you know Roger is not interested in you. He doesn't want to be with a crazy whore. He is with me now. Stop calling him and don't call me either. If you don't leave us alone, I'm going to Mr. Davis and the superintendant. Get a life. Fake Christian." The connection was broken.

Misha chuckled. How could this woman be so vulnerable? Roger was lying to her. She had not called Roger since they broke up. He had called her numerous times and she did not return his calls. But, this phone call signaled one thing—Roger was up to his old tricks again. Probably mad because she did not speak to him at the store.

Her phone number was unlisted, which meant she probably got the number from Roger. It was time to change her phone number. Not only would it keep Roger from calling, it would keep the few Kingdom Faith people who called her from time to time from calling her with gossip. She took the tape out of her machine and labeled it in case she needed it in the future.

The next day she tried to avoid everybody by staying in her classroom all day. If she could make it to the end of the day she would have freedom, at least for a few days. She rushed to her classroom without speaking to anyone, including Judy. She did not go to the staff Thanksgiving breakfast that morning before school, trying to avoid Roger and Gloria. However, when she opened the door her classroom, Gloria was waiting inside, sitting on her desk.

"Gloria, what are you doing here?" Misha stood in the doorway.

"I'm trying to save your job."

"What are you talking about?"

"Did you get my message?"

"If you're talking about the message on my answering machine last night, I got it." Misha left the door open as she walked into the classroom and set her bag on the desk, refusing to be intimidated by the tall woman sitting on her desk. She watched as Gloria got up to close the door. "Don't close that. Leave it open."

"Whatever. If you want everybody to know your business, that's you," she said, waving her hand in the air.

"Gloria, what is it? I have a lot to do before class starts."

"Roger told me what happened at the grocery store."

"What happened?"

"Yeah, he told me he ran into you at the store and you attacked him. He said the store security had to escort you out of the store."

"I know you don't believe that." Misha started laughing and sat down at her desk. She opened the drawer and began to move her hands in it like she was searching for something. "Where does he get that stuff?"

"You're laughing. I don't think it's funny. If I go to Mr. Davis, you could lose your job. Roger told me you're on probation for the last incident."

Misha couldn't help herself. Her head flew back and she laughed even harder. However, she kept her hand in her drawer. "Please don't tell me anything else he said. I can't take this. He's using you. Don't be stupid. You're his little messenger girl. If you're not careful, he's going to do the same thing to you too."

"I know you're jealous because Roger is with me now. You know when he's with me, in my bed, he doesn't even think about you. He's mine. All mine."

"So you're telling me you and Roger are having a sexual relationship? Is that what you're saying?" Misha removed one hand and pointed at Gloria.

"You heard me. That's exactly what I said." Gloria walked closer to Misha's desk.

"He's a minister."

"He's a man. He loves me and I love him. We're going to get married. I go to his church with him."

"You ride in the same car with him?" Misha kept her hand in her drawer and continued her conversation with Gloria.

"I drive my own car because he has to be at the church early. You know he's a pastor. But, that's none of your business. The bottom line is if you don't stay away from him, I'm going to—"

"To what, Gloria? Are you threatening me?"

"All I'm going to say is you better stay away from him or you're going to be sorry."

Misha pulled her hands out of her desk. She held up a small handheld tape recorder that she kept in her drawer. "I'm sure Mr. Davis would love to hear this tape of you threatening me, Gloria."

Gloria stood there, shocked. "You heifer! You were recording me? Give me that tape." She lurched toward Misha, trying to grab the recorder.

Misha ran around her toward the door. "If you and Roger don't leave me alone, I'm taking this tape to Mr. Davis and Frank Wright at the City Development League and telling them how both you and Roger are threatening me. I'm also going to the police to get a restraining order on both of you."

"You think you're smart. You just leave Roger alone," she said as she walked out the room and down the hallway.

"Have a nice Thanksgiving," Misha shouted down the hall. She walked back into her class. She laughed as she looked at the tape recorder. It didn't have a tape in it. Gloria never noticed.

Misha walked to her desk and began unpacking her bag. "God, thank you for helping me defeat this enemy who tried to ruin my day."

He doesn't want her. He is using her too.

"God, please let both of them find a new job. They are thorns in my side and they need to leave this place," she prayed. "God, I don't know why Roger's doing this to me. But, if he has to stay, please make him stop. I need my job. I know he needs his. I don't know why he's lying so much. You know. I can't help him. I know you can. Let your peace be with me and let everything covered be uncovered."

The rest of Misha's day was uneventful. Her students were just as anxious as she was for the day to end. By the time the last bell rang, she had already packed her bag and was standing with the students at the door of her room. When the bell rang, she stood back to allow her students to push their way into the hallway. She followed the last student into the hallway.

"Hey, Misha, you in a hurry?" Judy called out from her classroom.

"Not really. What's up?"

"I hate to tell you this. Randy decided he wanted to spend the holiday at his parents' this year. So we're going to Memphis for the holiday. I wanted you to know I can't go shopping Saturday."

"That's okay. I need the rest anyway."

Misha and Judy walked down the hall toward the parking lot. They spotted Gloria turning on to the hall. She looked up and suddenly disappeared around the corner. They began to laugh and Misha told Judy about the phony tape. They laughed all the way to their cars.

On the way home, Misha stopped by the grocery store for what she knew would be the first of her many trips to the store for her mother during the next twenty-four hours. Although her mother was negative, she could cook and Misha was planning to enjoy every minute of it. She purchased the items and headed down Campbellton Road to her mother's home.

"Mom, I got the stuff on your list." Misha set the bags on the table as she entered the house from the garage. She could smell the pies and cakes her mother had already started baking. She peeped under the cake plate to see what type of cake her mother had made. She wanted to see the tale-tale signs of her father cutting the cake so she could have an excuse to cut herself a slice. Noticing the big hole in the cake, Misha reached for the knife sitting on the counter beside the cake plate.

"You just like your daddy. Leave my cake alone. That's for tomorrow," her mother said as she walked into the room.

"Daddy already cut it. Can I have one slice?"

"Your daddy did that before I saw him. You leave my cake alone. Did you get my cinnamon?"

"It wasn't on the list."

"I can't make my pie without cinnamon. You knew I needed cinnamon. Now, I'm going to have to go to the store."

"I'll go for you. Anything else?" Misha knew her mother had another list. She watched as her mother wrote out a completely different list and gave it to her. She picked up her purse and keys off the table as her niece and nephew ran in the door.

"Auntie Misa. Happy Thanksgiving," India screamed with her arms outstretched to Misha.

"India, Asa. My favorite niece and nephew." She put her purse down and ran to embrace both. She picked them up, one under each arm. She swung them around. They screamed with delight.

"Hey, Misha, Mama. Smells good in here. What you cooking?" Justin walked in looking like a younger version of their father. He went straight to the cake plate.

"You better leave that alone, before Mama go off on you," Misha warned.

He ignored her and went to the cabinet and took out a plate. He picked up the knife and sliced deep into the cake.

Misha lowered the two children, who ran toward her mother. "Mama, Justin cut your cake."

"Stop tattling," her mother said. "He's been working hard all day at that airport. Justin, cut these babies a piece. Not too big or they won't eat dinner."

"You let him have a piece of cake?" Misha was angry. Justin was her mother's favorite. There was never any doubt. Being the younger of the two, he was spoiled. Her mother always let him get away with murder. The sight of him enjoying the cake, licking the icing off his fingers, made her jealous.

She did not want to be that way. She loved her brother. There were times when pain of the past would spring forth. Justin never treated her poorly. He always found a way to show his love. There were times when they were young and her mother would not get her something that she wanted or needed. Justin always got it for her by somehow sweet talking their mother. She could never deny Justin anything. The older he got he became more like a big brother than her kid brother. But she wanted a piece of coconut cake and he was teasing her by pretending to give her a taste and then pushing the slice into his own mouth.

"Misha, you going to the store or what?" her mother asked.

"I'm going. Are you sure this is all you need?"

Her mother walked toward the stove. The children ran out of the room, looking for their grandfather. "Y'all come back here. Your Papa Joe is not here right now. Go in the den and watch TV." She looked over at Misha standing in the doorway watching Justin eat cake. "I thought you were going to the store?"

"Mama, get off her case. Come on, Misha, I'll ride with you. Mama, watch the kids."

"How am I supposed to watch two children and do all this cooking?"

"Bye, Mama. We'll be right back. Come on, Misha."

They walked outside and Misha noticed a new black SUV sitting in front of her mother's home. "Is that your car?"

"Yeah. Just got it last week. It's nice. Got it financed at the hospital credit union. I told Pam it was a good idea to join. Got a good rate, too. Wanna drive it?"

"Yeah." Misha took the keys and headed for the truck. She switched on the ignition. "It purrs." She pulled into traffic.

"Don't let Mama get to you." Justin said as they journeyed to the store.

"She let you eat a piece of cake right after she told me no. You know you're her favorite. She doesn't keep that a secret."

"You're the oldest, so she expects you to be more responsible. If I forget, remind me to get a six-pack of light beer for the holidays. I know Mama and Grandma are not going to have any."

"Now you know Grandma is not going to let you drink at the house while she's there."

"I can drink outside. Besides, I'm grown."

"Okay, Mr. Grown. We'll see how grown you are when Grandma takes her stick to you." They both laughed because they knew their grandma didn't play. She was firm about not having alcohol in her house or during family occasions. The people who drank beer usually did it away from her eyesight. "This truck handles nice. I've been thinking about buying a new car. Can't do it now. I got into Clark."

"You did? That's great. I didn't even know you applied." Justin reached up and gripped the handle over the door as Misha maneuvered a tight curve.

"I'm going to get my master's in education. I'll start in January."

"Are you going to be strong enough for that? I mean with the cancer and all."

"I'm fine. I told you they got it all."

"I know. But, I still worry about you. Pam and I prayed for you."

"You? Prayed?"

He started to laugh. "I know. I know. I haven't been the best example of Christianity but I do pray. I don't want anything to happen to my big sis. You're the only one I can talk to when I can't talk to Pam. I love her but sometimes marriage is hard. There are times when I think we were too young when we got married. Then there are days when I wonder why we waited so long."

"And today?"

"Today, I have the perfect family. We're happy. But I still worry about you. You need to find somebody to settle down with and have some children. My kids need some cousins to spend the night with."

"Or you need a babysitter. You know you can ask me to keep them anytime. I love it when they spend the night."

"We love it too." They continued talking and laughing as they pulled into the parking space in front of the grocery store. People were running into the store like they were giving away free food. "Misha, are you really all right? I mean, you're not holding anything back are you? Pam's a nurse and if you need our help, we want to help you as much as we can."

They sat in the truck talking. "I'm fine. Don't worry about me. I'm still going to the doctor on a regular basis. That's only for follow-up. So far, it's been good. If anything's wrong, I'll tell you. I won't tell Mama but I'll tell you."

"You need to sit down and talk to Mama."

"You mean sit down and argue with Mama. No, thanks. I want to have a good holiday." Misha shifted in her seat. "There is something I want to tell you."

"What is it?"

"I'm moving back to Washington."

"I thought you said you were going to Clark. When were you planning to move?"

Misha shook her head. "No, you don't understand. The Holy Spirit told me I was going back to Washington and I would be there awhile."

"Holy Spirit?" He sighed and shook his head. "I thought you were serious. You had me going for a minute there. Come on, let's get Mama's stuff before she calls." He reached for the door.

Misha reached out and took his arm, stopping him from leaving the truck. "No. Really. I'm moving to Washington. I have this gift. I know you don't believe. I know in my heart I'm moving back to Washington. I don't know when or how or even why but I wanted you to know in case it happens quickly so you won't be surprised."

"Well I know when you set your mind to something, you do it. Give me some time okay? Pam and I need to know how much babysitting time we have left." He gave a nervous laugh and hugged her. "Big sis, take care of yourself. I love you and don't want you to get hurt."

"I will. I promise you with God on my side, I'll be okay."

They opened the door and began the second of several trips to the grocery store for the day.

Chapter 16

It was Saturday after Thanksgiving and Misha was tired from her Friday all-day shopping experience with Pam, her sister-in-law. They purchased all the children's Christmas toys and a few gifts for other family members. Misha carefully placed the toys in her spare bedroom, pushing away some of the items she had stored there. Picking up the doll that crawled and cried, she pulled the string and placed it on the floor, watching it crawl toward a stack of boxes. Then, she heard in her spirit, *pack your suitcase and go where I tell you.*

This time she did not question that voice. She was ready to go wherever the Lord sent her. She was in love—in love with the Lord. He had protected her from the events of the past year. When she looked back, God always had her back. He always led her in the right direction. Now, she had no doubt God was continuing to lead her in the right direction.

Anyone else would have thought she was crazy getting into her car and driving, not knowing where she was going. Yet, she continued driving until she saw a sign that said Tuscaloosa County, Georgia. The next sign that caught her attention read Welcome to Cartersville, Georgia. "What in the world am I doing here?"

She continued to follow the voice that sounded as if someone were sitting on the seat beside her, giving her directions. She pulled into a hotel as instructed by that voice. She checked into the small hotel and was given a key to a room that looked clean but had a hint of stale cigarette smell in the air.

Having been on the road a long time, she walked to a small restaurant across the parking lot from the hotel.

"You know what you want?" a small Mexican woman asked, then took Misha's order and ran off to get her food. Misha sat at the table, wishing she had gotten a newspaper or magazine before she came into the restaurant. She busied herself reading the old, torn menu card that remained on the table. She looked around the restaurant and noticed she was the only African American person there. The waitress placed a glass of water and wrapped silverware on the table. Misha attempted to start a conversation. But, her English was not good and Misha's Spanish was even worse. So that idea went nowhere fast.

After her meal, Misha decided to do a little shopping while she was in town. She spotted a shop she wanted to look in. When she opened the door, immediately the lady behind the counter ran to meet her.

"Can I help you with something?" she asked Misha.

"No. I'm just looking right now. Thanks for asking." Misha walked around the store, looking at the different items as the lady followed her around the store. Misha picked up a blouse to get a better look and the lady took the blouse out of her hand.

"We have this blouse in another color. I don't think this suits you," she said. The clerk folded the blouse and placed it back on the table.

"Excuse me. I was looking at that."

"Oh, I'm sorry. Were you going to buy it?"

Misha's left brow arched as she noticed the smug look on the woman's face. "Look, lady, I'm a woman of God. I'm not here to steal anything from you. I have plenty of money. I don't need to steal," she said as calmly as possible, not allowing her anger to show.

"Were you going to buy something? Can I get it for you?" the lady replied, not being moved by Misha's speech.

Misha became so disgusted with the situation she shook her head and left the store, feeling insulted. This was the first time she had been found guilty of shopping while black. It was a weird and insulting experience. She quickly walked to her hotel room and stayed until the next day.

"God, why am I here?" Misha prayed aloud as she packed her bag, preparing to leave town Sunday morning. She really wanted to go to church that morning. Any church would do. She just wanted to hear the Word.

She checked out of the hotel and headed for the highway. As she drove through town, she noticed as small brick church with people going inside. MISSION BAPTIST CHURCH, the sign out front read. She found the scene interesting enough to make a three-point turn in the road and turn into the church parking lot.

Misha walked into the church and sat down at the end of one of the middle pews. The whispers of the congregation asking who invited her there resonated in her ears. Looking around the sanctuary, she noticed she was again the only African American person in attendance. She lifted her purse that sat on the pew next to her and stood to leave, when she was greeted by a middle-aged woman with big, blond hair.

"You're new here," she said matter-of-factly in her thick Southern accent. She reached her hand out to shake Misha's hand.

"I'm just passing through. I wanted to attend church before I got back on the highway."

"Isn't that nice. Well, we're glad you chose to fellowship with us this morning. Please come join me and my family. We're up on the second pew." She leaned closer to Misha's ear and continued. "I hope you're not one of those back-row Baptist who only likes to sit in the back of the church." She laughed at her own joke.

"No, I am definitely not a back-row Baptist. I would love to join you and your family."

The woman took Misha's elbow and led her to a pew in the front, where she was introduced to the woman's husband, son, and daughter.

Misha had never been in a church, Southern Baptist or otherwise, where no one said a thing while the service was going on. One could hear a caterpillar crawling across the floor. The pastor's preaching style was simple, yet powerful. She studied his movements, his commitment, and his passion as he ministered. At the conclusion of the service, she knew she had to meet him.

The pastor stood at the door, greeting the congregation leaving the church. He shook each one's hand and spoke to them as if he knew each one personally. When Misha approached him, he hugged her as if she was a regular parishioner. "Ma'am, I'm glad you came to worship with us today. Are you new in town?"

"I'm just passing through. I'm headed home to Atlanta. I wanted to go to church this morning and stopped when I saw your church. Thank you for that wonderful sermon."

"Well thank you, and if you are ever in town, come by and see us again." He patted her on the back.

"Thank you. I will."

Misha walked to her car. She could see a few people staring suspiciously at her. She started her car.

Go tell the pastor that it's time for him to start that church. No longer will he be restricted by man's laws. He will be free to be directed by the Holy Spirit alone.

*If he starts his church now, miracles, signs, and won-
ders shall follow him.*

She started to back her car out of the space. But, she
heard it again. She pulled back into the space and went
inside the church. She walked up to the pastor and told
him what she heard in her spirit. Stunned, he took her
hand and escorted her to a woman standing near the
pulpit.

"This is my wife. Honey, listen to what this lady
told me," he said, keeping a grip on Misha's hand. "Go
ahead, tell her," he said, standing between his wife and
Misha.

Misha's voice trembled as she told them what came
to her. "Well, the Spirit of the Lord told me to tell you
it's time to start that church."

Both of them grabbed one of her arms and escorted
her down a small hallway and into an even smaller office a short distance away. The pastor's wife closed the
door.

"I knew it was something about you when you walked
into the church." The pastor sat in a chair on the other
side of the desk.

"I did too. I was going to speak to you before you left
the church but you got away from me. You must be a
prophet," his wife said.

"I'm not a prophet. I only say what the Spirit tells
me."

"I know you don't know anything about me. By the
way, I'm Pastor Jack and this is my wife, Betty." The
pastor pointed at his wife.

"Nice to meet you."

"I know we're acting strange. But what you don't
know is the Lord had put in our hearts to start a
church. We had been praying about it for months. Last
week we started fasting and praying for clear direction
from God and you walked into our church."

Misha was stunned. She was beginning to understand the ministry God had placed her in. She had never seen anything like it before. No one ever talked about people like her. She stopped short of saying she was a prophet. But she was beginning to realize her job was to deliver messages from God. She decided that day to go where God led her and say what He told her, and she knew it would not always be in the pulpit.

Misha drove back to Atlanta feeling confident in her relationship with God. She felt stronger and empowered to do the will of God no matter what. When she arrived at her apartment, her spirits were high. She praised God for teaching her about the ministry He placed inside of her.

I am sending Matthew to you.

There was that name, her childhood dream that was coming back to her. This time was different. She heard his name again. She believed God that Matthew was soon to come and she would be alone no more. She danced all around her apartment until she began to worship. She fell on her knees and worshiped God for who He is and what He was doing in her life.

The next day she returned to school feeling refreshed and ready for her class. The calendar sat on her desk. The starred December 21st stood out. She could not wait. It was the last day of classes before the Christmas holiday began. She placed an X on Monday and began preparing herself for her class.

"Hey, girl. How was your weekend?" Judy asked, walking into her classroom, wearing a sweater with a snowman on the front.

"You're dressed like we are going to get a snow storm or something. Remember, they call it Hotlanta."

"My husband got me this sweater and I'm going to wear it no matter how tacky it is. So how was your holiday?"

"It was good. My mother and grandmother threw down in the kitchen."

"The food was that good, huh?"

"I'm not talking about the food. You should hear the two of them in the kitchen fussing when they're cooking. We all stay out of the kitchen. The food was good though. How was yours?"

"Well, it was kinda special."

"Oh yeah? How special?" Misha stopped separating the papers on her desk.

"Well . . . I . . . Well . . ." Judy began to pace the floor. "It's just that . . . I don't know how to say this."

"Judy, what is it?" Misha walked to her side.

"I'm pregnant again. I'm going to have a baby. I don't want you to feel bad because of . . . well . . . you know."

"You're pregnant? That's great! I'm happy for you," Misha squealed and hugged her. "When are you due?"

"In June. I didn't want you to feel . . . well . . . I wanted to tell you myself. We waited to tell our parents before we told anyone else. I hope I'm not making you uncomfortable."

"Don't be silly. I'm happy if you're happy. You guys are truly blessed. You guys are going to have four kids. Are you happy?"

"Yes. I never thought I would have a large family but it's probably one of the best things that has happened to me. It's what I needed. The kids are excited, too. They are already fighting about whether they want a little brother or sister."

"Judy, don't think about me. I'm fine. I'm so very happy for you. If you don't mind, I want to pray for you before class starts."

"I would like for you to pray for me. I'm not exactly in my twenties anymore."

"Twenties?"

"Cut it out, Misha. Okay, thirties and that's where I'm ending it." They began to laugh as they joined hands.

"Father, how excited I am for your goodness and how you send us unexpected blessings. We honor your love and grace over our lives. Right now, Father, I have one request—I place my friend, my sister Judy, and her baby in your hands. I pray she have a safe and wonderful pregnancy. I pray both she and her baby remain healthy and strong. Use them as an instrument for your glory. In Jesus' name I pray. Amen." Misha concluded her prayer with a hug for Judy.

"I better get to my class before the bell rings. Thanks for the prayer, Misha."

Misha returned to her desk after Judy left the classroom. She felt a tear roll down her face. *Why am I crying?* She could feel another one follow the first, then another. She raced to her door and closed it, wiping her face in the process. She walked to the back of her classroom to the corner and leaned her head against the wall so no one could see her. "God, I'm happy for Judy. Everybody's pregnant now—first Nicole and now Judy. I want a child, from my own body. Please heal my body so I can have my own child, and send Matthew to me. I'm tired of being by myself. I want to be happy like Judy and Nicole. I want a family like my brother. You promised me and I'm standing on your promises. Nevertheless, not my will, but yours, Father. In Jesus' name." She ended her prayer when she heard the bell ring. She wiped her face, took a deep breath, and walked to her desk as the first students began filing into her classroom.

The rest of the day, that voice, that negative voice, tormented her with the thoughts that she was never going to get pregnant. The voice teased her about Matthew only being a childhood fantasy and not real. It began to almost torture her as she tried to teach her class. She tried hard to focus on her lesson for each class, yet in her silent moments the voice taunted her.

During her planning period, she spent the time praying and ate lunch in her classroom. She began to think she was jealous. She prayed against the spirit of jealousy. She didn't want to be jealous of other people's blessings. She wanted her own. She had a promise from God and He was faithful. She decided to stand on what God had told her.

Later that night after grading some papers, she settled down to read her scripture and pray. The feeling of sadness overwhelmed her. Everything in her wanted to be happy about Judy's and Nicole's pregnancies. She thought about her brother's, Judy's, and Carlos's marriages and how happy everyone seemed to be. She understood marriage was not a fairy tale. There were ups and downs. But, with marriage, she would have someone to share those moments, whether good or bad, with her.

Why did God allow her brother to get married before her since she was the oldest? It seemed the true order of things would have allowed her to get married first.

She went into her storage room, picking up the container her grandmother had given her. She pulled out the quilt and looked at each piece. She decided, as a show of her faith, she was going to start her child's quilt. She sat down and tried to piece the different material together into something that may have resembled a design. Realizing she did not know what she was doing, she gathered everything together and put it back into the storage container.

The next day after school, she went to her grandmother's home. She parked in the driveway, opened the trunk of her car, and pulled out the storage container she'd placed there that morning, and walked into her grandmother's home.

"Hey, baby. I didn't expect you here today." Her grandmother was spraying furniture polish on the coffee table in front of the sofa.

"Well, Grandma, I decided to start on my quilt. But there's only one problem."

"What's that?" She set the dusty cloth on the table and greeted Misha with a kiss on her cheek.

"I don't know what I'm doing. Could you show me how to do this? I got some more material and I brought some old clothes of mine. Could you give me some more material? I don't think I have enough."

Her grandmother smiled. Misha set the container on the coffee table and lifted the lid. Her grandmother pulled out some of the old clothes Misha had placed there. Misha pulled out some of the cut pieces of cloth and sat on the sofa.

"Brang that stuff to the table." Her grandmother gestured toward the kitchen table. Misha picked up the container and followed her into the kitchen.

Misha placed the pieces of cloth on the table as her grandmother toyed with the pattern. Asking Misha her thoughts, she placed a bright yellow piece of material that was the shape of a star in the middle. Delighted, Misha squealed. Handing her the scissors, her grandmother began to instruct Misha how to cut the cloth so that the pattern grew from the center piece to a large star that reached to the sides of the quilt.

After a couple of hours of piecing together the pattern, Misha's stomach growled. "Grandma, I'm hungry. What did you cook?"

"Butter beans wit' ham hock. It's some cornbread in the oven."

"Why did I ask?"

"You hungry? Fix you up a plate whiles I work on this," her grandmother said, holding up two pieces of cloth she finished cutting.

Misha got up and went to the kitchen and fixed herself a plate of food. Walking back to the table she watched as her grandmother carefully cut each piece of cloth, stopping sometimes to rub her aching fingers. Her grandmother was patient, not rushing to cut the cloth. She took the time to match up every piece. Her grandmother hummed old hymns as she worked. The sound was so beautiful to her. Misha wished she had a camera so she would have a picture to attach to the quilt of them working on it together.

"Misha, you finish eating?" her grandmother asked after noticing the empty plate on the table.

"I'm full." Misha rubbed her belly.

"Go in the closet and get that old sewing machine of mines."

"I thought you made quilts with your hands."

"Not when I can use that machine."

Misha did as she was told and placed the old machine on a table in front of her grandmother. She opened a lid on the machine, reached in, and pulled out a spool of thread. Her eyes peeped over the edge of the machine as she got the thin thread in the small hole in the needle on the machine.

"Why you lookin' at me? Git over here and do this thing. I can't see this. You know my eyes not like they used to be."

Misha got up and threaded the needle on the machine and watched her grandmother slowly start the machine while explaining everything she did. Misha stood over her and watched every move. Her grandmother completed the first star out of several pieces of material and held it up for Misha's approval.

Misha could not hold her excitement. "It's wonderful."

Her grandmother stood and suggested that Misha sit down.

"Now, I's show you how to work this machine."

As instructed, Misha slowly turned the balance wheel. She reached for the pieces of cloth her grandmother handed her. She put two pieces together and placed them under the needle. She pressed the foot control, making the needle go up and down as the material moved across the plate. She continued sewing until each piece had formed a star similar to her grandmother's. Proudly lifting the piece from the machine, she smiled at her accomplishment.

Misha and her grandmother continued cutting material and pinning the pattern together the rest of the evening. Misha listened to her grandmother share stories of their family history and her upbringing in coastal Carolina. She especially loved hearing her grandmother sing the old songs. Some of them sounded like her grandmother were making them up as she sang.

At times, she would stop and share a funny story the song sparked about something that happened at church or a family reunion or other occasions. They continued working on the quilt until her grandmother became too tired and Misha went home satisfied and feeling everything was going to work out.

Chapter 17

The Christmas break had been just what Misha needed. Two weeks off had been like a gift from heaven. This past year had been a very trying year for her, to say the least. She was now glad that it was officially over. A new year was beginning. It was time to start fresh and new. She was sure this year was going to be better than the last. She was beginning her classes at Clark in a week and she was looking forward to earning her degree.

She returned to school feeling energized and enthusiastic about the new school year. She walked down the hall, feeling optimistic, with a smile so big on her face it was not hard for other people to notice it. She walked to the library and had a seat at one of the tables, waiting for the staff meeting to start. She reflected on the way God used her during the month of December.

Throughout December, everywhere she felt in her spirit she needed to go, she went. She saw how God would direct her and when she got there, the people were amazed how she spoke truth to them and declared her to be a prophet sent by God to give them hope. She had become more secure in her ministry.

She was also happy she was attending New Vision Worship Center, Carlos's church. The messages the pastor preached were so timely with the way her life was at the moment. She made up in her mind she was there to rest from all the things she had endured. She did not join any of the auxiliary ministries. She did tell Pastor Wells she was a minister. He did not treat her any differently than any other member. However, he never asked her to preach or even sit in the pulpit. Each Sunday, she walked into the church and sat near the back row. At the end of the service, she would get up and leave. Carlos and his wife had told some people she was a minister, but they did not acknowledge her ministry.

Misha thought on these things as she continued to wait for the other teachers and Mr. Davis to arrive for the meeting. Rummaging in her tote bag, she discovered the picture she'd taken with her grandmother during the holiday. They were holding up the quilt they were making. She planned to put the picture on her desk.

"Hey, Mimi, you got a minute?"

Misha looked away from the picture to see Roger standing in front of her. "Roger, you shouldn't be here."

"I don't mean to bother you. Did you hear about Bishop?" he asked.

"I'm not going to talk with you about Bishop."

"He had a heart attack."

"Oh no. When? How is he?" Misha's hands flew to her mouth. She was truly concerned about Bishop. She didn't want anything to happen to him no matter how he treated her. "No one called me."

"I tried. You changed your number."

"I did." She did not give Roger her new number on purpose. He could no longer call her or have someone else call her. That was one phone call she was glad she missed. "How is he doing?"

"He's back at home now. He's taking some time off." Roger stood in front of her, waiting for an invitation to sit with her.

"Well, Roger, I'm glad you told me. I'm gonna have to call to see how he's doing."

"Did you have a good Christmas?"

"Roger, thanks for telling me about Bishop." Misha reached her arm in her bag and pulled out a notepad and placed it on the table as Roger stood watching her. She secretly prayed for him to leave.

"Mimi, you look good."

"Roger, don't start. Please not here." She returned to her bag. He finally got the message and walked away and sat down at another table. *This cannot be some sort of omen as to how my year is going to go. No more foolishness. Not this year.* "Please, God, give me wisdom to handle any situation that may arise," she prayed. She opened her eyes and watched as the other staff members walked into the library.

Mr. Davis got up with his "new year" speech Misha believed he memorized and used every year. It was his version of a pep rally for the teachers. At the end of his speech, he introduced a man who looked familiar to her.

"As you all know, the state school board has hired consultants to look into the school system and see how we can improve the service we provide and also to see which areas could use a little help." There was a groan from the staff. People settled into their chairs with looks of disappointment on their faces.

Misha understood what was going on. Now they were going to have someone snooping in their classroom trying to find something wrong. This could only mean one thing: more work for the teachers. She listened as Mr. Davis continued.

"Each school has a consultant assigned to their school. I want y'all to meet Pete Heckler. He's the consultant the State has assigned to us." The man stood and faced the staff.

How do I know this man? Misha looked at this middle-aged balding white man, who looked very distinguished and well dressed as he stood and briefly addressed the crowd. *I know his voice. Where did we meet?*

Misha sat quietly, staring at the man until the meeting was over. Afterward, she walked to greet him as he spoke to Mr. Davis. "Hello, I'm Misha Holloway. I teach history here." She held out her hand to shake his. *His eyes, such a deep blue. How do I know him?* "Excuse me, I hope you don't think I'm being forward, but have we met somewhere? You look so familiar."

"I don't think we have. I think I would remember someone as beautiful as you."

Oh brother. "Maybe you look like someone I know. It's funny, seems like we've met before. It's your eyes. . . ."

"Miss Holloway, don't you have to get to your class before the bell?" Mr. Davis asked.

"I'm sorry, Mr. Davis. I thought we'd met before. Maybe not. Well, Mr. Heckler, I look forward to working with you." Misha gathered her things and walked to her classroom.

She placed the picture of her and her grandmother on her desk and watched as the room filled with students talking about all the great things they got for Christmas. Amber bounced into the classroom.

"Good morning. Well look at you, Miss Amber. Did you have a good holiday?"

"Sure did. We went to Montreal, Canada. It was beautiful with all the snow."

Misha listened attentively as Amber went on and on about her holiday. *God, why is this child living my dream life? Where did I go wrong?* The bell chimed. "Amber, please have a seat," Misha requested. She stood and began teaching her class.

***

Later that evening, after dinner, she decided to call Bishop Moore to see how he was doing. The phone rang several times and just as she started to hang up she heard First Lady Moore answer the phone. "First Lady. Hi, it's Misha."

"Well, Misha. I'm surprised to hear from you. How are you?"

"I'm doing well. I heard Bishop was sick. I called to see how he was doing."

"Sick? Well he did have a cold during Christmas. He's better now. He's not here. He's in Detroit preaching a revival. He'll be back at the end of the week. I'll tell him you called."

"He had a cold? I heard he had a heart attack." Misha twisted her mouth. She fell for another one of Roger's lies. She should have known better.

"Lord, Misha, where did you hear that?"

"Well, Roger said—"

"Roger? You two still seeing each other?"

"No. He works at my school. Today he told me Bishop had a heart attack and had just gotten out of the hospital. I'm pretty sure he told me that." She could hear First Lady Moore laughing over the phone. She felt like such an idiot to believe anything that came out of Roger's mouth. "Well, I don't want to take up any more of your time. I better go."

"Misha, I forgot Will got Roger that job."

Okay, this was news to her. Was Bishop trying to torment her on purpose? Were Bishop and Roger working together to make her lose her job, her sanity?

"You should stay away from Roger. He's up to no good. I've known him longer than you. Be careful around him. He'll do anything to get ahead."

"I'm learning that. I try to stay away from him but he keeps showing up. I've been praying he finds another job."

"I'll be sure to pray with you."

"Well, First Lady, I've got to go. It was nice talking with you."

"Misha . . ."

"Yes."

"Take care of yourself. Be careful. Okay?"

"I will. Keep me in your prayers. I'll talk with you later." Misha hung up the phone, feeling stupid again and wondering why Roger purposely came to her and told her a lie. It wasn't even necessary. She sat down on her sofa and turned on the television. She got lost in a documentary on the Spanish-American War.

Call Judy.

The feeling overwhelmed her. She picked up the phone and punched in the number. Her husband, Randy, answered the phone.

"Hey, Randy, this is Misha. How are you?"

"I'm doing all right, considering everything."

"What do you mean?"

"Well, Judy's having trouble with this pregnancy. I just got in from the hospital. They decided to admit her for a couple of days."

"That's why she wasn't at school."

"Yeah, she started cramping real bad last night and I took her to the hospital. I've been there all day."

"I'm sorry. I didn't know. How is she now?"

"She's doing much better. The baby's fine, too. They wanted to watch her. We still have a long way to go with this one. She's going to have to be careful and stop trying to do so much."

"She does do a lot. Well do you need any help? I can watch the kids for you."

"They're staying with Judy's parents right now. Thanks for asking. If you want, you can visit her at Northside Hospital. She's in room 312. She'll be glad to see you."

Misha quickly got dressed and rushed to the hospital. Judy appeared to be sleeping peacefully, not noticing the beeping sounds of the machines around her.

"Judy? Are you asleep?" she whispered.

Judy opened her eyes. "Hey, Misha. I'm not asleep. Come on in. Have a seat." She adjusted the head of the bed slightly upward and slowly rolled to her side to face Misha.

"Randy told me you were in the hospital. Why didn't you let anybody know?"

"Everything happened so fast. They thought I was having contractions but it may only be gas. The doctor wanted to keep me a couple of days to be sure. I never went through anything like this with the other kids." She shifted again. "I could use a couple of days off. But, not like this. How was the meeting? Did Mr. Davis give his 'this is going to be an exciting new year at Westdale' speech?" she said, imitating Mr. Davis.

Misha laughed. "You know he did. How are you feeling, really?"

"I'm okay. I'm a little tired. I've been up all night."

"Well I'm not going to keep you. I wanted to see how you were doing. Do you need anything?"

"No. Randy went to the house to get my bag. I don't think I need anything else right now. Thanks for asking." She lifted the head of the bed more and moved around to find a more comfortable spot. "Hey what else happened today at school?"

"Well, nothing really. The same old thing. Roger told me another super lie."

"And you're surprised?"

"No, this time he stooped low. He told me Bishop Moore had a heart attack. When I called tonight, First Lady told me it was a lie. He should be ashamed of himself. I also found out Bishop Moore got him that job at the school. I wonder if he did it on purpose to harass me. Oh yeah." Her hands flew in the air. "The State sent in an education consultant to review our work. He's going to be with us about three months, evaluating how we do things. You know what that means."

"Yeah, more work for us." Judy rolled her eyes.

"You should have seen that guy. He had the deepest blue eyes. They popped right out at you. I kept looking at him. I thought I knew him and asked him if we had met. He said no. But, something in me says I know him. I don't know where we met, but I'm sure I've seen him before. Anyway, I hope he didn't think I was coming on to him by using that old line about having met him before."

"Is he married?"

"Don't go there. I told you a long time ago that the Spirit of the Lord told me my husband's name is Matthew. I'm not seeing anyone until Matthew shows up. That guy's name is Pete something. I can't remember his last name. It looked like he had some money. He had on an expensive suit. Enough about work. You need to get some rest. I better go. I'll check on you tomorrow."

"Okay. Before you leave, can you pray for me?"

Misha could tell something was wrong with Judy. She looked worried. Not wanting to force her to talk, she placed her hand on Judy's stomach and prayed.

Arriving at school the next day, she did not say anything to Roger about Bishop Moore. It would not have served any purpose. Besides, she wanted very little to do with him. Apparently people were beginning to hear Judy was in the hospital and throughout the day she was asked how Judy was doing. Saying as little as possible, she did not want to stoke the rumor fire at the school.

Severe cramping filled Misha's abdomen as she walked to her car after school. She had plans to make a brief visit to see Judy, pick up a sub sandwich for dinner, and head home to take some pain meds and curl up on her sofa. She had almost reached her car in the parking lot when Roger stopped her.

"Mimi, I'm glad I caught you. I wanted to send Judy some flowers. What hospital is she in?"

"You can get the information from Mr. Davis."

"You don't have it?"

"I'm going to call her husband when I get home."

"Oh."

"I've got to go."

"Mimi."

"What?"

"I wanted to call you. I didn't have your number. You didn't give it to me yesterday."

"My number's private. Not many people have it."

"Well . . . can I . . . I mean . . ."

"If you're asking for my number, I don't think that's a good idea. If you need to get in touch with me, you can see me here at the school or you can call New Vision. That's where I go to church."

"Oh, it's like that."

"It has to be like that. If you'll excuse me, I have to go."

Misha brushed past him and walked to her car, wondering why he needed her number. She wasn't crazy enough to give him her new number. He needed to get a life and leave her alone. It felt good to reject him like he rejected her. Finally, he was out of her system.

Chapter 18

Misha was enjoying her classes at Clark Atlanta. She decided to start slow and only take two classes this semester since she had to find out how much studying she would have to do along with all the work she had to do at Westdale. Things were beginning to look up for her. The Westdale Eagles' blessing was its basketball team and, as usual, they were having a winning season. Her students were in a good mood because of it and were anticipating winning the state basketball title, an honor that had eluded them for the past three years. However, one thing continued to concern her: her period was still on after three weeks and it was still heavy.

She had waited as long as she could to see her doctor, but she knew something was wrong. Never had her period stayed on like this before. She waited nervously in Dr. Trinidad's office for the results of the ultrasound and lab tests. All kinds of thoughts ran through her mind. That voice that tormented her with the first surgery was back again, telling her the cancer had returned and she was about to die. This time, she found it difficult to convince herself of her healing. She looked at the crinkled paper in her hand. The sweat from her palms had begun to make the ink run the letters together. Yet, she could still see the "I believe I am healed" she had written on it. She recited it quietly as she sat on the hard exam table while the wrinkles in the paper cover pinched her buttocks.

"Well, Ms. Holloway, I have the results of your tests." Dr. Trinidad walked into the room. Misha looked at her body, which obviously looked pregnant. *Even Dr. Trinidad is pregnant. God, what about me?* She watched as the doctor placed the clipboard down and walked to the sink and washed her hands. "We didn't see anything abnormal on your ultrasound. However, you are very anemic. This may be due to the bleeding. You are bleeding pretty heavy. This has been going on how long?"

"Almost three weeks."

"Why didn't you come and see me sooner?"

"I've been very busy. I'm back in school working on my master's degree."

"Oh. Well, we have a couple of options." Dr. Trinidad sat down in the chair beside the sink. "One, we can go back in and do the same thing as the last time, with one exception."

"What's that?"

"Well this time we will do a D&C. This may stop the bleeding." Dr. Trinidad began to explain to her the procedure and that it was possible she may have to have a hysterectomy if something looked out of order, like if there were signs the cancer had returned.

"What's the second option?" Misha was concerned. She didn't want a D&C or anything like it.

"Well, we can go ahead and do a hysterectomy and this will probably solve all of the problems you are having now."

Shaking her head, Misha said, "No . . . no . . . I don't want a hysterectomy unless it is absolutely necessary. Are these my only two choices?"

"You can also sit at home and hope the bleeding stops and everything's okay. I'm not trying to scare you. I know you haven't had any children, so having a hysterectomy is a major decision. Why don't we go in and take another look to see if we missed something. I'll do the D&C and hopefully we won't have to do a hysterectomy."

Misha agreed to this option. She was tired of the cramping and bleeding. She was scheduled for surgery in two days. Although Dr. Trinidad wanted her to have the surgery the following day, she wanted to wait, to inform her family, job, church, and friends.

Misha left the doctor's office upset that, once again, she was going to have surgery and it was possible the cancer had returned. She cried as she listened to the voices in her head telling her she was going to die. This time, she did not have the energy to fight them. She let them beat up her mind. Crying, she found it difficult to drive with the tears that clouded her eyes.

She drove directly to her grandmother's house from the doctor's office. She walked throughout the house looking for her but the house was empty. She went in the kitchen and out the back door, where she saw her grandmother hanging clothes on the line. "Grandma, what are you doing out here? It's thirty degrees. Those clothes are not going to get dry."

"Sun's good for white clothes. They get dry." She picked up the empty laundry basket and walked into the house. She took off her old brown coat and hung it by the door. "Child, look at you. What's wrong?"

Misha laid her head on her grandmother's shoulder and began to cry, telling her the cancer may be back and she was scheduled for surgery in a couple of days. They walked into the living room and Misha sat on the sofa. Her grandmother walked over to the storage bin Misha had purchased to keep the quilting supplies in, and took out the partially made quilt and some material, and walked back to the sofa.

"Grandma, I really don't feel like working on that quilt now."

"Best thing for you." She picked up some material and began to thread the needle. "You know I had five babies before your mama come to this world." Misha followed her grandmother, picking up another end of the quilt and a needle, and began sewing. "All them babies died before they was ready to be born. Your granddaddy thought we would never have no children 'til your mama came. I was old then. We took in your Uncle Paul and raised him when his peoples put him out. He was four years old. Raised him like our own. We was happy. But Lord when your mama came, we had joy. Never felt like that before. Now I know how Sarah and Abraham must have felt." She screamed with laughter.

Misha listened quietly to her grandmother. She never knew her grandmother had five miscarriages. She knew her Uncle Paul was adopted. She didn't know why. "Your mama was old when she had you, almost forty. Then, she had Justin."

Misha watched her grandmother's hands carefully stitch each piece of cloth. She tried to do the same. Somehow her seams didn't seem the same. Silence filled the room. They continued to quietly sew each stitch that seemed so important to Misha. Her grandmother stopped sewing and leaned back on the sofa.

"Child, listen to me. When yo' time come for your baby, it gon' come. Not in your time. In God's time. Now tell me, do you believe God healed you of that cancer?"

"Yes, I do."

"Then the devil can't touch you. Believe in your healing. God's doing something in you. You need to find out what it is."

"Why do I have to go through so much pain? I've been in pain all my life. When will it stop?"

"You's special. Devil don't like it. Devil do things for evil but God make it good. You gon' be all right." She patted Misha on the leg. "You's gon' be all right."

It had been a long time since Misha had seen her grandmother so solemn. She didn't say much more after that.

Thinking about her grandmother as she drove to her class at Clark, she wished she had never told her. She didn't want to worry her. Her heart was heavy because of her grandmother, more than her surgery. It was unfair for her to put so many burdens on her grandmother. It was on her so much in her thoughts she couldn't concentrate on her class that night. However, she managed to stay until the end of the class. She informed her instructor about her surgery and that she would be out of class for a week, she hoped.

The next day, Misha sat in her classroom before school started, cleaning her desk in case she would be out of work for the next six weeks. She looked at her doctor's note she had for Mr. Davis. Mr. Davis paged her over the intercom to come to his office. When she arrived there, she saw Roger and Gloria sitting in the office with him. She groaned.

"Ms. Holloway, come on in." He got up and walked to the door and closed it after she entered the office. Wondering what they were up to now, she took the seat Mr. Davis pulled out for her. "Ms. Holloway, Mr. Williams and Ms. Bates have brought some very serious allegations against you."

"What kind of allegations?"

"Ms. Bates and Mr. Williams said you came to Mr. Williams's apartment last night and threatened to harm them. Is this correct?"

"What?" Misha shook her head in disbelief.

"They say you have been stalking them and they're afraid of you."

Misha looked at the two of them. Gloria leaned toward Roger. She shook her head again.

"Well, Miss Holloway, what do you have to say?"

"Mr. Davis, I don't have any idea what you are talking about."

"Where were you last night?"

Ask him what time.

Misha followed the instructions given to her in her spirit. "What time are you talking about?"

"They tell me it was about six," Mr. Davis responded. Misha laughed. "This is serious, Miss Holloway. They tell me they called the police on you."

Ask them to see the report.

Misha once again followed the instructions. "Do you have the police report?"

"We tried to protect you from going to jail. We didn't file a report with the police," Gloria chimed in. She sat up in her chair like she had proof of her allegations.

You called 911.

"So you called nine-one-one and didn't fill out a police report on me threatening you?"

"Roger—I mean, Mr. Williams—didn't want you to get into trouble. So we didn't file a report. You need to stay away from us. I know you have been in a mental institution and you may be off of your medication, we want you to get some help."

Misha screamed with laughter. She couldn't help it. With all that was happening in her life, a person with lesser faith would have ended up in a mental hospital. Not her. She believed God and it was this belief that she was holding on to. This was how she was able to make it each day.

"I'm sorry, Mr. Davis, but they can't be for real. Roger, how did you come up with this one? Better yet, tell me why? I haven't done anything to you or Gloria. But thanks, I needed the laugh, especially today."

"Miss Holloway, this is no laughing matter," Mr. Davis said.

"I know you don't believe them. Mental institution? That's funny."

"In our last meeting, Miss Holloway, I warned you not to bring this matter back into my school. These are very serious allegations and I must address them."

Misha began to get serious. She heard the seriousness in Mr. Davis's voice and on his face. "I understand this is serious. I am not the one who is bringing this into the school," she answered. Turning to her accusers she asked again, "What time was I allegedly at your apartment last night when the police were called, Mr. Williams?"

Gloria answered for him. "It was about six. You know what time it was."

"Mr. Williams, I believe I asked you what time it was," Misha asked him again.

"He said—"

"No, Ms. Bates, let him answer it." Mr. Davis leaned forward on his desk, looking sternly at Roger.

"She said about six," Roger answered, nodding toward Gloria. "I don't really remember."

What do you say?

Once again she followed the instructions. "What do you say?" Misha said, trying to force his participation in this accusation. "What time do you say I was at your apartment?"

"Six, I think."

"Mr. Davis, may I speak with you alone?" Misha requested.

"Yes. Ms. Bates, Mr. Williams, can you give us a minute? Please have a seat outside. I'll let you know when you can come back in." Gloria and Roger walked out of the office looking like two innocent children. "Now, Miss Holloway, what do you have to tell me?"

Misha handed him the doctor's note she held tightly in her hand. She watched as he read the note. "I'm having surgery in the morning. My doctor feels the cancer may have returned. She's going in to do more exploratory surgery. If I have to have a hysterectomy, I'll be out six weeks." He looked up at her. "I have been having problems for weeks. Yesterday, after school, I went to her office for the results of my tests. After I heard the news, I went to my grandmother's to tell her. By six, I was sitting in my class at Clark Atlanta."

"You're in school?"

"Yes. I didn't tell anyone I went back to school to work on my master's degree. I'm glad I didn't. Now you see they're harassing me. I have no earthly idea why. I haven't done anything to either one of them. I don't even speak to them. Mental hospital? I can't believe they said that."

"Can you prove you were in class last night?"

"Yes. I was there until eight. After class I spoke with my professor about my surgery and told him I would be out of class next week or possibly longer. I will give you his name and number. I never went to Roger's apartment. I was tired and emotionally drained. I went home and prayed and went to bed. If they had said nine or later, I would have been nervous because I was at home alone, but they said six. At six, I was in class."

"Why do you think they are saying these things about you?"

"I don't know. I'm too busy to stalk anyone right now. After tomorrow, physically, I won't be able to do anything for a little while."

"I'm sorry. I didn't know you were still having problems. I thought your last surgery was successful."

Misha could hear in his voice he was sincere with what he was saying. "I didn't tell anyone. Please don't say anything to anyone about this, especially Roger and Gloria. I only want people who are praying for me to know. They are definitely not praying for me. I think they want me to lose my job."

"Don't worry about them. I'll straighten this entire thing out." The bell chimed the start of the day. "Can you get me a copy of your schedule from Clark?"

"I'll give it to you before I leave today."

"How are you feeling? Do you need the day off?"

"I'm going to work today. I'll let my students know I'm going to be out a few days."

"Very well then, I'll stop by and see you before the end of the day. Don't worry about this. You just take care of yourself."

"Thank you, Mr. Davis." He walked around his desk and hugged her. He had never done this before, surprising Misha. He walked her to the door and opened it. Misha walked out of the office, trying to avoid eye contact with Roger and Gloria, who were sitting in the lobby as she went to her class.

Misha sat in her classroom, watching the video on the Civil Rights movement. As the film played she thought about the incident in Mr. Davis's office. The more she thought about it, the angrier she became. By the time her planning period came, she was furious. She sat down and penned a letter to Mr. Davis.

Dear Mr. Davis:
I am writing in reference to the incident this morning in your office when Mr. Roger Williams and Miss Gloria Bates accused me of stalking and harassing

them. As you know they accused me of threatening them at about six o'clock in the evening, on Thursday, February 6. They said they called the police but did not file a report. I would like to address their accusations.

As you are aware, last night I was in my Dynamics of Special Education class at Clark Atlanta University. This class begins at six and ends at eight. I stayed later after class to inform Professor Ernest Cooper of my surgery tomorrow morning. I have enclosed a copy of my schedule for your review. Therefore, there is no way I could have been at Mr. Williams's apartment last night, threatening him.

This is the latest in a number of false accusations Mr. Williams and Miss Bates have made against me. I am tired of this harassing behavior against me. There is no reason for them to be doing this. However, it is unfortunate that I must defend myself.

I am contacting my attorney to have him start proceedings against Mr. Williams and Miss Bates to sue them both for malicious slander. I am sure he will ask for the 911 tapes of them calling the police. Also, he will request the proof they have of me being in a mental institution. I am deeply troubled by these accusations and therefore want it to stop immediately.

As you are also aware, I have had a number of health problems in the past few months. These accusations only exacerbate my problems, thereby making my work environment hostile, and I will no longer tolerate it. When I return from sick leave, I expect to no longer have to face any more false accusations from these two people.

Over the past years, I have shown myself to be a vital part of Westdale High, with my students scoring in the top percentile in social studies and history. You even recognized my work by nominating me for rookie

teacher of the year. I certainly hope I can continue my
career here at Westdale, but not under these condi-
tions. Even though I would like an apology from them, I
don't expect to get one. Therefore, from this point on,
I will no longer address any other accusations of theirs.
I will let my attorney handle them all.

It is sad I have to go through this nonsense while I
am facing what could be the fight of my life. There is
still fight in me. Not only will I fight the cancer that is
threatening my body, I will fight to clear my name and
reputation.

Sincerely,
LaMisha Tramaine Holloway
Cc: Eric Davidson, Esquire
Frank Wright, City Development League

Misha used Judy's brother's name. He was the only
attorney she knew. She figured, if she had to, she would
be able to contact him quickly. She wasn't expecting to
have to contact him. Nor did she plan on sending the
letter to Frank Wright. She didn't want Roger to lose
his job. He needed his job and she was not going to be
responsible for anyone, even Roger, losing their job.
Wanting to live as the scripture tells us, to treat people
kindly even if they misuse you or abuse you, she vowed
not to treat him as he treated her. By doing so, the Bible
says you are heaping coals on their heads. She copied
the letter and her schedule and placed it in an envelope
to give to Mr. Davis at the end of the day.

Chapter 19

Misha returned to her classroom after two weeks off of work. She was ready to get back to teaching, although she was anxious of what might happen with Gloria and Roger. She was feeling better after her D&C. She was afraid this time when she signed away her uterus they would have to actually take it. Fortunately she did not have a hysterectomy. Yet, she continued to bleed and her doctor did not know why. Dr. Trinidad asked her to think about having a hysterectomy while she was out on maternity leave and they would discuss it when she came back. She was advised that if she had any problems to contact Dr. Trinidad's partner.

Like the last time, she went through the surgery alone. Judy was on bed rest and could not meet her at the hospital. Justin could not get off work. Pam said she was unable to leave her floor at the hospital to come down to the surgical area to check on her. She understood that but she did not know why no one at her church showed up. Pastor Wells told her he was going out of town and he was sending one of the associate ministers to pray with her before surgery, but no one showed up. Her mother said she was tired and her father was out of town driving his truck and could not make it back in time. She still did not know how she got home. Her car was in the parking space in front of her apartment when she woke up. She was extremely disappointed since everyone knew how she felt about being alone during the first surgery. She took it in stride and convinced herself that there were some things she had to go through alone. It hurt just the same.

But, she returned to work, still bleeding, although not as heavy, ready to drown herself in her work and her studies. She took an extra week off to catch up on her studies and rest. She didn't have the energy to return to work and she didn't want to face Roger and Gloria. She prayed they didn't call her bluff.

"Miss Holloway." Mr. Davis walked into her classroom. "How are you? I thought you would stop by the office when you came in."

"I decided to come to the classroom. I'm still moving kind of slow."

"I wanted to see how you were doing. How did everything turn out with the surgery?"

"Everything's fine. I didn't have a hysterectomy. They didn't find any cancer. I'm still having the problems. They asked me to think about more surgery. I don't know. I've already had two. Oh, thanks for the flowers and card."

"No problem. Do you need anything?"

"No. I think I'll be fine."

"Well, I wanted you to know I took care of that problem. They won't bother you again."

"You took care of it?" Misha was worried Roger and Gloria had gotten fired.

"Yeah, I let Mr. Williams know that if it continued, I would talk with Mr. Wright at the league about his behavior and have him removed from our school. Ms. Bates, well, with her, I had to follow disciplinary rules outlined by the district. I can't discuss that with you."

"What about the evidence I asked for, like the nine-one-one tape?"

"They told me they didn't actually call the police. They said they were thinking about it. You know, when all this was going on, I remembered Roger came with you to the Christmas social the first year you were here. He didn't think I remembered. I almost forgot until he mentioned it. Looking back, he had been telling a lot of lies. It's a shame. He's a good worker. The kids love him and he gets along well with the staff. His program is very successful here. I would hate to lose him."

"I didn't want them to get fired. I know, just like me, they need their jobs. I only wanted them to stop bothering me. If it starts again, Mr. Davis, I'm going to have to pursue legal action. I can't take much stress right now. I'll have to let my attorney handle it."

"I understand. Well, hopefully you won't have to do that. I'll let you get back to your work. Good having you back."

"Thank you. It's good to be back."

Misha lifted her hands in praise to God after Mr. Davis left her classroom. She finally had some peace on her job. She sang as she prepared for her day.

There was a light tap on her door. "Excuse me."

Misha looked up to see the school consultant standing in the doorway. His shockingly blue eyes peered down at her. *How do I know him?* She motioned for him to come in. "Hi. I'm sorry, I forgot your name."

"Pete, Pete Heckler. I'm the consultant for the district." He walked into the classroom and closed the door. "I came by to see you a couple of times and they told me you were out sick. Are you feeling better?"

Misha looked at him wearing a soft navy blue suit with a red tie. This was a man who knew how to dress. His suits and shoes looked expensive but he needed to get rid of that government-issued red tie. "Yes. I'm fine. Can I help you with something? Do you need my records or lesson plans?"

"I haven't gotten to you yet. I'm still collecting data from the math and English departments."

"Oh, well, how can I help you?"

He walked closer to her and casually crossed his arms in front of him. "Well, that day we met, there was something about you. I was wondering if you would like to go to a movie or something."

Misha's eyes grew large. She couldn't believe this man was asking her out. He was old. He looked like he was over forty. "Mr. Heckler—"

"Call me Pete. We can go get drinks or something after work. We can get to know each other."

"I'm sorry, Mr. Heckler, I don't drink. I'm a Christian, a minister at that." She smiled and placed a stack of papers on her desk.

"You're a minister?" He released his arms and pocketed his hands. "I would have never guessed."

"I don't know if that's a compliment or what."

"Trust me, it's a compliment. You're very beautiful. Well, we can go to dinner. How 'bout it?"

Misha smiled and stood up from her seat and began erasing the blackboard. "I'm sorry, Mr. Heckler, I don't date coworkers. Your offer is quite tempting. I've got this policy and I'm going to stick with it."

"Is it because of what happened between you and Roger?"

She stopped wiping the board and faced him. "Roger? What does he have to do with anything?"

"Well, I was told you two were an item at one time. I asked him if he would mind if I asked you out. He said no and told me to go for it. So here I am being shot down." He placed his hands on his chest and bent over as if he had been hit in the heart.

Misha laughed at his silly gesture. "That was a long time ago, before we worked together. Besides, if I

wanted to go out with you, you don't need Roger's per-
mission."

"So are you saying you'll go out with me?"

"No, that's not what I'm saying. Thank you for the
compliment and the offer but the answer is still no."

He let out a long sigh. "Well, if you change your
mind, you know where to find me."

"Have a nice day, Mr. Heckler." She watched as
he left her room. Suddenly a nervous energy flowed
through her body.

Stay away from him. He's dangerous.

Her large tote bag fell over and the stuff inside fell
out. She saw a letter slide across the floor. She picked it
up and read it. "Oh my God, I forgot."

She had forgotten she had to preach Sunday at her
grandmother's church. She was going to have to find
the time to study for her sermon, study her school
work, and grade the papers she was already behind in
doing.

The day and the week went by quickly. There was no
trouble from Roger or Gloria. When they saw her in the
hallway, they turned and went the other way. Roger
stopped speaking to her unless he was with other people. She was delighted. It took some of the pressure off
of her. However, she could tell all the other staff members knew what happened among the three of them.
She did not care as long as they left her alone. With
Judy out the rest of the school year, she was lonely at
work.

Then there was Mr. Heckler, who was persistent in
asking her out. Each day, he came to her room to see
her. He started bringing her things like pastries for
breakfast, and had a specially prepared lunch catered
for her and delivered to the school with a note stating
she could have lunch on him and someday with him.

She enjoyed the attention. It took her mind off her troubles. But, she was still bleeding.

Tired of bleeding, she decided to go on a fast and pray during the weekend about her health. On Saturday, after she studied for her sermon, she began to pray and ask God to show her what was happening with her. She didn't want another operation and she definitely did not want a hysterectomy. Her fast was to last from noon until sundown for direction and clear understanding of what was happening with her.

When she began to pray, the severe cramping returned. She decided not to take anything for pain during her fast and asked God to help her because she felt the devil was attacking her babies. She fell to the floor and stretched out. She began to weep and ask God why she had to have so much happen to her.

As the sun was setting, she stood up and washed her face. She sat down in her Queen Anne chair and began to question God about all of her troubles. She no longer felt cramping. She sat alone in her quiet apartment, meditating on her healing scriptures, when the Holy Spirit began to speak to her.

You asked me to cleanse you. Don't you know you are cleansed by the blood?

Misha sat up in the chair. "What?" she questioned.

Don't you know you are cleansed by the blood?

She fell on her knees and began to repent for not trusting God and listening to the negative voices in her head. She knew the blood of the lamb cleanses us. She began to thank God for cleansing her and making her whole. No longer did she have to worry about her past, the bad relationships she had, or the health problems that occurred. God had cleansed her. The bleeding was symbolic of that cleansing.

The next morning Misha awoke refreshed. It was the first night in a long time she slept so peacefully. She walked into the bathroom to shower before preparing for church. She noticed she had not bled all night. The bleeding had stopped. She checked on herself before leaving for church, no blood.

She went to church and preached like she had never preached before. Her grandmother was so proud of her. She sat back in the amen corner like the queen mother she was. Misha was filled with the Holy Ghost. She began to prophecy like never before.

Tell Pastor Smith to stand and do as I instruct you.

She called out Pastor Smith and began to do everything she heard in her spirit to do. She spoke to him with authority and ministered to him about church growth.

"Hold out your hands," she asked and he complied. She placed her hands on top of his. "God is giving you new hands to heal." She removed her hands and used them to wipe the sweat from her forehead. Then she wiped Pastor Smith's forehead. His body dropped to the floor.

After service, people rushed to talk with Misha. After the small crowd left a man walked up to her. Misha looked at him dressed in a mustard-colored suit talking to her with much seriousness.

"Minister Holloway, I don't really know any other way but to just say this." The man swallowed. "When you were preaching, the Lord spoke to me and told me you were my wife. I think we should get together and talk about it."

"The Lord told you that?" Misha smiled.

"Yes, He did."

"What's your name?"

"Alonzo Stephon Black. Can I call you?"

"Brother Black. It is a pleasure meeting you. However, if the Lord said you were my husband, He would have to tell me too."

"The Bible says the man finds a wife."

"Well, brother, it also says that the woman chooses her husband. You pray about that and ask God for direction. He will let you know what to do."

Misha walked away from him and took her grandmother by the arm and began walking toward the door. An usher ran toward them with an envelope. She handed Misha the envelope. Misha knew it was money for preaching.

Give it back. Sow it into the building fund.

She was obedient and gave the envelope back and told the usher to put it in the building fund.

She and her grandmother left the church and went to a buffet restaurant for dinner. While they sat at the table eating and enjoying each other's company a man walked up to them.

"Excuse me, aren't you Minister Holloway?"

"Yes, that's me." Misha set her fork on her plate and quickly swallowed the food in her mouth.

"Hi, I'm Lamont Stokes. I was at church this morning visiting my aunt and I heard you preach. Girl, you turned it out." The man jumped up in the air. Misha tried hard not to laugh at his comical reaction. "I'm sorry, Minister Holloway. I didn't mean to call you girl."

"That's okay. I'm glad you enjoyed the service."

"I did. Girl, you know, I'm going to marry you one day. Yes, I am. We are going to get married. I saw it when you were preaching. I told my aunt that was my wife up there. She said you were good people. She said you was smart and you was a teacher."

"I am a teacher. What did you say your name was again?"

"Lamont Stokes."

"Well, Mr. Stokes, I'm glad you enjoyed the message. I don't think I'm your type but I appreciate the compliment."

"Can I get your number? Maybe we can go out sometimes or we can go to church or something."

"Thank you for the offer. I'm sort of seeing someone right now. But you keep praying about that okay? It was good talking to you. I've got to get my grandmother home. She's tired."

"Yeah, wo'e out," her grandmother said.

"Well, I don't want to take up your time. I'll talk to you later."

When the man left the table, Misha released her laugh. Her grandmother joined her. "I must have preached this morning. I got two husbands out of that one. People don't think men approach women ministers just like women approach men. I'm your husband . . . I'm your wife. Don't they know it's not me they are attracted to but the anointing?" She shook her head and took another bite of her banana pudding.

Her grandmother sat patiently, waiting for Misha to finish her food. "Are you finished?" Misha asked her.

"I'm done. When we get to the car, you can tell me about the guy you seeing." She screamed with laughter.

Both of them continued to laugh about Misha's husbands all the way home. Misha shared with her grandmother the miracle of her fast and prayer the day before. She told her grandmother the bleeding had stopped.

"God getting you ready for Matthew," her grandmother said.

"I hope he shows up soon. I'm ready. I am so ready."

Chapter 20

March came in like a roaring lion. A freak Southern snow and ice storm roared through Atlanta, giving Misha some much desired time off of work. The entire city was shut down for two days until the one inch of snow and ice melted on the roads.

Misha walked into her classroom, prepared to give her students their midterm exams she made multiple choice not for them, but for her. It was easier and faster to grade than essay questions. She was trying to make everything easier now. She had to study for her own midterm exams in her classes at Clark.

There was a small gift box on her desk wrapped with a large blue bow. She knew who it was from. It was not her birthday and only one person gave her gifts at work. She opened the box. Inside were two tickets to a gospel concert at the Civic Center. Misha was tempted. She loved Marvin Sapp and LaShun Pace. She could not accept those tickets. Misha turned to leave her class when she noticed Mr. Heckler leaning against the door. He startled her. "Wow, you're like a cat, sneaking up on me. Don't do that again."

He smiled as he walked into the room. "Well, what time can I pick you up?"

"Thanks for the offer. Looks like a good concert but I can't go." She handed him the box with the tickets inside.

"It's a gospel concert. Roger said you would like it."

"Please don't tell me anything Roger said. Besides, you know my policy: no dating coworkers. I've given you back everything you've given me, even the food. Please don't give me anything else. I'm not going out with you now or ever."

Mr. Heckler threw his arms out. "You don't have to sound like that. I thought it would be nice to hang out with you. I don't even know who these people are. I thought you would like it. I was thinking about you."

"Mr. Heckler, school is about to start. I'm going to ask you nicely not to send me any more gifts. It's inappropriate. Besides, I'll be married soon and I don't think my husband would like me accepting gifts from men."

"You're getting married?"

"Yes. His name is Matthew. He's a terrific guy. You'll have to meet him one day." Misha said with a deceptive crooked smile.

"Oh. No one said anything."

"That's because I don't tell everybody my business." Misha walked around her desk and sat down. "Now, Mr. Heckler, if you will excuse me, I have work to do." He left the classroom.

Heckler gave her the creeps. She hoped he got the message that time. She felt uneasiness in her spirit. She felt weak. She leaned against her desk trying to gain her composure. She knew that feeling. It was the same feeling she got each time someone in her family was about to die. She felt it when her grandfather and her great aunt passed away. She began to pray.

Later that day as she was sitting at her table in her apartment her phone rang. It was her mother. She let out a long sigh as she reluctantly picked up the phone.

"Hi, Mom."

"Has anybody called you?"

Misha knew that tone. She was going to say something bad. She stopped grading her papers and sat back. "Called me about what?"

"Aunt Lorna died this morning. They want you to read a scripture at the funeral."

A sense of relief came over Misha. Not that she was happy her aunt died, it was the fact that it wasn't someone close to her like her brother or grandmother. She didn't know if she could take news like that. Her Aunt Lorna was over ninety. She was her grandfather's sister. She had been in a nursing home since she had a stroke last year.

"When is the funeral?"

"Thursday. They want you to read the twenty-third psalm."

"I'll have to get off of work. I'll let you know tomorrow. Has anyone called Grandma?"

"Yes. She called me after they called her."

"Well, I'll have to call her and see how she's doing."

Misha pressed the end button and then punched in her grandmother's number. Aunt Lorna and her grandmother were close. They talked every day until the stroke left her aunt unable to speak.

"Hey, Grandma. Mama just told me Aunt Lorna died. I called to see how you're doing."

"I'm fine. Getting ready to go to bed."

"Well, I'm not going to hold you. You need anything? I'll be by your house tomorrow."

"Call first. Paul taking me over to the house. Don't know when we get back."

"Oh. Well, I'll call you first. I love you."

"I love you too. Good night."

Misha hung up the phone and released a long sigh. She wished she could be as strong as her grandmother. Memories of going to her Aunt Lorna's house with her grandmother when she was a child flooded her mind. Aunt Lorna always had pound cake waiting for company. Misha remembered her loud laugh and the conversations the grown-ups would have, and how scared she was to ask any questions. They talked for hours about the old days. There was always loud laughter whenever those two got together.

Leaning back on the sofa, thinking about the many times her Uncle Woodrow, Aunt Lorna's husband, would take her outside to ride the old bike with the shaky wheels they had in the broken-down garage in the back of the house, Misha smiled. Once when she fell off the bike, she watched as the two ladies jumped on Uncle Woodrow for letting her ride that old bike. They nursed her wounds and, as always, Aunt Lorna thought her pound cake would cure all diseases. Her smile turned to sorrow when she remembered how her Uncle Woodrow suffered from cancer and died ten years ago. Now her Aunt Lorna was gone. Things were beginning to feel different. There were not many elders left in her family.

She tried to refocus on the papers she was grading. However, she felt a nervous tension come over her. Tired, she rose and entered her bathroom. A nice, hot bubble bath was exactly what she needed.

She continued to feel uneasy as she slipped into the warm water breaking through the large mound of bubbles that were coming from her portable spa she purchased at the department store.

She laid her head back and tried to relax. She closed her eyes and listened to the quiet hum of the portable spa.

When you go to work, take all your personal items home. It's time for you to leave that job. It will happen suddenly.

Misha quickly opened her eyes and sat up in the tub. "I must be imagining things." She closed her eyes and relaxed back into the water.

It's time for you to leave that job.

She sat up again. She could no longer relax. "God, how am I going to pay my bills?" She waited for an answer. Nothing. She only heard the sound of the spa.

After her bath, she attempted to relax by reading a book. Nothing could stop the voice telling her it was time to leave her job. She returned the book to the shelf and eyed the book Judy had given her.

Something about the author's name caught her attention. She pulled it from the shelf. She stared at the author's name, M. Bernard Taylor. She tried reading the book on vacation. She couldn't get past the first chapter. She shook her head and returned the book to the shelf. She pulled out a Maya Angelou autobiography and walked to her bedroom. She stretched out on her bed and began to read. She laughed herself to sleep reading about Ms. Angelou's adventures with a traveling theatre company.

The next morning she awoke to the loud sound of her alarm clock going off. She rolled over, dreading going to work. She began to pray for strength as she tried to force herself to get up.

When she arrived in her classroom, Mr. Davis greeted her. A sinking feeling came in her stomach when she saw him sitting in her class. "Mr. Davis. I didn't expect to see you. How are you this morning?"

"I'm well, Ms. Holloway. Can I speak with you for a minute?"

"Sounds serious. What's up?" She closed the door and sat down sideways in a chair beside him.

"How have you been?"

"I'm okay. My Aunt Lorna died yesterday. By the way, may I have Thursday off? Her funeral is Thursday and they want me to read a scripture during the service."

"Yes. That's okay. Be sure to turn in your leave slip so I can sign it."

"Okay."

"Tell me. How are you and Roger getting along?"

"Me and Roger? There is no me and Roger. What's going on now?"

"Somebody said you told them you and Roger were getting married."

Misha shook her head. She knew where that came from. She only told one person she was getting married: Mr. Heckler. *Another liar. Creeps hang out with creeps.* Roger and Heckler were scheming to have her fired. "I never told anyone I was going to marry Roger. I did tell someone I was getting married to Matthew."

"Matthew?"

"Yes, Matthew. I've known him for some time. We're getting married. I only told one person and it was not Roger."

"This Matthew, is he a real person? What's his last name?"

"Is he a real person?" Misha could not withhold her laughter. "Are you suggesting I'm making this up?" She continued to laugh until she noticed him staring at her. "Mr. Davis, you can't be for real. Of course he's a real person. I've known him all my life. He's a special guy. Wait, you'll see. He's a very busy man. I'll introduce you one day." She stood up and tried to hold back her laugh. She placed her bags on her desk and turned and watched Mr. Davis try to squeeze his large belly out of the small student seat.

"I didn't mean to insult you. I'm on rumor control. I look forward to meeting . . . What's his name again?"

"Matthew. His name is Matthew."

"Matthew what?"

"Now, Mr. Davis, I don't want to add to the rumors. Someone may know him and try to interfere with our relationship. You'll meet him one day. I promise."

"Well, okay. In the meantime, keep up the good work. Don't forget to put your leave slip in my box."

"I won't. You have a good day." Mr. Davis left the classroom. "Okay, Matthew, it's time for you to come. I've got to introduce you to Mr. Davis." She said out loud as she laughed about introducing a man she never met to Mr. Davis. She continued preparing for her class.

Call him.

"What, Lord?"

Call him.

"Who?"

Matthew.

"Call Matthew?" Misha twisted her lips. How in the world was she going to call him when she did not know his phone number or his last name? She shook off the thoughts and began her day.

The voice telling her to call him stayed with her throughout the day. During her planning period, she prayed to God to give her his full name and phone number and she would call him. She promised God she would call him if she had the information.

After work, she drove to her grandmother's home. She did not call first, so she was glad when her grandmother greeted her at the door. She looked like she had on five layers of clothes and a coat.

"Hi, Grandma. Are you getting ready to go with Uncle Paul?" Misha asked as she entered the house.

"No. Just got back. Ain't had a chance to take off my coat yet. Sit down whiles I hang up my coat." She left the room. Misha spotted the kitchen table full of food.

"Grandma, did you fix all this food by yourself? Do you need me to take it over to the house?"

"That is food from the house," her grandmother said as she walked into the room wearing a thick sweater, a house dress, and bedroom slippers. "You should have seen all that food over there. Paul gone to the store to get some foil. I can't eat all this. He gon' take some home. You want some? Help yourself."

Misha sat down at the table and began looking at the big plates of chicken, ham, potato salad, green beans, corn, and other assorted vegetables and desserts. She took one of the plates that was filled with fried chicken, macaroni and cheese, green beans, potato salad, and corn and began eating. Her grandmother sat back, watching her enjoy her meal. She looked up briefly from her plate to ask her grandmother how she was doing.

"I'm fine. Lo was sick. God done called her home. She at peace now. I'm at peace with God." Misha looked up. Her grandmother's eyes filled with tears. Misha stood and hugged her. She pushed Misha away and quickly wiped her face. "Lo was funny. She could tell a joke like nobody business. Kept us laughing all the time."

Misha stayed with her grandmother after her Uncle Paul left. She wrapped the remaining food in foil and placed it in the refrigerator. Her grandmother sat in a chair in front of the television watching a Christian television show. Misha took a comb and carefully parted her grandmother's hair, scratching the scalp like she used to do when she was younger.

Her grandmother began to speak. "It's time you learnt something," she said to Misha. She stood and walked into the kitchen. She returned with a small piece of paper slightly hidden by her hands. "Now this is Lo's secret pound cake recipe. Don't let nobody see it. Promise."

Misha was excited. She was being trusted with one of her family's most highly prized secrets. Her heart beat wildly in anticipation of being let into the inner circle of great cooks. Even her mother did not have the recipe. She held up her right hand and said, "I promise I will not show the secret to anyone."

Her grandmother reached out, handing her the paper with a wry smile. Misha took the paper and looked at it. *Is she for real?* "Grandma, is this what I think it is?"

Her grandmother laughed loudly and sat down in the chair. "If you think that is a recipe off the back of a flour sack, it is. Lo got that a long time ago. It was so tasty, it became her specialty—what she known fo'. She only changed one thing. Look, she wrote it on there." She pointed to the paper.

Misha eyed the penciled-in instructions to add one teaspoon of butternut flavoring to the recipe.

"Thank you, Grandma. I will cherish it forever."

"Don't cherish it. Make it. Lo would want you to continue the tradition."

Misha picked up the comb and continued scratching her grandmother's hair as she listened to stories about Lo, Woodrow, and other long-gone relatives.

"Paul, he Woodrow son."

"What?" Misha was floored. She wasn't expecting that. She dropped the comb.

"He had Paul before he met Lo. His mama thought she was gone marry him. When he met Lo, he said she was his wife. They got married three months later. Paul's mama warned Woodrow to leave Lo. When he wouldn't she left Paul with them. Lo couldn't take in Woodrow's child. So your granddaddy and me took him in. Years passed and Lo accepted him as part of the family. She loved him."

"Does Uncle Paul know this?"

"Woodrow told him 'fo' he pass. They look just alike. You ain't notice?"

"It never dawned on me. I guess I was too young to notice."

"Your mama finds out when he did. She was upset. Don't thank she respect Woodrow no more. She was hurt. Paul her big brotha, now her cousin. It bother her still to this day."

"Is that why she fuss with him all the time?"

"She fuss with everybody." She leaned her head back and laughed loudly. It was always funny to Misha to see her grandmother laugh. Her grandmother enjoyed the act of laughter more than what she was laughing at. "I told you she spoiled. Too late to do anything about that." She suddenly stopped laughing and stared at Misha. "Chile, we all got to go when our time come. It was Lo's time. She at peace. She loved da Lawd. Now she making Him laugh." She returned to her laughter. This time Misha laughed as she remembered how funny her Aunt Lorna was. They both were going to miss her.

Chapter 21

Misha sat in Judy's family room, watching as Judy propped a pillow under her legs. She was delighted to finally have some down time with Judy. Her husband had taken the kids to the pizza fun park to give them some time alone. Judy had obviously gained weight and girth with the growing baby inside of her. Although she had strict instructions from her doctor to stay on bed rest, her smile never changed.

"Look at how big you are," Misha said as she sat in the chair across from Judy.

"This child is weighing me down. I can't wait until it's over. Make yourself at home. You want something to drink? Help yourself in the kitchen."

"I'm fine. Here, I got you something." Misha handed her a small box and watched as Judy opened it. Inside the box was a heart-shaped locket. Judy opened the locket and started to laugh. Inside the locket was a picture of Judy and her family. Judy laughed harder when she realized Misha had used her computer to put a picture of a baby into the picture of her family. "I thought you could use a laugh."

"Thank you. What is this, a picture of the baby Jesus?"

"I took it off a Christmas card." Both of them continued to laugh as Judy hugged one of the many pillows that surrounded her and pulled the blanket to cover her legs. "How are you doing? You look tired," Misha said.

"This child is doing a number on me. The only good thing about this is now I don't have to do anything around here. How's everything at the school?"

"Same old thing. That Heckler guy gives me the creeps. You know, he followed me after school yesterday."

"What? Did you tell Mr. Davis?"

"No. This guy is a friend of Roger's. The two of them are probably trying to make me look crazy. I'm not falling into their trap. But that doesn't stop the feeling this guy is bad news."

"You should report it to the police. Let somebody know."

"I won't give Roger the benefit of making me lose my job. I'm praying him out of my life. God will move him soon. Besides, this Heckler guy is only at the school temporarily. I think next month is his last. Then byebye Mr. Heckler." Misha waved good-bye.

"Well, be careful. I'm going to touch and agree with you in prayer this man leaves you alone." Judy put her hand on her stomach and let out a long sigh. "This baby is very active."

"He's moving?"

"He's always moving."

"Can I . . . Can I touch him?"

"Sure, everyone else does."

Misha walked over and bent down and carefully laid her hand on Judy's stomach. "I don't feel anything."

"Wait."

Misha felt the rise and fall of the baby inside of Judy. "Oh my God. I do feel him. That must be a weird feeling to you."

"This my fourth. You get used to it."

Misha put both of her hands on Judy and the urge to pray came over her. She began praying for Judy and the baby. Then she ended the prayer by praying for the entire household and speaking blessing over it. "This child will be different from your other children. He may be difficult to manage at first. Just wait. He will become a light for others to see and he will speak to many for the Kingdom of God because the hand of God is on him."

"He's going to be a preacher?"

"What?"

"You said he will speak to many for the Kingdom of God. Is he going to be a preacher?"

"Shoot, I don't know. You're going to have to ask God." Misha walked back to her seat. They began chatting about everything from work to men to food. When they mentioned food both of them got hungry. Misha went out to Popeyes and got the chicken Judy was craving. By the time she returned, Judy's family was back at home. She decided not to stay and left the food with Judy and headed home.

Misha spent the rest of her evening trying to catch up on the reading she had for her classes until she fell asleep. Early Sunday morning she got up and went to New Vision's eight o'clock service. She sat in the back of the church, listening to the pastor preach, although she wasn't really into the service.

She looked around the sanctuary and felt a spirit of slothfulness. She could see New Vision's pastor and members were stagnant in their worship and work. She could see they had become complacent because God had blessed them with a new sanctuary and they felt they no longer needed to work because God had already blessed them. Therefore, they had become slack in every aspect of the church. She could see and feel their slackness as she sat quietly during the service. She began to pray silently that God light a fire and desire in their hearts for ministry and return the sincerity in worship they had before.

Misha woke up the next morning, asking God if this was the day she was leaving her job. She looked at the clock and rolled over in her bed and prayed for strength to get up and go to work. She had been feeling weak and uneasy since her Aunt Lorna died. She thought she was coming down with something. She wanted to come down with something so she did not have to go to work. However, she repented for the thoughts and thanked God for healing her and rolled over and got up and began her day.

She arrived at school the same time the first buses began to roll onto the school grounds. A couple of her students met her at her car and offered to walk her to her class. Their upbeat attitude cheered her up and helped her gain the strength to make it through another day. She decided against giving the students the pop test she planned. Instead, she allowed them to use the test as a worksheet and watched as they opened their books searching for the answer to the questions.

During her planning period, Mr. Heckler walked into her classroom and informed her he needed a copy of her grade books and lesson plans to complete her segment of his review. He was surprised she already had a copy of all the information he needed. No other teacher was prepared.

"Are you this efficient with everything?" Heckler said with a flirty tone.

"Everything, meaning my career and ministry? Yes, I guess I am. Mr. Davis told us what you needed and I made the copies to be sure I had them when you needed them."

"What about . . . well . . . What if I need other things? Would you be just as efficient?" he said with a crooked smile.

"What other things are you talking about?"

"Just things. Thanks for the information," he said as he lifted the package. "I'll get this back to you as soon as possible."

Heckler walked out of the classroom with a slight smile on his face. *That guy is so creepy.* Misha tried to refocus and continued the day.

After work she drove to her grandmother's home. When she entered the house she could smell the chitterlings cooking in the kitchen. The smell turned her stomach. She hated chitterlings. She could not get past the smell and the way they looked. She was the only one in her family who did not eat them. But, her grandmother cooked them on every holiday and at least once a month and more if the church was trying to raise money. Everybody loved her chitlins plates she sold at the church. There were always early orders taken and they would sell out every time. Today Misha wanted to work on the quilt, but not with that strong smell in the house.

"Hey, baby," her grandmother greeted her.

"I wanted to work on the quilt and I thought I was going to get something to eat. I can tell you're cooking chitlins."

"Chitlins and rice. Good for you. I don't know why you don't eat them. Much as your mama ate them when she pregnant with you."

"That's probably why I don't like them. I had too much in vivo."

"In what?"

"Never mind. Grandma, where's the quilt."

"I slide it over there, by the fireplace."

Misha walked over and took the quilt out of the storage bin. She stretched it out over the sofa, admiring the work she and her grandmother had put into it. However, the smell was making her feel more nauseated, giving her a reason to leave.

"You can work on it if you wanna. Those 'itis boys are getting to me today. Don't feel like working on it."

Misha smiled as she listened to her grandmother call her arthritis "'itis." She often said that she had all the 'itis boys: arthritis, bursitis, sinusitis, and so on. She was the only one Misha had ever heard refer to their arthritis that way. She knew her grandmother did not know the difference between arthritis and bursitis. She only knew that, on certain days, all of them would attack her. "That's okay. We can do this another day. I had some down time and thought we could talk and work on the quilt."

"Talk 'bout what?"

"Nothing really. Just talk."

"Sit down a spell."

Misha sat down on the sofa, trying not to take deep breaths to let the scent clog her nostrils. "You know I went over my friend Judy's house. She's six months pregnant. I felt her baby move. It was the weirdest thing."

"Nothing weird about no baby moving. Good, healthy, strong baby. That's what that is."

"This child is going to be different. She's got three other children. Somehow I know this one is different from the others."

"God letting you know that."

Misha turned on the sofa to face her grandmother. "Grandma, what does it mean when God tells you to call someone?"

"I 'spect He wants you to pick up the phone and call. Something's up."

"No. That couldn't be it. What if you don't know the person's name or phone number?"

"What'cha mean?"

"Can I be honest with you? I mean I know I can. I don't want to sound stupid."

"Nothing's stupid. Tell me."

"Well, I've been having this overwhelming feeling to call Matthew. Once, I believe God woke me up in the middle of the night and told me to call him. Does that sound weird to you?"

Her grandmother patted her on the leg and started to smile. Misha felt relieved. She knew her grandmother would know what she was talking about and would not think she was stupid or crazy. "You know I's grows up in the country. We ain't had phones back then. When I was out in the yard and my mama wanted me she would go to the back door and holla loud as she could." Misha watched as her grandmother's face lit up with a bright smile as she remembered her mother and the things she did when she was a child. Misha listened intently as her grandmother continued her story.

"'Ida Mae, git yo'self in the yard.' Her voice so loud, everybody could hear her a mile away. I'd hear her and run fast as I could to get home. And I could tell by the way she yell if she be mad or happy or whatever. I could tell the difference."

Misha watched as her grandmother leaned back and screamed with laughter.

"One time our goats got out of the fence. Me and my brothers were supposed to keep the gate locked but we were down at the next farm, playing with our friends." She laughed again. "When I heard my mama's voice yelling for us, it sent chills down my spine. I almost wet on myself. I knew we done something wrong and we were in big trouble." Her grandmother stood and scrunched her face and placed her hands on her hips, showing Misha how her mama looked when they got home.

Misha continued laughing as her grandmother described how it took them all night to find all those goats. Then, her grandmother returned to the chair.

"What the Lawd want you to do is call Matthew like my mama call me."

"You mean He wants me to stand at my door and yell for him?"

"If that what it takes. Next time God tell you to call him, do what He says."

"I think I'll feel stupid doing that."

"You wanna get married? It's power in the tongue. You call him. He hear. He come."

"So all I had to do was call him? That sounds like Dorothy from *The Wizard of Oz*. Should I click my heels three times?"

"If the Lawd tells you. Do what He tells ya."

"I never heard of anything like that. It's worth a try. I don't know his last name or his phone number. All I got is my voice."

"Pray God open Matthew's ear to hear you when you call. He hear. He come. You watch. God never lie. He faithful from generation to generation. Let me git up and take an aspirin. This 'itis got my hands aching today."

Misha took in a deep breath and remembered her grandmother was cooking chitterlings. She folded the quilt and placed it back into the storage container. "Well, Grandma, I better go. You need me to do anything for you?"

"No, child. Take that quilt home with you and that sewing machine. You can work on it at home. You know when my 'itis is like this it take a few days to feel better."

"No, Grandma. I can leave it here. I'll be back in a couple of days. I have class tomorrow night. It'll probably be the day after before I can get back over here."

"Child, take that stuff with you. Bring it back when you come back. I'll let you know how I feel."

Misha took the storage container and the sewing machine and placed it in the trunk of her car and returned to the house. "Grandma, I'm getting ready to go. You sure you don't want anything?"

"No. I'm going in here and fix me a plate of them chitlins. I know you running from them. They good to me."

"That's your stomach. Anyway, are you sure all I have to do is yell for Matthew?"

"When God tells you, you call him like my mama call me. That's when the anointing on him to hear. He hear you and he come."

"Well, I'll give it a try. Thank you, Grandma. I love you."

"I love you too, baby."

Misha hugged her grandmother and made sure the door was locked behind her. As she drove down the busy streets of Atlanta, she heard the voice telling her to call Matthew.

"Matthew, come to me." She was embarrassed to say it aloud in her car. She thought the other people in the cars would think she was crazy talking to herself. She placed her Bluetooth in her ear.

Say it again.

"Matthew, come to me."

Command him to come to you in the name of Jesus.
She was nervous sitting at the red traffic light. She looked at the cars on her left and right to see if anyone she knew was looking at her or if anyone was looking in her car. The man in the SUV on her right waved at her and smiled. She quickly pressed the gas pedal as the light changed to green. She screamed out loudly in her car, "Matthew, I command you to come to me in the name of Jesus."

A sense of peace came over her. It was the same peace she had when she knew she was walking in the will of God. Satisfied she had done what God told her, she hoped Matthew would show up soon and she could go forward with her life.

Chapter 22

Two weeks had passed since Misha got her grand-mother's sewing machine and the quilt. During this time, she enjoyed the Easter holidays with her family and spring break at college and at Westdale. She was returning to school early for a teacher's meeting before school. She expected the same thing, the "preparing for exams" speech, at school. However, this meeting was different.

Mr. Davis informed the teachers they would have a report on Mr. Heckler's findings and they would meet with some of them to discuss how they could improve their teaching skills. He said this would end Mr. Heckler's time at the school. He would continue to analyze his findings and, after discussion, have a complete report for the State.

The sound of that man's name made Misha grimace. She disliked him even more than she disliked Roger. He never quit asking her out and sending her things. He even began sending her notes without signing them. She knew they were from him and not Roger. She knew Roger's handwriting and she compared it to the sympathy card she received from Mr. Heckler.

He started saying things to her that were inappropriate, not only for work, but for her as a woman. She was relieved his work was complete and he would be leaving the school soon. This announcement made her day. This was an answer to her prayer. Now, she only wanted to get rid of Roger.

After work, she called Judy with the good news that Mr. Heckler would be leaving soon. However, her joy was erased when she learned Judy had to go back to the hospital for premature labor. She rushed to the hospital to be by her friend's side. When she arrived in the room, Judy looked like she was really worried.

"Hey, girl. Your mom told me you were here." She walked to Judy's bedside.

"Just wanted to get out the house." She slightly laughed as she leaned back on the bed with her eyes closed.

Misha looked over at Randy, who was sitting in a chair near the window. When she looked at him, he shrugged his shoulders and shook his head. "Hey, Misha. I'm glad you came. We've been here all day. They're just watching her now. They gave her something to stop the labor. I told her to stop doing all that work around the house. She's hardheaded. Maybe you can talk some sense into her."

"You've been here all day? Have you eaten?" Misha asked Randy.

"I skipped lunch. I didn't want her to be here alone."

"Why don't you go to the cafeteria and get something to eat. I'll stay here."

"How long do you plan to be here?"

"Well, how long do you need me to be?"

"I need to run home and get my computer to do some work. We kinda left the house pretty quickly. I also need to check on the kids and get Judy some stuff."

"I can stay until you get back. Go ahead. Take your time."

"Thank you, Misha. I'll get back as soon as I can. Honey, tell me what you need."

Judy rattled off a list of items she needed and her husband left them alone. Judy offered Misha a seat. A

nurse came in and checked the long printout coming
from the machine that sat on a table on the right side
of the bed. She asked Judy several questions. She adjusted the IV and left the room.

"How are you feeling? What's going on?" Misha
asked.

"I started having contractions this morning. They
gave me something to stop them. I haven't had one
since this morning. The doctor is going to keep me in
here a couple of days anyway."

"What kind of work were you doing?"

"Nothing heavy. I was so bored. I had to do something."

"You know you're supposed to stay off your feet."

"I know. I know. Please, don't you start too. I've
heard it from everybody today. It was one simple mistake."

"Okay, I won't get on you. I'm worried about you."

"I've learned my lesson. I didn't have these problems
with the other kids. I don't know about this one. I just
don't know."

Misha looked at her friend lying back on the bed with
a look of worry on her face. She didn't want her to be
down. Silence filled the room. She prayed to herself,
asking God to show her how to cheer Judy up.

"Guess what?" Misha tried hard to make her voice
sound cheerful.

"What?"

"Mr. Stalker Heckler is leaving."

Judy sat up in the bed and adjusted the head of the
bed so she could sit up comfortably. "What happened?"
She listened as Misha filled her in on all the information they received in the meeting, including some juicy
gossip one of the teachers told her. Judy started laughing when Misha told her one of the counselors said

Roger was telling everyone Gloria was stalking him and Gloria had gone off on him in the office in front of everybody. She threatened to go to Mr. Davis and tell him about all the lies he told on Misha. "What goes around comes around," Judy said.

"Girl, it's a big mess. She hasn't apologized to me. I don't expect her to. I'll pray for her."

"Pray for her? Remember, you're the one who prayed for the truth. When truth is revealed, people involved are affected and guilty parties are uncovered and always get hurt. That's God's vengeance. Now if she comes to you, it'll be up to you how you handle it. You can do the 'I told you so' thing or you can forgive and minister to her. It's up to you." Judy adjusted herself in the bed as she spoke.

"Look at you, Miss Teacher. I thought you were sick."

"I don't know where that came from." She leaned back in the bed. "You better listen. Have you forgiven them?"

"A long time ago."

"Good, so if she comes to you, you can receive her in love."

"Preach on my sista." Misha laughed and Judy threw a pillow at her. She caught it in midair.

"Oooo, stop making me laugh. It's putting pressure on the baby."

"I'm sorry. What's wrong?" Misha jumped up and ran over to the bed. "Are you okay? Should I call the nurse?"

"Calm down. I'm fine. Put that pillow back behind my head. I needed to laugh." She smiled as she leaned into the pillow. "Misha, sometimes you have to go through some pain to give birth. It can be at the beginning, end, or even during the process. Either way, you're still going to have pain when you're pregnant. This is the order of things if you want to birth something important. I'll get through this. This child is special. We both know that."

Misha sat down in the chair, listening to Judy minister to her at a time when she needed ministry.

She will preach the gospel.

They continued their conversation until Randy came back into the room. Misha left the hospital, inspired by the words Judy said. She taught her a lot that night about enduring pain and hardship.

The next morning Misha walked into her classroom and was greeted by a note from Mr. Davis stating he wanted to meet with her during her planning period. She was prepared to be called into the office because of Roger and Gloria. She prayed for both of them before she started her day and asked God to help her minister when the time came.

She walked to the office confident that the truth had been revealed and she would be vindicated of all the lies that were told on her by Roger and Gloria. Instead, she found Mr. Heckler and Mr. Davis waiting for her in the office. Mr. Heckler looked and acted very professional as he greeted her when she walked into the room.

"Hello, Ms. Holloway. Come on in. Close the door behind you," Mr. Davis requested.

Misha did as instructed and sat down in the chair closest to the door. She looked around the office at all the plaques on the wall and the large desk she was too familiar with this year. She glanced over at Mr. Heckler dressed in a black suit with a light green shirt with French cuffs. She stared at the emerald beetle bug-shaped cufflinks that protruded from underneath his sleeve.

"Ms. Holloway, as I informed y'all Mr. Heckler and I would be talking with some of you about his findings. Today, we want to go over your reports."

"Is that what this is about? I thought you wanted me for something else." Misha relaxed in the chair.

"Really? What?" Mr. Davis looked puzzled.

Misha waved it off. "Never mind. Go ahead with what you were saying."

Mr. Davis paused for a moment as if he was trying to think of what she may have been talking about. Then he continued talking. "I'm going to let Mr. Heckler go over his report with you."

"Ms. Holloway, how are you today? You look nice," Mr. Heckler noted.

"Thank you. I like those cufflinks."

"These?" He held up his forearm. "Can you believe I found these at an estate sale? This is the first time I've worn them."

"Well, they're nice."

Mr. Davis cleared his throat. Misha and Mr. Heckler looked at him. "Mr. Heckler, the report." Mr. Davis pointed to the notes Mr. Heckler held in his hand.

"Yes, the report. Miss Holloway, your students seemed to be doing well in your courses. I did an average of your tests scores and your students were in the upper percentile in both your class grades and standardized testing."

He gave Misha a copy of his report showing the averages in her classes compared to the school, state, and nationwide averages. They allowed her time to briefly read over the report. She was proud her students were scoring well on the tests despite their lack of real interest and enthusiasm in the classes. Mr. Heckler continued discussing her scores as she read the report.

"Miss Holloway, why do you think your scores are so high compared to others?"

"Well, Mr. Heckler, I take time with my students. I encourage them to study and be creative in their assignments. I don't want them to remember only dates and events. I want them to know how it affected history and things around them. If they learn that, then they're more likely to remember the information. Looks like it's working."

"A little too well," Mr. Heckler said.

"What do you mean by that?"

"Well, in comparison to your classroom tests scores, your students shouldn't be scoring so high on standardized testing."

"What are you saying?" Misha watched as Mr. Heckler stood and began walking the floor like an attorney interrogating a witness.

"Well, based on your classroom scores, your students should be scoring significantly lower on the tests. Can you tell me how that is?"

"What are you suggesting? Are you saying I'm coaching my students with the tests?"

"I'm not saying that."

"What he's saying is it appears there are some discrepancies in your report. We are not accusing you of anything," Mr. Davis chimed in.

"Why do I feel like you are, Mr. Davis?"

"I have no reason to think you're cheating for your students. Mr. Heckler will talk with some of your students about your teaching methods and add their comments to his report before he submits the complete report to the State. We wanted to make sure you were aware of this."

Misha looked at both of them. They were suggesting she may be cheating on standardized testing. She never cheated. She could not explain why her students did better on the standardized tests than her classroom work. She concluded they were probably looking at the pop quizzes she gave her students on a regular basis to make sure they were studying. This could have been the cause of the lower test scores in her class.

"I feel you are questioning my integrity. Mr. Davis, I have never given you any reason to believe I would stoop to cheating on tests." Misha inched to the edge of her chair.

"We're not saying that you're cheating. It could be you have a lot of pop tests that many of your students don't do well on and that lowers your students overall grades," Mr. Heckler said. He knew that was exactly the problem.

"Are you suggesting I stop giving pop tests? That's the only way I know to make my students study."

"There are other ways to teach them other than giving pop tests," Mr. Heckler responded.

"What do you suggest? Are you a teacher? How many years of teaching do you have?" Misha fired back.

Mr. Heckler returned to his seat. "I don't have to be a teacher to know how to teach children. The State hired me to do a job. Based on research, there are more effective ways of teaching," he said.

Misha's breathing deepened. She felt as if she were strangling trying to keep what she felt on the inside. Deciding not to argue with them, she stopped commenting on everything they told her. She was being ganged up on. Remembering God told her it was time to leave her job, she tried to relax. This was part of the process, but she did not want to get fired. If this was the way God had arranged it, then she would have to submit herself to His will, even if she did not like it.

"I will start talking with some of your students tomorrow," Mr. Heckler informed her.

"Thanks for telling me. Will there be anything else?"

"No. You may leave," Mr. Davis said. Both of the men stood as Misha stood to leave the room.

Misha left the office fuming mad. She looked at the report she held tightly in her hand. She decided to analyze the figures for herself when she got home. She was convinced it was only Mr. Heckler getting back at her for not going out with him. She was determined to find problems with his report.

The next day, Misha came in armed with notes she made about the report. She was prepared to discuss her findings with Mr. Davis and Mr. Heckler. When she entered her classroom, Mr. Heckler was looking out the window.

"Hello." She hesitated. "Didn't expect to see you here this morning," she said. He turned around. Misha walked to her desk and placed her bags on her desk. "Can I help you with something?"

"I don't want you to get the wrong message about what happened yesterday."

"Oh you mean the way you decided to get back at me for not going out with you? That's very childish, Mr. Heckler. I expected more of you."

"I was only doing my job."

"I reviewed your little report and my numbers don't match yours."

"Are you suggesting I was lying?" He walked closer to her desk.

"I'm only saying my numbers don't match yours." Misha was on the defense. She was ready for him. She stood looking at him with her hand on her hip, ready to defend herself on every hand.

"So you are saying I'm lying?"

"Look Mr. . . ." Misha suddenly became weak. She felt like she was going to faint. She leaned forward and gripped the desk.

"Miss Holloway, are you all right?" Mr. Heckler asked as he rounded her desk to catch her in case she fell.

"What?"

"Are you all right? You look like you're about to pass out."

"I only got a little lightheaded. School is about to start. I need to prepare for my classes. If you don't mind, please leave me alone."

Heckler turned and walked out of the door. Misha gripped the edge of the desk like she was trying to break off a piece. She began to pray to herself. Finally, she gained enough strength to sit down in the chair. She put her head on the desk and prayed silently until the first students walked into her classroom.

Misha made it through first and second period, even though she was feeling weak and nervous. She stood up to begin teaching her third period class. She walked between the lined seats holding on to each one as she passed. Once again, she felt extremely weak and she gripped the back of two of the seats and bent over. She had a severe pain in her chest.

"Miss Holloway, are you all right?" one of her students asked. The student left her desk and ran to Misha when she did not answer her.

Misha could not move. The pain in her chest was crippling. She felt weak. Then the pain hit her sharper. Misha grabbed her chest and fell to the floor.

Misha awoke and looked around her surroundings. She was no longer in school. She edged up slightly. She was in a hospital room. She looked at her arm. An IV had been placed on the back of her hand. She tried to push herself up. She looked to her side and spotted her

Aunt Mattie, Uncle Paul's wife, sitting in a chair in the corner.

"No, Misha. Just lie there. I'll let the nurse know you're awake." She stood and walked to Misha's bedside.

"Aunt Mattie? What happened?"

"They said you passed out at work."

"Aunt Mattie, you may not believe this. Something happened. Something bad. I could feel it." Misha sat up on the bed.

"No, Misha, lie back down." Aunt Mattie patted her hand.

"No, you don't understand. Something's wrong. I've got to get out of here." Misha pressed the nurse call button. She wanted the nurse to remove the IV so she could leave the hospital. "Aunt Mattie, you don't understand. I could feel something bad is going to happen. I just know it. I've got to get back to the school."

"Misha, be quiet. You're getting yourself all worked up. Now your brother is on his way here. The doctor will be in here momentarily."

Misha lay on the bed, knowing something was really wrong. She didn't know what it was but she could feel it in every part of her being. The sooner she got out of there, the sooner she would be able to find out what was happening.

Chapter 23

The following day Misha returned to her class after having been diagnosed with severe anemia and told to take iron pills and eat food loaded with iron. Dr. Trinidad had already told her that but she neglected to do it, preferring to eat fast food instead. She had finals coming up and she wanted to do her best both at her school and at Clark.

Although things were winding down with school, Misha still felt that something was wrong—out of place. She saw Heckler walking down the hall and that nervous feeling in her stomach came back with a vengeance. He only had a few days before he left and it was not soon enough for her. *The sooner the better,* was all she thought about. She was depending on the Word from the Lord that she was leaving that job soon so she did not care if Roger stayed or left. If God told her she was leaving, then another job for her was coming open soon.

At school, she tried hard to delve into her work, although sometimes during her planning period, she would think about Matthew and the way he would come into her life. She would call him when the feeling hit her. She was young and full of life. She did not need to be sitting home alone with no one to hang out with.

She joined the singles ministry at the church but it was not the same. There were too many women chasing after the eight men who dared to be a part of the ministry. It was not what she wanted. She loved going to jazz clubs, museums, festivals, and other special events, including church. But, she had no one to go with. In addition to that she had no one to talk to other than her grandmother and she couldn't talk to her grandmother like she would talk to a man. She wanted someone who made her voice change and made her feel like a woman. Her grandmother did not do it for her.

To add insult to injury, Roger continued to use Mr. Heckler to harass her. He knew her too well and called her bluff. And, Bishop Moore told the pastor of a church she was scheduled to preach at not to let her preach. As a result, they cancelled her speaking engagement. What was it about her that made these grown men bent on destroying her? She had no clue.

One day as she was sitting at her desk, she heard a voice in her spirit.

I have prepared a love to heal your heart. Call Matthew.

She wiped her eyes. "God, I have called him. He didn't show. God help me. I want my husband and a baby from my own body. Only you can help me. Give me someone to love. Give me someone who loves me."

Call Matthew.

She shouted as loud as she could for Matthew, not caring who heard her.

She watched as the students began to file into her classroom. She sat back and took a deep breath and prayed silently for the strength to get through two more classes. As the bell rang, Bethany ran into the classroom.

"Just in time. Miss Holloway, Amber is going to be late. She ran down to the dungeon to get her book bag she left there this morning."

When Misha heard "Amber" and "dungeon" something shocking went all over her body. Her hands trembled. Goose bumps rose on her arms. "Where is Amber?"

"She went to the dungeon to get her book bag. She left it there after gym class."

Misha sat down at her desk and began class. After calling the roll, she handed out a worksheet and sat quietly at her desk, watching the students trying to locate the answers in their book. Suddenly, she heard a scream and jumped. This startled the class.

"What's up, Miss Holloway? Did you go to sleep?" one of her students asked her and the class laughed.

"No. Did y'all hear that?"

"What?"

"Did y'all hear a scream?" No one in the class heard the scream. Misha sat back and tried to grade some papers. She heard it again. "Did y'all hear it this time?" Once again she was the only one who heard the scream. She sat at her desk and an urge came over her to go to the dungeon. She told the class to continue working and she walked out of the school toward the dungeon.

She cautiously walked into the dimly lit building that smelled like something had died in there. She yelled out for Amber. No one answered her. She decided to check the showers before she left. As she walked around the corner she saw Amber. Her hands and feet were tied with jump ropes. Her mouth had duct tape on it. She ran to Amber and removed the tape. She then untied Amber's hands and was working to untie her feet when she heard Amber scream her name. Misha turned around and saw a man with a ski mask pointing a gun at her.

The man directed her to move away from Amber. When she heard the voice, she immediately knew who it was: Mr. Heckler. He had on a jump suit but she noticed the emerald beetle bug-shaped cufflinks sticking out from underneath the arm of the jumpsuit. She stood her ground. He demanded her to move. She stared deeply into his eyes. She knew it was him. She knew those blue eyes.

"Mr. Heckler. I'm not moving. You're going to have to shoot me. I know it's you. I know your voice, your eyes, and those cufflinks. They're the same ones you wore that day in the office. I'm not going to let you touch this child."

"Well, you know who I am? I'm just going to have to kill you," he said, pulling off the ski mask.

Amber screamed. He yelled to her to shut up and pointed the gun at her. Misha ran toward him and grabbed his arm. His arm flew in the air and the gun went off. Misha fought him with everything she had. He punched her in the face so hard she fell to the floor. He began hitting her repeatedly. Misha lay on the floor, screaming for God to help her.

Misha yelled to Amber to go get help. Amber struggled to untie her feet and ran out the door. Misha swung at Mr. Heckler with all her might. She wasn't going to let him kill her. After a few minutes, she could no longer struggle with him and lay helplessly on the hard, cold cement floor, crying and praying.

"Shut up," Mr. Heckler told her as he stood and looked around. He noticed Amber was gone and he began yelling profanities and kicking Misha in the side. He ripped her clothes off her. Misha closed her eyes and prayed. The pain of his body pressing against hers ripped throughout her every being. She tried to push him off of her. But, he kept violating her body as if he were trying to penetrate her soul. She continued to fight him with all the strength she had left, hoping and praying that someone would arrive soon. Her strength was failing her.

It seemed as if hours had passed as she endured his repeated abuse when she heard someone calling for him to come out. Her arms flung in the air. Weak and distraught, the room got dark. Her strength left her and she could only call on the name of Jesus to help her. Each time she said "Jesus!" she felt empowered.

"Shut up. I'll kill you. I promise. Shut up." He stood up and began pacing the floor. Misha continued to call the name Jesus. "Shut up. I told you. I'm not playing with you. Shut up."

Misha did not stop. She continued to call Jesus as loud as she could. He leaned down and put the gun to her head and pulled the trigger. It did not go off. She continued to call the name of Jesus. He pulled the trigger again. It still did not go off. He looked up and jumped back as if he had seen something that frightened him. He crawled backward to the opposite wall.

They could hear the people outside pleading with him to release her. He sat on the floor against the wall, breathing hard. He pointed the gun at her again, pulled the trigger, and it did not go off. He dropped his hand into his lap, staring blankly at her.

He stood with the gun in his hand and laughed. "You should have gone out with me. We could have had a good time." He turned and walked toward the door.

Chapter 24

Misha's year had started with such optimism. She had just known God had worked and would continue to work things out for her. She had been enrolled in college. She was learning how to quilt and had finally gotten over her breakup with Roger. She'd even found a church she liked. Her ministry and life appeared to truly be looking up. Then of course, out of nowhere, the bottom fell out again.

She had health problems. A man who had a history of being a sexual predator had raped her. To make matters worse, she had been out of work over a month due to the rape and the school district denied her workers' compensation claim, stating she should not have been in the dungeon at the time of the attack.

Judy's brother, Eric, who was her attorney, tried to reassure her that this was common in workers' comp cases. He filed an appeal of her claim and was planning to sue the consulting firm the State hired. They never checked the background of Mr. Heckler before they hired him.

She was slipping into a deep depression. She had no one to talk to. She did not want to burden Judy. She had her own problems with her pregnancy. She was still having difficulty communicating with her mother. Whenever she tried to talk to her, her mother accused her of being a big sinner and told her God was punishing her. She definitely did not want to worry her grandmother.

She sat in her apartment, feeling the full impact of being alone. She looked at her arms and legs. The bruising from the beating was gone. Her face did not show signs of being hit. Yet she still felt naked and exposed to the whole world. She asked God what she did that was so bad she had to be punished like that.

She had not attended church. Sherrell, the singles minister, came by once and prayed with her. She also called at least once a week to see how she was doing. She encouraged Misha to return to church. Misha did not want to call her because she knew Sherrell was a single parent and probably had a lot going on in her own life.

Misha dared not to venture out of her house alone. She was afraid that everyone could see straight through her. She felt so naked to the world, as if everyone knew she was the teacher who was held hostage and raped. The media ran the story over and over. They even ran connecting stories about school safety and background checks. It was weeks before they finally let it go. One thing she was glad of in the whole situation was she did not have to face a trial. Heckler was dead, killed by the police after he shot at them. She did not think she could survive a long public trial. Two good things came out of this horrible situation: police told her Mr. Heckler was HIV-negative, and Amber was not raped. This is what God had been showing her for months.

One night as she lay crying in her bed she began to question God about everything that had happened to her. She became angry with God. She told God how she saw people living in the worst possible way being blessed all around her. Yet, she was trying to live a life that would glorify His Kingdom and she had so much pain and was alone.

Get up and encourage yourself in the Lord. I am sending you back to Washington to minister the gospel to the sick. You will not have to do it alone, for I have appointed you to be a help for such a time as this.

"God, you've been saying that. Yet I don't see anything happening. I don't know if I can take much more of this." She began to cry.

I am all that I am. I would not let you die for I am faithful. I will do what I said I will do. Call Matthew and he will surely come. The two of you will go forth and preach the gospel to this generation.

Misha fell off to sleep with God's promise in her spirit.

The next morning she awoke and sat up on the side of her bed. As she stood, she felt lightheaded. She sat down on the bed until the room stopped turning around. She reached for her robe that lay across the foot of her bed, pulling it on as she walked into the kitchen and fixed a bowl of cereal. She sat curled up on the sofa, watching a morning news show, trying to eat the cereal. The taste of the cereal was making her nauseated. She smelled the bowl to see if the milk was sour. This made her even sicker and she ran to the bathroom and vomited everything she had eaten.

She lay down on the bed, trying to make the room stop turning. She asked God to help her. After a few minutes, she tried to stand up but the room kept spinning. She was afraid to call anyone. Everyone she knew would assume the worst. She couldn't deal with any negativity today. She concluded in her mind she probably had a virus and decided to stay in the bed the rest of the day.

She rested until the early afternoon. She was feeling much better so she decided to get up and eat something. Her stomach was growling loud enough she thought the people in the next apartment could hear it. She looked in her cabinet for something light, like chicken soup. She did not want to upset her stomach again. Unable to find soup, she made herself a sandwich and waited for it to come back up. She tried to busy herself moving the boxes around in her spare bedroom, when she heard her phone ring. She saw it was Judy.

"Hey, Judy. How you feeling?" Misha tried to sound cheerful for Judy. She did not want to upset her in any way.

"It's not Judy. It's Randy. Judy wanted me to call you and let you know she had the baby."

Misha gasped. "She had the baby? She's not due now. Is everything all right?"

"Judy's fine. She's up and walking around. Our son, he's tiny. But he's doing good. He weighs three pounds, five ounces. He's going to be in the hospital a little while."

"How are you doing?"

"As well as can be expected. Tired. We've been here all night."

Misha wanted to run to the hospital but she remembered her stomach virus and told Randy she was sick and would try to make it the next day. She called Judy's room to see how she was doing and told her she would visit her later. She went online and ordered some flowers to be sent to Judy. She sat around her apartment, debating whether she should go out and purchase a present for the baby or stay at home. She couldn't stay in her apartment forever. The thought of going outside frightened her. She decided to stay at home and order a gift online.

The next morning when she got up she felt sick again. She groaned as she got back into her bed after rushing to the bathroom to throw up. She called Pam and asked her to come over because she was sick. She stayed in the bed until she heard a knock on her door. She slowly walked to the door, not bothering to comb her hair. She opened it and Asa and India ran into the apartment grabbing her legs in a tight hug.

"You shouldn't have brought the kids," Misha said.

"I wanted to make sure you were okay before I took them to daycare."

"I think I have a stomach virus. I keep throwing up. I hope they won't get it."

"Did you take your temperature?"

"I don't think I have a fever. I just feel weak and nauseated." Misha walked over to the sofa and sat down. "This has been going on a couple of days. How long does a stomach virus last?"

"That depends on what type of virus you have. Have you called your doctor?"

"Not yet. I wanted to see what you said."

"Call your doctor. I think you'll be okay until I get back from the daycare. Put some clothes on. I'll take you to the doctor."

Misha watched as Pam pulled the children away from her and left the apartment. She groaned and fell onto a pillow on the sofa. She didn't feel like getting dressed. She forced her body up and called Dr. Trinidad's office. She was told they would work her in and she should come as soon as possible.

Misha sat on the exam table in a room she was so familiar with. Pam tried to make conversation, but she wasn't listening. Dr. Trinidad walked into the room.

"Well, Miss Holloway, I have the results of your tests. Your body healed well from the attack and the surgeries."

"Then what is it? I was feeling bad when I came in. Now I'm feeling much better. I think I may be able to eat something now."

Dr. Trinidad walked over to her. Misha could see the look of concern on her face. "Miss Holloway, based on your symptoms, I decided to run a pregnancy test."

"Pregnancy test? You told me I couldn't get pregnant."

"I told you it would be difficult for you to get pregnant naturally. The test was positive. You're pregnant."

"Pregnant?" Misha and Pam yelled at the same time. Pam jumped up from the chair she was sitting in. "Pregnant. How can she be pregnant with the cancer and all?"

"Well we can run the test again. I'm pretty sure you're pregnant."

"Oh my God. I'm pregnant by a rapist. No, this is not happening. What did I do that was so bad I'm being punished like this?" Misha said shaking her head from side to side. She cupped her face in her hands and began to cry. Pam walked over and rubbed her back, trying to console her.

"Could you be pregnant by anyone else?" Dr. Trinadad asked her.

Misha shook her head no. "Before the attack, I hadn't had sex in years. I was trying to be a good Christian. No one will ever let me preach now that I'm pregnant."

"As your doctor, I need to advise you of your options."

"Options?"

"If you decide to keep this baby, I will classify you as a high-risk mother and we will follow you more carefully than we would someone without your medical history. This could be a difficult pregnancy." She took a deep breath and continued. "Then, there is abortion if you choose to terminate this pregnancy. I don't do them here. Under the circumstances, I can refer you to a clinic that does them."

"Pregnant? Abortion?" Misha placed her face into her cupped hands and continued to cry. Pam caressed her shoulders.

"Doctor, I think Misha needs some time to think about this. Can she get back to you?" Pam asked.

"I understand. Here's some information about the clinic if she decides to terminate the pregnancy." She handed Pam a brochure, some discharge instructions, and prescriptions for prenatal vitamins and medication for nausea. She left them alone in the room and Misha wept bitterly.

"It's going to be fine. Come on. I'll take you home."

Misha lifted her head. "Pregnant? How can I be pregnant?"

On the ride home Misha sat silently, crying. Just when she thought her life could not get any worse, it did. Now she was a single female minister and pregnant. How would she explain this to everyone? She never thought she would ever consider abortion. But today, this was her one and only option.

"Misha, it's going to be all right. We're here for you," Pam said. She reached over and gripped Misha's hand.

"I don't know what to do. I'm pregnant by that crazy man. How could this have happened?"

"Whatever you decide, I got your back. If I were you, I would get an abortion as soon as possible."

Misha knew Pam was only trying to console her. But it wasn't helping. *If you were me? How could you say something like that? This is my body. My baby,* Misha thought as she sat in the car, looking out the window. Pam reached down and turned on the radio to break the silence in the car.

"Whatever you're going through, God's worked it out for you. He's never let you down. He's there . . . all the time." The voice rang out from the radio. Misha listened to the words of the song as tears flowed down her face.

"That Bernard Taylor can sing," Pam said as she turned the radio louder.

"Who?" Misha sniffed and wiped the tears from her face.

"Bernard Taylor. That's him singing this song."

"Oh."

They continued their journey when they came upon what looked like a mob scene outside the Remnant Church. The police had the traffic stopped and news trucks were parked alongside the road. Misha sat up in her seat, looking at the mass of people with picket signs. For a brief moment, it made her forget her troubles. Pam rolled her window down and asked someone what was going on. They found out someone had secretly videotaped the pastor talking about the congregation. He referred to the black members as dumb niggers and laughed about how he got people to give their money to fund his lavish lifestyle. The angry lady told them they were demanding he resign as pastor and asked the police to do a criminal investigation of him and the church.

"That's what they get for running with every wind that blows," Pam said as they watched the angry crowd in front of the church.

Misha remembered what God had told her to say that Sunday. They were warned. These are the same people who treated her like a common criminal and kicked her out of the church and warned her not to return. She did not feel sorry for them. She only felt sorry for herself. After a few minutes, the traffic began to move and Misha finally made it home.

She paced the floor, asking God for clear direction. Her mind was so confused. She wanted to do the right thing. What was the right thing? She did not know. She wanted her child to grow up in a loving home with two parents who loved him and cared for him. She never wanted to be a single parent. She certainly did not want to conceive a child in this manner.

As the days went by she found it harder and harder to sleep. The morning sickness kept her from eating in the morning. But by late afternoon, she ate everything in sight. She was now eight weeks pregnant and she had to make a decision soon. She tried talking to Judy. She did not give her any answers. She told Misha she would have to seek God's face for the answer. She avoided her grandmother, embarrassed by her predicament.

Finally, after a long discussion with her parents, Justin, and Pam, she decided to have an abortion. In her mind, it was her only option. She didn't want a reminder of the rape. She wasn't working and could not afford a baby. What if the child turned out crazy like its father? Abortion was against her religious and moral beliefs and she never thought she would consider it, until now.

After her decision was made, she could not get any sleep at night. She tossed and turned all night long. She slipped off the side of her bed and on to her knees.

"Lord, I need you now. I love you and I know you love me. I may not understand all your ways or even why my life is like it is. But, if I am doing the wrong thing, please stop me. Give me a sign or something. I'm not happy. Please restore me to the joy of my salvation," she prayed.

Arising from her prayer she continued to have a nervous feeling that made her body shake each time she thought about having an abortion. However, she fought to convince herself she was doing the right thing.

Finally, the day had arrived for her abortion. She woke up with morning sickness that she could not get used to. She got dressed and waited for Pam to pick her up. She heard a knock at the door. She opened the door and gasped when she spotted Aunt Mattie standing in front of her.

"Aunt Mattie. I didn't expect to see you here. Come on in. I'm waiting for Pam to pick me up. She should be here in a few minutes." Misha frowned. She felt so bad and nervous she could not fake being cheerful. Aunt Mattie stepped into the room, and before Misha could close the door, her grandmother appeared carrying a large shopping bag. "Grandma."

"Misha, how you feeling?" her grandmother asked.

"This morning sickness is rough. It'll be over soon and I won't have to worry about it anymore."

"You know I don't get in everybody's business. But I have something for you," her grandmother said, reaching into the bag and pulling out a box and handed it to Misha.

"What's this?" Misha asked.

"About a month ago Miss Ida Mae called me and asked me to take her shopping. She purchased this gift for you," Aunt Mattie said as they rounded the sofa and sat down.

"Can I open it?"

"It's fo' you," her grandmother said.

Her aunt nodded her head yes and watched Misha open the package. Misha started to cry when she saw the contents of the box. There was a pink blanket with a small newborn outfit that had a small hat. There was also a blue one in the box. There were matching pink and blue booties. She picked up the items and pressed them to her chest.

"Misha, I wanted you to have these today," her grandmother said. "You been believing God for a baby."

Misha nodded her head.

"Doctor said you couldn't have none. But, God said different. Now I can't tell you what to do. But, seems like God done His part. He waiting for you."

"Misha, sometimes our greatest joy comes after our deepest pain. I'm not telling you what to do. Everybody's telling you this child's going to be crazy because of what happened and how he was conceived. I want you to remember one thing: this child is also a part of you. He may have your smile, your intelligence, and even your sassiness. Do you want to go the rest of your life asking yourself what if? You prayed for a child. This may be the way God answered your prayer and how He's restoring your joy. Don't let other people convince you to abort everything you have prayed and worked so hard for just because it didn't come the way everybody expected," Aunt Mattie said.

There was a knock on the door. Aunt Mattie and Ms. Ida Mae stood up and walked to the door. "This must be Pam. Remember what I told you. This baby is a part of you. Do you want to give that up?" Aunt Mattie said as she pulled open the door to see Pam standing in the breezeway.

"Whatever you do, we love you. But, I can't support killing no babies. That's my great-grandbaby. There is a reason why this child come to this world. Only God knows," Ms. Ida Mae said. She reached out and hugged Pam. "Mo'ning, Pam. We was just leaving. Misha, I'll call you later to see how you're doing." Aunt Mattie and Ms. Ida Mae walked out of the apartment.

Pam walked into the room closing the door behind her. "What did Aunt Mattie and Grandma want?" she said, spotting Misha clutching the baby clothes tightly and crying. "What's wrong?"

"I can't do it. I won't do it. I'm keeping my baby."

"Somehow, I knew you were. I told Justin you wouldn't have it done."

"Why didn't you stop me?"

"You had to make the decision on your own." She sat down beside Misha on the sofa. "Aunt Mattie bought you baby clothes?"

"No. Grandma did, a month ago. She gave them to me today."

Pam looked down in the box and saw the card. "What's this?"

"A card from Grandma."

"What does it say?"

Misha opened up the card. She was too emotional to read it. So, she gave it to Pam to read.

My baby Misha. You a very special child. Special from the day you born. Now you have special children. One suit is for Elizabeth 'cause she is a star and she will speak to many people. One is for little Matthew. He named after his daddy and will preach the gospel to many nations like his daddy. Raise them to know and love God. I love you.

Grandma.

Both of them began to cry as Pam struggled to read Grandma's handwriting. Although the grammar and spelling were bad, they knew she had written it herself. Misha knew this was God guiding her in the right direction.

"Just like Ms. Ida Mae. She's still bossy." Pam started laughing. "How's she going to name your children?"

"Elizabeth and Matthew. Grandma has faith. I wish I had the faith she has." Misha took the card and read it again. "I'm sorry I had you get off of work for nothing."

"Don't worry about it. What you want to do now?"

"I guess I better start taking those vitamins Dr. Trinidad gave me and call to schedule an appointment with her."

"You're going to be showing soon. Let's go shopping. They make cute maternity clothes now."

"Maternity clothes. I didn't think about that. I'm on a tight budget now. My comp case was denied by the State. My attorney is appealing to the commission. Hopefully, I'll get a check soon."

"Don't worry about money. I'll buy you a couple of outfits. You need something new. Then we can go to my house and see if you can wear some of my old maternity clothes."

Misha laughed.

"What's so funny?"

"I just thought about what Mama's going to say when she finds out I didn't have an abortion."

"Oh my goodness. I didn't think of that. We'll at least wait until after lunch to tell her. We don't want her to ruin your day. Come on, let's go."

Chapter 25

Misha sat in her apartment, having her own pity party. She had promised Judy she would help her with the baby but she didn't feel like going. She was now twelve weeks pregnant and her clothes were beginning to fit a little snug. She stood in front of the mirror, trying to imagine herself at eight months' pregnant. She stuffed a pillow under her blouse and turned from side to side.

She sat on the bed. She didn't want to go through this pregnancy alone. Her head snapped at the sound of her phone ringing. Checking the caller ID she saw it was her attorney.

"Good morning, Misha."

"Good morning, Eric. Hope you are calling with good news."

"Indeed I am. The Workers' Compensation Commission approved your case."

Misha jumped up and did a little dance around the room, waving her hands in the air, until she heard Eric's voice calling to her.

"Misha, are you still there?" Eric asked.

Misha placed the receiver to her ear. "Yes, I'm here. What does that mean?"

"You didn't hear what I just said. Did you?" He laughed. "That's okay. I know you are happy to hear this. It means you will be getting a weekly check until your case is settled. Your first check will cover all the back payments they owe you from the time of your injury. It's a pretty sizable amount."

"This is minus your twenty percent, right?"

"No. I don't get anything until we fully settle your case. All the weekly checks are yours to spend as you need to. You should be getting the first check by the end of the week."

"What about medical coverage?"

"I'm still working on that. But it's nothing to worry about. You are getting your checks now. The medical coverage is soon to follow."

"Thank you, Eric, for everything." She punched the end button on her phone and threw her hands in the air. "Thank you, God, for making a way." She placed her hands on her belly and leaned forward to talk to the growing baby inside her. "Hear that, little miracle? Mommy's going to have some money now. We've got to go to Aunt Judy's and help with Rafael. Please let Mommy enjoy her breakfast so I can have strength to make it." She rubbed her stomach as she talked to her baby. Her spirit brightened and she felt the strength to visit Judy.

She arrived at Judy's house feeling much better than she did that morning. She was looking forward to seeing the baby. She had not seen him since he was born. He had only been out of the hospital a couple of days. With so much going on in her own life, she just hadn't been up to going to the hospital or visiting with Judy.

"Hey, Judy. Where's the baby?" Misha rushed past her into the house.

"He's over there in the bassinet. Please don't wake him. He was up all night."

Misha walked over to the bassinet and watched Rafael sleeping peacefully. "He's so cute. He looks like you."

"That's what everybody says. Look at you. You're beginning to get a little pooch." She walked over to where Misha stood, gazing in the bassinet, and placed her hand on Misha's belly. "Here. I've got some of my maternity clothes for you. I'm not going to need them anymore." She walked toward a basket of clothes near the fireplace, picked it up, and placed it near the door. "I'm setting these here so you won't forget them."

"Thank you," Misha said as she leaned into the bassinet to get a closer look at the sleeping child. "He's so tiny. What's this?" she asked, pointing to the small white box at the lower end of the bassinet.

"That's the apnea monitor. He has to wear that to be sure he doesn't stop breathing when he's asleep. So far, the alarm hasn't gone off. Come on. Sit down."

Judy waved her over to the sofa. Misha sat down beside Judy and began a conversation that flowed from one subject to another, not staying on any topic for long until they heard Rafael cry. Misha walked to the bassinet. "Can I pick him up?"

"Go ahead."

Misha slowly picked up Rafael and held him closely to her body. She smiled when he barely opened his eyes, squinting as if the light was hurting them. Misha squealed with delight at the sight of him smacking his lips. She sat down and rocked him back and forth, watching him twitch from side to side.

"I think he likes me," Misha said. She continued rocking him until Rafael's face twisted like he just ate a sour lemon and he opened his mouth and let out a loud scream. She held him up against her chest and patted his back. This did not calm him down. She became nervous. "What's wrong?"

Judy leaped from the sofa and walked toward the kitchen. "He's probably hungry. I'll go get his bottle."

"You're not breastfeeding?"

"After three kids? No way. Let me get his bottle before he really gets mad." Both of them walked to the kitchen. Misha tried everything she knew to get him to calm down. She tried rocking him from side to side. She sang. She talked baby talk.

Finally, Judy lifted him from Misha's arms and placed the nipple of the bottle into his mouth. This silenced Rafael as he sucked the milk out of the bottle. He calmed down and desperately began drinking the milk. Judy cradled the baby in her arm and walked back to the family room. Misha eased down beside her on the sofa.

"You do that so well. I hope I'm as good a mother as you."

"I've had lots of practice." Judy lifted the bottle from the Rafael's mouth and glanced at it to measure how much the baby had eaten. Satisfied, she placed the bottle on the end table. Then, without missing a beat, she lifted the now-sleeping baby on her shoulder and patted his back until a loud belch emerged from the baby's mouth.

"Judy, sometimes I wonder if I'm doing the right thing. I wonder if I'm going to be a good parent. I wonder what I'm going to tell this child when he asks about his father. I get so depressed with it all."

Judy stood with the sleeping baby and walked to the bassinet, where she lowered him inside. "You shouldn't think about things like that. It'll come naturally. As far as his father is concerned, God will direct you when the time comes."

"I know. I get so worried sometimes." Misha watched as Judy returned to the sofa.

"You've got too much time on your hands. What do you do all day?" Judy crossed her legs underneath her.

"Not much. I don't go anywhere. I've got a lot of things on my mind."

Judy took Misha's hand. "Misha, let me give you a hint to a good pregnancy. A happy mother equals a happy baby. If you're sad all the time, your baby is going to be sad. But if you're happy, your baby is going to be happy. You should get out the house. Join an exercise class. Go to the movies. Do something. Don't stay in the house."

"I don't think I can do something like that."

"Why not? Misha, look. I know the past year has not been a good one. You've had the cancer, and the rape, but it'll get better. It always does." She stood and walked to the kitchen island where her purse sat. She reached in and pulled out two tickets. "Randy and I got these tickets to Bernard Taylor's concert at the Fox Saturday night. We can't make it though. We were going to give them to my sister and her husband." She walked back to Misha. "Here, take them. You go to the concert. Relax a little. It will be all right."

Misha reached out and took the tickets from her. "Bernard Taylor? Who's that?"

"It's a gospel concert."

"I can't take your tickets." She handed them out to Judy.

"Girl, take the tickets. We can't go now that Rafael is at home. Come on. Go to the concert. It'll take your mind off things."

"Well, okay. How much do I owe you?" Misha placed the tickets in her purse.

Judy's eyebrow arched. "Now I know you didn't ask me that."

Judy sat down and their conversation continued until Misha became tired and left for home. Finally feeling better about being out of the house, she decided to stop by the grocery store before she went home.

At the store, she walked down the aisles, trying to look confident. Yet, she felt so exposed. After only going halfway through the store, her nerves overwhelmed her. She went to the self-checkout, trying to avoid the long lines, and drove as fast as she could to get to her apartment.

She quickly ran into her apartment and slammed the door as if someone were chasing her. She paced the floor in her apartment, chanting Judy's words: "A happy mother equals a happy baby. God, I want my baby to be happy. I want to be happy. Help me," she cried out.

Saturday morning Misha woke up expecting the usual weakness and nausea. To her surprise, she felt like she had some energy. She bounced from the bed and cooked some grits, scrambled eggs, bacon, and toast. She had so much energy, she washed her clothes and cleaned her apartment without complaining.

She walked downstairs to the mailboxes and pulled out a stack of envelopes and returned to her apartment. On top of the stack was her first workers' compensation check. Misha ripped open the envelope and gasped at the amount. Now, she could pay her rent on time without asking for help, and still have money left over.

"A happy mother is a happy baby. Come on, miracle, we're getting a makeover."

She quickly dressed and headed for the mall, where she knew she did not need an appointment to get her hair cut. On the way there, she stopped by the bank located across the street from the mall and deposited her check.

The salon was crowded with ladies in various stages of getting their hair styled. Misha listened to the hodgepodge of conversations in the salon while the stylist wrapped her newly cut hair. She noticed three distinct themes in the salon: men, church, and hairstyles. The television and radio blasted over all the noise in the salon.

A stylist wearing latex gloves and holding a long, thin comb in her hand shouted for everyone to be quiet. She quickly turned off the radio and picked up the remote for the television and pressed the volume control.

Misha turned to focus on the television screen. She looked around the salon. It seemed as if everyone stopped what they were doing to look at the screen. It was a music video. She couldn't believe a music video would make the entire salon come to a standstill.

"That's my song," the lady said as she danced around the salon with her hands in the air. "Look at him. Y'all, that's my husband."

The women in the salon laughed at the woman's antics. "Girl, Bernard Taylor don't want you," another stylist screamed.

Bernard Taylor? That guy looks familiar. How do I know him? I haven't seen this video before. Misha thought as she stared at the video, *I know I know that guy.*

"You watch. Tonight at the concert, he's going to pull me out the crowd and he's gonna sing a slow, sweet tune in my ear. . . ." The stylist wrapped her arms around her body and pretended to slow dance. Then she screamed and threw her hands in the air, sending the comb she was holding flying across the room. "I got my tickets early. I'm in the third row."

Misha couldn't help but laugh at her antics too. The woman was so animated. "You ought to be ashamed of yourself. That man's a preacher. Besides, he don't want no black girl anyway."

The conversation went to whether he was white or black or both. They debated about his hair being natural or processed. They debated about everything they could think of about him. Then they began loudly discussing whether gospel artists were taking Jesus out of their music and trying to sound and look like hip-hop artists. Throughout the intense conversation, Misha kept wondering how she knew him. She had been down that road before and did not want to return.

Finally, after several hours, her hair was finished and she drove back to her apartment. She looked at the clock. She looked around her empty apartment and decided to go to the concert to avoid sitting alone one more night. Besides, the tickets were free and she might enjoy herself.

She tried on clothes to see which outfit she was going to wear. Soon realizing many of her clothes were fitting snugly around her waist, she sat on the bed, wondering if she should try to put on maternity clothes. She looked in the basket of clothing Judy had given her. She found a simple black skirt with the elastic panel on the front. She had her own fuchsia-colored tunic blouse that still fit her. It would go well with the skirt and would cover the front panel.

After dressing, she looked in the mirror. She did not look pregnant. That was good in case she ran into someone she knew. She did not want to explain anything to anyone who did not know her situation. Looking at her toes, admiring the free pedicure the salon gave her while she sat under the dryer, she chose a pair of black strappy heels to wear.

Misha left her apartment and drove to downtown Atlanta. As she got close to the theatre, hoards of people jumped out in front of her, trying to cross the street. She drove slowly until she found a parking space and followed the large crowd to the Fox Theatre.

There was a long line outside the box office. A large sign read SOLD OUT. A lady at the front held up the ticket line, trying to convince someone inside to sell her a ticket. Misha looked in her purse and pulled out the two tickets. She walked up to the lady and gave her the extra ticket she had. The woman looked at the ticket and started jumping up and down.

"Thank you. Thank you. Thank you. A front-row seat? You got to be kidding. How much are you selling it for?" the woman screamed.

"You can have it. Be blessed." Misha walked away. She looked at her ticket. She didn't realize Judy had front-row seats. She hated sitting in the front row at concerts. The speakers were always too loud. If she had known, she would have worn pants instead of a skirt. She didn't want Bernard Taylor to get a free show too. She stood back from the crowd and wrestled with going in the building or going back home. Since she was already there, she decided to stay, and if the music became unbearable, she would leave. She walked into the building and an usher escorted her to her seat that was in the center of the front row.

Misha looked around the beautifully decorated auditorium. People came in, filling the balcony and box seats. The lady she gave the ticket to came and sat down beside her.

"Hi, I'm Tequala. Thank you again for the ticket. All three of his shows are sold out." She reached out her hand to shake Misha's.

"Three shows? This guy is that popular? I never heard of him until a friend of mine gave me the tickets."

The lady's mouth flew open. "You never heard of Bernard Taylor? He's one of the biggest gospel singers in the country."

"Really?"

"Yeah, you'll like him. I have all his CDs."

The lights dimmed and the audience became silent. The opening act was a local group that sounded good to Misha, but the music was too loud and Tequala talked the entire time. After they finished, someone started to clap. It wasn't a demanding, get-the-show-started clap, it was a church clap. It seemed to Misha like everyone joined in. Then all of a sudden three women and a man came out on the stage, clapping their hands and dancing around the stage. Then a tall, light-skinned man walked out and the crowd leaped to their feet. Misha looked around and joined them. The energy was high and Misha was enjoying herself.

She recognized Bernard Taylor from the video she saw earlier at the salon. She watched him as he danced around the stage with the others. Then the women and the man walked over to some microphones that were set up at the side of the stage and began singing. Misha looked over at Tequala and she was singing along with them, her head steadily bouncing. *Everybody knows this song but me.* Misha stood with the crowd listening to him sing the first song. After he finished he asked the audience to sit down.

Bernard Taylor worked the crowd like the professional entertainer he was. He had everyone laughing and dancing. Everybody was so into the concert. Misha sat, staring at him. *I know I know this guy. How?* Finally, he said he was tired and someone brought him a tall stool and he sat down on it. The backup singers did the same thing.

Bernard Taylor talked about the goodness of God and how God has the ability to heal. He stopped briefly and stared directly at Misha. She stared right into his big brown eyes. For a brief moment, she could feel his pain. She could see his sorrow. She placed her hand on her heart. Her heart went out to him. She lowered her head and began to pray for him. Did anyone else notice he was trying to encourage himself?

As he continued singing a slow worship song Misha somehow knew he was in a personal battle. She could sense he was struggling with being accepted by the audience. She could almost hear his heart cry out, "Is there anyone here who truly loves me, not my music, not my money, but me?" Misha lowered her head again and continued praying.

When she raised her head, she noticed he was no longer singing and had walked over to the backup singers. One of them was singing a brief solo. While she was singing, he was whispering in the ear of one of the other ladies. They then looked in Misha's direction.

He returned to the front of the stage after each singer had their solo. "I have an announcement," he said. "This is my last tour. I started a church back home in DC, where I will serve as pastor. Touring takes a lot of time. I now have to give that time to my members."

The audience gasped.

"I will continue to write and record music," he continued. "From time to time, I will accept a concert. But, I will no longer do full tours."

During the rest of his concert, he continued to stare in Misha's direction. When their eyes met, he would turn and walk to the opposite side of the stage. Misha stared at him too, wondering if he went to Howard.

After the concert, Tequala thanked her again for the ticket and disappeared into the crowd. Misha stood in front of her seat, waiting for the crowd to move out of the auditorium before she headed for the door. When it looked like the mass of people had exited the hall, Misha picked her sweater up off the seat and turned to walk away, when she noticed Bernard Taylor staring at her from behind a stage curtain. *What's up with this guy?* She waved to him and walked up the aisle toward the door.

Outside in the lobby, she noticed the vendors were selling concert T-shirts, hats, and booklets. She walked up to the table and noticed the rows of CDs on the table. She asked for the latest one and purchased it. She left the auditorium happy she went to the concert but wondering what was wrong with Bernard Taylor. She vowed to keep him covered in prayer. He needed someone who didn't want anything from him to pray for him. That someone would be her.

Chapter 26

Misha lay on the exam table, listening to the swooshing sound of her baby's heartbeat. She focused her attention on the ultrasound picture, trying not to feel the coldness of the gel the doctor applied to her stomach.

"Can you tell if it's a boy or girl?" she asked.

"Not today. You're only sixteen weeks. Maybe the next time. But it looks like everything is progressing well." Dr. Trinidad took a tissue and wiped the gel off Misha's stomach. She reached behind Misha's back and helped her sit up. "We'll see you back in a couple of weeks to see how everything's going. If you have any problems before your next appointment, call my office immediately." She tore off the picture of the baby from the ultrasound machine and handed it to Misha. "Here's the picture of your ultrasound. How's that nausea doing?"

"It's much better. I barely have morning sickness now." Misha looked at the picture she held in her hand. She tried turning it around so she could get a better look, trying to see what the doctor saw.

After receiving her next appointment Misha left the office to face the August Georgia sun. She thought she was used to the Southern sun. But today it seemed hotter, hell hot. Misha walked to her car as fast as she could. She wanted to feel the breeze of the air conditioner. She started her engine and sat back and relaxed to the coolness of the air flowing in the car. She wiped the sweat from her brow and sighed. Her family had decided to have dinner at her grandmother's house. She was not looking forward to it. Her mother would be there. She did not want to face her mother's scorn, especially on a hot day like today.

Since she decided to keep the baby her mother had not had a good thing to say about it. Misha tried to avoid talking to her as much as she could. In the past few weeks, she had decided she was going to do things that made her happy and one of those things was to avoid her mother at all costs. However, today, she was unavoidable.

On her drive, Misha thought about how much she had grown with all the turmoil that had gone on in her life in the past year. Now, things were beginning to look up for her. She was studying for her exams in her classes at Clark Atlanta. She was pleased her professors had given her an incomplete due to the attack and not a failing grade. She planned to take her exams and a couple of classes until she delivered her baby. She had joined an exercise class for pregnant women that Dr. Trinidad referred her to. She was also in a support group at the rape crisis center. She became more involved with the singles group at her church, even though her pastor told her she could not preach at his church. She did not question it. It was probably some of Bishop Moore's doing.

She did not want anything negative in her life. She wanted a happy baby. She sang the alphabet song aloud in her car until she pulled into the driveway at her grandmother's home. Other family members were already there. She sat in the car and directed the flow of the air conditioner to her face. After sitting for a brief moment, she walked into the house.

Loud chatter filled the house as the family gathered to celebrate her grandmother's birthday. Her mother was fussing at everyone as usual. Misha tried to avoid her by talking to her aunt and uncle and her cousins. Children ran in and out of the house. Her mother screamed at them, telling them to stay outside. Misha sat next to her grandmother.

"Grandma, I am almost done with my quilt. I think I'll bring it over here next week and you can show me how to finish it up."

"That will be okay. Call first. I'm going on a trip with the group from the senior center next week. We going up to Chattanooga to the museums and shopping. Staying overnight. But, I'll help you."

Her mother stopped what she was doing and faced her with her hands on her hips. Misha looked at her and for the first time she realized her mother looked like a younger, fatter version of her grandmother. "Mama, I told you I could not go on that trip," she yelled.

"I know. That's why Mattie going with me." Her mother huffed and left the room again.

Aunt Mattie hugged Misha. "Look at you. You're getting out there."

"I just left the doctor's office. She said everything is fine. Look, I have the ultrasound." She handed the picture to her aunt and everybody, except her mother, stopped working and passed the picture around the room. Finally, Misha was able to get the picture and place it in her purse. "What y'all want me to do?"

"Sit down. You can't do any heavy lifting in your condition," Aunt Mattie said.

"Aunt Mattie, I can do something."

"Go in the bedroom and get that fan in the closet and bring it in here. All these people are overworking the air conditioning and we need to get the air circulating," Misha's mother demanded.

Misha walked into her grandmother's bedroom. She looked around. It looked so small. When she was a child, the bedroom and the whole house looked huge. She thought her grandmother lived in the biggest house in the world. But that day, it seemed so small and cramped. Her grandmother's handmade curtains still covered the tiny window that looked out into the backyard. She caressed the antique dresser and mirror her grandparents had since they had gotten married. She walked over to the bed and followed the seams of the handmade quilt that covered the bed. She took a long, deep breath and let it out to relax the memories that engulfed the room.

She opened the closet and pulled out one of her grandmother's house dresses she wore every day. Misha hugged and smelled it, trying to take in a hint of her grandmother's scent. It still smelled like her. She became overwhelmed with emotion. She looked on the shelf and spotted her grandmother's hats. She picked up one of her hats and walked to the mirror and tried it on. The hat was so small it did not fit her head. Misha stood, looking in the mirror, trying to see her grandmother instead of her reflection. She could feel herself about to cry. She was so emotional lately. *A happy mother equals a happy child.* She took the hat off and placed it on the bed.

"We don't have time for you to play dress up." Her mother was standing in the doorway, looking at her try on the hat.

"I only tried it on. I'm just getting the fan." Misha flipped around and headed for the closet where the fan sat.

"That don't look like a fan to me. Step aside. I'll get it. You don't need to be lifting anything. You might hurt the baby." Her mother reached on to the shelf and pulled down the small desk fan and left the room.

What just happened? Her mother helped her? Misha could not believe it. And, she mentioned the baby. She usually didn't have anything good to say.

Ask her if she wants to see the picture.

Misha followed her mother out of the room. "Mama, I had an ultrasound today. Do you want to see the picture?" Misha did not wait for her to answer. She handed her the picture. Her mother stared at the picture. Then, she turned it in different directions. Misha started to laugh. "That's the same thing I did when Dr. Trinidad gave me the picture."

Her mother handed the picture back to her. "Here. We're wasting time. Food should be ready in a minute."

Misha's cell phone rang. She looked at the caller ID. It was Eric, her attorney. "Hi, Eric. Give me the good news." She closed the door to her grandmother's room and sat on the bed.

"I wish I had some for you. The State is refusing to pay for your prenatal care. Their attorney says they can't determine if the baby belonged to Heckler. But that's okay. It's just legal maneuvers. When the baby's born, we can do a DNA test. Are you absolutely positive your baby is Heckler's?"

"I told you I had not had sex in years before the rape. I have not had sex since. He's the only one who can be the father." Misha's hand trembled. She needed the State to pay her medical expenses. Trying to pay her health insurance on the workers' comp check was taking a toll on her finances.

"Calm down. I'm on your side. I have to ask you these things. One more thing. We scheduled a deposition for you, Amber, and several students who were in your class the day of the attack. Your deposition will be next week."

"Deposition? What's that?"

"It's nothing you need to be worried about. The attorneys for the State want to ask you some questions about what happened that day. They want to know why you were in the field house the day of the attack. I'll be there with you. I'll probably ask you a few questions to clarify your answers to them. It's routine in most comp cases. You'll be fine."

"If you say so."

Eric gave Misha the time and date of the deposition and ended their conversation, trying to assure her everything would work out. He told her he thought she could possibly get $1 million from the consulting firm for the assault and the baby. Somehow, this information did not make her happy. She sat on the edge of the bed and began to pray God move the State attorneys to allow her to get assistance with medical care and pay for her insurance premiums, at least until the baby was born.

"We don't have time for you to sit around daydreaming."

Misha looked up. Her mother was standing in front of her. "I wasn't daydreaming. I just finished talking to my attorney."

"What did he say?" Her mother eased closer to her.

"Looks like I'm going to get a lot of money to take care of Miracle." Misha stood, her head hung low.

"How much money?"

"He doesn't know yet. I've got to do a deposition first. He thinks I could probably get a million dollars."

"A million dollars? What?" Her mother wrapped her arms tightly around Misha, startling her. "Y'all, Misha's attorney said she's going to get a million dollars for the baby." People ran into the room, excited and congratulating her.

"Wait a minute, everybody. It's not a done deal yet. We have a long way to go first and the State can decide not to settle."

"Oh they can't deny my grandbaby the money she deserves."

Your grandbaby? Who is this woman? Misha looked at her mother hugging Uncle Paul. She almost laughed out loud. She knew her mother was only thinking about herself. "Everybody calm down. We still have a long way to go. They need a DNA test to be sure it's Heckler's. So I won't know anything until after the baby's born."

"Well, they're going to give my granddaughter everything she deserves. I'll see to it." Her mother swung the towel she held in her hand over her shoulder.

"Your granddaughter? How do you know I'm having a girl? My doctor couldn't even tell."

"You showed me the picture. Besides, you're carrying high. It's a girl."

"No. Looks like she's carrying low to me. It's a boy." Aunt Mattie chimed in, setting off a debate on the sex of the baby as everybody returned to their chores. Misha sat on the edge of the bed. Her father came up to her and hugged her.

"What was that for?"

"Making up with your mama."

"I was never mad at her. I don't want anything negative or any negative people around me. I want a happy baby."

Her father sat down on the bed beside her. "Your mama worries about you. I know. I live with her. She talks about you day and night. When everything happened, I thought I was going to have to put her in a mental hospital. She took it real hard and it wasn't one of her acts. We've been married a long time and I can tell when she's putting on."

"I don't want either one of you to be worried about me."

"You're our child and we do worry about you and Justin. After your attack, your mother changed. I've never seen her like this before. She doesn't even want to shop."

"Mama's not shopping?" Misha's eyes stretched.

"She hasn't been shopping since you got hurt. I had to take her to the doctor. He put her on some pills for depression. She don't take them except when she can't sleep."

"She's on medication?" For many years Misha thought her mother should have been on medication for what she thought were mood swings. She did not want her to be on medication because of what happened to her. "Dad, why didn't you tell me?"

"We didn't want you to be worried. She's coming out of it though. She's excited about the baby."

"How can you tell? She hadn't said anything positive until today."

"That's because you're beginning to learn how to speak her language."

"Her language?"

"Yeah: money." Both of them laughed as her father struggled to get up from the edge of the bed. "Let me get in here before she comes looking for me. You need anything?"

"Is the food ready? Miracle's hungry."

"No. I'll tell your mama you're hungry. I'm sure she'll get this party started." He walked toward the door and stopped. "Missy, if you need anything, money or anything, call us. We want to help you, and remember your mama the next time you go to the doctor okay?"

"Okay." Misha sat on the bed, surprised about the conversation she had with her father. She had no idea her mother was on antidepressant medication and was having problems because of her. She repented for everything she thought about her mother and she prayed God heal her mother's heart and their relationship.

Chapter 27

The excitement of the Sunday morning message left Misha inspired and encouraged. Her heart was happy as she eased her way out of the pew toward the aisle. She wanted to beat the rush to the media desk to purchase a recording of the morning service. However, it did not look like she was going to make it. People kept stopping her, telling her how big she was getting. She was also getting used to the debate on whether she was having a girl or boy that she heard at least three times each Sunday before leaving church.

She finally arrived at the media desk. They were sold out and she would have to wait until they made some more tapes. While she waited, Sherrell, the singles minister, approached her.

"Misha, girl, look how big you're getting. Walk over here with me for a minute." Misha followed her to the other side of the room. Sherrell moved in close to her and began to whisper. "I'm having a cookout at my house tomorrow. You're invited if you don't have anything to do. I'm whispering because I don't want everybody to know. I can only invite a few people. Do you have any plans?"

"School's out for Labor Day. As far as I know, my family hasn't planned anything."

"Good. We should get started about four."

"You want me to bring anything?"

"No, I got everything. Just come and relax. It should be fun."

"Thank you for inviting me."

Sherrell gave her directions to her home and walked away. Misha returned to the desk in time to purchase the last CD and left the church. She thought about Sherrell's invitation. They were not close friends. Why would she get an invitation when no one else did?

When she arrived home, she went to her closet to see if she had anything to wear to a cookout. She wanted to look like a cute pregnant woman. She was tired of wearing the overalls Pam and Judy had given her. She tried on several outfits until she was satisfied with a sundress she had purchased.

The next day, she debated on whether she should go to the cookout. She wasn't really close to anyone at the church. She barely knew Sherrell. She felt going to the picnic was the least she could do for all the support Sherrell had given her since the assault. She was the only one from the church who called her weekly to see if she needed anything.

She got dressed and went to the picnic. As she neared the house, she saw a grocery store and decided to run in and get a cake, strawberries, ice cream, and whipped cream to make strawberry shortcake. She didn't want to go to the house empty-handed.

She walked into the store and took a cart and began her shopping. She turned the corner on to an aisle and almost rammed her cart into Roger. "Roger? What are you doing on this side of town?" Roger was standing beside a woman who took his arm when Misha spoke to him, obviously letting her know she was with him.

"Misha? You're pregnant?" He stared at her large belly.

"What? I'm pregnant? How did that happen?" Misha started laughing. "Funny seeing you here."

"Oh we're having a private cookout at my place. Hi, I'm Alexis. Roger's girlfriend."

Roger continued staring at Misha's pregnant belly. "I'm sorry. Misha, this is Alexis. Misha and I went into the ministry under Bishop Moore."

"You're a minister?" Alexis asked. She turned up her nose as if she smelled spoiled milk.

"Yes, I am. Roger, how's everything at Westdale? I sure miss my kids."

"Huh? Westdale?" He lifted his head to focus on her face. The conversation was too much for him, or was it the pregnancy?

"He's a guidance counselor there now. He left the City Development League. It's a better job with better benefits."

"A guidance counselor? Congratulations."

"I bet your husband is excited about the baby." Misha could tell Alexis sensed something more was going on between her and Roger.

"I'm not married."

"You're not married?" Misha could see her face turn up like she was looking at low-life trash. "But you're pregnant and in the ministry?"

Misha grew tired of the conversation and excused herself from them. She decided against the strawberry shortcake idea she walked into the store with. Instead, she purchased an ice cream cake and left the store.

"Misha, wait." She heard Roger's voice behind her.

Not today. She unlocked her car and placed the ice cream cake on the floor on the passenger's side. "What do you want, Roger?"

"So I guess you are not as perfect as everyone thought you were. You are still the same old woman I met at Howard."

Misha slammed the passenger door and walked around her car to the driver's side. "I'm not going to entertain you today, Roger."

"You wouldn't have sex with me. Obviously, you found someone else to your liking. Maybe you had someone else all along."

Misha wanted to remind him what happened to her. She hesitated, and then opened her car door. "Roger, you have a nice life."

"Everybody thought you were so perfect. You took my life away from me. I rescued you and what did you do? You took my life." Roger grabbed the car door, pinning Misha against her car.

"Roger, stop it. What are you talking about?"

"You were nothing but a whore when I met you. I cleaned you up and took you to church. Suddenly, everything was all about you." He stepped back. "Everybody was saying, 'Misha can do this. Get Misha to do that. Misha is so great she is a blessing to the body of Christ.' It was like I wasn't raised in that church. Before you, it was me. Then, you took over and I had to sit back and watch you get all the awards and praise for the work I spent years doing."

"I can't believe what I am hearing. You were jealous of me? Is that what this is all about?" Misha shoved him away from her. "Is that why you tried to destroy my life and make everybody think I was crazy? Jealous?"

Misha pointed her finger in Roger's face. "Let me tell you something. I was *never* anybody's whore. You didn't do *jack* for me. You didn't take me to church. I was *raised* in the church." She lowered her hand and held on to her car door. "As for the other stuff, I worked my behind off because I loved the Lord. Not you, but God. I cannot help it if He rewarded me openly. If you hadn't been such a lying slime ball, God would have blessed you too."

Roger balled his fist and drew back as if he were going to punch Misha.

"Try it. I dare you. You know where I came from. Don't let this baby fool you. I can still protect myself."

Roger laughed. "Like you did with Heckler." He laughed again.

"I'm here. He didn't kill me or Amber. I saved her life." She looked toward the store and saw Alexis fast approaching them. "Here comes your girlfriend. You need to get your life together and stop blaming other people for your problems. I've got to go."

She dipped into her car and started the ignition. The wheels on her car squealed as she exited the parking lot. She was not far from Sherrell's home and quickly arrived in the small subdivision.

It was almost four-thirty and a lot of people were already there. She took a deep breath. She was not going to let Roger ruin her day. Reaching up and flipping the sun visor down, she popped up the small mirror. She peered into the mirror making sure her hair was in place and there were no signs of the confrontation with Roger on her face. She leaned on the passenger's side and picked up the now-soft cake and exited her car.

She walked to the door and rang the doorbell. No one answered. She knew people were there because she could hear a lot of people talking. She walked around the house and saw a large crowd of people in the backyard. There was loud music playing and children were running around everywhere. She noticed Sherrell coming out of the back door of the house, carrying a large platter of food to place on the grill.

Although she was more on the heavy side than skinny, she was casually dressed in a tank top and shorts. Sherrell yelled at some children running around on the wooden deck. She looked up and spotted Misha holding her cake.

"Hey, Misha. Glad you came. Come on over."

Misha walked up on the deck as Sherrell handed a man the large platter she was holding. After they hugged Misha informed her she had an ice cream cake that needed to be placed in the freezer. Sherrell took it and invited Misha into her home.

Misha looked around the kitchen. It was beautifully decorated. It looked like something out of *Better Homes and Gardens*. Misha did not expect Sherrell to live in such a large home. She was a single parent taking care of two children on her own. Misha thought she was struggling like all the stereotypes of single parents. She surely did not expect a large home in a beautiful subdivision.

"Thanks for the cake. The kids are going to love this," Sherrell said as she placed the cake in the freezer.

"I didn't expect so many people to be here."

"It's just family. I'm careful about who I invite to my home from the church. Some people talk too much."

"Why did you invite me? I mean, we haven't known each other long."

"The Lord told me I can trust you and to invite you. You're a prophetess and I know a lot of people don't understand you. But you're a woman of God. Pastor must be crazy not letting you preach."

"How did you know about that?"

"When you're over a ministry, you hear everything. I think Pastor's scared people would like you more than him. He knows you're a prophetess."

"I'm not a prophetess," Misha said.

Sherrell invited Misha to sit down with her at a small table in front of a bay window that looked out over the deck and backyard. People were scattered throughout the yard talking and laughing. Two small children played in a small plastic pool near the deck.

"I've watched you and listened to you since you walked into our church. The Lord told me you were a prophet and you were ordained to be at the church. I don't know why you're there. It's none of my business. I know God has a mighty work for you," Sherrell said.

"I enjoy attending the church. Pastor preached to me yesterday."

"Pastor can preach. Today, no shop talk. We're going to have some fun. Come on. I'll introduce you to everybody." Sherrell stood.

Misha followed Sherrell outside and she introduced Misha to her parents, aunts, and cousins. Misha was talking with Sherrell's uncle at the grill when she noticed Bernard Taylor walking into the yard. *Bernard Taylor's here? How does Sherrell know Bernard Taylor?*

Everybody stopped what they were doing and ran toward him. He picked up Sherrell's daughter and hugged her, smiling. He spotted Misha standing behind his uncle, next to the grill. Their eyes met. A wide smile spread across his face. He knew exactly who she was. He never forgot her face. Suddenly she spun around and faced his cousin, Sherrell.

At the grill, Misha was stunned. "What is Bernard Taylor doing here?" she asked Sherrell.

"He's my first cousin. My mother and his mother are sisters. I invited him. He's in town a few days finishing up his new CD."

"I thought he was going to pastor a church or something."

"He is but he still has his music. You want to meet him?"

"Maybe later." Misha throat went dry. She reached for a cup of lemonade when she heard his voice.

"Hey, cuz. Look at you. I went by Jenny's house and she wanted me to tell you to stop by and see her sometime." Bernard voice was so close behind her.

"I know you're setting me up. Jenny who?" Sherrell twisted her mouth.

"Jenny Craig." He laughed as he hugged Sherrell.

"You tell Jenny ain't nothing like a big black booty to satisfy a brother." They began talking trash back and forth.

Misha was afraid to turn around. She slowly started walking away.

"Hey, Misha, wait. I want you to meet my cousin."

Misha turned around.

"Misha, this is my cousin, Bernard Taylor. Misha goes to my church."

He stared at her. He looked down at her obviously pregnant belly and looked at her face again. "You're pregnant?"

Misha's hand flew to her mouth. "What? Is that what's wrong with me? No wonder Jenny didn't want me to drop by her house." Misha tried to talk the same trash they were talking. It did not work. He continued to stare at her. His mouth curved to a frown. He looked disappointed.

"Spanky, Mama wants you," Sherrell said to Bernard.

"What?" He focused on Sherrell.

"Mama's calling you."

"Oh. Well, it was nice meeting you, Misha."

They watched him walk away. "What did you do to my cousin? It's rare he's quiet like that. He acted like he's never seen a pregnant woman before."

"I don't know. I was trying to be funny. I guess that was an inside joke." She took a sip of her lemonade.

"I don't pay him any attention. He's always talking about somebody being fat. Not everyone can be like those anorexic celebrities he hangs around." She embraced her uncle's shoulder as he perched over the grill, flipping hamburgers. "Uncle Jake, is that food ready?"

"Five mo' minutes."

"Good because I'm hungry. Come on, Misha, let's go sit down."

Misha was enjoying herself, although the hot Labor Day sun was beaming down on her and she was sweating horribly. She enjoyed the two plates of food Uncle Jake gave her that were filled with a sample of all the food he had prepared. People were laughing at Misha, telling her she was "down-home folk" because she wasn't afraid to eat in front of them. She did not care. She played along with them, telling them that Miracle was hungry.

A couple of hours in the hot sun were doing a number on Misha. She had to get into some air conditioning. After getting the okay from Sherrell, she walked into the house for some cooling relief.

She stood in Sherrell's spacious family room and looked at the pictures and degrees that filled the room. She was surprised to see that Sherrell had a PhD in biomedical engineering. She knew she worked for the Centers for Disease Control but she did not know she was Dr. Sherrell Cunningham. The tap of footsteps on the hardwood floor caused Misha to turn around.

"Excuse me. I didn't know anyone was in here," Bernard said as he turned toward the door.

"No, don't leave. I came in to cool off some. But, I can leave if you want me to."

"I heard pregnant women are hotter than anybody else."

"I heard that too. It's true. I'll only be a minute." She looked over at the degree on the wall. "I didn't know Sherrell had a PhD."

"She's real smart. She's doing what she likes. I don't understand how she does it. She's a strong woman."

"I know."

Bernard walked into the room and sat on the sofa. "When's your baby due?"

"In January. I'm twenty weeks now. I'm already waiting for this to be over." Misha rubbed her belly.

"Your husband must be excited. Is this your first?"

"I'm not married. This is my first child."

"You're not married?"

"No. My baby's dad is dead."

"Dead for real or in your mind?"

Misha chuckled at his question. "No, he's dead. He was killed. So I'm doing this alone."

Silence filled the room as both of them wondered what to say next. Misha headed for the door.

"You don't remember me do you?" Bernard asked.

Misha stopped. "Well, you're Bernard Taylor. I went to your concert at the Fox a couple of months ago. I was on the front row."

"I know. I remember you. That's not what I'm talking about." He stood and walked up to her.

"You know, there's something about you. I thought you looked familiar. How do we know each other?"

He put his hand on his hip and walked in a circle. He said in a high-pitched voice, "Not every woman who sees you wants you. Not every woman who hears you sing wants you."

"What?" Misha was confused.

He repeated himself, walking around the room with his hand on his hip. He stopped and approached her with outstretched hands. "Don't you remember? We met at a rib joint one night. You told me not every woman who sees me wants me . . ."

"Ooooooooh. That was you? I didn't recognize you without the two goons who were with you." Misha laughed so loudly she reminded herself of her grand-mother.

"Well?"

"Well what?" Misha asked.

"Aren't you going to apologize to me?"

"For what?"

"For insulting me?"

"I didn't insult you." She continued laughing and sat down on the sofa. "I offended you?"

"Yes, you did. You didn't have to go off on me like that. That was cold."

"I apologize for how I said what I said. I won't apolo-gize for what I said. You were trying to pick me up with that lame line about the time. I'm not a one-night stand no matter what it looks like now."

"What about now?" He sat down on the sofa beside her. "Did you love him?"

"Who?"

"Your baby's father."

"You are getting too personal. I don't want to talk about him." She stood up again and walked to the op-posite wall and leaned on it. He stood.

"I'm sorry. I didn't mean—"

"I know." Misha folded her arms on top of her belly.

"I guess I better go back outside." He started walking toward the door.

Tell him I love him.

"What?" Misha questioned the voice.

He stopped and turned to face her. "Did you say something?" She shook her head no. He turned to con-tinue his trek toward the door.

Tell him I love him.

"Pastor."

Bernard turned to face her again.

"God loves you."

"What?"

"God said to tell you He loves you."

He walked back to her.

"God loves you. You have to believe that deep in your heart. God loves you."

"You know, I prayed this morning that God show me He loves me. I needed to know for more reasons than I want to explain. Then you say something like that to me and you didn't even know what I prayed this morning."

"Since your concert, I've been praying for you."

"You have?"

"I saw you up there dancing and joking around as if nothing were wrong. But, I could see you were in a struggle. It was almost like I heard a cry from your heart seeking to know if there was anyone in the building who loved you for you and not for your fame or money. I prayed for you during the concert and have prayed for you every day since. I believe we were ordained by God to meet. You need to know there is someone out there praying for you. Someone who doesn't want anything from you in return."

Misha walked to him and touched his shoulder. His eyes were filled with tears.

Tell him to take out his contacts.

"Pastor. Could you take out your contacts?"

He looked at her for a brief moment. Then he walked to a mirror over the fireplace and took them out and turned around.

Misha gasped. "Wow." Misha stared into his eyes, his deep blue eyes. "You have beautiful eyes." There was something familiar about his eyes, sea blue and inviting.

Ask him if he needs the contacts to see.

"Do you need those contacts to see?"

"No."

Misha walked over to him and turned him to face the mirror. She looked at him as he tried to hold back tears. Her heart went out to him. She looked at his curly dark blond hair that was cut so evenly and neatly lined up around his face. The deep dimples that lined his cheeks were pleasing to her even when he wasn't smiling. This was one good-looking man. But, she had to focus and get back into ministry mode.

"Pastor, we all have struggled with things in our lives. Right now, I'm in a personal struggle being a single, pregnant minister."

"You're a minister?"

"Yes. I'm a minister. However, it's been awhile since I've preached anywhere. God has me in individual ministry now. He sends me places to minister to people in need. You know it's amazing how God moves. He said in His word he would not leave us without a comforter."

"I know."

"It's like every time we get discouraged he sends someone or something to encourage us. He sends that comforter."

Bernard listened intently as she ministered to him. Finally he allowed himself to cry and she caressed his back to let him know everything would be all right.

"Pastor, I don't know what your struggle is but I want you to know one thing."

"What's that?"

"You're a beautiful person. One day, it is my prayer you see the beauty that lies in you."

He sniffed back tears. She looked at him. Somehow she knew he needed to cry to release his struggle and to be free from the bondage he was in.

After he calmed down, she decided it was time for her to leave. She felt she had done the will of God and her work was finished. "Everybody's probably wondering where we are. I better get back outside. Besides, Miracle is hungry."

"Miracle?"

"My baby."

"That's your baby's name?"

"No. I call my baby Miracle because one day a doctor looked me in the face and told me it would take a miracle for me to get pregnant. So I call this child Miracle."

"You are a woman of great faith."

"I am who God says I am and nothing more. I better get outside and feed Miracle. If you need a listening ear, Sherrell has my number. I'll keep you in my prayers." Misha walked out of the house, leaving him standing alone, wondering about this incredible woman he just met.

Chapter 28

"I knew it." Misha's mother screamed with delight of the news the doctor had given them. "You were carrying high. I told you. I carried high when I had you."

"Miss Holloway, you should have listened to your mother. Looks like it's a girl all right. Let me get this gel off of you. Then you can sit up."

Misha waited until the doctor finished wiping the gel off her stomach and she sat up on the exam table. She looked at her mother, who seemed like she was glowing in her victory. Misha was happy she was having a girl. She would have been happy having a boy. She was happy because everything looked normal and her pregnancy was progressing without incident.

"Is this your first grandchild?" Dr. Trinidad asked.

"No, my third. My son has a girl and a boy. This is different. This is my daughter who's having a baby. It feels different. It's so exciting to have a new baby coming into the family."

Misha looked at her mother and the doctor talking to each other, wondering who was talking to the doctor. Her mother's face shined with excitement. Her father told her she was doing much better since Misha had involved her in everything about the baby. Her mother wanted to go shopping for the baby after the doctor's appointment, but Misha had a class at Clark.

Now that she was twenty-four weeks pregnant she was beginning to feel the effects of her pregnancy.

There were days when she would have a lot of energy and there were other days when she did not have any energy at all. Every day she was hungry. She had never eaten so much. Dr. Trinidad warned her about gaining too much weight during her pregnancy. Even with her exercise class, she could not manage to stave off the weight gain.

Misha pushed open the door to the doctor's office when her phone chimed. The caller ID number was unavailable.

"Who's that?" her mother asked.

"I don't know. I better answer it." Misha pressed the button and placed the phone to her ear. "Hello."

"May I speak with Misha Holloway please?"

"This is Misha."

"Hi, it's Bernard Taylor."

Misha quickly turned to see how close her mother was to her. This was one phone call she did not want her mother to hear. In a very professional, proper tone, she said, "Hi, Pastor. How are you this morning?"

Her mother turned and walked toward the car. Misha walked slowly behind her.

"I hope I didn't catch you at a bad time."

"My mother and I just left the doctor's office."

"Doctor? Is anything wrong?"

"No. Just my monthly appointment. What can I help you with?" Misha got into the car and continued her conversation as her mother drove her back home.

"Well, I'm in town for a few days. I was wondering if we could get together."

"What's wrong?" She could hear the hesitation in his voice. For some reason, she could tell something was wrong with him. He had been heavy in her spirit and she prayed harder for him each day. She knew he was going to call. She could not tell him because her mother was in the car listening to every word coming out of her mouth. Misha knew she was trying to determine what the conversation was about. That's just how her mother was and that was something about her that hadn't changed.

"I just wanted to talk."

"Okay. Can you call me later? I have a class in about an hour. Then I can get back to you on that matter."

"You're not alone."

Misha switched the phone to her other ear. "That's right. My class at Clark ends at noon. I should be at home about thirty minutes after that. I can call you . . ." She remembered she did not have his number. "Or you can call me back. If it's urgent we can discuss it now."

"No. I'll call you back. You said about twelve-thirty?"

"Yes. I should be back home by then."

"I'll call then. Thanks. Have a good day in class."

Misha closed her phone and waited for her mother to ask about her conversation. *Five, four, three, two, one . . .*

"Who was that?"

"That was just Pastor. Sherrell, the singles minister at the church, gave him my number. He's going to call me back after class," Misha said nonchalantly. She was surprised this seemed to satisfy her mother's curiosity.

"So what are we going to name her?" Her mother glanced over at her.

"We?"

"We can call her Julia."

"Julia? Mom, that's such an ol'-timey name. Grandma wants me to call her Elizabeth."

"Elizabeth?"

Misha told her about the day she was going to have an abortion and how Aunt Mattie and her grandmother came over and gave her the gift.

"Mattie should mind her own business. If Mama had bought you a gift, I would have known about it."

Misha wished she had not told her about the gift. Her mother returned to her normal self and she was so negative. Misha could not wait for them to reach her apartment. She definitely did not want to go shopping with her mother acting the way she was acting. She felt so free when she finally reached her apartment. Her mother had a way of draining her energy.

When she walked into the apartment she was so tired she decided not to go to class. She had a craving for dry Honeycombs. She walked to her kitchen and opened her cabinet door. She took out the box of Honeycombs and reached her hand inside. As she placed the dry cereal in her mouth, she thought about the phone call she received from Bernard. She put the box down and sat on the sofa and began to pray.

It was after two when he called her back. Misha had settled into her afternoon nap and was awakened by the sound of her cell phone ringing.

"Did I wake you?"

"No, I'm up. How can I help you?" She struggled to get up from the bed.

"Well, I was in town and I thought about the last time I was here, our conversation. You didn't tell Sherrell."

"I didn't think she needed to know. It was between you, me, and God. Did you want me to talk to her?"

"No. I'm glad you didn't. Thank you."

"Pastor, you may not believe this but I knew you were going to call me. You have been heavy in my spirit the past few days. I have been praying hard for you. I don't know what's happening with you right now. God has assigned me to intercede for you."

"Thank you for praying for me. I don't want to talk on the phone. Can we meet somewhere? Are you at home?"

"Uh. Pastor, I usually don't let men in my apartment." Misha could tell from the sound of his voice he needed someone to talk to.

Invite him to your apartment.

"We can meet somewhere."

"Pastor, I'll tell you what, why don't you come over here? I think you're safe. Besides, I feel you need some privacy right now. I don't know you. I trust the Holy Spirit and I feel in my spirit it will be fine."

Misha gave him directions to her apartment. When she hung up the phone, she looked around her apartment. "Oh my goodness. Bernard Taylor is coming to my house." Misha began running, moving things around in the apartment. She checked her plug-in air freshener to make sure her apartment had the calming scent of vanilla. She made up her bed. "I know he's not coming in my bedroom. But, Miracle, if he tries, we can clock him." She talked to her baby as she cleaned her apartment.

She continued doing little things around the apartment. She wanted it to look perfect. Bernard Taylor was used to going into mansions of celebrities, not a small apartment of someone living on a teacher's salary. She placed her Bible on the coffee table, opened it, and placed an ink pen inside. She set her Bible Study notebook beside it to make it look as if she was studying. Placing a finger to her lips, she looked at it. *Too fake.*

Moving the Bible, she put her Dynamics of Instructional Learning book on the table alongside her book bag and her notebook from class. Then she turned on her CD player. Mary J. Blige's voice rang out. She quickly stopped the music and looked for another CD. She put in CeCe Winans and played the music softly until she heard a knock on the door. She hesitated and looked around her apartment. Confident that it was presentable, she opened the door.

"Hi, Pastor, come on in."

He entered her apartment, wearing baggy jeans and a long button-down striped shirt. She looked at his shoes. He was still wearing those cheap tennis shoes. She watched him look around her apartment as she closed the door.

"Have a seat. Make yourself at home."

He moved to the sofa and sat down. She saw him looking at her books on the coffee table. "I was trying to catch up on my studying."

"So you went back to college?"

"I'm working on my master's in education at Clark Atlanta. I'm in my second semester."

"You're a teacher?"

"I'm on medical leave right now. Can I get you anything to drink? I think I have some milk and bottled water. The strongest thing I have is probably diet, caffeine-free soda. Can I get you something?"

"No, I'm fine."

Misha sat down in the side chair. "So, Pastor, what can I do for you?"

"I don't know. I wanted to talk. You said if I needed to talk . . ."

"Pastor, let's pray." Misha sat down beside him on the sofa and took his hand and began to pray. She could feel him squeeze her hand hard. The more he squeezed her hand the harder she prayed. When she finished and opened her eyes, she noticed his blue eyes. "You're not wearing your contacts today."

"I thought you would ask me to take them out. You're the only one who told me to do that. I thought I would save you the trouble."

"Why do you wear those anyway? I mean you have beautiful eyes. Why would you want to cover them up?"

He stood and walked around the room. Stopping in front of her framed degree he asked, "You went to Howard?"

"I did my undergrad there. I wanted to get as far away from Georgia as I could. I was younger then. I didn't appreciate the area."

"That's the same thing my mama said. She went to Howard too." For a short time they compared notes about Howard and all the activities, especially homecoming and the band.

"You went to Howard?"

"No. I went to FAMU."

"That was my second choice. It was too close to Georgia. I knew I wanted to go to an HBCU." Misha walked to him and stood beside him. "So your dad's white?"

"Why would you say something like that?"

"Are you embarrassed?"

"No. My dad is great. He went to Georgetown."

"Are your parents married?"

"Almost thirty years."

"Then what's the problem? Why are you here?"

He looked at her and moved back to the sofa. "Can I have some water?"

"Sure, come on in the kitchen with me." He followed her into the kitchen. She reached into a cabinet, pulling out a glass and handing it to him. "Would you like ice?"

"No, I can drink it from the bottle." He handed the glass back to her. She directed him to sit at her small dining table.

She sat for a moment, watching him drink the water straight from the bottle.

Tell him your baby is biracial.

Misha took a deep breath and released it. "You know our meeting was not by chance. I believe God ordained us to meet for such a time as this."

"What do you mean?"

"Miracle. Well, she's biracial. Her father was white. I know people are more tolerant now. But, I can't imagine what she's going to go through in her life. People can be so cruel sometimes. I believe God sent you to me to prepare me to mother this child."

They sat at the small table and talked about Bernard's life growing up as a child of an interracial couple.

"The children called me all kinds of names: ghost, white boy, and red. Because my eyes were blue they called me cat. I hated those names. I used to fight all the time." He lifted the bottled water to his lips and took a sip. "It got so bad my parents took me out of public school and put me in private."

"I bet that helped," Misha said.

"Not hardly. The private school was predominately white. The kids there had different names like baboon, jigaboo, and let's not forget nigga."

Misha could tell he still had trouble with his identity. He was on the brink of tears talking to her about the abuse even teachers and family members placed on him. She allowed him to release all that kept him in bondage throughout his life.

"That's why I went to FAMU. There, I was a light-skinned black man. I started wearing the brown contacts then. My eyes were the first thing people noticed."

"You have beautiful eyes."

"I didn't feel like it. I wanted to be as black as I could. I think I went overboard a little. That's why I pledged—to be a part of the black experience."

He went on to explain how he thought the ridicule would end once he became a celebrity; instead, it got worse. Now, he had the media questioning his blackness. People still came up to him and asked him what type of chemicals he had in his hair. Even when he appeared on Christian television, people would question his sincerity and ask him questions about white people trying to act black. It was bondage he had never told anyone before.

Misha listened as he released his emotions about his struggle. His mother was black and she was a student at Howard when she met his father, a white student at Georgetown. His parents were very successful, both of them doctors. They faced many obstacles while dating and during their marriage. However, they tried to protect him and his sister. But, when he went to school, the abuse started. Not only did it come from the students, but from some of the teachers, too. Some of the adults and children alike in the community treated him as if he were diseased and if they got close, they would catch it.

He felt alone. He never had anyone to talk to until he met Misha. He could tell her how it felt having to wrestle with being too dark to be white and too light to be black and not being accepted by either, even some members of his own family. But she did not look at him that way. He released years of pent-up emotions, thoughts, and feelings.

"Look at the time. I've been talking over three hours," Bernard said, looking at his watch.

"What? Really? It didn't seem like it. Can I get you some more water?" Misha said, noticing his empty water bottle.

"No. May I use your bathroom?"

"It's down the hall—first door on the right."

Misha stood to stretch her legs and tossed the empty bottle into the recycling bin. She thought about all she had heard from him. How could someone hold in so much pain and, yet, try so hard to please people all around him?

Misha stood at her door, rubbing her stomach, as Bernard prepared to leave. Thanking her for listening to him, he asked her for a hug. He reached for her. She felt the connection. The heat spread from his touch throughout her body. Apparently Miracle felt it too because she began moving wildly inside her. Bernard stepped back, still embracing her shoulders with his hands. He looked at Misha's stomach.

"Hey, I felt the baby move." He smiled. "Can I feel it again?"

"Sure. Thanks for asking. Most people put their hands on me without asking."

He placed his hands on her pregnant belly and Miracle moved again. He looked up at Misha, his smile widened. "Wow. That's something."

"It is isn't it?"

"Well, I guess I've taken up enough of your time. I better go."

"Hey, if you need me you know where to find me."

"Thanks for everything." He turned and walked out the door.

Misha closed the door and leaned on it. She could feel the intensity of the conversation and the embrace. She began to pray and ask God to cover him and heal the broken pieces of his life. She also thanked God for all he said. He had ministered to her too. She had a better understanding of what Miracle may experience, and prayed her child didn't suffer the abuse Bernard had.

Chapter 29

Bernard showed up at Bible Study the following week, surprising Misha. She laughed as everybody flipped out seeing him at the church. Their eyes connected and they smiled at each other. Misha could hardly focus on the lesson because Bernard kept making faces at her and making her laugh. After Bible Study, he tried to push past the crowd of people who wanted to meet him. Misha pretended to not see him walking toward her, and headed for the door.

"Hey, Misha, wait," he shouted over the crowd. He excused himself from them and walked over to her and greeted her with a hug. "Look at the beautiful pregnant lady."

"Hey, Pastor. I didn't expect you here. Don't you have your own church?"

"My assistant pastor is teaching tonight. I still have some work I need to finish up here. I'll be back home by Sunday." A young boy interrupted them and asked for an autograph. Misha watched as he autographed the back of an old church program for the child. The little boy thanked him and rushed off to show his friends his trophy signature. Bernard laughed with delight.

"I see you aren't wearing the contacts again."

"I decided not to wear them anymore."

"Are you here with Sherrell? I've got to catch up with her to get my ticket to the play on Saturday. The singles group is going together and we got a discount rate on our tickets for buying them as a group."

"Oh, I forgot. I have your ticket. She gave it to me to give to you. She had a brief meeting after Bible Study tonight." He handed her the ticket and she placed it in her purse.

"Thank you, Pastor."

"Please, call me Bernard."

"Okay. Well, it's late and I've got a test in class tomorrow. I'll talk to you later."

"I'll walk with you to your car."

They walked toward the door when a group of ladies ran to meet him. He stopped to chat with them. Misha watched as he put on his game face and began to flirt with them, all of them at the same time. They giggled with delight. She shook her head at the sight and laughed. He was always the entertainer. Misha looked at him being the Bernard Taylor she saw at the Fox. She caught his attention and waved good-bye to him and left him standing with the women.

While driving, her cell phone rang. She looked at the number. It was a 202 area code. She wondered who was calling her from DC. She answered the phone and was happy to hear Bernard's voice on the other end.

"Hey, why did you leave?"

"You were entertaining your fans. Miracle's hungry. I've got to get home to feed her."

"You wanna go somewhere and get something to eat?"

"I can't tonight. I have a test. I need to study and eat at the same time."

"Oh. Well, you have a good night."

"You too." Misha hung up the phone. *He has a Washington phone number. He lives in Washington? I know he said his parents went to college in DC. I wonder if they still live up there.*

***

Misha was looking forward to going to the new gospel play. She needed a good laugh. At twenty-six weeks, she no longer cared about wearing something that made her look pregnant. Everything made her look pregnant. She was at a stage where she could not hide it. But she was sick of people rubbing her belly like a good-luck charm. She hoped no one did it at the theatre.

She arrived at the theatre and waited for the rest of the singles group. She spotted Sherrell and other members waiting outside. An usher looked at Sherrell's tickets and escorted them to a row of seats. Misha sat down with the group. Then a couple came and told her she was in one of their seats.

"There must be some mistake. We're all together." She handed her ticket to the usher.

"Miss, your seat is way down there. I'll escort you."

"There must be some mistake. We got our tickets at the same time. We're a group."

"I don't know what happened, but you're in the front row."

"The front row? I want to sit with my friends," Misha said, looking back at the singles group she was with.

"Miss, I'm sorry. The show is sold out. You'll have to sit in your reserved seat."

"Misha, it's okay. We'll meet up after the show," Sherrell told her.

Something's up. Sherrell was smiling a little too hard.

Misha picked up her purse and jacket and followed the usher to the front row and sat down. Staring at her ticket stub, she was unaware of Bernard walking up to her with two men.

"Hey, Misha, you look terrific." He hugged her. "Let me introduce you to my associates. This is Antonio and

Bruce." Misha shook their hands. They walked to the row behind her and sat down. Bernard sat in the seat beside Misha.

"You planned this didn't you?"

"Planned what?" Bernard said, smiling and doing a poor job playing innocent.

"You purchased this ticket. That's why I'm not with the group."

"I didn't like those seats way back there. These are better seats."

Why am I always ending up in the front now? First at the Rock, then the concert, now the play. God, what are you up to? Misha prayed to herself.

"You look really nice tonight."

"Thank you, Pastor. You look nice tonight too."

"I thought I told you to call me Bernard."

"You did." Misha felt awkward. She wanted to get comfortable but she couldn't with Bernard sitting beside her and his two associates sitting behind them.

She quickly forgot about them as lights dimmed and the play began. Misha had tears in her eyes as she watched the antics of actors on the stage. She hated to see the play end. After the cast exited the stage, Bernard was swarmed by people. Antonio and Bruce quickly jumped into action, making sure the crowd of people did not crush Bernard. They made a path for him. He reached out and took Misha by the arm. "Come on. I'll introduce you to the cast."

"You can do that?"

"My lady, there are some benefits to being Bernard Taylor." They walked the path cleared by his associates and went backstage, where Bernard introduced Misha to the cast members. Misha remembered the group and excused herself to call Sherrell to ask where they were meeting to eat. Sherrell gave her the name of the restaurant and Misha agreed to meet them there.

Bernard and his associates walked her to her car and stood by it until she drove off. When she arrived at the restaurant she did not see the rest of the group. She waited until she saw Bernard walking toward her.

"You and Sherrell planned this whole night didn't you? Why didn't you just ask me to attend the play with you tonight?"

"Because I knew you wouldn't accept my invitation."

"Where are your associates?"

"They went home I think. Come on. They have a table waiting for us."

They were escorted to a table in the back of the restaurant. Misha watched and listened as people whispered, recognizing him, as they walked between the tables in the restaurant. They sat down at their table and ordered something to drink.

"You didn't have to go to all this trouble. I would have considered it, if you asked."

"Considered isn't the same as accepting. I enjoyed talking to you the other day and I wanted to do something nice for you."

"Excuse me. Aren't you Bernard Taylor?" A lady interrupted them. She seemed so happy as she smiled at him.

"Yes, I am."

"I'm one of your biggest fans. I have all your CDs . . ." she said rapidly.

Misha smiled at her excitement.

She waved to her friends to come over. Misha watched as the entire table of people got up and headed in their direction.

"Can't you see we're trying to have dinner here? We would like to be alone if you don't mind," Bernard rudely said.

Misha was surprised he would speak to a fan in such a manner. She had not seen him like this before. He was always the entertainer. She watched the smile go away from the lady's face just as her friends arrived.

"Come on. Let's go back to our table," she told her friends, and they began to whisper to her, asking her what happened.

Misha called the waiter over to the table. She asked him to bring them the check from the table where the lady sat with her friends. She could tell they were talking about them because some of them turned around and looked at them.

"You're going to pay for their meal?" Bernard asked.

"No, you are. You were rude to that lady. It was uncalled for," Misha whispered.

"Don't you think she was rude interrupting us?"

"She's a fan. Tell me something. Are you absolutely sure you are in the will of God when you sing and minister to people all around the world?"

"I know I am." Bernard adjusted his napkin in his lap.

"So you're obedient in doing what God has told you to do?"

"Yes."

"The Word of God says if you're obedient in what He tells you to do, God will send men to your bosom to bless you. That lady, her friends, and all the people who buy your CDs and attend your concerts are walking in obedience to what God sent them to do. The same as when you are standing on that stage."

He stared at Misha as she spoke firmly to him. Misha did not hold back anything she was feeling.

"Now, what you're going to do is pay their check and go over there and apologize for your behavior. Make up some excuse if you have to about what you said.

But apologize to her. Sign autographs, take pictures, or whatever. Because at any moment, God can command those very same people to stop blessing you. You need to be grateful for their obedience to God."

The waiter handed her the check and she gave it to Bernard. He got up from the table and walked over to the group. Misha could tell he turned on the charm. She watched as he motioned for a waiter. People began taking pictures of them with their cell phones. Before he left, Misha could hear the people laughing and talking loudly, breaking the silent atmosphere of the restaurant. He waved good-bye to them and headed back to the table and sat down.

"Now where were we?" Misha asked.

"I think we were about to order." Bernard lifted his menu in front of his face.

Bernard was silent the rest of the evening. As they walked down the sidewalk toward her car she had enough of his silence.

"Are you mad with me?" Misha asked.

"No. It's just that . . . well . . . I never looked at it that way. You were right."

"Right about what?"

"Everything. Well here's your car." They stopped next to the driver's side door. Good night, Misha."

He stood by the car until she drove off. Misha figured that was the last time she would see him. She began to question if she had done the right thing. She knew he had issues and was sensitive about them. He must have been really upset with her. Why did she even care?

The next morning, Bernard called her to thank her for her honesty and told her he was boarding a plane so he could get home in time for Sunday service. She hung up the phone glad he called, but concerned he sounded down.

Maybe she should not have spoken to him so harshly. After all, he was an international celebrity. He had his pick of people he could hang out with. Yet, he chose Misha. *Why?* Misha pondered. Did he feel sorry for her? She could afford her own ticket to the play. She had already paid for it. She even had money for her meal. No, that wasn't it.

Did he have any real friends, people he could depend on even if he was not famous? Or was everyone around him a hanger-on depending on him for a living? Was he now feeling the pressure of being a pastor and entertainer at the same time? Both careers could be very trying. Being a pastor alone was enough to drive anyone nuts if God was not protecting them.

What's wrong with him? What's wrong with me, Misha wondered. God sent a saved, handsome, independently wealthy, straight man to her and all she could think about was how to minister to him.

Maybe it was her and not him. She always had to minister. Just once, she would like to be the woman God placed her on this earth to be: feminine and sweet and able to hold a conversation without preaching. *No one likes to be preached to all the time. Sometimes it's just good to have a pleasant conversation.*

Misha searched for answers as she dressed for church and the baby inside her kicked.

Chapter 30

It was the end of October and Misha had not heard from Bernard since the morning after the incident in the restaurant. She continued her daily routines occasionally thinking about him and praying for him. She did not want to ask Sherrell about him for fear she would think she was interested in him. She was interested in him. There was something special about him that she could not put her finger on. It bothered her on occasion. She continued to ask God to show her what it was.

Being alone and pregnant was getting hard for her. She had to get her extra bedroom cleaned out to get it ready for the baby. Justin had promised her he would help her move some of the boxes in there but he had yet to do it. She walked into the room, feeling overwhelmed with the task that faced her.

She heard a knock on the door and when she answered it there was a man delivering roses to her. She looked at the card. It was from Bernard. He was going to be in Atlanta on Friday and wanted to have dinner with her. Friday was a bad time for her. She had promised one of her students she would attend the homecoming game at Westdale. The Eagles were having a winning season and they could possibly make it to the playoffs. She wanted to call him. Having never saved his number in her phone, it was automatically deleted after he called. She set the big vase of roses on her small table and returned to the task at hand when she heard another knock on the door.

"Well what about Friday?"

She smiled when she saw Bernard standing in front of her.

"You just drop by without calling? Look how I look. You could have given me a chance to put on some clothes." She ran into the bedroom, slamming the door behind her and pulling off the scarf that covered her hair. In record time she pulled off the torn sweatpants and oversized T-shirt with paint stains on it and put on jeans and a pull-over top.

Bernard was standing outside with the front door wide open when she returned to the living room.

"Why didn't you come in?" she asked.

"You didn't invite me."

"Come on in here. You should have called first. I was getting ready to clean my spare room to get it ready for Miracle. Goodness, I look awful." Misha smoothed down the wrinkled blouse.

"You look beautiful. Well how about it?"

"Oh so you think you can come into Atlanta and I'm going to drop everything and go with you. I had plans for Friday."

"Oh yeah, what?"

"I was going to Westdale's homecoming. I ran into one of my students and she invited me. I'm going. They're having a winning season. Besides you only gave me twenty-four-hour notice. You should have said something earlier in the week."

"I'll go to the game with you. Then we can have dinner."

"You attract too much attention. What are you in town for anyway? Before I forget, thank you for the flowers. They're beautiful." They sat down at the table and continued their conversation.

"You're welcome. I'm here for the Empowerment Day Parade."

"Oh I love that parade."

"You want to go with me?"

"Are your associates going with you?"

"No, not this time."

"Sure, I'd like to go with you."

He looked around her apartment. "Don't you have class on Thursday?"

"The professor cancelled the class today. I'm glad. I really need to clean out my spare bedroom."

"Maybe I can help. I don't have any plans today."

Sounded like a good idea to her. Since Justin never showed up, she decided to take him up on his offer. "The bedroom is across from the bathroom." She stood up and took his leather jacket and hung it up in the hall closet. He followed her down the short hallway into the spare bedroom.

"Whoa. You need some help with this. You can't lift these boxes," Bernard said, eyeing the large number of stacked boxes in the room.

"My brother was supposed to help me. He didn't show up and the clock's a-tickin'." Misha rubbed her belly.

"Well, I'm here. What do you want me to do?"

For the next several hours they worked in the room, separating items into three different piles—donations, keepers, and trash—while Bernard told stories of his travels around the world. Misha sat in a chair, or the royal throne as he called it, listening to him and admiring his passion and commitment to ministry. Bernard took the trash to the Dumpster outside her apartment and placed the items to be donated in his car to take to the charity on his way back to his hotel.

Afterward, she prepared lunch of ham sandwiches and canned soup for them and they sat down at the table to eat.

"You live in DC?" Misha asked him.

"Yeah. How did you know?" he said in between bites of his sandwich.

"Well, the last time you called me, I saw it was a DC number."

"If you had my number, why didn't you call?"

"You said you were going to call me. Besides, I didn't want to bother you."

"You could have called me. To be honest, I was disappointed you didn't call me."

"I thought about it. Once I got up the nerve to phone you, but my cell had already deleted your number. I wanted to know how you were doing. How are you doing?" she said, placing her hand on top of his. He stopped eating.

"I've been busy."

"That's not what I asked you."

He sat back in his chair and sighed. "I'm thankful we met."

"I'm thankful we met too. You don't realize how much you ministered to me the last time you were here."

"Ministered to you how?"

"Well, several ways. Most importantly you're teaching me how to minister to my child. You look troubled. Anything wrong?"

Looking toward the spare bedroom, not wanting Misha to see his pain, he asked, "What are you going to put in that room?"

"I'm saving my money to buy a bed I saw at the Baby Mart. Hopefully, my family will buy the rest or I can buy it on credit."

"Is that where you're registered?"

"Yes. I just did the registry last week. I still have about three months to go. Thank you for your help today. I don't know if I would have gotten it done without you."

"I'm glad I could help. What are you doing the rest of the day?"

"I don't have any plans."

"You wanna hang out with me?"

"And do what?"

"I don't know. Maybe we can go to a museum or something."

"Okay. You'll have to let me get presentable first."

"You look fantastic," he said, taking his fingers and lightly moving the strand of hair that fell from under her scarf. "I'll take the donations to the Goodwill and come back and pick you up. Will you be ready in twenty minutes?"

"I think so."

"I'll be back."

Bernard left the apartment and Misha ran into her bathroom to take a shower and put on some nicer clothes. Bernard attracted a lot of attention and she wanted to look good when she was around him.

She picked up the remote and flopped down on the sofa to take in a little television while she waited for Bernard to return. An hour passed and he was not there, nor did he call. After the second hour she gave up on him returning. Three hours later, she heard a knock on the door. She opened it and Bernard was standing in front of her.

"Before you say anything, I know I'm a little late," he said, holding up his hand. He held a small box in the other.

"A little late?"

"I'm sorry. Please forgive me. I brought a peace offering." He handed her the box wrapped in baby paper.

"What's this?" She held the beautifully wrapped gift in her hand.

"Open it." He smiled.

Misha invited him in and they sat down on the sofa. She pulled the ribbon off the box and lifted the top. Inside was the baby intercom system that was on her registry.

"Thank you. But, you didn't have to do this."

"I wanted to. Before I forget, I have something else out in the car." They walked outside and down the stairs to a moving truck waiting in front of her building. Bernard lifted the back door. Misha's mouth flew open at the sight of baby furniture, and what looked like all the items on her list. "Surprise."

"Bernard, I . . ."

"You're welcome. I was so late because they had to put some of this together and I had to find a truck."

"I don't know if I should accept all this stuff." She looked at the items stacked inside the truck. *Did he purchase everything in the store?*

Bernard stepped up into the truck and began shifting the packages closer to the door.

"Bernard, I appreciate all this. I really do. But, I don't think I can accept it."

He stopped and walked to her and hugged her. "I wanted to do something special for you since you did something special for me."

"What did I do?"

"You don't treat me like everyone else. You treat me normal."

"Normal?"

Misha's neighbor walked out into the breezeway between the two apartments and stopped at the sight of Bernard Taylor. He volunteered to help Bernard carry in the items from the truck. Bernard thanked him by promising to stop by his apartment to surprise the man's wife.

Misha walked into the nursery and looked at all the stuff Bernard purchased for her, not knowing how to take his generosity. No one had ever treated her this nicely.

Caressing the expensive bed she wanted but did not have the money to purchase, she could not imagine having a nursery this nice. God had truly blessed her even before this child was born. She knew this child was special.

She hoped she looked like her. She did not need the constant reminder of the rape staring at her daily. She prayed for the unconditional love a mother should have for her child. *God, I know this is selfish, but please let this child have all my features,* she prayed silently.

Bernard stepped into the room. "We can put all this away tonight or tomorrow."

"Bernard, this is too much. You shouldn't have."

"I wanted to. Looks like you're ready. Let's go."

"Go? Go where?"

"You'll see." He held out his hand. She reached for it and he led her to the door.

They left the apartment and drove to a small restaurant near Lenox Mall. He escorted her to a private dining area in the back. The people in the restaurant treated them like royalty. He had already planned everything. The meal was perfect. He entertained her like he did on stage. But she could see he was covering up. He was standing, acting out his jokes and laughing like nothing was going on. She stared at him but she could not laugh. She could feel his pain.

Tell him he doesn't have to entertain you.

"You don't have to entertain me."

He stopped and stared at her.

"You don't have to entertain me." She stood up and took his hand. "You don't have to entertain me." He hugged her and Miracle began moving around. He stepped back.

"I don't think she likes me."

"When Mary and Elizabeth came together, the Bible says the babies in them leaped because of the spiritual connection. Miracle only leaps when you're around. It's spiritual. Now, what's wrong?"

He shook his head as if nothing were wrong. But Misha knew differently. She knew something was up. "Come on. Let's go."

They arrived at Misha's apartment and Bernard remembered his promise to the neighbor. They walked to the man's apartment. Apparently, he had not told his wife Bernard would be visiting. When she opened the door, the lady started screaming. Misha watched as Bernard jumped into his "Bernard Taylor, gospel superstar" routine. They took pictures with him and their family. The neighbor repeatedly thanked him for surprising his wife as they left the apartment.

When they arrived in her apartment, Misha excused herself to go to the bathroom. When she came out, Bernard was sitting on the sofa watching television.

"You know, people ought to live right," Bernard said.

"What are you talking about? What are you watching?"

"The news. Some bishop is being sued by a lady saying he fathered her two children."

Misha focused her attention on the screen. There on the television was an old video of Bishop Moore at a City Development League rally. Then they showed the woman. It was the same woman Misha had seen in her visions before she talked to Bishop. She picked up the remote and turned the television off. Once again God had confirmed something He showed her. However, right now her focus was on one man: Bernard. "You've been avoiding something all day. What is it?"

"My sister, Brea. She's leaving the ministry."

"Why?"

"She and her husband are starting their own ministry. She said the Lord told them to leave."

"You know they have to be obedient to what God says. You shouldn't try to stop them."

"But, what am I going to do when I have to travel? Who's going to stand in for me? I need their help. Why would they do this to me? After all I did for them?"

"Aren't you being selfish?" Misha sat beside him on the sofa. "You think it's all about you, don't you?"

"I'm not being selfish. It's about God and how He's working in our lives."

"If it's about God, then why are you upset that they're doing what God told them to do?"

"I'm not upset."

"Yes, you are."

Bernard stood up and headed for the door.

"Do you always run when people are trying to talk to you? Stop being stubborn and sit back down." She patted the seat next to her. He returned to the sofa. "I know you're feeling uncertain about change. But you can do it. Hasn't your sister helped you thus far?"

He shook his head yes.

"Well, she and her husband won't grow spiritually as long as they're in your ministry. She's done all she can do for you. Now, it's time for her to help her husband. You've got to let them go."

"What am I going to do?"

"God will send the help you need."

For the rest of the evening, Misha ministered to him about the goodness of God and she corrected his selfish behavior. He sat and listened quietly to her. His mood went from sadness to anger to conviction. Misha prayed for him and asked God to open his eyes and give him direction on what he should do in his ministry.

"God is changing your focus. You must change with it. If not, God will surely correct you. You're a man of God and He loves you. God will chastise whom he loves. Therefore, you have to walk in obedience. So does your sister."

"You know, you're the only one who seems to understand me."

"It's not me. It's the Holy Spirit using me."

The following day, Bernard arrived early to pick up Misha for the Empowerment Day Parade. When they arrived at the parade site she found out Bernard was riding on a float in the parade, and he asked her to ride with him. Before they boarded the float, several photographers gathered around them, taking pictures. He spoke to one of the photographers and the man agreed to take a picture of them posing together.

Misha sat back on the float feeling like the queen of the parade. She waved to the people who filled the streets while Bernard lip-synced to one of his songs blaring from a speaker. He glanced back at her and smiled. She returned his smile and continued waving at the crowd. Misha had to admit she was enjoying the star treatment. It was something she could get use to.

After the parade, as they walked back to their car, a young man walked up to them and asked for an autograph. Misha couldn't help but see his hurt and pain. Misha took the young man aside from the crowd that had gathered to meet Bernard.

"This may sound awkward. But you are a good kid. I see it in you," Misha said to the young man. "You have a lot on your shoulders right now trying to study and take care of your mother."

Startled, the young man stepped back. "How did you know about my mom?"

"The Holy Spirit told me. When she gets out of rehab, this time, she will be a changed woman. You'll see."

"I'm trying to do the right thing. I had to quit school to take care of my little brother. I work during the day and study for my GED at night." The words poured out of the young man's mouth. "My mom has been in and out of rehab, eight or nine times. I don't want my brother to end up in foster care. Somebody's got to take care of both of them."

"This time . . ." Misha hesitated. She looked toward Bernard, who was staring at her. She returned to the young man and continued, "This time it will be different. Your mother is sincere and has been praying for healing. God is going to honor that prayer. As for you, there is a college scholarship waiting for you. Look for it. It will surely come."

"Thank you. Thank you," the young man exclaimed. He hugged Misha tightly. "I've got to go. Thank you so much for the word." The young man turned and disappeared into the crowd.

"You're a prophet," Bernard stated after the young man walked away. "I saw the way you ministered to that guy. You looked right into his soul."

"I am who God says I am."

He smiled and hugged her. Her baby moved again. This thrilled him and he laughed louder. He was happy with this woman and her child, who kicked him every chance she got.

When he was away from her he was miserable and he made up excuses to come back to Atlanta just to see her. How could he leave her again? It was getting tough. She was special. Her baby was special. He felt at home in her apartment—cleaning and eating ham sandwiches. No one would ever let him do that. Everyone was always fussing over him. But Misha—she let him be himself. She let him be a man, the man. He was a happy man with his Misha and her karate kid.

Chapter 31

Misha's dreams had come true. She sat back at her parents' home, watching her mother throw commands at Justin. It was Thanksgiving and she was thirty weeks pregnant and growing larger every day. Her mother did not want her to do any work, including the multiple trips to the store she always sent her on. This year was Justin's turn and Misha was enjoying every minute of it.

Justin returned, singing, from his third trip to the only grocery store that was open on Thanksgiving Day. He placed the bags on the table, pulled a *Jet* magazine out of the bag, and sat down at the table beside Misha. "You know, Mama, there are people in our family that love to keep secrets from us," he said as he flipped through the pages of the magazine.

"What you talking about, Justin?" his mother asked.

"I'm only saying someone in here has been keeping a secret from us."

Misha looked up from a magazine of her own that she was reading. "What are you talking about, Justin?"

"Well, I was standing in that long line at the store when I picked up this *Jet* magazine to kill some time. Lo and behold there was a very interesting picture in it. So I bought the magazine."

"Let me see." Misha snatched the magazine from him. She flipped the pages. "What picture are you talking about?"

Justin leaned back in his chair with a big smile on his face. "Keep looking. You'll know the one I'm talking about when you see it."

Misha continued flipping the pages and stopped at a picture of her and Bernard Taylor. The caption read: "Bernard Taylor and his gal pal Misha Holloway at the Atlanta Empowerment Day Parade." Misha's mouth flew open. She stared at the picture of the two of them hugging each other around the waist, smiling and waving to the crowd. She briefly remembered the moment and smiled. Then, she noticed Justin looking at her.

"Well, do you have something to tell us?"

"Oh, this is nothing. I met him and we took a picture at the parade." She couldn't tell them she knew him personally and had been spending time with him. She knew how her mother would act. Her daughter knew Bernard Taylor. She would be asking him to do programs at her church for the next fifty years. She couldn't tell them they were friends and spoke to each other almost every day, sometimes two or three times a day. She definitely could not tell them she was attracted to him.

"You met who?" Her mother walked over, wiping her hands on her apron. She lifted the magazine and looked at the picture. "You know Bernard Taylor? Why didn't you tell us? It's just like you to keep this a secret from us."

"Mom, I met him. That's all."

"The book says you're his gal pal. Look at what you're wearing. You couldn't find anything better to wear for a picture in *Jet?* Oh my goodness, I'm going to have to call Mama." She wiped her hands on her apron.

"Mom, think how upset Aunt Mattie is going to be when she finds out your little girl is in *Jet* magazine with Bernard Taylor," Misha said with a crooked smile. "We can wait until she gets here with Uncle Paul or we can call her now and tell her."

Her mother raced to the phone on the wall. Misha laughed when she heard her mother telling Aunt Mattie about the picture. She had never seen her mother so excited about anything she did.

"So how long have you known him?" Justin asked Misha.

"A little while. Listen to Mama. By the end of the day, all of Atlanta will know about the picture in *Jet*."

"You don't tell anybody anything do you? You could have told me."

"I didn't want anybody to know. Besides, Bernard is very private."

"You two dating?"

"Naw, it's not like that. We're only friends. That's all." Misha returned to her magazine.

Misha forced herself up from the chair just as Pam and the children walked into the house. After greeting them, she stepped into the carport and punched in Bernard's number. A loud scream came from the house. Apparently someone showed Pam the picture.

"Happy Thanksgiving," Bernard said when he answered the phone.

"'Gal pal,' Bernard?" Misha walked out into the yard.

"Aren't you going to wish me a happy Thanksgiving?"

"Why didn't you tell me about the picture?"

"I wondered how long it was going to take you to find out. Who told you?"

"My brother saw it. Now my mother is telling everybody who will listen about it. I'm sure she's going to send Justin to the store to get more copies."

Bernard laughed.

"What are you laughing about? It's not funny. You should have told me."

"You're right. I should have. I wanted to surprise you."

"Please don't do that again. If I had known, I would have worn something else. That outfit made me look fat."

"You looked like a beautiful pregnant lady. They asked me if your baby was mine and when she was due."

Justin walked out of the house, putting on his coat. "Misha, Mama's sending me to the store to get some more copies of the magazine. Do you want one?"

"No, I'm fine."

"Who are you talking to?" he asked, noticing the phone to her ear.

"None of your business."

"You're talking to him aren't you?" He ran to the door leading into the kitchen, telling Pam and his mother that Misha was talking to Bernard Taylor. Her mother and Pam ran out of the house, screaming and smiling.

"See what you did?" Misha returned to her phone call.

"Is that Bernard Taylor? Let me speak to him." Pam reached for the phone and Misha twisted away from her.

"Bernard, my mother and sister-in-law want to speak to you."

He laughed. "It's okay. Put them on the phone."

She handed the phone to her mother and listened while she interrogated him. Misha knew he was enjoying every minute of the conversation without hearing his voice.

"Mama, you better check on your food," Misha reminded her.

Her mother handed the phone to Pam, who tried to act as if she spoke to celebrities every day. Speaking to him briefly, she handed the phone back to Misha and walked into the house.

"See what you did? You should have warned me."

He continued laughing. He seemed so thrilled about the picture. Misha was excited too but she did not want him to know. They looked good together, like a couple in love. She sighed. He was not Matthew. *God, if this is not what you ordained, please stop it now. This guy is too good to be true.* Misha was falling hard. She had to stop it and trust God that Matthew would be with her soon.

"I'm getting ready to go to my parents' for dinner," Bernard said. "Call me when you get home this evening. I should be home about eight."

"Do your parents know?"

"I told my parents about you before we were ever introduced."

"What do you mean by that?"

"Misha, I've got to go. Call me this evening." That was one thing she did not like about him: he had a way of avoiding questions. She stared at the phone in her hand. What did he mean by telling his parents before they met? The question would have to wait; Miracle was hungry.

This Thanksgiving, Misha was the center of attention. Not because she was pregnant, but because she knew Bernard Taylor. Her family wanted to know every detail. Her mother asked her if he could do a concert for her church.

Misha rushed home from her parents' house to call Bernard. She wanted to set him straight and make sure he knew not to do that again. Thinking about the parade, she realized Bernard had arranged the picture the day of the parade when he asked the photographer to take the shot. But when she heard his voice on the phone, she forgot what she was going to say. He apologized for not telling her about the picture and promised not to do it again.

They continued their conversation until Misha became too tired to talk. They had so much in common. She could talk to him, unlike Roger. He wanted to know her dreams and vision. No one had ever asked her that before. She told him every detail of her completing her master's degree and probably opening up a private tutorial school. She shared with him that God told her she would be moving to Washington. She did not know when or how. All she knew was God sent her places to minister and she did what He said. She talked until she had nothing more to say.

The following day, she decided to call Judy to tell her about the picture. She did not want Judy to find out like her family. To her surprise, Judy already knew about the picture and said she was wondering when Misha would tell her. Her husband stopped her from calling several times to ask her about Bernard. She could not convince Judy they were only friends. Judy insisted there was chemistry between them that showed up in the picture.

"You're putting too much into that picture," Misha said.

"I know what I see. There's something going on between you two."

"I'm in my third trimester. I could deliver any day. No man in his right mind would be interested in me."

"A man in love is not in his right mind."

"Bernard doesn't love me. Besides, you know my husband's name is Matthew."

"I know what I see. The two of you were glowing."

"You have a vivid imagination. I've got to go."

She hung up the phone. *Glowing? We were not glowing.* She was in total disagreement with what Judy said. Everybody was reading too much into the picture. As she lifted the magazine, she could see it too. How could she be so obvious? He was such a nice guy; she would have to tell him about Matthew soon. Then it will be left to God. She hated to lose him as a friend.

Chapter 32

The growing baby inside of her was stretching, trying to find room in her compact space, and pressed herself into Misha's lungs. Misha found it difficult to breathe. There were times when she had to sleep sitting up just to be able to breathe. She was bigger than she had ever been in her life. Even her maternity clothes felt too small. She felt miserable and to top that off she had a doctor's appointment. She did not feel like being poked and prodded by the doctor. Nor did she feel like going out in the cold, breezy December air. She could not even get excited about having her last ultrasound to see if Miracle was developing without problems. She knew in her heart that Miracle was fine, healthy and strong. She just wanted to stay in bed.

Luckily, her classes were over and her mother decided not to go to her appointment with her. She could not face any more questions about Bernard from her. Today, she was irritated and did not know why. Everything was getting difficult for her, even sitting, standing, and walking. She was about to leave the apartment when her phone rang.

"Hey, I'm in town. What are you doing today?" Bernard's voice rang out over the phone.

"Why didn't you tell me you were coming when we talked last night?"

"I decided this morning. I wanted to see you. Besides, it feels like I'm being drawn here, like I'm supposed to meet somebody. It's almost as if I can hear someone calling me here. Most importantly, though, I wanted to be with you."

"I'm on my way to the doctor's office. I have to go every week now. After that, I have a birthing class at the hospital."

"Who's going with you?"

"I'm going by myself."

"I'll go with you."

"You don't have to. If I wait for you, I'm going to be late."

"I'm right outside your door." She opened the door and he was standing outside. She shook her head and walked past him. "Hey, wait for me," he said.

"Come on, Bernard. I'm going to be late."

At the doctor's office, Bernard and Misha sat patiently, waiting for her name to be called. Bernard looked in the many magazines about pregnancy and child rearing that sat on the table next to him. They heard Misha's name and he helped her get up from the chair and joked about the way she wobbled toward the exam room. She gave him a look that let him know she was not in the mood for jokes. Against Misha's protests, he followed her into the exam room. *Why?* They did not have that type of relationship. She introduced him to Dr. Trinidad and began her exam.

Misha watched as Bernard's face brightened at the sound of the baby's heartbeat. A proud father he would someday be. He was getting enough practice asking Dr. Trinidad questions. Misha wanted him to leave but did not want to be rude to him since he had done so much for her. She wished he was out in the lobby, especially when Dr. Trinidad checked her cervix.

"Mr. Taylor, aren't you that preacher on TBN?" Dr. Trinidad asked as she pulled the latex gloves off her hands.

"You've seen me on TV?"

"I thought I recognized you." She walked to the sink and washed her hands.

The thought of her doctor knowing Bernard irritated Misha more. How would her white doctor know a black gospel singer?

"Come on. We're going to walk down to the ultrasound room. We're going to do the last ultrasound. Your baby has turned and is getting ready to make her appearance. Let's see what she looks like."

They walked to the small, cramped room where the ultrasound machine was stored. Misha lay down on the exam table and grimaced when Dr. Trinidad placed the cold gel on her abdomen. Bernard and Misha watched the screen on the machine and oohed at the same time when they saw a face come up on the screen.

"There she is. Look, she's looking at you."

"That's Miracle?" Misha looked at the face—a clear, defined face—of her baby on the screen. She did not expect to see a real face. Her eyes were barely open. A tear fell from Misha's eyes.

"She's beautiful, Misha. She looks like you." Bernard caressed Misha's forehead and bent down and kissed her on it. He returned his stare to the picture.

"Looks like everything is fine. I guess I'll see you back next week." Dr. Trinidad gave the picture to Misha and left the room.

Bernard embraced Misha as she began to cry. She was glad he was there after all. The impact of seeing her baby's face was too intense for her to handle alone. He held her hand as they left the doctor's office, leading her to their car. She stared at the picture. Bernard said

Miracle looked like her. That's the best news she heard all day. God knew exactly what she needed to brighten her day.

After the birthing class and lunch, Bernard took Misha back to her apartment. She was tired and had to go to the bathroom. She did not feel like talking to him. She wanted him to leave but he sat down on the sofa and made himself at home. When she returned to the room, she sat down beside him, trying to be nice.

"Have you decided on a name for her?"

"Not yet. I told you my grandmother wanted me to call her Elizabeth. I'm sort of leaning toward Courtney."

"How about Taylor?"

"You're saying that because it's your name. Taylor is a pretty name for a girl though. I'll think about it."

"I don't think you understand. I'm asking you to name her Taylor, not her first name."

"Elizabeth Taylor, you've got to be kidding." Misha started laughing. That was the funniest thing she'd heard all day. "My grandmother did say she was going to be a star. Elizabeth Taylor Holloway. That's funny."

Bernard was not laughing. He seemed frustrated. He stood and walked around the room. "Misha, I'm asking you to name Miracle Taylor. Not her first name. Not her middle name. But her last name. Name her Taylor."

Misha stopped laughing and stared at him pacing nervously around the room. She stood and walked to him. "What are you saying?"

"I'm saying I want her last name and your last name to be Taylor."

"You're asking me to marry you? I have to say no for a few reasons. You're overwhelmed by the doctor's visit and birthing class. Give it a few days; you'll get over it."

"Misha, sit down." Both of them walked to the sofa and he helped her sit down. "I've been praying about this. No one understands me like you do. I can talk to you about anything. It's not about today. It's about every day I've known you. I look at you and see the most beautiful, understanding woman I have ever met. You're an anointed woman of God. I love you with all my heart. I want to be wherever you are." He stood and began pacing the floor again.

"I don't know about your relationship with Miracle's father. You never talk about him other than to say he's dead. But, I promise you, I'll be the best father she could ever have and love her like my own." He sat back down on the sofa.

Misha knew she had to tell him about Heckler. However, she had learned to let him talk. She could see he needed to. She sat quietly on the sofa, caressing her large abdomen.

"I know we haven't known each other long. I need you. I love you." He leaned over and kissed her. Miracle began moving. He leaned back. "I don't think she likes me. She kicks me every time I'm near you."

"See if she does it again."

Bernard smiled and moved closer to her. Their lips slowly met and Misha felt herself being drawn deeper into his embrace. Then, Miracle moved even more. Misha pulled away from him and struggled to get up from the sofa. "Bernard. I can't do this. I can't do this to you. There are some things you need to know about me."

"What things?"

Misha walked over to her computer desk in the corner of her living room. She opened the drawer and pulled out a scrapbook. "I was raped. Miracle's daddy, if I can call him that, was a consultant the school hired to do an evaluation on my school. I walked in on him while he was attacking one of my students and he raped me instead."

She told him how she kept having visions about Amber being attacked by Mr. Heckler and calling her name and how she knew she had seen him somewhere before when he came to her school. She told him how he kept asking her out and saying inappropriate things to her. She even told him about Roger and his friendship with Heckler.

"You said he was dead."

"The police killed him. He tried to kill me three times but the gun would not go off. Then, he took the same gun and went outside and fired two shots at the police and they killed him." She handed him the scrapbook filled with newspaper stories about the incident.

"I thought about aborting Miracle when I found out I was pregnant. But, I couldn't do it. She is a miracle." She continued telling him about her cancer and how her doctor said it would take a miracle for her to get pregnant. She told him everything, how she prayed for a baby from her own body and God blessed her with Miracle.

"I can't marry you. You're not my husband."

"How can you say that?" Bernard asked.

She sat down in the Queen Anne chair in front of him. "Well, since I was a child, I've known my husband's name is Matthew. After all this happened, God confirmed this to me. He told me to call him here. He said if I call him, he will come. So I've been calling him. I know he's going to show up one day. I'm sorry if I led you on. It was not my intention. But I can't marry you. I can only marry who God ordained for me. He will understand my ministry and the call on my life."

Bernard stood up and walked toward the door. "Is that how you feel? You will only marry Matthew?"

"That's the way it has to be. I have to be obedient to God. I'm sorry."

"Thank you for being honest with me." He opened the door and walked out of the apartment.

Misha started crying. "God, this is too much for me. I'm about to give birth and one of my closet friends just walked out on me. Are you sure my husband's name is Matthew? I liked Bernard. No. I love Bernard. Can you change your mind about this one, God? Look how he has helped me. Look how you used him to bless me. I still want to be his friend. Now, I don't think I will ever hear from him again." She wept bitterly.

Chapter 33

It was Christmas Day and Misha was returning home from celebrating the day with her family at Uncle Paul's house. It was loud as usual. Everyone kept asking her questions about Bernard. She didn't tell them what happened between them and that she had not heard from him in several days. She was tired and ready to go to sleep and her back was bothering her. She looked forward to a long night's rest. She hoped Miracle would allow her to get the good night's sleep that evaded her in the last few days.

As she reached the top step leading to her apartment, there was a package outside her door. She struggled to lean down to pick it up.

"Wait. Let me help you with that."

Misha looked up. It was Bernard coming out of her neighbor's apartment. She could see her neighbors standing behind him with big smiles on their faces. "Bernard. I didn't expect to see you here."

"Did you think I was going to miss spending Christmas with you?" He looked at the neighbors and thanked them for allowing him to stay with them until she arrived. Misha unlocked her door. She and Bernard walked inside.

"You could have called me," Misha said.

"I wanted to surprise you."

"How long have you been here?"

"In Atlanta?"

"At my apartment."

"Not long."

"I'm glad you're here. I've got something for you." Misha walked to her small Christmas tree that stood on a table in front of a window. She took the lone gift from under it and handed it to him. "This is for you."

"Thank you." Bernard opened it to find a thick gold engraved men's bracelet. "This is nice. Thank you. I'll wear it every day. Open yours."

Misha wobbled to the table and sat down. She opened the package. It was the book Judy had given her. "Oh."

He saw the expression on her face. "Why you look like that?"

"I'm sorry. A friend gave me this book a long time ago."

"You read my book?"

"Your book?"

She looked at the cover of the book. *M. Bernard Taylor*. She looked at him. "I didn't know this was your book. Did you autograph this copy?"

"No. So you read my book. Did you like it?" He sat down beside her.

She did not want to tell him it was not one of her favorites. "It's been so long. I don't really remember. I'll have to read it again."

"Before you do, I have something else for you." He handed her another beautifully wrapped package.

"Do you always go over the top with gifts?"

"Stop asking questions and open the box."

She opened it and unfolded the tissue. She could see what looked to her like copies of his birth certificate. She looked at the name. She looked at him. She looked at the other papers. A copy of his social security card and a copy of his driver's license were in the box. Tears began to flow down her face.

"Misha, I told you my father's name is Matt. His legal name is Matthew Bernard Taylor. My name is Matthew Bernard Taylor Jr. I didn't think you would believe me. That's why I copied all this for you. I started calling myself Bernard when I went to college. I thought it made me sound black. My family calls me Matthew or Spanky."

"Spanky?"

"Yeah. I used to get into a lot of fights when I was young. My parents whipped me so much, some people began calling me Spanky. It sort of stuck. I want you to call me Matthew. I love you. I love Miracle."

He knelt down in front of her. "I have one more gift. You said the Lord told you to call me and I would come. I heard you. At first I didn't know why I kept coming to Atlanta. I kept making up excuses to come here. After I met you, I wanted to be here with you. But my ministry in Washington needed me. I'm still their pastor and I had a commitment to fulfill. But, I also wanted to be with you. So now I'm asking you to come with me, back to Washington, and be my wife. I know I can trust you. You're an important part of my life and I don't ever want to leave you here again. I don't know what I would do without you. You complete me. Please marry me." He opened the ring box. Misha could see the ten-carat diamond ring he held before her.

"You're Matthew?" she questioned him in disbelief.

"Yes. I'm Matthew. I heard you call me. I'm here. Marry me. Go back to Washington with me."

"I'm pregnant."

"Really? I haven't noticed." Both of them laughed. "So what do you say? Yes or No."

"I'm pregnant. I can't get married now."

"We can get married after Miracle's born."

She wiped the tears from her face. "Okay. After Miracle's born?"

"Yes."

"Then yes, I'll marry you."

They stared into each other's eyes. Then Misha burst out laughing.

"What's so funny?"

"You just put my mother on the map. Aunt Mattie will never outdo this one. You'll find out about that rivalry later."

He stood her up and passionately kissed her and Miracle kicked him.

It was New Year's Day and Misha's back was still bothering her. Dr. Trinidad told her she had started dilating. She was miserable. Her misery could not destroy her excitement. Bernard was flying back into Atlanta to be with her until she had the baby. His plane was landing in an hour and she could not wait to see him. She decided she had enough energy to meet him at the airport. She got dressed and drove to the small private airport to wait for his plane.

The door of the Learjet opened and Matthew stepped out. Then, out of nowhere, pain started in Misha's back and she could feel its squeeze all around her abdomen. She bent over in pain. The pain took her breath away. Matthew walked into the small waiting area and noticed Misha bent over in pain. He dropped his bags and ran to her.

"Misha. What's wrong?"

"I think I had a cramp."

"I didn't expect to see you here. You shouldn't have come down here." He hugged her and another pain hit her. She squeezed him so hard he couldn't breathe. "You're in labor. We need to get you to the hospital."

"No. It's over," she said as the pain eased. She stood straighter. "In the birthing class, the instructor said I'm supposed to wait until the contractions are two minutes apart." Then a gush of water flowed down her legs. "Oh my God. I think my water broke."

"We're getting you to the hospital now," Matthew said as he held Misha around her waist and began walking toward the door. Along the way, he asked an attendant to collect the luggage he dropped on the floor and take them to his car. The attendant met them at the door.

"Sir, would you like me to call an ambulance?"

"No. I have a car waiting for me." Matthew spotted the long black sedan with the driver waiting outside. He hurried Misha to the car and instructed the driver to take them to the hospital.

Matthew sat on the edge of Misha's bed. The room was quiet now and she was asleep. Her labor went quickly and she delivered Courtney Elizabeth Holloway three hours after arriving at the hospital. She was a healthy seven pounds, two ounces. Her skin was a bright pink and her eyes were as blue as Bernard's.

The room was quiet now. Misha's family had left an hour ago. Bernard sat in the rocker beside the bed, watching Misha sleep peacefully. Although he was not Courtney's biological father, he was just as proud to cut the umbilical cord and hold her for the first time.

The sound of a whimper came from the bassinet that sat on the other side of Misha's bed. He walked over and picked her up. Cradling her in his arms, he returned to the rocker. He picked up a small glass bottle filled with baby formula and started feeding her while rocking back and forth in the chair. He began to sing softly to her. She opened her eyes and looked at him. Eventually his singing woke Misha up and she sat up in the bed to watch the two of them.

Misha watched the scene play out in front of her. Bernard was going to be a good father. He seemed at peace feeding Courtney. He was not nervous during the delivery. She recalled the shock on her mother's face when she walked into the room to see Bernard coaching her with the horrible contractions she was having. Although she did not say anything, Misha could tell her mother was disappointed not to be coaching her. She simply stood back and watched the birth of her third grandchild and stepped up to deliver the news to the other family members waiting in the lobby.

"I didn't mean to wake you." Bernard glanced at her.

"No. I'm fine. How's Courtney?"

"I think she's hungry." He held up the empty bottle. "She eats like her mother." He laughed and stood. He handed Courtney to Misha and sat on the edge of the bed.

"Bernard, she's so beautiful. Look at all this curly blond hair. I wonder if it's going to get darker."

"It might. Mine did." He stared at the two of them. "You are beautiful too."

"I look a mess." She lifted her hands to her head and brushed back her hair.

"No, you don't. You're so beautiful and so is our daughter." He leaned over and kissed her but was interrupted by someone clearing his throat. They looked up and saw two men and a woman standing in the doorway.

"Eric. Hi. Bernard, this is Eric Davidson, my attorney. Is it ten already?" Misha said.

"Actually, it's after ten. This is Ivan Haselden, the attorney for the State. This is Jennifer, the lab tech," Eric said, pointing to the people with him. Bernard reached out his hand to shake theirs. Bernard lifted the sleeping Courtney from Misha and placed her in the bassinet. The attorneys watched his every move.

"Say, you look familiar. What's your name?" Eric asked.

"I'm Bernard Taylor."

"Bernard Taylor the gospel singer?" Eric's smile widened. "Misha, you didn't tell me you knew Bernard Taylor. Well, it's nice to meet you. We're here this morning to do the paternity test on Courtney. We won't be long. Are we ready?"

Misha watched as Mr. Haselden whispered something to Eric and they excused themselves and walked into the hallway. When they returned, Eric said they wanted to do a paternity test on Courtney and Matthew.

"He's not Courtney's father." Misha sat up in the bed.

"It's not that I don't trust you. However, we can't help to notice the similarities in your baby and Mr. Taylor. You two are in a relationship. I mean you were kissing when we walked into the room," Mr. Haselden said.

Misha could not believe this man was standing in her hospital room making accusations and smirking at her.

"But, he's not Courtney's father. Heckler raped me. It's his baby."

"Well, if it's not Mr. Taylor's then you have nothing to be worried about."

"But . . ."

Bernard held up his hand. "No, Misha. I'll do it. What do you want me to do?"

Jennifer began opening a small package. She stopped and looked at him. "I need to see some identification." He pulled his driver's license out of his wallet and gave it to her. She wrote the information on a sheet of paper and handed it back to him. "Open your mouth." She pulled out a very long Q-tip-looking stick and rubbed the inside of his mouth. She did the same to Courtney after checking her hospital bracelet, waking the sleeping baby.

"I guess in a few days we will know exactly who this baby's real father is," Mr. Haselden remarked.

Misha, disgusted with the man's remark, replied, "I guess you will."

Chapter 34

"Bernard, we have a lot to do before your family gets here." Misha rushed around her apartment trying to organize everything. Bernard held Courtney as he rocked back and forth in the rocker. Courtney twisted her lips at him, trying to make sounds as he made faces and talked to her in a high-pitched tone. "You're spoiling her. Don't hold her all the time."

"Look how cute she is. Besides she wants me to hold her."

"She wants you to hold her? How do you know that?"

"She told me." He held her close to his face. "Tell your mama you asked me to pick you up." He smiled and continued playing with the baby, who kept her focus on him.

"I'll remember that when she's screaming in the middle of the night. She'll be screaming just for you. Now I've got to go to the grocery store to make sure I have food in the apartment. A lot of people are going to be in and out of here in the next few days for the wedding. I've got to have something to feed them." She looked at Bernard ignoring her. "Bernard, are you listening to me? Bernard?"

"We've got to get some groceries," Bernard repeated.

Misha shook her head and walked out of the room. There was so much to do before their wedding in two days and all Bernard wanted to do was play with a two-month-old baby.

It had been a whirlwind two months. In that time, she and Courtney flew to Washington to meet Bernard's family and announce his engagement to his church. Then, the media came knocking with questions about her sincerity with their relationship. Before, no one knew who she was. Now everyone had something to say about her on the Internet. She learned to ignore the hype. There were a couple of engagement parties given by his celebrity friends. She had to withdraw from Clark Atlanta and apply to attend graduate school at University of Maryland. She had to do all this in addition to planning a wedding and packing to move to DC.

She stopped and took a deep, relaxing breath. Her phone rang. She looked at the caller ID. It was Eric.

"Hey, Eric. I hope you're calling with good news."

"I heard from the attorney representing the consulting firm. They have offered to settle with you. Since the paternity test showed Heckler was the father of your baby, they have agreed to pay all your medical expenses. I have already forwarded them the bills."

"That's good. It's about time." Misha folded a baby blanket and tossed it into a laundry basket.

"They also offered to settle your claim."

"For how much?" Misha walked to her kitchen and lifted the top off the bottle sterilizer.

"Three million dollars."

She stopped. Her hand stayed in midair above the sterilizer.

"Say what?" Misha was stunned. "I don't think I heard you. How much did you say?"

"Well, they want to give you two million for the attack and one to take care of Courtney. So in all, they offered three million to settle your claim."

"Three million dollars? What do you think?" Misha tried to hold back her excitement.

"I think it's a fair settlement. But, it's up to you."

"If you think it's fair, then I'll take it."

"Now we haven't heard from the Workers' Compensation Commission. I'll send them an offer. The school district could still want to go to trial. They probably won't since the consulting firm is settling. I should hear from them before you get back from your honeymoon."

"Eric, thank you so much for your help. I appreciate all you did."

"That's my job. I'll see you at the wedding."

Misha hung up the phone and began jumping up and down, praising God. Bernard stepped out of the nursery, still holding Courtney in his arms. "What happened? Who was that on the phone?"

"It was Eric. They gave me three million dollars. The consulting firm settled for three million dollars. Praise God. I can't believe it!"

"I'm so happy for you." He reached out his free arm and hugged her. She continued her praise. She looked up at him and it looked like he wanted to cry. She pulled back.

"What's wrong with you?"

He held her close again. "I'm so happy. Now you can pay for the wedding." He started to laugh.

"Get away from me." There was a knock at the door. "You better make sure you have your checkbook tomorrow when we have to pay the last of the vendors." Courtney whimpered. "I'll get the door. Did you call Bishop and tell him about rehearsal Friday night?" Misha asked as she walked toward the door.

"He'll be here early Friday morning."

Misha opened the door and saw Bernard's family standing in front of her. "Dr. Taylor. I didn't expect y'all here until this afternoon. Come on in." They hugged Misha as they walked into the apartment. "I thought your flight came in this afternoon. Let me take your coats."

"Spanky chartered an early flight for us so we could all come together. Where is my granddaughter?" She watched Bernard's mother race through the apartment, looking for Courtney.

Matt Sr. settled into the sofa. "Misha, you don't have to call us Dr. Taylor. You're going to be a part of this family in two days."

"Misha, look at all the weight you lost. You don't look like someone who gave birth two months ago. It took me months to get rid of that baby fat." Bernard's sister said, noticing Misha's weight loss.

"I got a personal trainer," Misha replied. "Where are your husband and kids?"

"They'll be here tomorrow."

"Look who I have," Bernard's mother sang as she entered the room holding Courtney, who was wide-awake and looking at her.

Bernard followed her into the room and greeted his family. His father and sister walked to greet Courtney.

"Bernard, if I didn't know any better, I would think you fathered this child. Look at her blond hair and those big blue eyes. She looks just like you when you were a baby." His mother sat down on the sofa, holding the baby while everybody else surrounded them.

"That's what everybody says. But we have the results of the paternity tests. She's not my biological child. But she's all mine. Funny how God works things out."

"Can I get y'all some coffee?" Misha asked them. They ignored her and she decided to go into the kitchen and start the coffee anyway. She smiled as she peeked into the living room, seeing her new family cooing over the baby. Her beautiful little girl whom God blessed her with had no resemblance to her or Heckler; for that she was thankful. Ironically, she looked like Bernard: blond hair and soft blue eyes. She literally jumped whenever she saw him and cried when he was not around. There was a special bond between the two.

Misha was at peace. She was in a great relationship and was about to marry the man God had spoken to her about so many years ago. Bernard had helped heal her and understand her ministry gift. He even mended the rift she had with her mother and taught her how to forgive. He loved her unconditionally. She loved him and her baby tremendously.

She leaned against the counter, waiting for the water in the coffee to be brewed. She glanced at her new family. She was happy. Long gone were the trials of the past. Each event led to this moment. The Bible was right—all things do work together for the good of them who love the Lord. She loved the Lord with all her being. Without Him she would not have made it to this day. His strength and guidance gave her what she needed and gave her unexpected blessings.

Laughter rang out from the living room. "What's so funny?" she asked as she walked out of the kitchen, holding the tray filled with cups of coffee and setting it on the table in front of them.

"You know how Bernard is always telling those silly stories. Talking about Courtney looked like she was robbing a bank," his sister said.

"What?" Misha didn't understand.

"I was telling them when Courtney was born she looked like she was robbing a bank," Bernard answered.

"I don't get it."

"When she was born, you couldn't see it. But she had this piece of thin skin over her face. She looked like she had a stocking over her face, like a bank robber."

"Oh my God no!" Misha felt faint. Not her child too. She stumbled. Bernard ran to catch her before she hit the floor.

"Misha. What's wrong?" he asked.

The Veil.

Discussion Questions

1. Do you think it is true or an old wives' tale that people born with a veil have a special gift of prophecy?

2. If Misha had known about her gift as a child, would she have been better prepared for the ministry?

3. What role did Ms. Ida Mae, Misha's grandmother, have in teaching her about the gift?

4. Misha studied for hours and preached for church events. Was it fair for the church not to pay her a fair wage?

5. Why would Roger stay with Misha so long if he was jealous of her?

6. Do you feel Misha went through so much because of her gift?

7. Misha always felt her mother favored her brother, Justin. Do you think parents have favorite children? Why?

8. Should the church be better prepared to teach its members about spiritual gifts?

Discussion Questions

9. Bernard knew who Misha was the moment he met her. Do you feel he had the gift or people automatically know when they meet their spouse?

10. Misha had the gifts of prophecy, exhortation, administration, and teaching. What is your spiritual gift and how are you using it to glorify God?

ABOUT THE AUTHOR

K. T. Richey is the bestselling author of the Lady Preacher Series. K.T. is a former pastor and social worker. Her books have been featured in Black Expressions and are listed as Amazon.com Indigo Love bestsellers. She has been nominated for author of the year by several book clubs. She is the recipient of several writing awards including the L.G. McGuire Literary Award in poetry. She holds a bachelor's of arts degree in social studies and a master's degree in counseling.

K.T. Richey is a prolific speaker, popular with women's groups, churches, and book clubs. In her spare time she enjoys travel, photography, and reading. She currently lives in Maryland.

For speaking engagements, book clubs, et cetera . . . go to www.ktrichey.com, www.facebook/ktrichey, or on Twitter @AuthorKTRichey.

Notes